AN UNCERTAIN FUTURE

To

Natasha

With best Wishes

David

AN UNCERTAIN FUTURE

DAVID HEMSLEY

An Uncertain Future
David Hemsley

Published by Aspect Design 2014
Malvern, Worcestershire, United Kingdom.

Designed, printed and bound by Aspect Design
89 Newtown Road, Malvern, Worcs. WR14 1PD
United Kingdom
Tel: 01684 561567
E-mail: allan@aspect-design.net
Website: www.aspect-design.net

ISBN 978-1-908832-64-1

For my wife, Gillian

CONTENTS

Main Characters

Gareth (Gary) Owen – Megan (girlfriend)

Alf Reynolds – married Jennifer (air hostess)

Ted Watson – married Penny;
    children, James and Harry

Harry Watkins – married Helen (nurse)

Oliver (Ginger) Markham – married Caroline;
    children, Gareth and Megan

Brian Walker (lost contact)

Fred Jarvis (died in training)

Colonel James – married to Molly;
    daughter, Penny, marries Ted Watson

Christine and her daughter Sophie (Ted's sister and niece)

Mr Townsend (Ted's neighbour, a farmer and horse breeder)

Mr Williamson (a solicitor and Ted's employer)

Captain Harper (Rex)

Peter Holmes – married? (lost contact)

PREFACE

In the 1950s Australia and the Pacific were chosen to test nuclear weapons ranging from the atom bomb to the hydrogen bomb. The UK launched operation Grapple.

To provide all the necessary infrastructure and services required for such a monumental operation members of the Australian, New Zealand, Fijian and British armed forces were employed. Many of the British contingent were eighteen- to twenty-year-old national servicemen who were expected to carry out extremely arduous work under very dangerous conditions—although it has always been claimed that it was perfectly safe. This story gives an account of what it was like during the first two hydrogen bomb tests carried out in 1957–58. It is often the case that memories can fade over the years, leaving one with a distorted view of what really happened in the past, but with experiments of this magnitude one is unlikely to forget.

All the characters in this book are entirely fictitious. They portray the typical experiences of a group of national serviceman who were conscripted into the Royal Engineers before, during, and after their deployment to a nuclear test site on Christmas Island (Kiritimati) in the late 1950s.

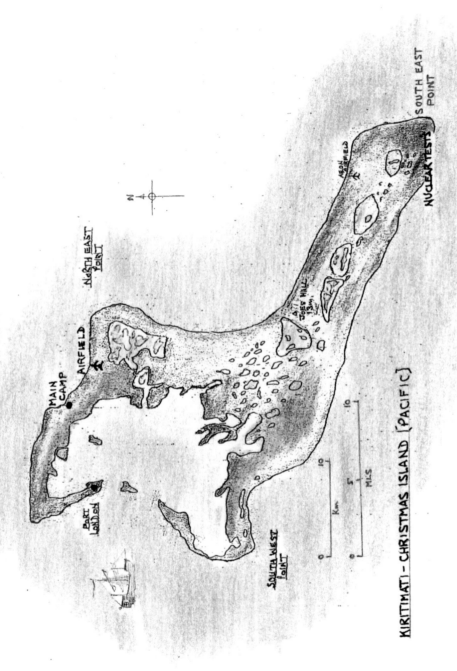

KIRITIMATI - CHRISTMAS ISLAND [PACIFIC]

NORTH EAST POINT

MAIN CAMP

AIRFIELD

PORT LONDON

SOUTH WEST POINT

JOES HILL 13m

NGON AIRFIELD

SOUTH EAST POINT

NUCLEAR TESTS

N

Km

MLS

5

10

INTRODUCTION

During the Second World War, the UK research into nuclear fission was passed to the USA. Known as the Manhattan Project, by July 1945 it lead to the first nuclear bomb being tested in the New Mexico desert.

In August 1945 the USA detonated an atomic bomb over the Japanese city of Hiroshima. Three days later a second atomic bomb was detonated over Nagasaki. Both bombs caused terrifying loss of life and left survivors with serious health issues for many years to come.

All hostilities soon ceased and the world was at peace, but there was an uneasy truce between the superpowers—the USA and the USSR—over political ideologies and power. By 1949, Russia had developed the atomic bomb and the world was plunged into the race for military and political supremacy known as the Cold War. The superpowers had embarked on an arms race with astronomical budgets which no other countries could afford, or indeed had any interest in, except the UK and France.

To become an independent member of the nuclear race would be costly, but in spite of this, the UK embarked on its own nuclear test programme, thus assuring it had its own deterrent against any aggressor. It was known as mutually assured destruction, MAD. There could be no winners in a nuclear exchange, the final result being that the world may well be plunged into a nuclear winter.

In 1952, the UK detonated its first atomic bomb on Mote Bello Island in western Australia with two more tests in 1956. In 1953–57 the UK also carried out nuclear tests in the Emu Field and Maralinga Range in the Woomera area of South Australia, once home to some of Australia's Aboriginal people.

Much to the dismay of the world, in 1952 the USA announced that it had successfully tested a hydrogen bomb, more or less rendering the atom bomb obsolete, and by 1954 the USA tested a hydrogen bomb something in the region of a thousand times more powerful than the Nagasaki bomb.

Russia replied with its own hydrogen bomb, and eventually produced an even more powerful bomb than the USA.

The UK and France decided to pursue their own independent programme to develop the hydrogen bomb, even though it would cost a fortune—to put it mildly.

Christmas Island in the Pacific was chosen as the main base with Malden Islands four hundred miles away chosen for the atmospheric nuclear tests. It was known as Operation Grapple. Initial trials proved to be unsuccessful, and with time running out before a test ban treaty to be agreed by the superpowers, it was decided to carry out more trials on, or near, Christmas Island, now known as Kiritimati.

The people living on the island would have to be kept well out of harm's way, but this was not the case for the servicemen working and living there.

In November 1957, the first bomb was dropped by an RAF Valiant jet bomber over the end of the island, it was much more powerful than expected and caused damage around the island. It demonstrated that the UK had the hydrogen bomb, but at a considerable cost. In April 1958 a second, more powerful bomb was tested with four more tests to follow.

Many health issues have been raised by the local people of Kiritimati, the servicemen who witnessed the tests and those that had to remain on the island after the tests. The claims of ill health suffered by the veterans have been vigorously contested in the courts and remain unresolved to this day.

Whatever is said about these hideous weapons, one thing is certain, they have maintained peace throughout the world, but with more countries in possession of these nuclear weapons, international terrorism, and one country after another falling out with one another, it still adds up to a very uneasy truce.

1. The Dreaded Letter

The fifteenth of November 1956 was a date Harry would not forget. He had received his marching orders, his mother had handed him the letter with OHMS on the envelope.

'Come on, Harry, you will be late for work, read the letter and tell me what's going to happen.'

'Alright, Mum, stop nagging, please give me a chance. I will read it to you.'

As if he did not already know; it was exactly what he expected. After being registered he had passed the medical examination and interview; so it had only been a matter of time before he received an enlistment order. His training as an electronic and electrical engineer had now come to an end, so there was no way he could be deferred any longer. So, with a sinking feeling, Harry opened the letter with his mother looking over his shoulder, eager to know what the Army had in mind for her son.

'How nice of them, Mum, they have invited me to spend two years with them and they have even sent me a rail warrant. At least I will be here for Christmas.'

'Come on, lad, off to work, we can talk this evening.'

On the way to work Harry thought of his two friends who were already serving their two years. One was in Singapore and the other in Cyprus. What about me? What happens if I end up in some outlandish place abroad, how will my girlfriend react?

Harry was in a hurry as there was just a chance he might meet his girlfriend, Sophie, and explain the situation. But Sophie saw him and was in before Harry could say a word.

'Yes, I know, Harry, I have all the details, and before you say another word, the manager wants to see you right away. We can talk this evening, now do not keep Mr Baker waiting, he is not in a good mood with your time keeping.'

Mr Baker was a patient man and a reprimand was long overdue, but he simply reminded Harry what he already knew.

'I am certain of one thing, young man, your time keeping will have to improve somewhat otherwise the Army will not be as patient as me, do you understand, Mr Watkins? However, if your time keeping becomes as good as your exam results, then I do not expect you will go wrong, I have no hesitation in recommending you for a degree course while you are in the Army.'

Mr Baker shook hands with Harry, wished him luck, and said he looked forward to seeing him in two years time. Harry was surprised to realise that he was appreciated so much, and was over the moon with his City and Guilds results, but he had to be honest with himself, his heart was not in electronics at all, he would much prefer working on engines and cars. Why on earth had he not said so in the first place? If he had, maybe things would be different. He felt so unsure of himself, and although he felt grateful, the idea of a correspondence course while in the Army didn't exactly cheer him up. Next he had to face Sophie; a much more daunting task. Sophie worked in the administration office, so a quick phone call would be in order—but he was mistaken.

'I will see you this evening, I am far too busy now, so stop worrying,' she said and hung up.

He should have realised, Sophie dealt with all the mail and therefore knew all about his departure for the Army. If he was not careful he would loose Sophie before he even left for the Army. Maybe Sophie was right, he thought, I am not thinking straight and it is all down to that wretched letter.

The day dragged on, but time waits for no man and it was time to go home. His mother had prepared a very special dinner table, thinking that Harry needed all the support he could get, after all he had never travelled far and never on his own. All the family sat round the table and there was endless talk of his future and so on.

'You will have to explain everything to your girlfriend,' his mother said.

His father said only one thing, 'I spent five long years in the Army during the war, so two years will go like the wind, enjoy yourself, any problems let me know. The first few weeks will be hell, stay with it and don't let me down.'

He then congratulated Harry on his brilliant exam results. With that the door bell rang. His two brothers were out to the door like greyhounds.

'Guess what?' said his brother to Sophie on answering the door. 'Harry is going into the Army for two years and he's terrified.'

'Terrified of what?' Sophie replied. 'It's me who ought to be upset. In any case, that's why I have come to see you all.'

Harry's mother made a place for Sophie.

'It's good of you to come, Sophie, and it is comforting to know that you have taken to heart the fact that Harry has difficult times ahead, but I am sure you will get through the next two years together.'

However, Sophie had worked out her own plans and had already realised that Harry was unable to work out his own future—let alone her own, otherwise his mother would not be treating him like a child. With that, Harry's father tried to take everybody out of the room leaving Sophie and Harry to work things out for themselves, but Harry's mother was reluctant to leave.

'Come on, leave them alone,' said his father.

But Harry's mother was insistent, until Sophie said that, if it was okay by Harry's mother, they would rather be on their own.

'Don't worry, Mrs Watkins, we can sort everything out, won't we Harry?'

Harry just sat there, not saying a word, which hardly impressed Sophie—his mother fussing and treating him like a child did not help either. At last everybody left and Sophie came straight to the point

'Look, Harry, I am happy for you, and I realise how difficult it must be for you, in fact it's very difficult for us both, you understand. I will write to you and will always be thinking of you, I hope you will do the same for me.'

'Of course I will,' said Harry. 'I will write to you just as soon as I arrive, I am sure the Army will insist I write home immediately.'

'Don't worry, Harry, I will always be there for you, I am fond of you, I think you know that and I will wait for you.'

It was that very point that bothered Harry's mind, both his friends already serving had received 'Dear Johns'. I will wait for you until hell freezes, as the old saying goes, and hell froze solid for both of them. Harry, on the other hand, felt that he could really trust Sophie. It was for that reason he felt a little more confident in himself, along with Sophie's support.

The time soon came for Harry to say farewell, it was just Sophie and himself waiting for the train. They never really heard the train arrive, they just held onto each other, then came a loud whistle and a voice, 'Come on lad, all aboard.'

The guard was eager to get moving, but Harry was not. Nevertheless, he climbed aboard the train. With another blast of the guard's whistle and a wave of his flag, the train jolted and moved forward.

Sophie let go of his hand shouting, 'I love you, Harry, write every day, won't you?'

'Of course—and I love you Sophie.'

She disappeared in a cloud of steam as the train picked up speed. He closed the window. Gosh it was cold, really freezing weather. He sat down feeling very low, in fact he felt so depressed he could not remember where he was supposed to be going. Everything was changing all around him, his life had been turned completely upside down by that letter. He stared out of the window but saw nothing. His mind was still back at home and with Sophie. An overwhelming urge came over him to get off of this train to nowhere. It was the most sensible thing to do, get out at the next stop. Why should his life be turned upside down by some official who had signed that letter? I'm not even thinking straight anymore, he thought, then suddenly the door of the carriage opened with a bang, pulling him out of his stupor.

'Tickets, have your tickets ready, please.'

Harry held out his ticket.

'Hello, what's this, you have a second class ticket and you think you are entitled to first class travel do you? Unless you want to pay up, then I must ask you to move, sonny boy.'

'The name's Harry actually, and I'm off to serve my country.'

'Well now,' the ticket man flexed his muscles and bellowed back, 'You will serve time with the magistrate if you don't shift yourself *now*, sonny boy. Now 'op it.'

Having settled down again in second class he really couldn't make out the difference, but he did notice the rain on the window. By now Harry was passed caring. The train rumbled on making him feel very tired. He was totally exhausted, he closed his eyes and left his depression behind.

2. The Train to Nowhere

On and on the train sped, taking Harry to a new beginning. Then it started to slow down to make its approach to the city of York. He soon became wide awake as, according to his information, this was where he changed to another train. He checked his itinerary, but he need not have bothered; it seemed he was not alone. Many others of his own age got off the train.

His first glimpse of uniformed soldiers was of them ushering these poor unfortunate young souls into another train to nowhere. Harry remained silent, he just followed all the other reluctant conscripts.

'Come on you lucky people,' yelled a soldier.

Nobody said much except one, he had a cockney accent and he seemed to have a natural talent for telling jokes. The look of depression was evident on the conscripts' faces so a joke or two was the tonic they needed. All seemed to be reasonable until a sergeant came on the scene.

'I'm looking at *you*, funny boy,' he said, staring at the comic.

The comic replied, rather foolishly Harry thought.

'That's okay, mate, there will be a signed photograph of me in the post.'

The sergeant grinned and said, 'I will remember you, funny boy, in fact, I will remember *all* of you.'

He moved away, checking his paper work he proceeded to ask all of their names and other details. Next they boarded the train—this was the beginning of an adventure they were unlikely to forget.

The rain was joined by a bitter cold wind. Many of the conscripts were ill-prepared for such weather. The light faded quickly as the train moved on, slowly at first, but then picking up speed, with what looked like sleet hitting the windows.

'Hello, my name is Gareth, call me Gary, what's yours?'

'Harry, from just outside London. Where have you travelled from?'

'Betys-y-Coed, Cymru,' said Gary in a strong Welsh accent. '*Croeso*, welcome to the hills of Yorkshire.'

Harry could not share Gary's feelings of welcome, in fact he feared the worse.

'Quite frankly, Gary, I don't think we are going to get a welcome; what I mean is, I don't expect them to shake hands with us when we arrive.'

'Cheer up, mate, it can't be that bad,' said Gary.

The train rumbled through what looked like vast area of wild country, finally the train slowed to a halt.

'Everybody off! Come on, let's be having you, we haven't got all day. Move it, you useless bunch of no goods,' the sergeant's voice was raised somewhat from their last encounter.

'I don't think I like the tone of that idiot's voice, what do you think?'

'I'm inclined to agree with you boyo, somehow I don't think they intend to shake hands,' said Gary.

The rain turned to snow with a biting wind. Harry remembered his mother had packed a flask of tea. After being bundled into the back of a lorry, Harry produced his flask, and to his surprise the tea poured out nice and hot. He glanced over to Gary and the rest of the lads all looking at him. He knew instantly that these lads would be his companions for the next two years, it would be only fit and proper to share the tea, after all, they must be feeling the same as himself.

'Pass the cup around please, Gary, only one mouthful each mind.'

The flask soon emptied but it was an act that even surprised Harry. He never knew that he could bring himself to share. It was an act that seemed to bring everybody together.

Then Harry remembered his uncle, whose entire family had been interned into a German concentration camp during the last war. The first chance he got he made a cup of tea. How he had managed to cope under the extreme pressure, Harry had no idea. All he could remember was his uncle saying, 'A good cup of tea relaxes the nerves, old son.' Under the circumstances, that had to be an understatement in anybody's book. Harry thought his own situation was a holiday camp compared to what his uncle's family had gone through—it was something like four years before they were liberated. They returned to their home in Jersey where nobody in the family had faired much better. And what was the first thing his uncle had done? He had tried to make a cup of tea with herbs. Nothing could be as bad as that. But remembering this true story temporarily took away the feeling of being so cold, thanks to his uncle.

'Three cheers for Harry,' shouted the comedian. 'The name's Alf, by the way. That tea tasted like nectar, many thanks.'

Suddenly lights came into view, lots of them, with huge fences and barbed wire. They passed through a gate with soldiers everywhere. This was the moment of truth for all of them.

The lorry moved forward and then backed into a huge shed and stopped. They were told to stay put and acknowledge their names as they were called out. One or two lads answered feebly and the response was swift to say the least.

'Louder, louder, I haven't got all day. When I call your name I expect to hear you loud and clear, do you understand?' yelled the corporal.

When all the shouting was over they waited, shivering with the cold and nerves at breaking point. Nobody said a word, one lad was crying and looked more like a twelve-year-old rather than an eighteen-year-old. He got short rift from some of the others and was labelled with some very colourful names, which will no doubt stay with him for the rest of his two years.

Harry started to have flashbacks of home. The lorry moved on, then suddenly his mind ran wild. Harry wanted out of this madness, and with a sense of panic he was going to get out of the lorry and make a break for it. His entire routine had been broken, as soon as the lorry stopped he was going to get out and make a run for the fence. However formidable this place was, he wanted out and nobody was going to stop him.

It was already dark, then more lights came into sight. The lorry passed what looked like barriers, high fences and barbed wire and then came to a halt. Once again nobody said a word, but Harry was only interested in jumping out, he was just about to when a soldier screamed at him.

'Going somewhere, soldier? Get back in and wait for your name to be called out you useless idiot.' The soldier wore a red hat and was much taller than Harry. Two more of these giants appeared, saying, 'We will remember you,' and then a barrage of verbal abuse came Harry's way. He was called just about all the names under the sun.

'I have an idea your parentage is being called into question, you're not going to stand for that are you?' said Gary.

That was enough for Harry, 'Who the hell do you think you are? Take that back you lousy bastards, and in any case, where's the toilets, or don't you pigs have any?'

'I don't think you should have said that,' said Alf. He was right, it was a very big mistake, but that was all Harry heard. Screaming and shouting, the two soldiers dragged Harry from the lorry, he fell down on the wet snow and was told to relieve himself.

'Who are you calling bastards, what's your name? Come on, relieve yourself and get back in, ya big nancy boy.'

Shear panic and fear overcame Harry, causing him to relieve himself in his pants. Humiliated and trembling, he climbed back in the lorry, which again moved on, and finally stopped by a row of huts. More shouting and screaming followed, most of which was not fully understood, then they all climbed out of the lorry and were told to line up. Gary had to remind Harry, who was still smarting from his encounter with the military police, that it was time to get out.

'Most unfriendly people I have ever met,' said Gary.

'You can say that again, I won't forget this in a hurry, they made me relieve myself, and I wasn't laughing, believe me.'

'Come on, Harry, just forget it. I guess we have to learn their ways from now on.'

Gary's turn was next for some colourful language. It seems he had to keep his mouth firmly shut. The corporal was beginning to wind himself up.

'How do *you* feel now, Gary?' said Harry feeling a little better.

They were informed that this was to be their home whether they liked it or not. Everybody was lined up and marched into a building. They were measured up to be issued with military clothing.

'Remember these measurements, or you will regret it,' said the corporal.

Next, each new conscript was sent into a huge building. Inside the building was a long counter behind which there were soldiers asking for the conscript's size and shouting at the same time. It appeared to be bedlam, but it seemed to work with most of the lads getting it right. At the end of the counter one couldn't help feeling amused at the stragglers who seemed to have forgotten their measurements. It was nothing short of a comedy show.

Next came the haircut, which wiped the smile off everyone's faces. Most of them tried to object, but they were quickly rebuked by the corporal. Harry had groomed the perfect DA [duck's ass/tail], so nobody, not anybody, was going to touch *his* hair. When it came to his turn he was firmly told to sit down by the barber.

Harry hesitated and proceeded to explain how he wanted it cut. The barber's name was Colin, he had a sinister-looking smile and looked as if he would cut your ears off for nothing; but he had a job to do. He nodded to the corporal. Harry sat down out of shear fear of getting into another confrontation. He could still feel his wet pants and wanted to get out of his soiled clothes as soon as possible. In seconds his beloved hair had gone, all he noticed was the barber wielding his shears ready for the next victim and still smiling.

In spite of the misery of it all, some of them felt the need for some sort of refreshment, for hours all they had had was a mouthful of Harry's tea. Although it was late, they were taken to the cook house for a quick meal. On the way they passed the parade ground and were reminded that this was where they would be spending a great deal of their time in the next few weeks. Nobody was allowed to speak. Only the corporal was allowed to say anything. Little did they realise that for the next few weeks this parade ground would be their playground, starting first thing in the morning, but only after all the kit they had been issued with had been inspected.

The cold air cut right through them, but the rain and sleet had stopped when they entered the cook house with its smell of food. It was warm, and the food made up for the misery they had just been through. With a warm drink inside them they felt somewhat recharged.

When they went back outside the air seemed even colder. Stars covered the night sky, which would mean a hard frost. One of the lads was eager to know where they were going to sleep. The corporal fell on him like a ton of bricks, reminding him not to speak unless spoken to. His name was taken down under the threat of a charge if he stepped out of line once more. None of this meant much at the time, but later on it certainly would. It meant extra duties which became onerous to say the least.

They were lined up again and somehow managed to march with all their kit across the parade ground to their living quarters. It was a row of wooden huts, twenty to a hut with a coke stove at each end.

The corporal quickly allocated them to their accommodation and reminded them that bedding had to be collected from another building close by. Before he dismissed them, he reminded them that all their kit had to be laid out according to the diagram on the wall. There would be a roll call at 0600 hours followed by the kit inspection. All other duties were posted on the notice board. Before he left, the corporal appointed two unsuspecting recruits to take charge of the two stoves unless they wanted to freeze to death.

It was a tall order and one which made them extremely tired in spite of their youth. Harry just had to get out of his clothes and find a bath. The bathrooms were freezing, but at least the water was hot. Laying in the bath he realised that he would have to be up very early. Something like four in the morning, if he stood a realistic chance of laying out his kit for the inspection.

Tiredness had caught up with them and Harry found most of them had slumped on their hard mattress and were fast asleep.

His berth felt like a feather bed to Harry, but then it suddenly occurred to him, how do you make a bed? Making a bed had always been his mother's job. He took it for granted that she would always make the bed—and many other things come to think of it. What would he do without her? Well he was about to find out. Looking around the room he noticed Gary and Alf had ended their traumatic day. To hell with it all, let's end this miserable day, he thought. He found the light switches and pulled a couple of blankets over him.

The move from comfortable beds at home to hard and cold beds in a hut marked a change in the conscripts whole life. Why, Harry thought, didn't I jump from the train when I had the chance?

3. Please, Sir, I Want to Go Home

It seemed just minutes and the lights were back on. The fires were both giving off heat, courtesy of Gary, who was an accomplished climber of the Welsh mountains. He knew how cold it could get.

'You tend to slow down, and you don't think straight when you're cold boyo,' he said.

Harry was grateful that everybody else was struggling with trying to lay out their kit according to the picture. Most had forgotten to fold their bedding into a pack. It was a pantomime of gross incompetence. Hardly awake, they all missed the comforts of home, but their efforts where beginning to take shape. They began to help each other when the door opened with a bang. Their stood the corporal, his uniform was immaculate, with boots shining like glass. He stared straight ahead with a pace stick by his side. Why did he not move or speak?

'When I, or any other senior rank, enters the room you will stand smartly to attention, you will not speak unless spoken to, do you understand?'

Nobody said a word, and then he yelled so that everybody including the entire camp could hear,

'You address me as "Corporal" and stand to attention when I speak to you.'

He was staring at Harry, who was the closest to him.

'I didn't quite hear you, what is your name soldier?'

'Harry Watkins.'

'Stand up straight, you insolent man. Watkins, is it? Well, you have just made your first mistake, Watkins. Now let's try again. What is your name soldier?'

Alf was beyond himself. 'Please say, "Corporal",' he murmured to himself, 'for all our sakes.'

'I won't ask you again, now, soldier, what is your name?'

Standing to attention, this time Harry answered correctly. 'Watkins, Corporal.'

'Louder, Watkins, so that the entire camp will hear you.'

Harry had to repeat himself a few more times and then the corporal moved to Harry's kit which he had laid out, but had not completed according to the diagram.

'What's this, Watkins?'

Before Harry could answer his bed was turned upside down, with his kit flying everywhere.

'Stand to attention, Watkins, if you ever present a kit layout like this again you will have a kit inspection every day for the next eight weeks. Do you understand?'

Harry, standing to attention, replied with a very loud, 'Yes, Corporal.'

With that the corporal caused chaos in the room with just about all the beds being turned over. Nobody was spared the indignity of a judgement of incompetence.

'Do it all again, you have half an hour,' the corporal shouted as he left the room.

Half and hour later, bang on time, the corporal entered the room, this time he was accompanied by a sergeant and an officer. Few of the lads understood these ranks. The sergeant joined the corporal who was inspecting the kit layouts and shouting all the time. It was at this point Harry seized his chance by making an official complaint.

He tapped the officer on the shoulder, 'Excuse me, I don't know who you are.' That was all Harry said.

Screaming like a man possessed the officer shouted, 'Don't you ever touch an officer again. Take his name, Sergeant.'

Quick as a flash, Alf said laughing, 'Don't worry, Harry, you can wash your hands later.'

'Take that man's name as well, Sergeant.'

The problem was that they had no idea just how serious these disciplinarians were. Alf and Harry were quickly dispatched outside into the freezing cold. They were marched to the parade ground and given an early lesson in drill. Then both Alf and Harry were summoned to headquarters where charges were levelled against both of them for insubordination, among other trumped up charges. They were given a quick lecture on Army rules and the purpose of strict discipline. It was tough, but necessary in order to maintain team spirit and leadership. Nobody was allowed to break the rules, breaking the rules could lead to chaos, and make no mistake about it, if you step out of line, expect to be punished. They were given three days of extra duties, or 'jankers' as it was known. Three days of nothing but misery, running around the parade ground with full kit three times a day, reporting to the guard room twice a day, and finally washing up in the cook house during the evening. All this on top of their normal training schedule. It was highly probable that they would unwittingly offend again. But at this rate, the urge to oppose the system would soon fade away.

On their next visit to the guard room Alf reminded Harry that they would have to be ultra careful. One mistake, such as a wrong word, sloppy uniform, or one wrong move, and it would almost certainly mean seven more days of this misery.

As they stood to attention, the orderly officer made his appearance, and not before time as their legs were beginning to go numb with the cold. With them still standing to attention, the officer made his inspection. He seemed to be slightly disinterested, and handed the responsibility to the sergeant—who really was interested. His inspection was thorough. He made Alf remove all his webbing so that one slight imperfection, or one word from Alf, would almost certainly mean seven more dreaded days. Next came his boots, which came in for some criticism.

'I need to see my face in them,' the sergeant shouted at Alf, who was, by now, close to breaking point.

In addition to Alf's friendliness, he never complained, and without doubt he was the life and soul of any situation. But at this moment, Harry sensed a change in Alf's ability to cope. His actions declared that he was becoming less willing to respond, which prompted more shouting and abuse from the sergeant. Something was wrong, Harry felt the need to intervene for Alf's sake, but he already knew that one false move would mean more abuse.

'Stand still, you useless soldier,' this, along with less adoring words, was Alf's reward.

Suddenly, Alf went down on his knees and slumped forward.

'Get up, you useless idiot, what the hell do you think you are playing at?'

That was enough for Harry, who moved to help his friend; he was not going to watch him suffer any longer.

'Get the hell out of my way,' yelled the sergeant.

Harry was pushed to one side before he could do anything. Military police came from nowhere and carried Alf into the guard room. Harry was left standing to attention and dismissed to the cook house for more spud and onion peeling. He was joined by six other victims of trumped-up charges. One turned out to be a student of law. He started to go on about justice and the law.

'Justice is metered out according to the law,' he said.

'Rubbish,' was the response.

But the student continued to explain where he thought things had gone wrong. He went on and on until one of the lads had just about had enough.

'If you don't shut your mouth, law man, I will shut it for you,' which was endorsed by the others, except for Harry. He found the subject interesting, and thought that this barrack room lawyer should act in their defence. If he could explain where the sergeant had gone wrong, then he might be interested in taking Harry's case further.

However, he was not that naive, 'This is the Army, their laws are obviously written in blood, they do not have time for barrack room lawyers, so I think the lads are correct, they ought to tread carefully when taking advice.'

Nevertheless Harry was still interested in what he had to say about justice and the law.

Harry was overtaken by his emotions once again, then the room suddenly became darker. Standing in the doorway, a military policeman somewhere in the region of six-foot-six yelled out, 'Come here you, yes, *you*. Come out here now. So we have a barrack room lawyer do we? Well let's see, where shall we start?' said the military policeman.

The law student, who was frightened to death, received a lecture on Army law for about five minutes, accompanied by some very colourful language.

'Have I made myself clear? Because if I haven't then we can resume this conversation in the guard room.'

'I understand perfectly, Corporal,' replied the law student. The budding lawyer thought it would be very unwise to offer any form of defence in this slight misunderstanding, he also thought it best not to advocate in any further misunderstandings with the Army.

The military policeman then turned his attention to Harry. 'Your friend is recovering in the sick quarters. The medical officer said he has the flu which is bad news for all of us.'

'Why all the bullying?' Harry asked, half expecting more shouting, but the corporal spoke in a more humane way.

'You find just about everything complicated, even yourself, don't you?'

'I don't,' said Harry, his voice suddenly went up a notch.

'If I say you do, then you do. Stand up straight when I am talking to you. What is your name soldier? Come on, your name?'

'Watkins, Corporal.'

Harry's heart started to beat uncontrollably.

'Listen, Watkins, take some advice. These instructors are professional disciplinarians who, in time, will change you and your colleagues into a team of disciplined soldiers, so the need for their expertise is paramount. What faces you when you leave here is anybody's guess, but rest assured you will be able to cope with whatever faces you.'

Perhaps an overstatement in Harry's case, for he and his colleagues were about to face an experience beyond comprehension.

The corporal took his leave by saying, 'Don't let yourself down, soldier, in doing so you will let us all down, and come hell or high water, we won't let you do that.'

Once again Harry's mind was confused and frightened. What would happen when they left this place? Surely nothing could be worse than this? The corporal, on the other hand, seemed human—just like anybody else—but a few words from him had changed his whole way of thinking. Harry was at a crossroads, would he continue to rebel, or would he accept the rules?

Alf recovered, along with many other soldiers suffering from flu. The bitter cold wind lingered on, giving them all a very hard time with their training. The assault course proved to be much more difficult. Heavy snow hampered their progress, but there was no time to lose. The training programme could not be set back. Every move across the assault course came very hard for Harry and his friends, all except Gary, who received special attention from the sergeant.

'Well done, Owen, how did you manage to climb the ropes like that?'

'Mountains, Sergeant, I climbed in the mountains of North Wales, Sergeant. I do mountain rescue in my spare time, Sergeant.'

'Believe me, young man, that skill of yours may save your own life one day. Right, get fell in,' yelled the sergeant.

Back to base camp with full kit and rifle, it was a long two-mile jog. Once again, Harry and Alf arrived at the parade ground way behind the rest, which made them slightly unpopular since they all had to be present and correct before dismissal.

At last some peace. Harry slumped onto his bed. Although the mattress was hard with no springs, it felt like a feather bed. The indignity of failing on the assault course faded from his mind. It all had to be repeated tomorrow anyway.

'Come on, Alf and Harry. Get up, you have to eat!' said Gary.

They joined the rest of the lads in the cook house.

'Blimey, look at this lads, I'd rather eat my socks. What is it?'

Wham!—a pace stick slammed on the table.

'You may have to eat your socks one day, soldier,' shouted their corporal. 'Eat what's before you and be grateful, you miserable whingers.'

They couldn't believe it, this man had been out on the assault course with them, and yet he was still watching over them. His uniform was immaculate, nothing out of place.

'Enjoy your meal gentlemen, I will see you in the morning, 0600 hours sharp.'

Harry was at last beginning to understand, his life was slowly being taken over. The constant interference in his life had been onerous from the start, but it seemed the corporal was gradually bringing them into his confidence. All of the recruits had managed to master this redoubtable few weeks, and tomorrow was going to be another one of these formidable days. Harry was determined to show his masters that he could finish the assault course, no matter what was thrown at him, punishing though it may be.

Harry decided that he would write to Sophie and his parents, which was long overdue. His mind seemed to be much more settled thinking of home. He would have to explain the delay in writing to them, but he was sure they would understand. After that he would join the lads for a well-earned pint.

The next day they were lined up for their final attempt at the assault course, with full kit and rifle, and they knew that they had to impress the instructors. They went for it, shouting at one another. Alf was ahead of Harry, with Gary urging him along, but the energy seemed to desert him— and then came the rope ladder.

Gary explained how to tackle the ladder, which to Harry's surprise worked really well. Feeling much better, the rest of the course seemed a little easier, until they came to the water. Machine gun fire sounded all around them with explosions not a million miles away. It was then Harry fell straight into the freezing water, the ice had broken under his weight. Somehow he managed to scramble out, helped by Alf and Gary. His rifle slivered across the ice and managed to stay dry. Who knows what the consequences would have been had he lost his rifle. Cheered up by the fact that he had retrieved his rifle it reminded him of shooting back home. Weekends would be taken up by shooting rabbits using a twelve-bore shotgun, which was rather different to an assault course. With his mind on shooting rabbits, wood pigeons, and the odd fox, he somehow managed to bounce back from being exhausted to being refreshed.

Up the nets, over the top, and onwards towards the rifle range. This was their final test: load five rounds and fire them into the target, then race to the final section of the course. First he had to fall to the ground and lie in the firing position, then load the five rounds, take aim, and fire. He achieved a close grouping in the centre of the target. With his pride restored, he ran to the finishing line where he was greeted by his mentors.

'You useless——,' and so it went on, this unrelenting expression of demeaning opinions about him. Anyhow, why should I care, Harry thought, I would have bagged five rabbits had this been at home. With this sudden recollection of home, he wanted to write home and tell everybody that he had mastered the assault course.

The recruits were all starting to grow up. Their adolescent days were over—or were they? This was only the beginning of much more rigorous training, but they felt primed and ready for anything.

Harry was twenty years old and felt slightly out of place with most of the lads, who had just turned eighteen. Their budding lawyer was the oldest, being twenty one. Ted Watson had studied law, but had not taken the final exam. Ted was a solicitor's clerk and offered his assistance and advice whenever any of the lads found themselves in trouble. He was not that popular with the lads since none of his advice came in useful, in fact it often made things worse. Ted, on the other hand, enjoyed being their advocate, or barrack room lawyer. Not one of the lads who was at the receiving end of an NCO's wrath had won their case; they were at the receiving end of military law. Ted never won a case, much to his embarrassment and the misery of the defendant.

Ted's worst advice was given to a lad called Fred. Full of apologies, Ted failed to console Fred's feelings when he was awarded seven days jankers with no hope of an appeal.

'Well, lets face it Fred, swearing at an officer may have given you fourteen days,' said Ted.

'Rubbish,' was Fred's reply. 'I was a couple of minutes late for parade, that's all.'

'I'm sorry, Fred, but when challenged by the officer, you shouldn't have said "bollocks"—it didn't help.'

'But it wasn't intended for the officer,' said Fred. 'The moment I acted on your advice it was all over in seconds. I had no rights according to the military, and if I opened my mouth once more it would be fourteen days. "March him out," and that was that.'

'Well there you are, Fred, you admit that it might have been worse. It is highly unlikely that the officer presiding had any formal legal training, and was therefore in no position to mete out justice. If I were you, I would appeal.'

By now Fred was in no mood for more advice.

'Well, if you so sure of yourself, why don't you appeal on my behalf?' said Fred angrily.

'Ah, well, perhaps it would be better if we dropped the whole affair. The least I can do is help clean your kit,' said Ted.

Several of the lads got together and promised to help Fred through this gross injustice. His webbing, uniform and boots would be taken care of throughout the seven days. 'Just call us your butlers from now on,' they told Fred. Once again this gross injustice meted out to Fred was a setback for Harry, and all the others, but they had learnt how to regroup. Without doubt, this was a miscarriage of justice.

But Fred's real problem was an upset stomach causing him frequent visits to the loo. It was recommended that he report to sick bay by one of the lads who was trained in first aid. His name was Pete. With his limited knowledge, Pete said Fred had a temperature, among other symptoms, which might be contagious. Fred was in agreement and would report the matter to the corporal. The next morning, Fred's kit was laid out in immaculate form. Everybody in the room made every effort to ease his pain.

The corporal, however, was not impressed; and neither was Fred when the medical officer prescribed him medication and told him he needed to see him in a week's time.

The very next day, Fred's kit was laid out as usual. Both the sergeant and the corporal turned up for the inspection, but this time Fred was missing. He may have been delayed from his morning visit to the guardroom. All the lads made every effort to impress, but to their surprise the officer in charge of them turned up. The officer was a man of few words, but this time he made it quite clear that much work had to be done to improve their performance, especially on the assault course. There had to be more team spirit and all that.

Ted was not impressed, he was thinking it was a pity he did not spend more time looking after the troops, especially when they were sick.

The officer walked out mumbling something like, 'Carry on, Sergeant.'

The sergeant saluted, slamming his foot down on their highly polished floor, which annoyed them all after they had spent hours polishing it. He then turned his attention to Fred's absence.

'Where is Jarvis?' he bellowed.

'He may well have reported sick, sergeant,' replied Ted, stepping forward and standing firmly to attention. 'May I point out, Sergeant, Private Jarvis has been the victim of gross victimisation and according to my information I have——' and that was as far as Ted got.

The sergeant came down on him like a ton of bricks.

'Get back into line, you insolent man!' the sergeant screamed at Ted.

'Let me remind you of Queen's regulations, soldier, you lot must think I was born yesterday, I have heard all about you, Watson, and I think it's about time you dropped this barrack room lawyer advice and remembered that this is the Army, because if you don't then I will personally see that you get fourteen days. You can throw your law books on the fire, do you understand, Watson?'

'Perfectly, Sergeant.'

While Ted was being hung out to dry, Fred walked into the room completely unnoticed by the NCOs. He obviously was very unwell and without doubt unable to carry on.

'Thanks, lads, for laying out my kit.'

The sergeant, already fired up, turned around, but the corporal had already spotted Fred and gave him no end of unhelpful verbal abuse.

'Stand up straight, soldier. Who gave you permission to be absent from kit inspection?'

Fred's kit, all laid out to perfection, was suddenly thrown into chaos. The corporal lifted Fred's bed and turned it on its side sending his kit all over the place. Nobody dared move, but it was too much for Pete. He stepped one pace forward and reminded the corporal and the sergeant that Private Jarvis was unlikely to have heard them since he was very unwell.

'Well now, we have a barrack room lawyer and now a doctor in the room, I never realised that we had such eminent talent here. Get back into line you useless halfwit,' said the sergeant.

With trembling voice Pete stood his ground and pleaded with the sergeant, 'Please, let me look at him.'

Harry felt distinctly uneasy, but he dared not vent his feelings. They had been standing to attention for some time when the sergeant told them to stand easy. The corporal had disappeared and the sergeant attended to Fred along with Pete. Fred seemed to be going down fast, then something quite unexpected happened, the sergeant ordered everybody outside, putting Harry in charge for a spell of drill on the parade ground.

Pete was ordered to stay with Fred.

'Come on, jump to it,' the sergeant shouted.

'Private Watkins will give you one hour's drill before lunch break, and don't let me catch any of you stepping out of line—you will regret it. Carry on, Watkins.'

It was all so sudden for Harry. What do I do next? His anger and frustration had changed to panic and incompetence. The fear of making a complete fool of himself was sensed by the lads, a massive test of his authority. This test of leadership would stretch him to his limits. Harry felt his incompetence embarrassing, he never realised just how difficult it could be to take charge. Then a real commander came to the rescue.

'Get fell in you disobedient rabble.'

It was the sergeant issuing a real lesson on how to command.

'Now march them onto the parade ground, drill them for one hour and bring them back here to me. Don't let me down, soldier.'

'No, sergeant.'

Standing firmly to attention, and still unsure of himself, Harry then did an about turn to face his room mates and the lads in the next hut: thirty-eight men in all. It was now or never. Humiliation was about to take over.

'Squad, Attention.'

This was his first command and a feeble one at that.

The sergeant yelled out, 'Louder man, you sound like a fairy's fart,' which brought roars of laughter from the lads.

'I will have the lot of you on a charge, stand still and wait for my command, shouted the sergeant. With a thunderous roar the sergeant demonstrated how to give the command, 'Squad, attention. Now then, soldier, let's hear you again.'

This time Harry had to do it right, and yelled at the top of his voice. To his amazement, it worked. Next he gave the command 'Tallest on the right, shortest on the left, in two ranks file.'

Yes, it was actually working. I really am in command, he thought. But was he? In actual fact, these untrained soldiers were still becoming an organised force, at any time they could revert back to an undisciplined rabble. One mistake and Harry would face a calamitous situation. At first sight they all looked correct, so he gave the next command, and so on.

Harry had completed the first stage, the tallest at each end with shortest in the middle. Brilliant, now let me march them onto the parade ground, he thought.

'Squad, come on, shoulders back, squad move to the left; left turn.'

'Actually, Harry, the parade ground is the other way, I just thought I would let you know,' said Alf.

'Just testing, Alf,' replied Harry.

This caused a roar of laughter.

'Keep it down, lads, or otherwise we are all in it,' said Harry.

'Okay, squad, about turn— by the left, quick march.'

They were on their way.

'Come on lads, get your arms up, let's show them what we can do.'

Then panic set in. That old saying came to mind, 'Easier said than done.' But there was no reason for him to panic, they all marched to the parade ground without any trouble. Left wheel, and they were there. Harry marched them all around the edge and then brought them to the middle. He halted them, brought them into line, and gave the order, 'Open order, march, right dress,' and finally, 'Eyes front.' Harry had unwittingly brought them into view of an ambulance with somebody being placed in the back. This completely unnerved them all, including Harry. He gave the order, close order, march, and marched them well away from view. It had to be Fred, since the ambulance was right outside their hut.

'Look lads, how about marching back for Fred? Come on, shoulders back, and do your best for Fred.'

Finally, they marched back to the hut lines where they were being watched by the sergeant. They seemed to be in perfect step when Harry took a bold step. He peeled off the front, about turned and gave the order, 'Squad halt.' He then ordered right dress and so on. He turned and faced the sergeant.

'Reporting for duty, Sergeant.'

The sergeant came over to speak to them.

'Regarding young Jarvis, he has been admitted to hospital for treatment. If anyone of you experience similar symptoms then you must immediately report to the medical officer. This afternoon is pay day, you lucky people. Don't spend it all at once. And by the way, your performance on the parade ground was very good, well done.'

After being dismissed they all made a dash for the cook house for lunch. The food was not what Mum would dish up, but when you were hungry it was a banquet.

There was much speculation over the nature of Fred's illness. Pete did most of the talking, and finally put an end to the endless rumours. 'None of us will know until the hospital has diagnosed him. Maybe we will never know,' he said. 'Now what's this on my plate?' moaned Pete, changing the subject.

'If you don't want it, I will have it, never look a gift horse in the mouth,' said Alf.

'When was the last time we had a decent meal? This is nothing short of a gastronomic disaster,' yelled one of the boys.

His voice was just loud enough for the cooks to hear.

That's done it, thought Harry, as the cook was about to descend on them clutching a ladle.

'Who wants to complain? Come on, speak up. Who said my cooking was a load of garbage not fit for a pig? Come on, speak up.'

The cook was enraged to put it mildly. Then Alf stood up and said in his normal jovial manner, 'I am sure I speak for my fellow guests when I say that this was a first class meal fit for someone who is on the brink of starvation. Not even a pig would turn his nose up at it. My compliments to the chef, be upstanding and raise your mugs.'

Most of the boys were already standing as the chef swung a punch at Alf—who had already spotted the sergeant major. Their corporal had also entered the fray, bringing his pace stick hard down on the table.

'Outside, the lot of you.'

Accompanied by more verbal abuse, everybody raced outside.

'Fall in, the lot of you.'

Lined up and standing to attention, Pete suddenly remembered Alf was still inside under the table, and maybe unconscious, but it was too late. The duty officer was summoned, and when he finally turned up, the sergeant major gave him all the details. The duty officer turned to face them.

'As I understand it there has been a complaint about the food causing a minor misunderstanding between the cook and at least one of you. This behaviour is taken very seriously, and unless the complainant comes forward, I will have no alternative but to hand you all over to the sergeant major.'

'Typical passing the buck, as usual,' murmured Harry.

'Ah, at least one of you has something to say, step forward that soldier,' said the officer.

Harry had no alternative, wishing he had kept his mouth shut from always criticising others. He took one step forward and shouted out his number, rank, and name.

'Now, perhaps you would like to repeat yourself, soldier,' said the officer.

'Sir, I said it was bad luck, as usual.'

Harry was waiting for his fate, since whatever the situation some form of reprimand would be inevitable. Then our barrack room lawyer, Ted, shouted out, 'Permission to speak, sir.'

The sergeant major was by now beyond himself. He walked up to Ted, and when they were nose to nose, he yelled, 'You speak when invited to, soldier, and not before. Do you understand?'

'Yes, sir.'

'What have you to say, soldier?'

Although attention had been drawn away from him, Harry felt like he would rather be handcuffed to a bear than be here.

Ted was incredibly brave or just plain stupid.

'Come on, soldier, speak up while you still have a chance.'

'Sir, it seems to me, having thought about all the facts, that the cook—who took exception to the alleged remarks about his style of cuisine had, in fact, completely misunderstood. Sir, the cook simply failed to understand that he was being complimented, using violence——'

'Yes, yes, that's enough soldier,' said the sergeant major.

'Thank you, sergeant major. March them off.'

The officer walked away, and although Ted's explanation was a clever one, he nevertheless let the sergeant major adjudicate, knowing that the food was indeed garbage. Harry was right, the buck had been passed down. Ted had shown real guts when he confronted the officer who may well have put them all on a charge for instigating a riotous situation. As it turned out, he suspected the truth, so he drew a fine line between an amicable solution, or a severe punishment for all of them. As it was, the sergeant major ordered the corporal to march them onto the parade ground for an extra drill until pay parade.

Pay parade for national servicemen was not exactly an exciting event. Something like twenty-nine shillings a week was paid out to each soldier. When your name was called, each soldier would shout out, 'Sir!' and march forward to the paying officer; slam his boot to the ground and salute; quote his number, rank, and name; collect his money; step back; salute again; about turn; and march smartly back into line. Harry was thinking what a difference to just a few weeks ago when as an apprentice he had picked up more money than that. Having said that, he did not have to pay board and lodging here, but there were deductions which left them way out of pocket. At least he had some money, which he would have to spend on letters home, toiletries, and what's left, a pint or two? Fortunately, Harry did not smoke, and by the end of the week he might have enough money for egg and chips in the NAAFI.

Pay parade was all but over when it began to snow with a bitter cold northerly wind. As usual, their faithful corporal explained the rest of the day would be in the classroom for lessons that would change their perception of mankind.

4. An Introduction to Hell

The weather was closing in to do its worst. Great coats were ordered to be worn with gloves, and surprisingly the difference was immediate. They marched through light snow, entered the classroom where a sergeant was waiting for them. Their mentor remained at the back of the room, watching over them and reminding them to sit down and keep quiet.

You could hear a pin drop, then the sergeant introduced himself with a life-sized diagram of what looked like an alien from another world. He immediately revealed the mystery of the being from another world by saying that this was what you would look like in the event of a third world war.

Remarks came thick and fast to this, but were stamped out abruptly by the corporal.

The apparel in the diagram was explained in detail by the sergeant. 'Without this you would surely die,' he said.

He then briefly introduced the subject of chemical, biological, and if that wasn't enough, nuclear warfare.

Chemical and gas attacks was first on the agenda. Nobody had any remarks, which was not surprising. Harry could sense that the sergeant had their full attention. Finally, the lesson was over, which was a relief since it left most of them with a feeling of nausea. Let us get the hell out of here, Harry thought to himself, but the sergeant had other ideas.

'You will have to get used to the possibility of hell on earth,' he said. 'Tomorrow we will have a drill for a gas attack.'

'Blimey, I can't wait,' said Alf.

They were all dismissed back to another gastronomic delight in the cook house. The mystery would unfold tomorrow. The topic of conversation was anything but chemical and gas attacks. The stunned looks on their faces said it all. Nobody would be mad enough to resort to this, or would they?

'Oh, forget it, I fancy a pint this evening,' said Ted.

'That's the spirit, what with these miserable eggs, chips and beans, and then a pint in the NAAFI later on, we should remind the sergeant that it's not necessary to theorise a gas attack—we have a practical demonstration most mornings.'

'I really don't know what you are trying to suggest,' said Pete with a guilty look on his face.

There was only one problem, most of them could not afford a pint, so they agreed to pool their cash and share. Being locked up in this camp was a miserable feeling; it felt nothing like home. In fact, home felt a million miles away. Only a letter from home would dispel this feeling of depression. That subject of their afternoon lesson gave them a completely different view of human behaviour, leading them to feel like 'Who cares anymore?' Their perception of mankind had suddenly taken a turn for the worse. Their mixed reactions were expressed over their single pint. The reactions ranged from, 'An eye for an eye, a tooth for a tooth;' 'Why haven't we learnt from the last two dreadful wars?' and, 'It all comes down to power and rival ideologies.'

Pete found the conversation very depressing and felt it was spoiling a good pint. It was a pitiful situation when the lads were discussing the possibility of the human race gassing one another into extinction. To Pete the whole business seemed totally immoral. They all seemed to think that it was an odious situation when one had to resort to gassing one another as a response to their appetite for power, greed, envy, and so on.

One of the lads, Oliver, nicknamed Ginger because of his hair, had a more religious side to him. He said, 'What's mine is mine, and what's yours is mine.' Ginger didn't exactly choose his words carefully. 'That's their motto,' he said.

Ginger was from the West Country, he was a quiet, unassuming sort of chap, but at times had a real sense of humour. He was very religious, although you would never have guessed by the way he went about his daily life, although he was famous for quoting from the Bible. In view of what he had heard this afternoon, he made himself perfectly clear. 'Read Romans, chapter seven, verses fourteen to twenty-five, you will find it gives a firm warning,' he said. 'Some of you may want to read on, you will find the Bible incredibly interesting.'

'Boring,' said one of the lads.

Ginger just smiled back.

'The odd thing about all this is that pretty well all that we have been arguing about is answered for you in the Bible. We all make rods for our backs and then wonder why things go wrong.'

'Okay, Ginger, you answer this: what would happen if we all obeyed the *heavenly law* by walking out of this hellish place and refusing to have any further part of coping with earthly disputes? I mean, act as a pacifist,' said Brian.

It was a fair point, one which Ginger would not shy away from. 'Who would have the guts to walk out of the gates in the name of peace and heavenly law? I suspect none of you, including me. I am scared of earthly law, but the one who walks out of those gates would dispel all possibility of being called a hypocrite. That depresses me more than you can imagine: I am a hypocrite. I am scared of earthly law, which of course leads me to sin. I try very hard, which I guess is all I can hope for.

'When I look at what is going on in the world, very powerful people East and West have a habit of making rods for our backs. They have no control over their own desire for power and wealth. We are no more than puppets being manipulated so as to keep us all in a sense of fear. "Do as your told, or else." I have desperately tried to stay within heavenly law and follow it, but earthly law keeps getting in the way.'

There was silence until Brian mentioned that his girlfriend could start a Third World War in seconds. 'I don't know why I bother. I'm ready to take my chances on this earth, follow my instincts, and live for today; I have no wish to harm anyone. I don't want to be the one who presses the trigger.'

Harry thought Ginger was right. 'I have to say, Ginger does have a point; he is not entirely in cloud cuckoo land, and at least he is honest, which is more than I can say. All these discussions are no more than a simplistic view of world events, disputes, and ideologies, and it equates to no more or less than an intellectual view. It really comes down to the fact that if these weapons are used, we will certainly be in queer street.'

'Cheer up, remember tomorrow is another fun day, with gastronomic delights in the cook house, what more could you want?' said one of the lads.

There could be no winners or losers in these discussions, but they had all briefly thought about a more spiritual life where, one day, all troubles and tears would fade away—something that was not written about in their training programme.

Ginger was not prepared to give up his soul, no matter

what passed his way, or the consequences of contravening earthly law. He had to obey his own conscience, and at the same time, he was saying out loud that there was another way, however difficult.

The devil and sin really do exist according to Ginger, and Harry was beginning to realise it. He would read Romans, and maybe much more.

Harry's conscience was beginning to upset him. Surely I have to come to terms with the way I conduct my life? I have been dishonest on occasions.

Walking back to the hut he felt so cold. Snow was still falling, but not enough to prevent business as usual. The corporal would be on parade, you could count on that. He was thinking he must write to home and Sophie again, perhaps more letters would cheer him up. Thinking of Sophie, she had not exactly over-stretched herself with the pen.

Inside the hut it felt bitterly cold.

'Who's turn is it to make up the fires?'

Ginger, who had finished his letters, owned up. 'Sorry about that,' he said.

Harry noticed Ginger had not even topped up the fires, and worse still, the bins were empty and that meant going back outside into the freezing cold.

'You know what that means, don't you?' said Harry.

'Yes, please don't remind me,' replied Ginger.

'Well now, Ginger, what is it to be? It seems you are between the devil and the deep blue sea, metaphorically speaking of course.'

'Please say what you mean, Harry?'

'I mean what I say, you had better think quickly before it's too late and the others come back. Look, Ginger, you either incur the wrath of the other lads when they return from the

NAAFI, or you risk seven days jankers by raiding the coke yard, which as you know is out of bounds this time of the day. Raiding the coke yard this time of night would be a serious business, and so a little divine intervention would be very welcome, wouldn't you say so, Ginger? So, what are you going to do about it?'

'Okay, you're right Harry, I will do my best. Explain everything to the lads and apologise to them for me will you?' Ginger picked up the four coke bins and made for the door. 'God help me, and forgive me,' he said as he closed the door.

Harry's conscience immediately told him to give Ginger a hand, regardless of being caught. 'Come on, mate, give me two of those bins.'

'No way, Harry, I don't see why you should risk yourself just because of my mistake.'

'Ginger, say no more, remember the snow will cover our tracks, don't say anything, and if you hear voices—keep down.'

'That's really decent of you, but I can't allow you to take this risk, Harry, it's so cold.'

'Don't waste time, Ginger, let's go for it.'

Fortunately, there was just enough light for them to find their way, but it was fading fast, not helped by blinding snow and a bitter cold wind.

'We will take the short cut, Ginger, and I hope the snow will cover our tracks by morning.'

It seemed ages before they reached the yard, which was very dimly lit. It was snowing harder by now.

Horror struck, they found the yard was locked. Ginger was beside himself.

'Pull yourself together, Ginger, we will have to find a way in, come on.'

There was no way over the top, barbed wire saw to that, no

it had to be under the wire, in any case they have four bins to fill. Feeling their way around the fence Harry was genuinely hoping for divine intervention. Then a vehicle was heard not far away, its lights shining their way.

'Down, Ginger,' but he started to panic.

'That's it, we will have to go back.'

Harry grabbed him and pulled him down.

'Shut up, Ginger, just stay here and listen.'

They could hear doors slamming and voices. Lights from the vehicle drifted across them as the vehicle drove off. Voices grew louder, but then faded away. The freezing cold had chilled them to the point where they could not feel their hands, but up they got, looking for that elusive way in so they could fill their bins and receive a warm reception back at the hut, which seemed a million miles away. Then Harry found what looked like a join in the fence which had been poorly repaired.

'That's it, Ginger, we are in.'

Obviously somebody had been here before, tampered with the fence and clumsily tried to put it back together again. Harry was in.

'Come on, Ginger, pass me the bins.'

With as little noise as possible, he filled the bins and handed them through to Ginger.

'For crying out loud, Ginger, grab the bins and keep quiet, let me repair the fence and we can make our way back.'

The snow had become heavy and the wind had got stronger, making life even more difficult. At last the fence was back in place.

'Okay, let's go, and keep down, don't say a word, Ginger. If we get caught, its number, rank and name only,' said Harry jokingly.

Just as they were about to enter the hut they heard a loud

voice, but they could not hear what was being said. Staying on the right side of caution, they peered through the window. Ginger, once again, started to panic, he was not thinking straight anymore. It was just what Gary said about being really cold, your mind starts to wander.

'That's it,' I am going in and owning up.'

'Like hell you are, it may be nothing to do with us.'

Huddled up together with four bins of coke, heavy snow, and a biting cold wind the minutes seemed like hours. Finally, whoever it was left their hut, but only to go into the next hut.

'Okay, we can go in', and you can redeem yourself. Good luck,' said Harry.

On entering the hut uproar took place, accompanied by extreme language. Ted explained that it was not the coke stoves that was the issue, although naturally they were not best pleased with the rooms being so cold, and it had been slightly embarrassing explaining why the room was so cold to the corporal. 'What with no coke bins, and the absence of two members of the room . . . well, it was not easy. I'm afraid the corporal will pursue the matter in the morning. He has both your names, and I must say he looked really wild.'

Ginger sat down on his bed, still shivering with the cold and his nerves shot to pieces. He failed to realise that Ted was joking. However, Ted explained that the corporal knew something was up alright, but was presumably prepared to overlook the fact that the room was stone cold and the coke bins were missing along with two members of the room. He no doubt knew what was going on simply because he was responsible: they were showing initiative, courage, and the ability to work together. His professionalism was paying off irrespective of the fact that these two men—who had only been in his care for a few weeks—were prepared to take a huge risk. Yes, he was pleased with their progress, but he dared not let them know.

Harry decided to keep his overcoat on while writing another letter to Sophie. There was not much to say, other than life in this camp was not exactly five star. The letter fell short of how he actually felt, but trying to compose a romantic letter to Sophie in this miserable camp made it nigh on impossible. At least he had written to her, and could only hope that she would understand. By now everybody was in bed with their overcoats over the blankets.

'Turn the lights out, please Harry.'

During the night the temperature plummeted, but the two stoves threw out just enough radiant heat to keep the room above freezing.

It was half five and time to get up. Ginger had topped up the stoves during the night, which saved him from further acrimony. It was still snowing when they made their way to the cook house, with snow drifting across the road. The chef pointed out that breakfast would be late, so take it or leave it. They elected to stay, feeling that nobody could possibly make their way in this weather, but to their amazement there stood Superman, it was their corporal, as immaculate as ever.

'Look who's here; it's Father Christmas,' said Alf.

'Alright you lot, number two shed—now.'

Once inside he handed responsibility to Harry for drill. After an hour everybody had warmed up, leaving Harry's voice a little hoarse.

What I wouldn't do for a nice, hot mug of tea, thought Harry.

Just then the corporal turned up. 'Okay, lets have you outside in single file back to the cook house.'

He had organised a late breakfast, and then it was back to the classroom for another lesson on how to end the world as we know it in less than a day. We have come a long way since the bow and arrow, and in a very short time, thought Harry.

Breakfast consisted of porridge, an egg and bacon sandwich, and a mug of hot tea. Under the circumstances the cook had done a good job, especially considering that only two cooks had turned up. One of the cooks who had turned up was the one that had put Alf under the table, and he was not happy at all.

'Give me the chance and *he* will be under the table next time,' said Alf.

'In your dreams, Alf, he is twice the size of you: you have no chance. In any case, what happened to you, Alf, we didn't see you outside, I thought you had been layed out?' replied Pete.

Alf laughed and said that no one had noticed him lying under the table, not even the cook, so he decided not to get involved.

'You crafty devil, so what did you do?' asked Pete.

'I went back to the hut and sat by the fire until pay parade,' replied Alf.

'Blimey, Alf, you really are sailing close to the edge, what if the corporal had caught you?'

'How could he, Pete? He was with you, enjoying a walk around the parade ground in the snow. As it was, you all ended up in number two shed just in time for me to slip in unnoticed for pay parade.'

'I have to hand to you, Alf, you have guts.'

The winter continued with a vengeance, but it appeared it was quite normal for this area.

'Remind me not to come to this place for a holiday,' said Ted.

'You have got it wrong there, Ted, it's a fantastic place for camping in the summer,' said Brian.

'Well, I am sure you are right, but I have no wish to be stuck in a tent and being reminded of this place, thank you very much,' replied Ted.

Then an announcement was made by the sergeant chef. There would be no midday meal, instead there would be a hot meal between five and six. All the recruits stood up and cheered.

The NCOs soon put an end to their momentary feeling of cheerfulness. They were ordered outside again, then it was a single file march to the classroom for lessons on how to wipe out the world.

Inside they were told to sit down and keep quiet. The senior NCO introduced himself and wasted no time lecturing on the dreaded subject of a gas attack.

'You will be issued with a gas mask, so familiarize yourselves with it, you will have no time to waste once the alarm has been sounded. Every one of you will do well to get this exercise right first time, so listen up, all of you. Failure to do so could cost you your life.'

After the theoretical demonstration it was time to carry out the practical exercise in getting the mask on in seconds.

Their first attempt was nothing short of a pantomime, which incurred the wrath of the sergeant, who threatened a charge for anybody making a mess of it the second time. Alf rather bravely suggested Harry take his boots and socks off. That would be a practical demonstration and would help to improve their time.

'I can assure you, Sergeant, the gas masks will be on in a second,' said Alf.

Harry was not amused, but he had to admit his feet

needed some urgent attention. Everybody laughed, except the sergeant. 'Listen up, all of you, Watkins's socks are not up for discussion here, but I have to explain to you that a real gas attack will pale Watkins's socks into insignificance.'

The sergeant became deadly serious and began to explain the types of gas that might be used; just listening to his descriptions was enough to make them vomit.

Nothing much was taught about biological weapons, but it was enough to make Ted whisper to Ginger, 'If you are interested, I can do you a deal on your last Will and Testament.'

'What's the point, there won't be anybody left?'

Then when they felt like bringing up their breakfasts, they were introduced to nuclear weapons. By now Ginger was beside himself, and no longer could he just sit there and say nothing.

'Isaiah, chapter two, verse four. They shall beat their swords into ploughshares, and their spears into pruning hooks; nation shall not lift up sword——'

He got no further when as the sergeant yelled, 'Well, that is sound advice, soldier, but if you don't shut up I will beat *you* into ploughshares. We have to move on. Now pay attention.'

He went on to say that Britain now had got the atomic bomb. Then he showed them a diagram, it was something like a giant dartboard with the bull's eye being ground zero and the bomb being detonated well above the ground.

'Now then, what would be the effects of gamma radiation, fireball, blast, and fallout? Let me explain.'

'I don't want to know,' said Ted.

'With all due respect, Sergeant, you have demonstrated that it would be highly unlikely for anyone to survive the gas, or some deadly bug, and now an atom bomb? Surely we would all be circumnavigating the globe in bits?'

'Fair comment,' but I aim to demonstrate how you might just survive.'

At this Ginger became more vocal. The sergeant tried to rebuke him, but Ginger persisted before being moved and threatened with a charge.

It was a lance corporal that received Ginger's sermon, 'As a result of man's folly, God will vanquish the earth, He will decide who survives to rebuild a stable society—which is what was intended in the first place.'

Ginger was taken outside into the freezing cold snow and made to run around until he was exhausted. Unable to move another step Ginger was ordered back into the lecture room.

'Ah, look who's here, a survivor of man's stupidity, perhaps now you will keep quiet and vent your feelings at the right time and in the appropriate place? But not here, do you understand, soldier? What was that? I didn't quite hear you.'

Ginger looked as if was about to collapse, but managed to acknowledge the sergeant—but not in a very convincing way. He sounded more unrepentant than ever.

Harry was not impressed with these bullying tactics. Ginger showed little courage at the coke yard, but he had certainly made up for it today. In Ginger's absence they were shown a diagram of the impact of a twenty kiloton atomic bomb. Next, if that was not enough, they were shown another diagram of a one megaton hydrogen bomb, which only the USA and Russia possessed. In comparison, the atomic bomb looked insignificant. By now everybody was stunned by the destructive power of these weapons, a power the enemy had— and could deliver. Britain had no such weapon, but they had all those other evil weapons, so what would they want with it, thought Harry.

Lecture over, everybody was ordered outside, which came

as a welcome change. The snow covered the road making it almost impossible to walk, let alone march. The sky had cleared, making for a bitter cold night with a hard frost.

'Who's turn is it to make up the stoves?' wondered Harry.

* * *

The days passed with more lectures and training on the assault course. Sophie had not kept her word, she had barely written to Harry. By now Harry was past caring, perhaps he could make things change with another letter, but his heart was not in the right place for passionate letters. Maybe this was the problem. What he could not understand is why she had not written. If she explained her true feelings, he would feel a lot better.

It seemed that most of the lads had parted company with their girlfriends and were feeling free. Harry had not realised how much he had changed in this short period of time. Given time, his whole life could change, he thought.

Most of the snow had melted away by their final passing out parade rehearsal, which they all felt could not come quickly enough. Then they would have a few days leave before the next phase of training. It had been a bitter experience, what with the cold winter and the loss of Fred. Nothing had been heard of him since. They all agreed that they had learned a great deal about themselves and felt fit. Most of all they were looking forward to know what the Army had in store for them during the next few weeks.

The snow had cleared for the final day, they spent hours on their uniform and polishing their boots, for they had no intention of letting their corporal down.

Looking out the window, Harry noticed a pair of blackbirds

looking for worms and anything else they could find. Flying away with a beak full of food for their young fledglings, they were soon back for more. How on earth they managed to build a nest and keep their eggs warm was a marvel to Harry. How relentlessly they looked for food, it was a question of survival, especially during the bitter cold weather. They were seriously territorial and would drive out any other bird from their patch. What a contrast to the human race, who in order to drive out any aggressor from their patch, have to resort to using dreadful weapons of mass destruction. Harry was still watching these magnificent birds when Alf came over, with his boots looking like glass and putting Harry's to shame.

'Stand by your boots with your bed in your hand,' he said, laughing as usual.

'Congratulations, Alf, I am sure you will catch the general's eye, but just take a look at these two birds and watch how they work as a team.'

'The only birds I am interested in are not of the feathered kind; just think, in two days time we will be home and at it,' replied Alf.

He moved on showing the others his highly polished boots. Harry could not care less, he was more interested in these two blackbirds. He could not help wondering how they managed to build a nest, lay three or four eggs, hatch them out, and then look relentlessly for food for their young fledglings, with little or no sunshine to keep them warm. After all that, they would go on to bring up a second brood. *That* was what Harry understood as survival. The blackbirds were in harmony with mother earth, unlike the human race which seemed to be hell bent on destroying the earth as we know it, along with everything else. It seemed incredible that the human race had become the victims of their own intelligence.

Harry's philosophical pondering on mankind versus the world was broken by the arrival of the corporal. He entered the room in his usual manner, eyeing every detail without saying a word. Before leaving he turned and faced them all.

'Tomorrow, as you know, will be your final day. There will be high ranking officers and members of the public all watching you, but more importantly, *I* will be watching you. If I find anything to so much as raise an eyebrow you will not only incur *my* wrath, but also that of the Army, and I think that by now you know what I mean. Remember, you will not only let yourself down, but everybody else.'

With that he left in his usual ceremonious fashion, shouting so that nobody would misunderstand, 'On parade, 0600 hours.'

That morning Harry received a letter from Sophie, but due to pressure he was unable to read it properly. With all his uniform ready for the big day, he laid back to take in all of Sophie's words, one by one. Alf came over to talk just as Harry had finished reading.

'By the look on your face you look as if you have just lost five quid,' he said.

'You could say that, Alf. You know what she said before I left? "I will wait for you until hell freezes over." Well it looks as if this winter was cold enough to give him the impression that it had. She is not interested anymore. I was going home in a couple of days, and I must confess I have missed her.'

'Who are you talking about?' said Alf.

'Oh, forget it, I don't want to talk about it.'

Harry was about to feel really sorry for himself when he realised there was another letter from home. His parents and his two brothers wished him well and were looking forward to seeing him again. This more than made up for the lack of interest Sophie had shown. His family meant so much to him, and it made him feel that however long he was away from home they would always be there to support him.

Looking around the room, everybody was in bed and no doubt were trying to get some sleep in this freezing cold room. The fires had been made up, but it had little effect on the temperature of the room. Switching off the lights, Harry jumped into bed with his feet feeling like blocks of ice. He laid there thinking for a while, and then he thought of the two blackbirds. How do they cope with the freezing cold and also keep their young fledglings warm? He gave Sophie's letter some thought, thinking that there might be a possibility that she had met somebody else. What could he do about it? He just could not understand her change of attitude, what had he said that could have possibly upset her? Nothing that he could think of, in any case, what would she think if he was sent abroad, which was a distinct possibility? He had so much to think about, and what with Sophie's unusual behaviour, he felt that the time to sort it all out would be when he returned home. He simply could not afford to worry about things he had no control over, and in any case, things might not be as bad as they seemed.

It seemed he had only closed his eyes for a brief moment when he heard voices.

'What's going on?'

'Come on, Harry, shake a leg, it's ten past five and nearly time to go home.'

Getting out of bed was always a problem for Harry, but this time the fear of being late for the final parade made him shoot out of bed and take a quick shower.

The ablutions (the washing and toilet facilities) were fairly basic, a line of wash basins, showers and toilets. Often as not the showers were out of order, and this morning was no exception. In any case, it was freezing cold, so Harry had to make do with a quick wash and a shave with barely warm water. Back in the room the lads were already dressed and were frightened to move in case they spoiled their uniform with creases. To Harry's horror, the corporal had already been in the room, but Alf had already made Harry's bed, which gave him time to dress and join the others for an early breakfast. Harry grabbed a piece of toast and a mug of tea while the others were about to leave. It was enough to keep body and soul together, but would it be enough to keep out the bitter cold wind? There was no chance the parade would be cancelled what with the snow all but gone. Right on time, the corporal was sorting out the lads next door. It was the turn of the sergeant to start shouting, hopefully for the last time. He ordered greatcoats to be worn, which came as a welcome relief from the cold. With everybody outside and lined up he gave a quick inspection,

'You will do,' he said.

Before marching to the armoury for their rifles they were marched into one of the sheds to be informed on their next training programme. Their drill echoed around the huge shed, but getting out of the cold wind was more than welcome.

Right on target their corporal halted them where the senior NCOs joined them. They were inspected by their captain and given an assessment of their performance, which he had to admit was very hard due to the adverse weather.

'You have done exceptionally well and your presentation today is excellent; well done all of you.'

The captain went on to explain that on their return from leave their next phase of training would be a transfer to the Royal Engineering training establishment. Further instructions would follow after their leave.

You could feel the buzz among the lads. Excitement took over, all of the hard times, tears and feelings of utter despair were replaced with absolute jubilation.

At last, we are released from the shackles of hell, Harry thought.

He was already wondering whether this training with the Royal Engineers would assist in any way with his degree studies, or was there something sinister behind this opportunity? Only time would tell. Once again, Harry had no choice in the matter, he wanted to question this future his mentors had prescribed. In spite of all the strict disciplinary training, he had not fully succumbed to accepting an order without question. Britain somehow managed to continue its involvement in a host of other conflicts around the world— although the country could hardly afford it.

Why should I be denied an answer when it concerns my future? After all, it is my life, he thought. Then a loud voice jolted him from this rebellious turn of mind.

'Squad! Squad attention, move to the right in threes, right turn.'

Many highly polished boots came crashing down in unison sounding perfect.

'By the right, quick march.'

They were on their way to the armoury for rifles no matter what, Harry thought.

The snow had finally cleared from the roads, but there was still a biting cold wind, and ice, which was bad news for them. Each soldier was equipped with a rifle, then they waited patiently for the order to march on. They could hear the band strike up.

They must have guts playing in this freezing cold, Harry thought, and yet they sounded perfect. Finally, the order was given to march on, which they were all happy to go along with. The parade dragged on and then came the march past. Eyes right, and off the parade ground for the last time. It was the culmination of much hard work, and today marked a knew beginning for all of them.

With a late visit to the cook house they had a meal before a final brief from their corporal. He made no secret of the fact that he was extremely proud of their performance, and that in just a few weeks he and others had turned them into competent soldiers ready for a variety of possibilities. Their next phase of training would be an interesting one, leading to skills that could give them an entirely new way of life.

What sort of training? Harry thought. He had heard rumours that he could end up being trained in a skill entirely different to that of electronic and electrical engineering.

The engineers had a wide variety of skills, being masters of building roads, bridges, airfields, and so on. Perhaps they also trained telephone or electrical technicians, he would find out after a few days welcome leave.

The corporal brought them to attention for the last time. He shook hands with all of them and wished them luck.

'I would like to be able to give you news about young Fred Jarvis, but I am afraid I have no idea what happened to him, perhaps if you have any news of him you could let us know.'

As he left the room they thanked him for all his help and patience. Suddenly the atmosphere had changed, they were free for a few days leave. They were once again responsible for their own actions with nobody breathing down their necks.

Harry found it difficult to sleep that night, the thought of Sophie's lack of interest in him kept going around in his mind. How he was going to approach her? What had gone wrong? He sensed that something must have changed, or was it he who had changed? What Harry and all of the other conscripts had not realised was that the last few weeks had undoubtedly changed them. Even perhaps their whole personality had changed, and for the better. They could take care of themselves and were able to handle a crisis somewhat better than before. Without doubt they had found pride in themselves and respect for others.

With the thought of going home it was not surprising that nobody had difficulty in getting out of bed, even though it was still cold. Harry had noticed that the blackbirds were still busy hunting for food. He would miss them and was grateful to them for giving him so much pleasure. More than anything else, he had learnt a great deal from them.

'Goodbye my magnificent friends,' he said.

Transport was provided to the station after breakfast. They were all in uniform carrying very little luggage. Getting into the back of the lorry Harry suddenly remembered that dreaded day when they entered the camp, perhaps the worse moment of his life. That sinking feeling of having all your freedom taken away from you had been turned around. Yes, Fred was right when he said the sun will always come up smiling.

'Come on, Harry, shake a leg.'

The lads were impatient and wanted to be away to the station. On their way Ted raised the question about the corporal asking what had happened to Fred. Then one of the boys spoke up.

'I thought you all knew,' he said.

'I wrote to Fred and I received a letter back from his parents telling me that Fred had been medically discharged from the Army and that he was still in hospital. I am afraid Fred is terminally ill and may only have weeks to live.'

'Why on earth couldn't you have told the corporal?' said Ted.

'I am afraid I get rather emotional about it and I just couldn't bring myself to tell him in front of all of you.'

'Fair enough,' said Ted.

'Somebody give me a pen and I will write to the corporal, the driver will deliver the letter.'

Nobody said a word except Ginger, who said a prayer quietly. Pete followed with, 'May God bless and love him forever, Amen.'

5. Too Cold for Sophie

Bang on time, the train rumbled into the station, black smoke rising up from the funnel and steam everywhere, it looked absolutely brilliant. There were lots of goodbyes, and Alf cheerfully as ever yelled out, 'When I get home I will embrace my girlfriend in the back of the taxi, well that's if I can afford a taxi.'

Everybody laughed and Harry was no exception, although he was not at all sure that Alf *would* have his eagerly awaited, mad, passionate embrace in the back of a taxi. Why am I not like Alf? Harry thought. Maybe things would be different with Sophie. He was stuck with a personality totally different to Alf's. Why couldn't he be a little like Alf? Then maybe he could charm the girls, or was Alf all talk and none of his conquests were true. Well, it would be a very boring world if it were not true, thought Harry. Alf always used to say there are plenty more fish in the sea, an old metaphor which often cheered people up when one felt that all was not well in their nest.

Harry was miles away in his thoughts when the train rolled into the station. 'All change,' was about all he understood from the tannoy, the rest was mumbo jumbo, he never understood what was being said, and by the look of the lads nobody else did. He had no choice but to ask. The porter obliged by saying if he got a move on he might just catch the train to London which was running late due to fog. There was a stampede up the stairs to the other side for the 11.30. Two months ago they would have had no chance in catching that train, but their training had made them fit so they were soon seated on the train to London. Several lads made the dash and it was almost certain the guard delayed blowing his whistle.

Harry found a seat and watched the countryside pass by before falling asleep, only to be jolted as the train braked to slow down for dense fog. The journey became frustrating as the train crawled along almost to a standstill. Not to worry, they were on their way home, no matter what the weather.

Not expecting anybody to meet him, Harry decided to walk home from the station. A taxi home was out of the question since the money in his pocket had to be spread out over two weeks, and he had to pay for his keep to his mother. So start walking, soldier, he said to himself.

He passed places he knew only too well, it felt as if he had been away for a decade, then he spotted away in the distance a small group of people. It had to be his Mum, Dad and two brothers. No Sophie to be seen, his disappointment was soon forgotten in the outstretched arms of his mum. His father shook his hand along with his brothers.

'Come on, lad, we are going out to celebrate and your paying,' said his father, with a broad grin on his face.

'Ah, there is just one snag, Dad, where can you get a meal on twenty-nine shillings?' Harry replied.

'Good question, lad, but this one is on me, you deserve it. Come on lets start in the Maidens Head, then we can look in on the new restaurant on the way home.'

Harry's brothers could not help asking questions about Army life. Had he seen tanks and would he drive one? Harry did not let them down, he felt like telling the truth, but decided to tell them what they wanted to know. He just wanted to forget the last few weeks.

Arriving home was like stepping into a palace compared to an Army hut and his room was just as he had left it.

'When you are ready, Harry, I have made a cup of tea,' his mother called out.

Gosh, what a change, hearing his mother calling him rather than somebody shouting at him all the time. He could just imagine one of his mentors back in the Army calling him for tea! There was a fire lit and right beside his father a suitable bottle of refreshment.

'Drink your tea, lad, and then we can settle down for something a little stronger, and you two can get ready for bed,' said his father, pointing at his other two sons. Then he relented, 'Maybe you can have a wee sip since you brother is home, just a sip mind, then off you go.'

Harry's father poured a glass of wine for Harry's mother, handed Harry a large glass of whisky, and his brothers two small measures.

'Well, here's to you, lad, welcome home.'

'Many thanks to you both, you have been very supportive of me and I can't thank you enough,' replied Harry.

'Which is more that you can say for that young lady who promised this that and the other,' said his mother.

'Now, now, he doesn't want to know all that, I am sure,' replied his father.

'Well, he might as well know the truth. Quite honestly, I don't know why you bother with somebody like that, you deserve much better.'

Trying to hide his disappointment, Harry responded by simply saying, 'Dad's right, I don't want to know.'

His father changed the subject by bringing him up-to-date with all the news, there was the possibility of his being made redundant due to a restructuring exercise. 'It seems the old civil engineering company is being taken over, so everything is up in the air at the moment, and quite frankly it's chaos for all of us. What about yourself, Harry, do you know your next move?'

'As far as I know, Dad, we are being transferred to the Royal Engineers, but I have no idea what sort of training they intend for us.'

His father was delighted and explained to Harry's mother what it may well mean for their son. He raised his glass again, 'Good luck to you, son, drink up and let's have one for the road.' He topped up Harry's glass saying, 'So you will be a sapper, by Jove, you could do a lot worse. Take full advantage of what is on offer lad.'

With his glass topped up it was inevitable that Harry's tongue would become loosened and temporarily remove the shackles from his troubled mind. His mother then saved him from saying something he would later regret by talking about Sophie.

'She never came to see us once since you left, Harry, has she ever written to you?'

'Look, Mum, she did write, but not that often and I have to tell you Sophie has her own life to consider, much the same as I have to. In two or three months time I could be anywhere, and I don't really want to be tied down just at the moment. It was never serious between Sophie and myself, and as I explained, I have much to do and I am sure I am not the same person as I was before, the Army has seen to that.

'Come on lad, you look tired, you must get some rest,' she gave him a big hug and a kiss.

That is one thing the Army has not changed, he thought: the loving care of his mother.

'Goodnight, Mum, Dad, thanks for everything, and God bless.'

The night passed in a flash and he was woken by his two brothers bringing him a welcome cup of tea, just like in the Army, he thought, laughing to himself.

'Breakfast in half an hour Harry, see you when we come home from school.'

Was this all real? he thought, or was it the Spirit of Christmas Past? Apart from a slight sore head, he felt a million dollars. After breakfast he would ask his mother for a walk around the park. His father, a construction engineer, had long gone to work and his brothers to school. He thought he might call into his old place of work to check up on his degree course. Maybe he might catch up with Sophie, but he was disappointed on both counts.

The sponsorship towards his degree course would not be in place for at least a year, and according to his colleagues they had not seen Sophie for some time. Rumour had it that she had moved on. Empty-handed, he wandered off back home rather disappointed about his degree studies since he had ideas about studying the thermionic valves used in radio sets. Maybe he would build his first valve amplifier leading to his very own wireless receiver and perhaps even a transmitter. All very interesting, but perhaps a little ambitious. His plans had been interrupted by the Army, and who knew where that would lead him.

On the way home, he realised that electronics was not his first choice of subject to study, even though he had achieved excellent City and Guild results. It would seem a complete waste to change his mind at this stage of his career. How he would feel after two years in the Army he had no idea. His mind was suddenly reminding him of those bitter, cold days at the training camp when a blackbird flew just in front of him. No, he had no wish to go back, but the blackbird said it all. He had no choice.

The walk home had done him good, he had forgotten Sophie, as Alf would say, there are plenty more fish in the sea.

Spring was beginning to show its face with snowdrops being replaced with crocuses and daffodils. He then thought of his two blackbirds still looking for food, and no doubt it was easier to find in better weather. He was almost home when he suddenly realised that Sophie was not constantly on his mind. He had so many things on his mind now, what with the Royal Engineers and studying whatever, things which could change everything. He would be fully occupied for almost two years. Now, let's see if Mum has time for a walk, he thought.

His mother had already returned home and was preparing a real treat for dinner.

'I have no time for walking at the moment, my love, but tomorrow I'll have plenty of time. Come on, you can help prepare the vegetables and tell me what you have been up to in the last few weeks.'

'Well for starters, Mum, we—or should I say most of us—did our fair share of spud peeling.'

'Serves you right, I dare say you had all been up to something,' she said laughing.

'I have to say though, Harry, you look very well on what ever you were doing and your father is very pleased about you going into the Royal Engineers, and so am I.'

With that his two brothers came in from school arguing

over football, a subject in which Harry was not all interested. Cricket was more his interest. Then his father came in looking not quite his usual self. He took Harry's mother to one side and started to explain something that looked rather serious. None of the boys took any notice until he turned to Harry. It was grandfather, who they were all so very fond of.

'Your grandfather has been taken ill, Harry, and is in hospital. Maybe you would go to the hospital with me tomorrow, I really would appreciate it?'

Harry immediately reassured his father and said they must make an early start.

Under the circumstances the evening passed very pleasantly, what with his father talking about his pet subject, the local flower and vegetable show and competition. He had a large garden with a small orchard and chickens running around. One year a fox killed all the chickens, and as usual only took one away.

'It was my fault,' said Harry's father, 'I should have penned them in properly.'

It was obvious Harry's father was feeling low, but the talk did them all good.

'Time for an early night, boys and girls, it's an early start tomorrow so come on, off you go.'

'Gosh, Dad, it's like being in the Army,' said Harry. That cheered his father up no end, and he laughed all the way up the stairs.

They left early the next morning, hoping to miss the rush hour and skirting around London and then heading south to the hospital. But the traffic was just as busy as usual with the journey taking longer than anticipated. Wandering around the car park they eventually found a space and headed for the hospital. Following the signs through a maze of corridors they found the ward. On entering, a nurse pointed to grandfather sitting up in bed. He was over the moon to see them, especially Harry in uniform. To see his grandson in uniform seemed to cheer him up, although Harry could not share in his enthusiasm. It was his father's idea, not Harry's, but it gave the old chap some memories of his days in the home guard during the war.

Harry thought he would wander off and leave them together for a while. The nurse was sitting at her desk so he thought a nice little chat with her would be in order until he noticed she was wearing an engagement ring, or was it? She was extremely attractive and certainly caught Harry's eye, however the attraction was not reciprocated and Harry was given short shift.

'If you want to go outside then do so, I am very busy,' she said.

I wonder what Alf would do under these circumstances, thought Harry. He was not going to be pushed outside just like that.

'Look, nurse, I haven't got much time, I could be anywhere in the world in just a few weeks time, so I thought perhaps you would tell me what's wrong with my grandfather.'

The nurse looked at him and said, 'I thought you were going to ask me something else, soldier boy. Well your grandfather will be going home shortly and rest assured he will be looked after.'

'Many thanks, nurse, and whoever put that ring on your finger is incredibly lucky. My best wishes to you both.'

'What's your name, soldier boy?'

'Harry', he said very quickly, 'Harry Watkins of the Royal Engineers. What's yours fair lady?'

'Helen, and I am very busy,' she replied, 'and don't keep

your grandfather waiting. In any case, have you come to see *me* or your grandfather?'

'Now that I have seen you, that's a very difficult question to answer, Helen.'

Then, without warning, she was down the ward attending to a patient, curtains pulled and that was that, Harry saw nothing more of her.

Harry took his grandfather's hand and wished him well. He promised to see him again on his next leave.

On the journey home he no longer felt the urge to see Sophie, even though it seemed increasingly unlikely he would ever see her again. Helen had completely changed his feelings towards Sophie, but how could he get back to the hospital and try his luck with Helen? Time was not on his side with two long years in the Army in who-knows-where. Suddenly he had become completely besotted with Helen, but what could he do about it? Although he felt a better person, being more responsible and caring for others, he still felt that his time was not his own, his freedom had been taken away from him. He wanted a meaningful relationships with girls, but the chances of that had been narrowed down somewhat. Who could blame Sophie or Helen for their reluctance to miss out on their youth by tying themselves down with somebody who might be here one minute and gone the next?

His father seemed to be much more relaxed now Harry's grandfather was coming out of hospital. But time was running out for Harry, with little or no chance of ever meeting the nurse again. Never mind, he thought, it was a very pleasant memory and perhaps he should make more effort to see her again. With time running out, he thought he would go back to his old work place and meet up with some of his pals. He had already learnt that his degree course had been put back due to a lack of funding. Perhaps tomorrow he would visit the library and research the life and works of famous scientists and engineers who worked with electronics during the war. He wanted to know more about the development of communication. Everything seemed to be moving so fast and unless he could keep up with the latest techniques then he would fall behind with his studies while serving in the Army.

The next morning Harry's father left for work very early and his brothers were soon away to school.

'Fancy a visit to the library this morning, Mum, and then a cup of coffee?'

'Yes, my love, perhaps I will find a book myself.' Walking to the bus stop Harry spotted a car with what looked like Sophie driving. He stopped for a moment, but said nothing. However, his mother did speak, 'Yes, that was her alright, Harry, and don't get yourself upset about it. Rumour has it that she left your place of work and moved on. She has been seen with somebody else who is thought to be her new employer.'

'Well, who cares, Mum? To be honest I don't much care, and who can blame her?'

Harry's mother was a lot less forgiving and went on to say that she should never have made such promises. Harry, on the other hand, was thinking of the nurse who had changed his whole way of thinking.

'There is plenty of time, Mum, and besides who knows where I will be going after training? In any case, her letter virtually said it all: she was never interested.'

Finally the bus turned up, much to Harry's relief. His mother had said her piece and left it at that. The library was disappointing to say the least. Having searched the library, it seemed that luck was not on his side since he found little or no information on famous scientists or engineers who had worked with electronics during the war. Surely there must be something wrong that nothing was to be found about these famous people? Harry thought perhaps a larger library would be the answer, but he did not have the time to travel further afield.

Harry's time soon ran out, and it was not long before he was back in uniform on a train and bound for an uncertain future.

6. The Fight

Meeting up with all his mates in uniform and back in D hut, everything seemed to be much easier than before. Everybody seemed to have had a good time back home. All the recruits now knew the drill and they observed discipline to the letter. The disciplinarians had done their job by creating a team who would obey instructions without question and would support each other at all costs.

Their instructions were to assemble at 0900 hours the next day for transport to take them on to a Royal Engineers training school. That seemed straight forward enough, and it was unanimously agreed they would have a pint in the NAAFI before lights out.

The next day, after a quick breakfast, they were assembled in one of the huge sheds. It was here they got their first instructions for the Royal Engineers. The usual roll call was made and then they were each called upon to enter the waiting transport. With all their kit it was no easy task climbing into the back of a lorry. Soon they were on their way, like cattle to the abattoir—that was how Alf described it. Moos sounded throughout the lorry as it left the camp. They were glad of their overcoats and gloves since the cold draught chilled them to the core, but with their collars turned up they felt reasonably warm.

As they drove through a small town, they saw a group of girls standing outside what looked like a bakery. The response was immediate with whistles and banter coming from both sides. Alf was up and almost out the back, yelling, 'Meet me tonight, darling, and I'll show you my testimonials.'

Alf laughed when one of the girls yelled back, 'Why you are only a boy, I doubt if you have any, or even if you have, I doubt if they will be interesting enough for me.'

Even Ginger, our resident lay preacher, had to laugh. Unfortunately, they were soon out of range of the girls and that would be the case for some considerable time to come.

The convoy of lorries drove on and on. It was colder than ever as they made their way over high ground into the mist. Later on the convoy pulled over for a break and other needs. Stretching their legs the recruits had begun to admire the magnificent show of wild flowers in the woods when they were ordered back on board for the final leg of the journey.

Late in the afternoon the convoy finally turned off the main road and carried along a concrete road for at least a mile. They came to the camp gateway and drove on, being escorted all the way to a large compound. On the way Harry heard one hell of a noise and felt sure he saw a tank behind some trees. What ever it was, it made Harry wonder what they might be in for.

The convoy came to a halt with the usual shouting of orders. 'Let's be having you. Come on. Get a move on. Line up, you useless shower.' By now they were used to being yelled at and it would have seemed odd without it. At times Harry felt like suggesting that unless they were shouted at, how could they be expected to react? It seemed absurd that only a few weeks ago most of them would have taken exception to being shouted at.

The momentary chaos was quickly turned into order by the NCOs, and later a warrant officer who stepped forward and addressed them. His voice was well above the normal requirement for the human ear and seemed to be omni directional. In no time he had everything under control, a masterpiece of organisation, Harry thought.

'From now on you are with the most elite regiment in the Army, the Royal Engineers, and don't you ever forget it.'

For one moment Harry wondered if that last statement would be hotly disputed by others in the Army, but under the circumstances he was not prepared to challenge the warrant officer. He did not fancy seven days jankers. The warrant officer seemed to be upset when nobody reacted to being the best in the Army, so he invited everybody to shout, 'Yes, sir,' loud enough for the whole nation to hear. This was repeated several times so that nobody would forget.

The accommodation was much the same as before. It was no more luxurious, but nothing could be as cold as the last camp, so they were happy enough. Harry was keen to stay with his hut mates and it seemed he was in luck. Nearly all of them turned up in the same hut, however there was no time to stand around. All their kit had to be laid out by early morning for inspection. Harry could not believe that in just a few weeks his life had been so turned around, and hopefully for the better. Several weeks of purgatory had been replaced with, relatively speaking, an easier life simply because they had been groomed for it. Harry was thinking, after this place what next? But one thing at a time.

Ginger, who never said a great deal, was looking more relaxed. He was their paragon of virtue and without doubt he had given some of them solace in their hour of need, even when he had problems of his own. Ginger was never organised, unlike Ted who was the complete opposite to Ginger. They were often seen helping each other, although Ted found Ginger rather frustrating at times. To the lads it was like watching a Laurel and Hardy film. Every time there was a kit inspection it was like a pantomime.

Their new identity had to be clearly displayed on their uniforms with new insignia, which made them really proud. It was now up to them to prove that they were worthy of displaying these famous badges. Many of them had never sewn on a button before, but with the help of one or two of them they made a first class job of it. Tomorrow would change the lives of these raw recruits forever.

Everybody was up before the scheduled reveille with all their kit laid out for inspection. They half expected the door to be kicked open by an eight-foot NCO. Instead, a sergeant and two corporals entered the room. The corporals quickly inspected each bed space. It seemed they had not much interest in the kit lay out, but were more interested in the cleanliness and hygiene of the room.

The sergeant stood in the middle of the room and made their acquaintance, 'I will be your instructor throughout the entire programme. My team will expect you to be presentable at all times, any one of you breaking the rules and instructions will answer to a higher authority.'

He went on for a while expecting a 'Yes, Sergeant' after he had said, 'Do you understand?' He then brought them a little closer to what they would be taught.

'Perhaps you have already caught a glimpse of some very large hardware,' he went on.

Alf had always wanted to drive a tank, or anything big and powerful. However, Harry was not so sure, he was far from being enamoured with the idea since he saw no connection with electrical engineering. What use would a tank be to him?

The sergeant ordered the corporals to march them to one

of the massive sheds. The inside was divided into a maze of classrooms, but first they had to be sorted into various trades. Everybody lined up, then name and classrooms were called out. Soon it would be the moment they had all been waiting for. Harry found himself in a classroom along with all his room mates: Gary, Alf, Ted, Ginger, Brian, and Pete.

'You stand to attention when I, or any other NCO, enters the room, do you understand?'

'Yes, Sergeant.'

You could hear a pin drop after that as they were about to know their future in the Army.

'You lucky people, you are to be trained as drivers.'

Harry's heart sank, and he failed to take note of what was said next. What on earth do I want with being a driver? I have already passed my driving test back home, he thought.

Harry was not at all interested, but having no car, and highly unlikely to own one for some time, perhaps keeping in touch with the road would not be a bad idea. Then he noticed a series of pictures showing very heavy-looking vehicles were on display, they showed these massive lorries with tanks on the back, earth moving equipment, and even cranes. Suddenly, Harry began to show much more interest, it was just like being back at college, except with added discipline.

They were dismissed for their lunch break and were told not to be late on returning, 1330 sharp, as there would be a very heavy training schedule.

Alf could not help replying, 'Was that meant to be a pun, Sergeant?'

You could say that, sapper,' he said smiling.

The cook house was buzzing with conversation in which the recruits exchanged their newly assigned trades. After a while the penny was beginning to drop. It seemed that they were members of a giant building team, or as Gary put it, a civil engineering company. Gary's father had a building business back home and so he was over the moon, unlike Ted who felt like a fish out of water, being a student of law. As it stood, they all seemed to be happy enough, especially Ginger who had no trade skills at all. The excitement grew even more when it was rumoured they would be taught the basics of building roads, bridges, and even airfields and so on.

That evening Harry wrote home, giving all the news on a subject his father would understand. The problem with money was still the same, twenty-nine shillings a week, but as he explained in his letter, the training, clothing, full board and lodging cost nothing. And at the end was another very useful trade. No, Harry at last was feeling grateful, and much more relaxed within himself.

Ted and Ginger invited Harry for a pint, but first they had to find the NAAFI. Alf joined them and showed them the way.

'How do you feel, Ted, being a student of law and all that?' asked Alf.

'Quite frankly, Alf, it doesn't bother me, I have my law books to study, and who knows, when this is all over there may be plenty of time, after all we are only here for a few weeks.'

'What about you, Ginger?'

'I am more than grateful, I have no trade and now I am being offered a chance of a lifetime.'

Pete joined them, and with no hesitation admitted out how lucky he was.

'I thought you may not be all that happy, Pete, being a nurse.'

'I'm not a nurse, and never will be, a nurse is a profession in which it takes years to qualify,' replied Pete.

'We are here for just a few weeks, and I must say my first

aid knowledge may come in useful when you clumsy lot start driving these massive machines.'

'Don't tempt providence, Pete,' said Ted who seemed to be more terrified of driving these machines than the rest of them. 'Maybe all this knowledge of plant machinery will be useful if I become an industrial lawyer, so we all seem to benefit one way or another,' said Ted.

They still remained tired after yesterday's long journey in the back of a draughty lorry. The afternoon lessons in the classroom left some of them with tired eyes which their instructor was fully aware of. He very soon drew their attention by threatening them with a charge if he caught any one of them nodding off.

There would be homework and exams, which caught all of them off guard. Nobody had expected this level of tuition, but it seemed there was no time to lose, which none of them could understand. What is the rush, they thought.

By the end of the first week the classroom was abandoned for a more practical demonstration of earth levelling. Ginger was the first to climb up, and without persuasion or permission, started it up and drove off with the corporal running after him. Ginger had plenty of space to turn it and bring it back safely.

The corporal was beyond himself and gave Ginger another lesson in uncomplimentary language. Ginger apologised and said he failed to hear the corporal and then asked if he could have another go. To his surprise, the corporal allowed Ginger to demonstrate his natural driving skill once again, but this time only when the corporal was ready. He asked Ginger to move forward slowly, with the others walking by the side. Ginger was then shown how to lower the blade and so forth. As it turned out, not even Ted managed to make a mess of things, mainly due to Ginger and the corporal walking alongside and helping him.

The corporal was most pleased with their willingness to learn quickly in the practical lessons and had no hesitation in moving them on to the next phase of the training programme, which would prove more difficult for some of them.

Enter the giant transporter which could carry tanks and all sorts of military hardware with ease. This proved to be more difficult, with reversing being the hardest. Nevertheless, they proved themselves to be more than competent.

Days turned into weeks. Exam time was upon them, there were both theory and practical exams. Nobody found the theory that difficult, however the practical test proved more demanding. Driving huge transporters with several tons gave Harry a hard time, but he made up for it by a neat performance moving earth. Afterwards, they were all told that they had passed. Next would be stripping down the engines and putting them back together. This pleased all of them as they had had no idea that they would be taught to this level. Would all this lead to building bridges, roads, and so on? Who knew. One thing they *did* know was that their pay was still derisory by anybody's standard.

Back in the hut, Ginger pointed out that they had a right to feel bitter, but the training—with free board and lodging—was compensation for the low pay.

'Be honest with yourselves, lads, in my case I feel as happy as Larry, I will never have a chance like this again. The Bible clearly states that being honest with yourself allows you a clear conscience and self-respect. I would be the first to admit that our pay and conditions are not exactly in line with some others in our society, but just for argument's sake, let's say at pay parade you are paid your usual twenty-nine shillings, but when counting it you find that you have been paid an extra shilling. My question is, do you hand the extra shilling back, or turn the other way? Never look a gift horse in the mouth you might say, especially when you only receive a pittance. Remember, though, the extra shilling represents a fair percentage of your pay and the paying officer will not rest until the shilling has been returned. We may all suffer the wrath of our mentors. Would you want that on your conscience? Knowing all of you by now, I think not. However, if you were paid a realistic wage, say twenty pounds a week, the extra shilling would equate to a very small amount and no doubt would go completely unnoticed, which seems extremely unfair on us lesser mortals. Always remember, being honest allows you a clear conscience; knowing that not only are you not incriminating yourself, but that you may be saving others from a whole shed load of misery. Be contented with what you have been presented with in the last few weeks, your reward will come later.'

Ginger had the ear of a few of the lads, but others were scornful, saying that their whole way of life had been turned over, and in any case the extra shilling was the paying officer's fault. Besides can you imagine returning the shilling and reminding the officer that he should be more careful in future?

There was no doubt Ginger had created mixed feelings and confusion. The message was slightly flawed, but at least it made everybody think of not just the training, pay, and conditions, but a more moral aspect of their new way of life. Alf, comical as ever, said he wanted to know more about this guy called Larry which brought the roof down with laughter and lights out.

Harry could not help feeling Ginger was right, even though he sounded a little mixed up. In time the training could potentially be very rewarding, and the opportunity to learn about engines was indeed an added bonus, besides being taught how to operate these massive machines.

Tomorrow was pay day with just the slight chance of Ginger's hypothetical scenario being put into practice, but somehow Harry did not think it would happen as the paying officer was as tight as a drum. Alf would have more chance meeting happy Larry.

All of them being broke, pay day was more than welcome. None of them had much spare cash at the best of times. The twenty-nine shillings pay certainly stretched them, since out of their pay came stoppages which left them very annoyed at being billed for their cleaning materials. Ginger's theory that they should feel grateful for all this free training suddenly made no economic sense. As far as Harry was concerned, he was paying for all this training out of his own pocket. The only concession he would make was that National Service taught you the real value of money.

Social life on the camp was limited to the NAAFI for a pint or two, and then there was the occasional dance. It seemed that Alf scored at every dance, but nobody believed him. All the lads went to the dance night, and as usual made promises that none of them could keep. One girl asked Ted if he knew a chap called Vic, who had been posted to Mexico. If he came across Vic, would he tell him to write as it was rather urgent. Ted could see by the size of her that it was a little more than urgent. Ted met an extremely attractive girl, but she was dating somebody else and he caught up with Ted. He came back one night looking badly beaten up by the boyfriend and claimed he had been set upon by two others, as well as the boyfriend. He looked a dreadful mess, which brought about an urgent meeting. The word spread that there would be a mass retaliation at the next dance that would extend to the local town.

The following Monday morning was classroom work on engine maintenance which cheered Harry up no end. Diesel and petrol engines would be stripped down and put back together again, but first the theory of engines and so on.

Ted's face soon became the subject of discussion and did not go unnoticed by the instructor.

'What the hell have you been up to, sapper, and stand up when I am speaking to you,' yelled the sergeant.

Poor old Ted could hardly stand up, he had been badly bruised in the ribs. He mumbled something like, 'There was a slight misunderstanding with regards to the dating arrangements of a certain young lady which led to an altercation with three apes, and before anybody asks, "Does it hurt?" Yes, it damn well does.' Ted sat down, which turned out to be another mistake.

The sergeant was on him like a ton of bricks. 'Stand up, who told you to sit down? You should date more carefully in the future you useless, romantic idiot. Never enter my classroom with a face looking like a piece of bloody steak. Get out and report to sick quarters.'

Ted left the room much quicker than he entered it. Later on he came back patched up with a couple of stitches, and one eye and his mouth partially closed.

With no hesitation the sergeant showed little or no sympathy. 'I have to say, sapper, I don't remember your face or even if you had one, but don't keep mumbling, just try and stay with us or your feet won't touch the ground. And sit up straight.'

Everybody burst out laughing. The sergeant, having lost patience and still looking pan faced, said, 'I don't believe it, what a state to get into, you look as if you have been in a fight with a bear.'

Ted tried to mumble, but decided to stick up three fingers.

'You mean to say you have allowed yourself to be duffed up by three teddy bears? Don't you ever let the Army down again, or I will send you on another picnic, now all of you, pay attention, we have lost too much time due to lover boy.'

That evening Ted laid on his bed thoroughly exhausted, even though he was fit, he had taken one hell of a beating. His pride was hurt even more, and he felt the sergeant was right, but it was three against one. GBH came to his mind, if he had been practicing law he would have nailed those bastards to the floor, but now he had other ideas. 'Don't let the Army down again, sapper,' was still fresh in his mind as he crawled into bed.

Battle plans had been discussed not only in their hut, but in all the huts. Ginger pointed out that two wrongs did not make a right, but Gary answered back, 'An eye for an eye, a tooth for a tooth, boyo. War has been declared.'

The lessons on engine maintenance passed quickly and the lads enjoyed every minute. To see the engine start after dismantling and re-assembling it was most satisfying for all except Harry and Alf, their engine just coughed and gave up. The instructor gave them extra time to find the problem and reminded them that they could be crossing a desert with sand blowing everywhere, including into their engine. It was a clue as to what might be wrong. Unknown to Harry and Alf the instructor had replaced the air filter with a clogged up one. It was up to them to locate the fault and fix it. With everybody looking on Harry did not find it funny to have an audience poking fun at you. Alf was no help at all, and considering his father owned a large car repair garage and showroom, one would expect him to have no trouble. Instead he turned it into a comedy show. Harry felt very incompetent until the instructor intervened by calling them two useless idiots. Gary came to the rescue and fixed the problem with no trouble. The instructor seemed to be happy enough and advised them to work as a team in future.

'In the case of Sapper Reynolds and Watkins I strongly advise you to work together and learn from the others, otherwise I doubt if you would ever get out of the yard, let alone the desert. Learn from each other from now on, we must move on, there is no time to lose, he said.

Fresh instructions came through that afternoon, they were to assemble outside the clothing store at 0830 in the morning. They were to return to the classroom by 1000 hours.

'Is that understood?'

'Yes, Sergeant.'

Nobody dare ask questions, they had learned the hard way before, speak only when you are spoken to and not before.

Back in the hut the fires were made up, and without much money nobody could afford a pint. There was every opportunity to play some sort of sport, which most of the lads had taken up. Ginger went his own way by taking Bible lessons at the invitation of the camp padre. Pete would normally go to the gym with Ted, but something was wrong. Ted was missing. He was nowhere to be found. Harry had no idea and neither had the others. Of course, said Pete, he has probably gone to sick quarters for more treatment on his face, or what is left of it.

7. No Time to Lose

Ted was nowhere near the gym and had no intention of any exercise, it was agony just to walk, let alone to participate in sporting activities. His priority was to find out where these thugs lived that beat him up. He wanted information before he went to the police, and the only way he thought he could do that was to find the girl that led him into the mess in the first place. He wanted a witness, plus the fact that there could be a disaster at the next camp dance and in the town. The last thing he wanted was a rampage through the town for which he would feel partially responsible.

Ted thumbed a lift into town from an Army driving instructor he had met during lessons. He explained briefly his intentions, and the instructor agreed with him, something had to be done, although he thought Ted a little naïve to think that he would get a result from the girl, after all, she certainly would not admit to any involvement or that she knew any of them, but it was up to him.

'Perhaps the police will be interested and then, of course, you might need a solicitor. Have you got that sort of money? I think not, my advice is tread carefully, by all means meet up with the girl, but as I said, tread carefully. I can drop you off near the town centre if that's any use.'

Ted was grateful for his support and owed him a pint.

'You will get to know the Army with time, sapper, we look after each other, no matter who you are, good luck,' and he was gone.

Ted felt much better with one of the problems solved. The instructor would see to that. Now for the second problem, which to a certain extent had almost been solved by the instructor, and that was to tread carefully. He should not automatically assume that she would give him the whole story. Gathering information was one thing, but would it be genuine? After all, she was hardly a reliable witness. How could her statement be substantiated? He was beginning to change his mind about the whole business of pursuing revenge, however, he was in the town now, so he might as well meet the girl again. In any case, he was fully aware of his rights, and in view of his injuries he had almost been beaten to within an inch of his life. Only his fitness had pulled him through.

At last he came to the chemist shop where she worked, or at least that is what she had told him. Ted was beginning to have doubts, but he was not to be disappointed, out she came with two other girls. He could not be mistaken, she was very attractive—unlike himself, it must have been quite a shock for anybody seeing his face looking like a werewolf.

'My word, you really have been in the wars, soldier boy, I'm sorry we are closed for the day, but can I help you? Let's take a look at you.'

Ted fell apart, she was so attractive, and just looking at her made him forget what he was there for.

'What's your name?' she said.

'I'm okay, really I am,' replied Ted.

Suddenly, the pain in his face really hurt, and he remembered how he was set upon. Flashbacks raced through his mind and he turned to her without thinking, he wanted answers.

'My name is unimportant, I just need to know the name of your boyfriend and his two accomplices who were responsible for re-arranging my face and ribs. I am not surprised your boyfriend was jealous, but how was I supposed to know you had a boyfriend. Having studied law, I know my rights. I could bring serious charges against all of them, or face your boyfriend on a level playing field. Not only would there be very serious consequences at the next camp dance, it may even affect this town, you understand? It's up to you.'

Somehow Ted felt better for getting all that off his chest, he had regained his self-respect, even though she had very nearly charmed him off his perch. The other girls left without saying a word, leaving the girlfriend apologising for all the distress she had caused, but she had had no idea that this sort of thing would happen. She had heard that a soldier had been hurt at the dance, but it had been nothing to do with her, she had no boyfriend, and certainly did not know someone capable of this. But then she contradicted herself by saying, 'Why have I been singled out as being involved? I admit that he is known to me, and that I have been out with him, and so perhaps I am partly responsible, but I swear I would have had nothing to do with a person who could do such a thing if I had known. I am truly sorry.'

'That is as maybe, but the fact remains, if you know who and where these people live then you must tell me, or the police, these people are dangerous.'

By now she was visibly shaken and started to cry. 'My name is Penny James and please don't take this any further, I am due to be picked up by one of my parents any minute now, I must go, and please don't say anymore.'

Ted had to act fast, he was almost lost for words, things got really complicated when Penny shed more tears. She came over to Ted and kissed him gently on the only unmarked part of his face.

'I am so sorry,' she said.

Without hesitation, Ted asked her if she would meet him again, but under different circumstances. Saturday, same place and time, he would take her out, that was if she could put up with a werewolf. She agreed and said she would bring something for his face.

'You mean a mask,' he said.

Penny gave a sympathetic smile and said she would be there and with that she was gone.

He stood there for a moment trying to take stock of what had just happened. For starters he had made a date with a very attractive girl, but nevertheless, he still wanted the truth, was she implicated, or was she just the innocent party? One thing was for certain, he had averted a third world war, and for that reason alone he felt satisfied. He found his way back to the main road, thumbed a lift back to camp and was in the hut before all the others.

He started to look up cases of GBH in his law books and it was not long before he realised that, unless he could prove beyond all reasonable doubt that these men were the ones responsible for his injuries, then he would have no chance in bringing a case against them. All the cases he read made it clear that one had to be aware of all the relevant facts, and in his own case he most certainly was not. Penny, on the other hand, may know more than she was letting on. Nevertheless, she may be innocent of any intentional involvement, and that he had merely frightened her into believing she was implicated. He must tread carefully, but what about those tears? Were they genuine or not? What about the sudden desperate plea not to involve her parents? He certainly did not expect a kiss from her, especially the way he looked. Ted was confused, or maybe he had simply been taken in by her looks, after all, she was very attractive. So the burden of proof beyond all reasonable doubt would not be easy, one way or the other, in fact, he could end up in a worse situation. He had to ask himself this question, was he seeking justice according to the law, or was it revenge in the form of a re-match with the hypothetical boyfriend? On the other hand, he had made a date with the boyfriend's girl, so maybe he would settle for that. But the question he could not answer was whether he was making a rod for his back?

The lads came back in, all wanting to know were he had been.

'If you really want to know, I have made a will leaving everything to my pet dog, Humphrey. One more kick the other night and—had my will been in place—Humphrey would have been the sole beneficiary of five shillings and a well-thumbed law book. However, I am still here and perhaps I could join a fairground and put myself on display as the ugliest creature on earth.'

'Come on, Ted, somebody loves you out there, maybe a pint will cheer you up,' said Pete. 'Your face will heal in time, so cheer up. Why don't we take Ted for a pint, there is still time?'

Alf suggested that a mask might be the answer, just like the Phantom of the Opera.

Harry wrote home, wanting news of his grandfather, while Alf made up the fires. The temperature was dropping like a stone, even though it was the middle of May.

'Don't you fancy a pint with the lads, Alf?' asked Harry.

'Not on your nelly, what with the Phantom roaming about,' he said laughing.

'Though to be serious for one moment, we have to support Ted. I think he's taking things very hard, and quite frankly we don't really know him that well. Even though he may not want any interference, we should keep an eye on him, and that's not meant to be a pun.'

'Yes, you are right, and I agree his eye looks a mess. Apparently he has an appointment at the hospital.'

The next day was frosty and so was the sergeant, who almost kicked the door in. 'Come on, outside, the lot of you. Move, there is no time to lose, outside now!'

Breakfast came first and then a march to the clothing store where measurements were taken and they were quickly issued with what looked like tropical clothing, including sunglasses. They never had time to blink, or ask questions. Back in the hut they only had time to put all this clothing away and it was back to the classroom.

There was no hint from the instructor as to where they would be going for the simple reason he had no idea himself. Nevertheless, it was pretty obvious they were going somewhere in the tropics. What failed to please them was that the training had been cut short and that the syllabus had to be completed, therefore lessons would be extended into the weekend. That did not please Ted at all.

Harry was once again called upon to fix an engine. This time it was the water pump, which he managed to replace. Then he had to drive the low loader to pick up a load of crates and bring them back to their base. Then one of the other recruits would return them. This went on until they had all completed the exercise. That completed their exam, but time was not on their side.

On Saturday they had classroom work on the theory of concrete mixing and a practical demonstration. Finally, they would have a lesson on electrical components and wiring, accompanied by a booklet for them to keep and study. All of them thought that their training was being carried out with indecent haste, why all the rush, and why was nobody being reprimanded every other minute? What was even more bizarre was that nobody knew why their training was being rushed.

That evening several of the lads joined Ted thumbing a lift into town. Once in town Ted gave them the slip and went his own way. It was important to Ted that he was making every effort to see Penny again, he wanted to know more about this girl, but with a face like his, he really did not rate his chances.

Penny came out of the chemists bang on time. At first she was surprised to see him, but then that smile, it took Ted's breath away.

'I really am pleased to see you, Ted, but as usual one of my parents will be taking me home and——'

'It's okay, Penny, I just wanted to see you,' interrupted Ted.

Penny's face suddenly looked very pensive.

'It's not about——' she stuttered a little.

'No, Penny, please forget all about that, I should never have bothered you in the first place, and I am sorry. It's about Saturday evening, I may not be able to make it, but I would like you to be here just in case. I know it's asking too much, but to be honest I was really looking forward to seeing you and talking things through. It seems every body is in a hurry all of a sudden. I have been issued with all this tropical clothing and all that. And what's going on? I really don't know.'

He was beginning to babble on a bit, then Penny stopped him. 'By the way I have got some cream for your face.'

She started to look into her bag when something caught

her eye. Without giving Ted the cream she moved away, whispering, 'Don't worry about going away, I will know how to find you, and I promise I'll write to you.'

She blew him a kiss and that was that. Ted stood there for a while thinking, who is this girl? How on earth could she possibly know where I will be? No, she's having me on. Nothing adds up, but perhaps Saturday will answer more than one question.

Walking back to the main road hoping for a lift, the gang turned up. It was Gary, Ginger, and Harry.

'Heard the latest, Ted, we are on the road tomorrow. The instructor reckons we are good enough to drive on the public road. Great, isn't it ,Ted?'

'I'm ecstatic,' said Ted. That is my date out the window, he thought to himself.

It was Saturday morning and Harry was not exactly enthusiastic about driving tons of hardware around the countryside. However, he was chosen to be second driver to Ginger who was judged to be the top driver in the class. Ted played second fiddle to Gary, and Pete was to assist Alf.

Breakfast dragged on for Ted, he tried getting everybody out and to the convoy, but the lads felt an extra cup of tea was in order, and in any case, they had until 0900 hours before they had to report for duty. The convoy was due out at 1000 hours, provided they could fix all the faults which had been placed in the engines by the instructors. It would be a serious test of their skills after just a few weeks of training. The convoy would not move until all the vehicles were serviceable and it was not long before the frustration showed on their faces when a vehicle refused to start. They were way behind time when Ginger got the nod from the sergeant to lend a hand. He took no time in getting all the engines running, much to the delight of Ted. Most of the problems were in the fuel line and Ginger insisted that they all take note of what he was doing.

'I don't want to perish out in some outlandish desert place,' he said.

They were all given a packed lunch consisting of a corned beef sandwich and a hard boiled egg. Large flasks of tea were also provided. Estimated time of arrival back at camp would be approximately 1630 hours, maybe just in time for Ted's date with Penny.

The weather was fine and fairly warm with spring flowers showing their faces along the route. Harry sat back admiring the magnificent countryside and wondered about his blackbirds back up north. He marvelled at how they had engineered such a magnificent nest for their new family, and in weather that humans could not endure for long. Not only that, they had to find all their food and then, at various times of the day, the cock bird would put up a magnificent song. Harry was suddenly jolted by Ginger slamming on the breaks.

'Hello, something's up at the back,' he said. Looking in the mirror he could see the convoy falling behind. It had come to a halt. Ginger reversed with great skill and beckoned to the corporal for instructions.

'Would you give these clowns behind you a helping hand?' the corporal said.

Ginger and Harry jumped out of the cab and noticed the weather was about to change with rain not far away. They wasted no time and enquired as to what the problem might be.

'The damn thing just coughed, spluttered and stopped,' said Alf.

Pete was still half asleep, but managed to jump out and walk around the back.

'What's the point of looking up its backside?' yelled Harry. 'Have you looked at your gauges, what do they tell you?'

'Ah, I was about to mention that, Harry, that's a good idea,' said Alf.

'Look carefully and tell me what you see, Alf.'

'Wow, there's no fuel,' replied Alf.

Ginger wasted no time. 'Right, come on, let's fuel this thirsty engine and get this show moving.'

'The crafty devils, they deliberately done this,' said Alf.

'Well, of course they did, that's their job,' said Ginger, thinking Alf was heading for a reprimand—and he was right. Each vehicle carried spare fuel so it was easily refueled. While this was going on, the instructor gave Alf and Pete a reprimand, and unless they took the exercise more seriously they would find themselves on a charge; it was not a laughing matter, they had failed the entire convoy.

'If this was for real in some hostile place, and you were ambushed, then there would be a strong possibility that your privates would be hanging from a tree. If I had my way you would most certainly get fourteen days jankers for gross incompetence and insubordination, now get in and start moving,' said the instructor.

Alf was decidedly quiet on the way home and apologised to them all. Perhaps this time he had gone too far. Ted, on the other hand, was delighted in arriving back only about half an hour late. He wasted no time after being dismissed, making straight for the local town.

It was well past six before he arrived, not expecting to see Penny and he was right. He waited for a while and then found shelter out of the rain, which was when he spotted Penny walking away. She had also been sheltering from the rain and neither had seen the other.

'Come on, race you to the coffee shop, last one in buys,' she said, laughing as he walked over to her.

Ted still had difficulty with his leg and he fell over the curb just outside the coffee shop. He managed to get up and realised he was in one hell of a mess, and was beginning to feel in pain once more. He sat down with Penny, who had not noticed him falling over.

'Are you buying, or shall I?' she said smiling.

'No, no, that's down to me,' said Ted, with just a few shillings in his pocket.

Ted limped over to the counter, ordered two coffees and asked for the toilet. He knew something was wrong when he noticed blood seeping through his uniform. Cleaning himself up he managed to tie a handkerchief around his leg. By the time he got back to Penny she had almost finished her coffee and wanted to know what on earth was going on. Ted had no choice but to explain when Penny noticed blood on his face. Thinking that an old wound had opened up again he then showed his leg to her.

'Don't get any fancy ideas, young lady, I am not in the habit of showing a leg.'

Ted got up from the table and hunched himself up. Looking at Penny he really did look more like the phantom from the local camp. Screwing his face up he said, 'Help me, fair maiden, they call me the man with no financial means and I am in great pain, please help me.'

He then fell back into his chair. Penny being more emotional than he thought, took Ted's little comical act seriously and gave him a hug and a kiss.

'Don't worry, my love, I will take care of you.'

She went over to the waitress who very soon turned up with a bowl of hot water and a first aid bandage. With tears in her eyes she cleaned up the wound and applied a dressing. Ted was beginning to wonder, why on earth would a beautiful girl waste her time on somebody with a face like his? Pete was right, somebody out there did love him.

'Now I don't want you to say another word, just stay where you are and I will order more coffee and whatever you want to eat, I have something to explain to you.'

Ted was amazed at her kindness. Penny sat down again and reminded him that he needed building up, his system would be working to repair his wounds and so she had ordered something nice for both of them.

'Oh, I forgot the cream for your face, which I must say has started to heal nicely.'

She was not looking at him when out of her shopping bag she produced a small cake.

'This is for you, it's not much, but I thought you would like something to remind you of home, as I am sure you miss your home life, which reminds me, can I ask your name?'

Ted leaned across the table, and audacious as ever, he took a chance by kissing her, thanked her and said, 'My name is Edward, but please call me Ted.'

'Oh, I thought your name was "The man with no financial means",' she said laughing.

'If you're not careful, young lady, I can mutate into the phantom and chase you around the park.'

Penny giggled and said she could not wait, but first she must tell him who she was. She came round and sat next to him.

'Don't tell me you are that wicked old witch who makes cakes that turn people into frogs, or something.'

'Oh, it's much worse than that,' she said digging him in the ribs that sent him to the roof and back. It sent tears to her eyes when she realised what she had done.

'I am so sorry Ted, my love, please forgive me.' She kissed him this time with a lot more meaning and she held onto him as if there was no tomorrow.

'When you are quite ready, soldier, I will serve you your meal.' It was the waiter with two steaks and all the trimmings.

'I want you to eat plenty of vegetables,' Penny insisted. 'I want to see you fit and well before you go away, or otherwise I will be worried.'

Penny seemed keen on telling Ted all about herself while they enjoyed their meal. Ted had almost forgotten what a good steak looked like, but then Penny's candour suddenly changed the entire atmosphere.

'Not another word, my love, I have lots to tell you. First of all I have to tell you that my father is a serving Army officer, in fact he is probably responsible for much of your training. My mother thinks he will be promoted quite soon and may have to move.'

Ted, who was drinking coffee, nearly choked and had to apologise. He explained that there might just be a slight misunderstanding on his part. Penny explained she lived with her parents in the married quarter and that she had been traveling into town and back to the camp ever since she had been born. Her mother was aware that she was seeing a soldier this evening, and seemed happy enough so long as Penny continued her studies in pharmacology.

'I go back to university next month so it seems we will lose each other. My father does not know about you, of course, as it may well complicate things a little, and in any case he's gone away for a while. He retires in about six years' time.'

Ted was beginning to feel slightly uncomfortable, who was her father, and why would it not be a good idea for her father to know about him? Why on earth would he not be good enough for her father? Ted cut short Penny's background story by starting to give a little of his own. Penny, in the meantime, had ordered two magnificent cream buns with powdery icing on the top.

'By the way, Penny, what is your father's rank? Is he a sergeant, or something like that? I still fail to remember all the various ranks and so on. All I know is that I am at the bottom, known as Sapper Watson, with less than two years before they let me free.'

'My father is a colonel,' she said.

Hearing that, Ted nearly choked again, sending the powdery icing sugar up his nose and all over his healing face.

'Oh, I am sorry, please make allowances for this humble sapper who is beginning to wonder how I can settle the bill and now you tell me your father is a colonel.'

Penny burst out laughing and set about cleaning up his face. 'Don't worry about the bill, my love,' she said.

'Oh, but I do, Penny, I feel I am letting you down, and the very fact that you are a colonel's daughter worries me even more.'

Penny looked at him with tears in her eyes and said. 'So I am not good enough for you, is that it?'

'No, Penny, you have no idea how much I like being with you. Please, Penny, promise you will write to me, it's just you and me from now on.'

Penny reached for another tissue and explained how he was to use the cream. 'What are you going to do when you have completed your national service?' she asked.

Ted explained that he was a solicitor's clerk and was

studying law with the aim of becoming a lawyer. 'It's an ideal situation for studying,' he said and explained briefly his plans for the future. He told her about his parents and his sister, who was already a solicitor. His father had worked for a civil engineering company employed as a bricklayer until his health had forced him to take on less manual work. His mother worked part time as a cleaner in a shop, and his sister had just taken on a redundant shop.

'She aims to turn it into an estate agents, with my father helping to renovate the place, so you can imagine how I feel being forced out of my home when I could be helping my sister. Although a practicing solicitor, she feels happier selling property. I really don't know where she finds the energy and the time, she has a daughter to look after as well. Oh, I forgot, she also helped me with my studies until, of course, I was called up in the Army. Well, that's about it in a nut shell.'

Penny was intensely interested since she had no real family moving as she did from one place to another. Her life seemed to be almost blinkered by the fact she had no brothers and sisters, and if there were any relations, she had never met them. Nevertheless, Ted had met a real princess who not only had a heart of gold, she was incredibly attractive. He would love to take her home, but that was out of the question. He was thinking to himself what would happen if the colonel found out? It would raise more than an eyebrow, so it would be unwise to make any attempt at ingratiating himself. He certainly could not imagine going for tea at the invitation of the colonel and his wife. Ted knew it would be irresponsible to make big promises he could not keep, she was too nice. But in a short space of time, he had grown very fond of Penny and he did not plan to let her go; something would work out—with time.

'Why didn't you go to university, Ted? You would have been far better off when you came to do your national service,' said Penny.

'With hindsight, yes, you are right, sweetie pie, but for one thing, my parents could not afford to send me, and second, I would never have met such good pals as I have made. They are the salt of the earth. Finally, I would never have had the good fortune in meeting a truly magnificent girl called Penny. I am glad I forfeited my chances of qualifying, this day may never have happened and who knows what will happen in the near future?'

Penny was clinging onto Ted as if there was no tomorrow.

'I really love you, Ted, please see me tomorrow, and please don't let me down. You will come, won't you? I love you, Ted, and I want to be with you all the time.'

'Penny, don't worry, I will be outside your shop by ten o'clock to take you out for the day. I have ten shillings and fourpence, what do you think of that?'

'Oh well, if that is all you have, then don't be surprised if I am not there. I was expecting to be taken out to dine before going to the theatre.'

'Oh, that's not a problem, we can partake of fish and chips, then take in a film in the old flea pit. You know, pretty girl, you drive a hard bargain, I am not usually lavishing my money like this, but then you are very special to me.'

Penny looked at Ted and said, 'You are so generous, my love, I expected to be taken to the cinema, *but fish and chips as well*. Wow, I can't wait.'

'For you, darling, I would go to the other side of the world and bring you back riches.'

'I don't care where you go, so long as you come home. I really love you, Ted.'

Ted was not comfortable with that word 'love'. He had heard too much from the lads about falling in love in a relationship. It was only natural, but separation for long lengths of time always changed things beyond hope of recovery, leaving one of them hurt beyond measure. So many of these sort of relationships fell apart at the first hurdle. Neither of them would want that.

'Penny, I think we should steady ourselves a little, don't you? I mean, genuine love is a very emotive word, not to be taken lightly. I may well feel the same way as you, but I have to reserve my feelings for you until we know for sure. We have to see if we can hold onto each other through the pen while we are apart, if we can, then we can say we love each other. Personally, I can't wait for that day.'

Penny had hardly heard a word, it seems she was so tired and almost fell asleep holding onto Ted, but she was concerned, feeling that he was far from happy and that all this comical talk was just covering up his misery. She wanted to know more. 'Can I ask you something?'

Penny hesitated a little and then said she thought he was far from happy with Army life but was trying to put it to one side for her sake. 'That's why I think the world of you and I always say what I mean, so there.'

Obviously Ted was wrong, Penny *had* heard everything he had said. 'My parents live not far from here, so I am hoping to see them before I go away. Perhaps my sister has some more books on law, I will certainly need them. All my plans went out the window when I received the dreaded letter ordering me to report to the Army. As I have already mentioned, I was a solicitor's clerk, and with help from my sister, I had high hopes of achieving what she had; then bang goes my chance of studying to pass the law exam. When I received the railway warrant it was for a train that took me into a very dark tunnel indeed. It took me away from the comforts of home, all my friends, my leisure time, my studies, and most of all the chance of meeting someone. It was a transportation into a life of hell. Along that tunnel people shouted at me, punished me for the slightest mistake, and took away just about everything I had known before. They eventually made me a jack-of-all-trades, and, in my case, master of none, but I am a driver of massive lorries and I can fix minor problems on engines and electrical wiring. Give me the chance and I would be out of that camp like a shot, but I can't. On top of all these vagaries I get beaten to within an inch of my life, but I have to say it was worth it. You have no idea how much you have helped me.

'What do you mean?' Penny asked. 'What's really wrong, you're obviously very upset. Can I help you in any way?'

'Not really, Penny.'

Which, in a way, said everything, even to himself. He had become too independent, perhaps brought about by weeks of harsh treatment. His personality may well have changed and maybe for the better, only time would tell.

Ted realised it was a mistake turning down Penny's offer of help, but he had to think of the possibility of them not seeing each other again, he wouldn't want that for either of them.

'Can you see a light at the end of the tunnel, my love?' asked Penny.

'Yes, I can, there is an angel of love and mercy standing by me. When she speaks her words lift me up bit by bit. All my misery and pain fades away. She leads me out of this dark place where I can then see more clearly just how beautiful she is. She has a heart of gold and a smile that makes me feel alive again.'

'What does she really look like?' Penny asked.

'Well, as a matter of fact, she looks like one of those spring flowers I saw today, a bit ragged around the edges.' With that, and mindful of his ribs, she thumped him on the arm and said she did not believe a word of it. She held on and looked up at him. Ted needed no persuading and the rest was heaven.

'Oh, by the way, my love, the angel told me we would both have to go back into the tunnel and her advice was to make hay while the sun shines.'

'Now look here, soldier boy, I am not sure what you mean by that, but you can think again. On the other hand, it might be raining today, but the sun may shine tomorrow, I make no promises, you understand.' She pulled him closer to her.

It was home time for Penny, and Ted wanted her to go back on the bus with him, but she had other ideas. Penny ordered a taxi from the coffee shop and then asked Ted to take her home. To Ted it was acutely embarrassing, having no money and having to make excuses.

'Look, sweetheart, you know I can't pay for this and——'

For the first time Penny became a little annoyed. 'You keep saying that, don't you understand I am doing this for you, and us both, how on earth are we supposed to get on with each other when you won't let me do this small thing for you? Stop feeling sorry for yourself.'

On the way home they made plans for the whole of Sunday, perhaps their last chance of a really fun day for a very long time. To Ted's relief and embarrassment Penny settled the taxi fair and ordered the driver to drop Ted off at the gates.

'She's a lovely girl, just like her father, he's a real gentleman. I often take them about the town, as a matter of fact, I took him to the station only yesterday. He said he was off to London for a few days. You look after that girl, or you will have me to answer to, you know what I mean.'

He never stopped talking all the way to the gate. 'You look as if you've already been in a war, look at the state of you. You can't even stand up properly, what kind of an Army are you in? You make sure of what I told you, look after her, she's a lovely girl.'

'Yes, I am sure you are right,' and that was that, the driver was gone.

Ted stood there for a while and thought, why is everybody telling me what to do? I don't wish to interfere with other people's lives, so what's going on? It's a free world, isn't it? Then there was an almighty scream, a frightening sound and it seemed to be directed at him. Somebody wanted to meet his acquaintance.

'Come here you scruffy soldier, what the hell do you think you are doing hanging about looking like a tramp, come here on the double. Left, right, left, right, get those knees up you 'orrible man. Halt, stand still.'

Ted was back to hell on earth. The pain in his ribs and leg once again left him in agony.

'Now then, soldier, what's going on?'

Ted tried to explain the reason for his appearance, and that he had aimed to put matters right.

'As I understand it, you put up a very good fight, one of them has a busted nose. Don't involve yourself in this matter, do you understand, soldier? It won't be long before they receive a rail warrant and then they will be ours.'

'Excuse me, Corporal, I must get back and clean myself up, I can't be seen like this,' explained Ted.

'Well, I have seen you, and I don't like what I see, but under the circumstances I will make an exception. Just one more thing, soldier, the next camp dance has been cancelled, watch this space as they say.'

The military policeman had let him off the hook, but what did he mean by 'watch this space'? Walking back to the hut Ted felt relieved that his actions had potentially prevented a very nasty situation, but he felt that something was going on. Pete was already in and mentioned the rumour that the camp dance had been cancelled.

'That's no rumour,' said Ted, 'I have just been told officially.'

'Ah yes, but,' Pete continued, 'There may be a three-day pass, or leave, or something like that, starting from next week. I suppose we will find out on Monday. Your uniform looks a bit shabby, Ted, what the hell have you been up to?'

The lads drifted in at various times, some in the early hours. Harry lay on his bed looking a little depressed. Many of the lads were boasting of girlfriends and promises that had been made that none of them could keep. One or two lads boasted of a much higher level of experience with girls and it amazed Ted that they could be so open and callous about it. They seemingly had no feelings for these girls, or were they just bragging simply because there was not a shred of truth in their stories?

It had been a long, hard week and a day of rest was more than welcome. Sunday morning was busy for Ginger with all the church services, but he still found time for a game of football, which was his second passion. Gary and Alf's money had all but run out, but they still decided to thumb a lift into town. Ted had already left for his promised date, hoping the sun would shine all day.

Ginger came in early from the evening service with a little more news of Fred's death, but he waited for everybody to be present before saying a word. Ted, as usual, came in last looking happier than usual, until Ginger mentioned that he had been in touch with Fred's parents.

'It seems he died of stomach complications. Before he died he wanted to be remembered to all of you and wished us a happy life in this wonderful world. May God bless and love him forever.'

Everybody responded with 'Amen'.

Ginger made one last request of them all. 'I intend to collect for a wreath and cancer research.'

Harry came forward with his donation and remembered how Fred had been harshly treated, but Ginger quickly pointed out that Fred's life was over. 'Learn from it, and however hard it may seem, we should not blame this tragedy on the system. How do you think the people that shouted at him back in basic training feel? I suspect they feel the same way as we do and would do anything to bring him back, but they can't and neither can we. He left a message for us all.'

Ted's mind was on other matters, but he was listening to Ginger and he couldn't help feeling that the angel in the tunnel had taken Fred to a happier place. For a moment he had forgotten all about his sun-filled day with Penny. Ginger was probably right, Fred wasn't taken away because he was harshly treated, on the contrary, many people go through much harsher times. They should all feel very lucky that they still had a life and were capable of achieving many things, however hard it may be.

Ted's day with Penny would always be with him. Penny was his paragon of virtue, the angel had given him plenty to think about.

The morning came too early for them, and attempting to recover from the events of the weekend was foremost on their minds. Breakfast was brief but there was time to chat on the best of the weekends events. They all seemed to have had a great time, but the news of their next impending and mysterious move caught their attention. The bets were on with some saying the Near East, like Cyprus, and others the Far East, like Singapore. Others could not care less, but the sooner they got their two years over with the better.

It all got a bit personal when one of the lads said, 'You're bit of a dark horse, Teddy boy, have you been in another fight? You've a bruise on your neck, and what's with the limp, did she put up a fight? My advice if you have any sense is to lay low for a while, or you could hear from a solicitor, Teddy boy.' That comment brought the roof down with laughter, but Ted was not amused. He said nothing until they started on Pete, who had not left the camp all weekend. It turned out that he was seeing a NAAFI girl. Free cups of tea, sausage, egg and chips, it could not be bad.

'I freely admit she is not the most attractive girl, but she has a heart of gold. She really gives me a great deal of pleasure, and I must say I will miss her. I wouldn't give you a light for that lot in town you chase after.'

That comment was slightly unfortunate and one of the lads leaned over to Pete and said, 'Oh yes, so what's for afters, lover boy? What's that old saying, "You don't look at the mantelpiece when your po—"'

Harry intervened, 'One more word from you, big mouth, and your teeth will be kicked around the parade ground.'

'You and who else, you miserable bastard?' he yelled out. He was almost across the table, ready to grab Harry shouting, 'Come on, let's see *your* teeth fly first.'

The heated slanging match temporarily came to a halt when Harry said, 'It's none of our business what Pete and Ted get up to, and I think you should apologise.'

The reply was a punch which was wildly swung at Harry, but missed. The next attempted punch was halted half way through its swing when two military policemen appeared from nowhere, accompanied by a sergeant chef.

'Out, come on, get out of my cook house,' shouted the sergeant.

It took seconds to clear the room with the MP's bearing down on them—it was certain the culprits would be on a charge. The sergeant, brandishing a knife, paced up and down.

'I will have your vitals out, all of you, if you dare have a punch up in my restaurant again. Before I put you all on a charge I want the culprits to step forward.'

'It was me, Sergeant.' Ted stepped forward, then Ginger said it was him, followed by all of them. The sergeant made up his mind that they were obviously covering for each other. Perhaps a little more exercise on the parade ground would reduce their feelings for the opposite sex.

'Right, Corporal, make sure they get one hour's drill this evening, now get them out of my sight.'

One of the military policemen went over to Ted, and recognised him straight away. 'You always seem to be in trouble, soldier, you are in no fit state to march anywhere I can see that, go and make your way to the classroom, the rest of you, listen up. My colleague and me will be looking forward to drill you lot at 1800 hours this evening. You will present yourselves in full kit, do you understand?'

'Yes, Corporal,' they all chorused.

Knowing that they could be in real trouble, and the thought of losing there long weekend, filled them with horror. They had simmered down by the time they entered the classroom, but then another sergeant and a lance corporal burst into the room. An officer followed and the sergeant quickly brought them to attention.

'Stand easy, gentlemen, my name is Captain Harper and

I am sure you are eager to know your programme for the next two weeks.'

Alf leaned over to Harry and whispered, 'Ask him if we could have two weeks in the Caribbean.'

The sergeant, with a smile on his face yelled out, 'Stand up, you insolent joker. There will be no talking, do you understand?'

'Yes, Sergeant.'

'Now sit down and keep your mouth shut.'

Alf realised just how lucky he had been, and Harry tried hard to distance himself from Alf. This was not the time for jokes.

The captain thanked the sergeant and continued. 'As you may already know, you have been granted four days leave as of from Thursday. You will return to duty first thing Monday morning. The training programme ends Wednesday when you will be paid for two weeks. Your movements thereafter will be revealed in due course. Thank you. Sergeant, carry on.'

The officer walked out followed by the two NCOs.

The instructor walked back in and immediately started to lecture about electrical wiring, power generators, and power distribution. 'We have only three days so listen carefully.' He issued a book to each of them. 'Study it carefully, you will find it very useful and interesting,' he said.

After their evening meal the lads reluctantly prepared themselves for an hour's drill with a great deal of acrimony. They would have come very close to blows once more had it not been for Ginger intervening, 'We are all to blame, so let's get it over with,' said Ginger.

In the meantime Ted had disappeared once more, saying he was excused boots, rubbing it in a bit which did not help. 'Enjoy your walk about on the square,' he said with a big grin on his face.

The parade ground was massive, and was obviously used by tanks. Tracks were clearly visible, but now it was the turn of boots. Harry was elected to march them on, much to the surprise of the NCOs. Harry was in his element and by now he was quite prepared to show off his power of command. All worries and fears left him as they marched towards the sergeant major. Harry halted them and brought them into line facing the sergeant major.

Harry offered a few rebukes to the lads, saying they would never make top grade and here was a chance to show off what they had been taught. He then turned to face the sergeant major, stood firmly to attention and asked for permission to carry on. Permission was granted and they were reminded that they would be watched closely.

Harry took a gamble, hoping the lads would co-operate. His first order was tallest on the right, shortest on the left, in two ranks file. Having got the shorties in the middle, with the tallest at each end, he marched them off to give a performance worthy of any passing out parade. He then marched them back to the sergeant major, hoping they would be dismissed early. To their surprise, the sergeant major had nothing to say except, 'Well done, but don't let me hear of any more trouble, you understand? March them back Sapper Watkins, and well done.'

When they got back to their hut, several of the lads began to write letters home, but it was anybody's guess whether the letters would reach home in time. Harry thought that he really did not want any fuss when he finally returned home, he just wanted to see his grandfather again and enjoy time with his entire family. Sophie had gone from his life, and the nurse was too far away.

Harry joined the lads in the NAAFI and had just enough

money for a pint and cleaning products. Pete's girlfriend served him up a pint and then he caught a glimpse of Pete who was tucking into a meal, no doubt served up by his girlfriend. Good luck to him, thought Harry. Joining the lads he could not help mentioning the nurse he had met at the hospital.

'You should have got her telephone number, and in any case you should remember the name of the hospital and the ward, what's the matter with you Harry?' said Brian.

'You're really good on the parade ground, but useless at chatting up birds. Why don't you phone, make a few enquiries, and don't waste our time giving us hard luck stories, what do you say lads?'

Brian was joined by Gary saying he had no choice now since they all wanted to know what she looked like, that was an order, Harry.

'What about you, Gary, who have you got tucked away up in those mountains?' asked Harry.

Gary reached into his top pocket and produced a photograph of his girlfriend and himself up in the mountains. They passed the photo around and they all responded saying she was absolutely gorgeous, pity about the bloke with her, which caused a great deal of laughter. Gary snatched the photo back saying it was a bad day what with the weather and all that. They all thought he was very lucky, especially with a face like his. Even Gary laughed and had to admit it was not his best side.

'What part of Wales do you come from?' asked Brian.

'I come from North Wales near Betws-y-Coed and my girlfriend, Megan, lives in Llandudno. The mountain in the photo is Carnedd Llewelyn. Sometimes we climb around Yr Wyddfa, or Snowdon to you. I just hope where we are going has some mountains to climb.'

Gary was in full flow when time was called.

'Must take a holiday there sometime,' said Pete who had decided to join them.

'No doubt you have enjoyed your meal, Pete?'

'Well, I am certainly not complaining, the dessert was absolutely bang on. Where's Ted, by the way, he's always out chasing some skirt. Does anybody know what's going on? I mean, he never says a word of where he is going, or anything about this girl—I assume it's a girl.'

Everybody laughed, but all agreed it was his business.

Ted wasted no time explaining his four-days leave and Penny said she would try and take an afternoon off. Ted said he would have to go home, but would return Sunday. Penny was so excited, and said she would make a few arrangements of her own.

The next two days dragged on towards pay parade where they were dismissed until first thing Monday morning. Harry made straight for the phone box: maybe his parents would pick him up that evening? Being just over an hour by car he felt sure they would fetch him and Ginger, who lived not far from them. Ginger was so grateful that he offered to pay, but Harry would not hear of it, he knew Ginger needed every penny.

'God bless you, Harry, one day I will make it up to you.'

Gary was out of the blocks and gone. He was heading for the A5 thumbing lifts. Pete planned to take his girlfriend home the next day to meet his mother.

'Of course, I expect you have made alternative sleeping arrangements, Pete, I mean to say, I wouldn't want you to bring D-squad's entire reputation into disrepute,' said Ted with a large grin on his face.

'Talking of sleeping arrangements, Ted, what about your own?'

'Ah well, I have arranged for my sister to pick me up at the station tomorrow evening.'

Pete wished him good luck and told him, laughing as usual, not to do anything he would regret later. Ted stood there for a moment wondering about that last statement, he really should have visited the chemist rather than throw caution to the wind, but how could he, when all the staff knew Penny? His embarrassment had got the better of him.

Rumours travelled fast, and just maybe her parents would be very suspicious of their daughter's assignations with a sapper. Well, it's too late now to worry about it, he thought to himself. Before setting off to town to meet Penny, he had to phone his sister to arrange his lift from the station.

Penny would try and arrange to have Thursday afternoon off, and they planned to meet up again on Sunday. That nagging feeling of knowing that it would be there last chance of meeting one another had temporarily left them.

Harry and Ginger were well on their way home with Harry's mother. 'Your father is taking us out tonight, but your grandfather is not well again and he might have to give it a miss, hope you don't mind.'

'Of course not, has granddad gone back into hospital, Mum?'

'No, but I wouldn't be surprised if he did, he can't look after himself, so we have to look at alternatives.

Ginger was most grateful for the lift home—which looked very run down to Harry—but he seemed to be happy enough.

'Many thanks again, see you at six on Sunday evening, and don't forget to phone the hospital, Harry, you know what I mean, have a nice time.' He walked off, whistling as he made his way down the road.

'He seems to be a nice young fellow, Harry.'

'They don't come better than that, Mum. I must say he holds us all together.'

'What's it really like, Harry? I know you only too well and I have to say you don't sound too happy. Your father said it would be tough for you.'

'The thing is, Mum, we just cohere in a way that helps us to preserve our sanity. I don't expect people to understand how I feel, empathy is the last thing I want. You just get on with what has to be done. We are in a state now where we know an overseas posting is imminent, but we haven't been told where. Having said all that, I must admit I have, to a certain extent, enjoyed the last few weeks. The training has been first class. Well, that's it, Mum, there is no more to be said except it's great to be home.'

'By the way, young man, what did your friend mean when he said, don't forget to phone the hospital?'

'Oh, nothing, Mum,'

He then remembered what Ginger told them all about the merits of telling the truth; but Harry made a mistake: he chose to tell his mother about the death of Fred rather than the nurse he met at the hospital when his grandfather was ill.

'Harry, are you seriously telling me one of your friends is dead?'

'Yes, but it was an illness that put him into hospital.'

'Yes, I can understand that, but what did he die of?'

'I don't really know.'

'Well, I don't like it, my boy, and I intend to talk to your father.'

'Oh, come on, he's got enough to think about, please don't bother him now.'

Ginger was so right, always tell the truth, because if you

don't it tends to create misleading impressions leading to an embarrassing situation, which is exactly what he had done.

'Look, I should explain this chap really did fall ill and die, but of what I don't know. His parents told Ginger he died of complications of the stomach, the Army training had nothing to do with it. We all feel very sorry about it. What Ginger meant was, don't forget to phone the nurse at the hospital.'

'What on earth are you talking about? Are you talking about young Fred or your grandfather—neither of which are in hospital.'

'No, it is the nurse at granddad's hospital, I am supposed to phone her, but I don't know any details. We seemed to get on well, but I haven't got her address.'

'Well, I must say, you're a bit slow, my boy, and you certainly don't take after your father—he never gave anybody else a chance where I was concerned. I am sure we still have the phone number of the hospital and all the other details, and why didn't you say all that in the first place? What on earth are they teaching you in the Army?'

Harry's mother was much more relaxed when they arrived home.

Gary was well on his way home. He had reached as far as the A5 and was trying to thumb a lift when a lorry pulled over.

'Can you take me anywhere near North Wales?'

'Climb in, soldier, where are you heading for? I can take you right through to Holyhead if you want.'

'No, Betwys-y-Coed will do fine, thanks.'

'Okay, here we go, I hope to reach your home in a couple of hours or so, must have a break for a cup of tea on the way. Have you been in the Army long?'

'About ten weeks with the Royal Engineers.'

'Good on you, I was a sapper, national service,' and then he laughed, 'Spent most of my time on jankers. I ended up in Palestine, and then on my way home the troop ship turned round during the night.'

'What on earth for?' asked Gary. 'Don't tell me somebody had forgotten their kit bag,' said Gary laughing.

'No, it was no joke, the next stop was Alexandria to refuel and so on. Although we didn't realise it at the time, we were on our way to Korea. I had to do another six months. No, mate, I would not like to go through that again, believe me.'

Gary could have cut his tongue out. He apologised.

'You were not to know, young fellah, it was difficult at the time, but the Army has its compensations, I learnt my trade and now I have three lorries. I wouldn't be driving today, but one of my drivers has gone down with flu, so here I am.'

Gary was really tired by now and was about to go into the land of nod when the lorry came to a halt.

'Fancy a quick cuppa, mate?'

Gary thought it a good idea, but first he would phone his girlfriend. The driver had bought Gary a cup of tea with a cake.

'On me,' he said, 'I know what your cash flow must be like.'

He seemed to be ahead of Gary all the time.

'Will your girlfriend be picking you up in Betws-y-Coed? Well, I hope you told her what this lorry looks like,' he said.

'She will be coming down from Conwy.'

'Okay, I will drop you off just by the bridge.'

Then he started to sing, until the rain came down in torrents. Low cloud over the hills slowed him down, but it was not long before Gary knew he was home. As the lorry went over the bridge there was Gary's girlfriend waving at him.

'Wow! You lucky fellah, she's a real beauty.'

'Thanks, mate. I hope to meet you again one day,' said Gary climbing out the cab.

It was a bright, sunny Thursday and Ted set off for town hoping Penny had got the afternoon off. He had plenty of time before meeting her so he shopped around to find a necklace that would hopefully remind her of him.

Ted paced up and down, waiting impatiently and then somebody came up behind him. Penny, not being that tall, tried to put her hands over his eyes, but didn't quite manage it. He turned around and was relieved that she had got the afternoon off. Penny was more than excited, especially when Ted told her that she would meet his sister.

'But before that we have the entire afternoon to ourselves,' said Ted. He would have loved to take her home, but circumstances would never allow it, so he told her to close her eyes and made an attempt to put the necklace on her. In the end, Penny had to help him, she turned around so that he could see the necklace on her. It looked magnificent. Ted was surprised when Penny told him that she had never been given a present by anybody—bar her parents, of course. She gave Ted the hug of his life and said she would wear it at all times.

The afternoon passed quickly and Ted's sister, Christine, was bang on time. She was very friendly, but had little time to spare.

'Call me any time, it was very nice meeting you, Penny— but I must go,' she said.

Then Penny spotted Christine's daughter. She just had time to say hello before they parted and then she said softly to Ted, 'You will come on Sunday, won't you Ted?'

'Of course I will, you have my word.'

Christine overheard the conversation, and had to hurry

him on. 'Come on, lover boy. He's as soft as a brush, Penny, and we love him to bits.'

'Yes, so do I,' Penny said to herself softly. 'Bye, my love. Bye Christine.' Then she waved to the little girl. 'See you soon.'

At the back of all the recruits' minds was the nagging awareness that they would have to return to camp soon. This feeling was emphasised by their not knowing where they would be stationed. They had been held in abeyance for long enough and time was running out.

For Ted the nagging knowledge that he must return to the Army was slightly tempered by the fact that he knew Penny would be waiting for him. On his return, Penny ran towards him looking as pretty as ever and wearing the necklace he had given her. After lots of hugs, she said she wanted to take a walk in the park with him. During their walk, Ted pulled her leg about his mother saying that he must be careful of girls taking advantage of his innocence.

'Innocent my foot! All I can say is, your mother should know the truth about her own son. You wait till I meet her. As a matter of fact, my mother knows all about you as well, Ted Watson, and you don't want to know the rest. My mother went on about what my father would think, and that you are not right for me. I reminded my mother that you had your own future which has now been interrupted. How would my father react if his future was being compromised? I told her how hard you work, having to study and at the same time obey the Army.'

'I hope that is all you said, except, of course, how well behaved we are and that we have no intentions of taking advantage of each other.'

'Heaven forbid, but it's our lives, and I have found the life that I have missed so much.'

They talked about each other, but Ted was beginning to realise that Penny had led a very sheltered life, moving from one place to another. A very strict life was beginning to show through. Then, out of the blue, Penny asked about Christine's little girl.

'Oh, that's Sophie and she was two last month. Christine and Sophie live on their own—the boyfriend ran off.' No matter how much he loved his sister, Ted could hardly blame her boyfriend, his sister could be overbearing at times to say the least, but Penny did not want to know all that.

'She's very lucky to have a little girl; would you like to have children, Ted?'

'I certainly would, one day.'

Feeling a little uncomfortable, Ted then said jokingly, 'I tell you what, my love, why don't we have one together right now?'

'Ted Watson, what do you take me for? How dare you?'

Sophie was still clinging onto him, and Ted felt she was more relaxed and that perhaps she knew more about life than he had thought. The talk about children was cut short by the rain. Penny wanted to go home and ordered a taxi.

'Well, I suppose this is where we say goodbye, sweet girl, I will never forget you, no matter what happens.'

But Penny had other ideas, '*We* are going home,' she said.

'You must be joking, what about your mother? I am sure she hasn't invited me for tea,' he said nervously. 'I have fallen in love with you, Penny, but under the circumstances I think I will give it a miss.'

Penny asked the driver to stop short of where she lived and invited Ted to walk her home. It was dark so Ted agreed, but when Penny said she knew how to get into the back of the house, Ted stopped her and said he had to respect her parents' home.

'I know your father has gone away, but your mother is bound to see us and then I will certainly lose you. No, I have to draw the line.'

Penny insisted, and said she should have told him before that her mother was in London with her father. 'Come on, darling, I know there's a hole in the fence, nobody will see us. I have to be in by half six, they will be phoning me, so let's go.'

Checking up on her I expect, thought Ted. Well, let her have her freedom for once. It would be a very audacious move, but who cares? This would be their last few hours together. They had to make the most of it, however reckless it might be.

'Come on then, Penny, show me the way in and let's have some fun.'

Ted was thinking here he was, in the colonel's house, something which he would have found unthinkable only an hour before. There had been no chance of ingratiating himself with her parents in the past, but here he was with a beautiful girl and he intended to make the most of it, for both of their sakes.

Penny prepared a meal with wine and made certain that no trace would be left for her mother to discover. Time was running out fast, and all their past unhappiness had temporarily left them. Ted had given Penny a sense of freedom, it was as if she had a home of her own. Penny had, at last, found somebody that she loved and wanted nothing more than to look after him.

Ted woke up to see Penny, who was fast asleep. She was truly very pretty, but then he noticed the time—which gave him one hell of a shock. It was way past six in the morning. Ted was in a state of real panic, he was due in the classroom by eight sharp. It would be their day of reckoning, they would be told their new destination. Penny suddenly woke up, and realising Ted was getting dressed, she started to cry. She tried talking to him, but she was crying so much all he heard was, 'I love you.' The last thing he wanted was to see her crying, but what could he do about it?

Still dressing, and thinking of the consequences of being late to the classroom, he said, 'You lured me here on a false pretence, took full advantage of my innocence, and now I could be in deep trouble. I know what it was? It was that drink you made for me. It must have had a magic potion in it.'

'Yes, soldier boy, you are right, and there is nothing you can do about it, but it's all your own fault.'

'Don't you prevaricate with me, young lady, you will be hearing from me in due course.'

'Well, you had better get a move on, hadn't you? You shouldn't have got involved in such a complicated situation, especially one in which someone loves you and doesn't want you to go.'

The tears fell from her eyes, 'Please look after yourself, and do your best for me. Please write as soon as you can.'

Somehow he just had to stop those tears and reassure her, but sheer panic set in, being caught in the colonel's house would spell disaster for both of them. He had no time to waste, even Penny's charm could not delay him further. In his eagerness to dress he suddenly lost his balance and fell over Penny's dressing table. Penny stopped crying and helped him up. Scented powder, perfume, and more was spilt all over his clothes.

'There is no rush, my love, take your clothes off and I will clean them up for you.'

'You've got to be joking, I have to go now or it's curtains for both of us.'

With one last embrace he finally left. Climbing back through the fence he could hear the church clock strike seven. He looked back, and to his horror, there were two children looking at him from the top window next door. There was nothing he could do but make his way back to the main road and try and get a lift. His luck was in, a motorbike pulled up.

'Hop on, mate, I'm going your way.'

Passing through the main gate was a huge relief after the security check and a military policeman had waved them through. Making up his mind, Ted realised he would have to take a chance; time was not on his side, he had no choice but to go straight to the classroom. It would be highly unlikely he would get away without a charge levelled against him, but who cared? He would not change anything for the world.

The evening before had seen all the lads return from leave except Ted. Nobody had missed him at first. Their main thought being whether anybody knew what their next move was. Alf came in looking just like he had lost all his pay—which apparently he had. As he slumped on his bed he blamed the Army for just about everything.

'The Army can't even get its timing right.'

Pete, knowing Alf's reputation with the opposite sex, could not help saying, 'You don't think your girlfriend has anything to do with you current state do you, Alf?'

'I never have a girlfriend for more than a couple of dates, it's all this settling down business they want, and I'm not ready for that, give me freedom.'

'Well, how on earth can you blame the Army for that?

And what's more, you can't call this freedom can you, after all, we are all in the same boat, Alf.'

'I guess you are right, but as far as I am concerned this boat has no rudder, which brings me to ask, got any news as to where we might be heading in the next couple of days?'

'No idea, I guess they feel they are under no obligation to tell us anything.'

'You surprise me, after all, being a regular visitor to the NAAFI, the centre of Army intelligence, I thought you at least would know.'

'I can assure you I haven't a scrap of information,' Pete said.

Ginger and Harry were the next in, 'Any news lads?' asked Harry.

Gary and the rest all came in asking the same question.

The sun brought in Monday and time refused to slow down for anybody. At breakfast only one was missing. It was inconceivable that Ted would do a runner. Harry put an end to any notion that Ted would let himself down, or anybody else come to that. Ted would not let them down, and Harry strongly suspected what he was up to. The Army was not going to deprive him of one second of his time with his girl, especially as it could be his last for a very long time.

In the classroom, Ted had unwittingly brought with him Penny's perfume which permeated the room, he was unshaven, and looking as if he had been dragged through a hedge. He was sitting there with his eye's closed, mumbling something like, 'I don't know what's been keeping you all, I am dead keen to know my fate—and please don't ask questions. I would be grateful if you would just leave me to the devil's instructions.'

Ginger went over to him, 'Where's your case, young fellah?'

Ted was in no fit state to answer, but Ginger could see a case at the back of the classroom.

'Don't worry, Ted, I will look after your case.'

'Thanks, Ginger, you're a good man. By the way, it may not be the only case you can help me with.'

'What do you mean?'

'I mean what I say: guilty, or not guilty?'

'Oh, I see what you mean, or I think I do. You can rely on my support, but in the meantime lay low and mind your tongue.'

By now Ted had cheered up just enough to realise he was not alone. 'Do your best,' Penny had said. He needed his friends to get through the next couple of hours, otherwise he had no chance of doing his best.

Then in walked two senior NCOs followed by the captain. The recruits were brought to attention, but Pete had to prod Ted and bring him into the land of the living. Ted's failure to respond smartly caught the eye of one of the NCOs who was also sniffling the air.

'Stand up straight, you useless scruffy individual, look at the state of you, don't you dare turn out looking like a tramp. Hello, what's this, perfume? I think you have some explaining to do, you will report to me later.'

The captain simmered things down a little by thanking the sergeant and then he read out some simple instructions:

'You will return to your quarters, pack all your belongings carefully, and label your luggage with your number, rank, and name. There will be an early lunch at 1200 hours after which transport will take you to the station.'

No destination was given, but Ted was not prepared to let it go just like that. Foolishly, he failed to heed the advice of his friend Ginger to lay low and keep quiet. He said to the captain, 'We have been kept in ignorance for long enough, and we have a right to know what is going on, after all, I have arrangements to ma——'

That was all he was allowed to say. The officer quickly dealt with Ted by saying that he had no rights, but Ted seemed to flip and answered back to the officer.

'May I remind the captain that I *do* have rights and that I am on loan to the Army.'

That was all he was allowed to say, the sergeant screamed at Ted not to speak unless spoken to, he had no rights. The captain ordered Ted out of the room, he was to be marched straight to the guard room where he would speak to him later, but no other action was to be taken. The officer told the sergeant to dismiss them back to their quarters. Ginger made a dash for the door with Ted's case. On the way back to the hut he noticed Ted being marched to the guard room, arms shoulder high and constantly being shouted at. Ginger had mixed feelings about Ted's sudden outburst, but without doubt he had to admire his guts. He was the only one that was prepared to ask questions, even though he was in all kinds of trouble only known to himself. Ted's courage was one thing, however he seemed to be suffering and not being able to talk about it was making things worse. Ginger gave Ted's case to one of the lads and told him to pack all of Ted's belongings, he would go to the guard room and risk his own neck.

Ginger was challenged right away, but the officer told him his friend had been reprimanded and that Ginger and he must now return immediately to their hut and pack ready for transport.

'Escort them back to their quarters, there is no time to lose,' ordered the captain.

Ginger, although confused as to how Ted had escaped a

charge, wasted no time in stepping back and saluting.

Walking back to the hut Ginger pointed out to Ted that if he had no wish to talk then, rest assured, he would not press him, but that he would always be there if needed.

Ted was grateful for all the support and said, 'One day I will explain to you why I have isolated myself from you all. I have very sound reasons.'

Ginger was no fool, he could read Ted's face like a book.

'Look, mate, you're obviously upset, just like the rest of us. Most of the lads are suffering the loss of female warmth and charm, on the other hand, some of them can't get away quick enough.'

Ted laughed and was in full agreement, he was back to his old self once more. Ginger then quoted an old prayer.

'Please, God, grant us the serenity to accept the things we cannot change, the courage to change the things we can, and the wisdom to know the difference.'

Back in the hut all of Ted's belongings had been packed except a carrier bag. Brian and the sapper that took a swing at Harry in the cook house had packed everything carefully.

'Thanks lads, I really do appreciate this. Anybody got a knife? My girlfriend made a cake for me and I want to share it with my mates.'

The sapper came over to Ted and put his hand out, 'We don't know each other much, but my name is Bill and I would like to apologise for what I said.'

'Forget it, mate, you can have the first slice.'

Alf came over, eager for a slice and mentioned how good it tasted. 'Wow, that was good, but you don't think there is another little cake left behind, do you, Ted?'

Everybody knew Alf as the joker in the pack, but maybe this was a little over the top. Ted quickly turned the joke around by saying with a laugh, 'I really couldn't say, Alf, but I suspect we may well be leaving several little problems behind, but that would be a lot to look forward to—what do you think, Pete?'

'Ah well, I didn't throw caution to the wind, but somehow or other I wouldn't be surprised if a letter came which revealed as much.'

Brian just about had time to reveal his secret by announcing his engagement, but the transport had arrived before he could say another word. In any case, he was always falling out with his girlfriend so nobody expected it to last, his chances were not good, especially going away for months on end.

After enjoying their cake one of the lads from another hut came into the room. They had been told of their destination, an island in the Pacific called Christmas Island. We will all be told officially later on today.

'Cheer up lads, just think of all that sun on a tropical island,' said Brian.

Ted nearly threw his bed at him, but the others were quite excited.

8. No Turning Back

Feeling nervous about what lay ahead, the lads arrived at a holding point before transport was laid on to take them to Heathrow airport for the flight out of the country. Heathrow was new to them all. They were joined by four Airforce lads, all very young. None of them had much to say, and by the look on their faces, they were not at all happy. According to Alf the message over the tannoy mentioned their flight to a place called Goose Bay.

'That's in Canada, Alf, what the hell do we need shorts for? You will freeze your vitals off in that place, believe me. I thought we are going to a Pacific island?'

'So you are,' said one of the airmen. Once again there was an officer and a sergeant making sure everybody went through the gate to the aircraft. The Airforce lads boarded the aircraft last and sat up front in the aircraft, one of them seemed to be chatting up one of the air hostesses. With seat belts tightened, the plane took off, climbing into the night sky and heading for Goose Bay. Ginger was sitting next to one of the airmen and soon started talking.

'What's going on at Goose Bay, mate?'

'Oh, it's just a couple of hours to refuel and then on to Vancouver; I think we have a break there before moving on to

Hawaii, and then Christmas Island.'

The lights of London had long since disappeared and Ginger had settled down when the one of the cabin staff offered them a drink.

'I think a beer would be in order, thank you,' said the one airman.

'And I will have a double whisky,' said the other airman.

Ginger ordered an orange juice, which prompted the airman to say, 'You may need something a little stronger when I explain what you are getting yourself into, since it's obvious you have no idea what's going on. I can't understand it: I don't understand why you haven't been told. Perhaps because you might do a runner, absent without leave, or something like that. Mind you, I wouldn't blame anybody for not wanting to go. I asked for an alternative posting, but I was refused and reminded that there was nothing they could do about it.

'Why don't you want to go?' asked Ginger, who by now was getting a little agitated.

'We have all been ordered to a nuclear test site called Christmas Island in the middle of the Pacific ocean.

'Not on your, nelly,' replied Ginger who by now was out of his seat and getting really angry, which was totally uncharacteristic of him.

'I see that they may have been right,' said the airman, 'I think you would have done a runner.'

'You're damn right I would have,' said Ginger and he stormed off to tell the others.

Having passed the word he came back and settled in his seat. 'May God have mercy on us all,' he said softly to himself.

'I am not a volunteer, and I certainly would not have volunteered for this sort of depravity. It is deplorable.'

Then the airman went on to say, 'Of course, you may not

realise, they already have the atom bomb, so it looks as if they are going for something much more destructive and powerful, like the hydrogen bomb, I certainly wouldn't worry though, I expect we will be well away from ground zero, something like two hundred miles away.'

This was no consolation to Ginger though, it was the escalation of these terrifying weapons that filled him with absolute horror. The thought of being involved went against everything he believed in. No, it was wrong to be involved, and he would make it known at the first opportunity.

The airman, though, saw it differently, and although he also agreed with Ginger about being involved, he thought these weapons would deter any aggressor thinking of starting a war. 'It would be unthinkable,' he said.

'That is as may be, but what about us? According to what they have taught us, we should be nowhere near this island,' replied Ginger. He could not share the airman's confidence and reminded him of the nuclear tests which had been carried out elsewhere; only time would tell if there was a sting in the tail.

At last the drinks were being served up. Ginger was handed his orange juice, but kindly asked the young girl if she would be kind enough to fetch him a whisky instead, preferably the bottle. The two airman were highly amused, and apologised for breaking such ominous news to him.

It was a long journey to Goose Bay, but somehow sheer exhaustion put the recruits into semi-consciousness.

No wonder we have not been told, thought Ginger. Well, let's hope none of us suffer as a result of this. I wonder if nuclear testing is not a euphemism for something much more sinister? thought Ginger. His mind was racing away with him, the couple of drinks had worn off, and it was time for a meal in the cabin, which was like a long tube full of cigarette smoke. The air was stale and very warm, not the ideal place to take your boots off, one would have thought. Ginger thought the girls worked tirelessly, walking up and down this tube full of obnoxious air. At last, the pilot announced the arrival, which could not have come quick enough for Ginger. It was just about getting light when the plane touched down at Goose Bay.

Sure enough, there was snow either side of the runway. When the door was opened a cold blast of clean, fresh air refreshed the cabin. For Ginger it was the bitter cold air that made him realise he was on Canadian soil. He had never left his home before, other than reporting for Army training.

As the plane was being refuelled they were treated to a hot cup of coffee and a couple of biscuits. Everybody was impressed at the efficiency of the Canadians in spite of the intense cold and snow, and the plane was soon ready for the next part of their journey. Back home there would have be delays and everybody would be blaming each other.

The experience was short-lived as they were soon on their way again, heading for Vancouver. There was to be a one-night stopover, which would give them a chance to write home. Most of the lads made the most of this magnificent place, some were even shown around the city by local people. Being most grateful to the people of Vancouver, they set off once more, heading for the much warmer climate of Hawaii.

Once again the stop over was only to refuel, but they managed to catch a glimpse of an RAF plane. It was from Christmas Island, collecting mail and whatever. Ted wanted to send another letter to Penny, but this time they were not allowed off the plane for some unknown reason, but he spoke to a stewardess who willingly said she would post the letter for him.

Taking off again, they headed for the coral atoll called Christmas Island, it was just about one hundred miles north of the equator, so it would not take any longer than about three hours or so.

It was quiet on board with most of the lads sleeping when one of the stewardesses tripped over Alf's leg, which was right across the isle. She was not at all pleased and gave Alf a reprimand worthy of the regimental sergeant major.

'Alright, keep your clothes on, I can only apologise to you, allow me to help you,' said Alf.

'I can assure you I will keep my clothes on, who do you think you are speaking to? You have really hurt my leg.'

'Allow me to take a look at it, I am quite good at this sort of first aid,' said Alf.

'Yes, I am sure you are,' she said quite angrily. 'You can keep your hands to yourself, if you don't mind, and help me pick all this mess up.'

Alf never said a word as he picked up the mess. Having made a good job of it, he sat down, and for once in his life he became very anxious at the thought at what lay ahead of him. For some peculiar reason the very thought of getting closer to this island filled him with dread.

He wrote a quick letter to his parents, thinking perhaps the stewardess would post it for him and that he would apologise to her once more. Later on she walked passed him, and without doubt she was limping. She glared at him, leaving him in no doubt that he was not at all popular. Plucking up courage, he called her, and to his surprise she responded.

'What now?' she snapped at him.

'I was just wondering if you would do me a favour and post this letter to my parents. Look, I really am sorry for what has happened and I only wish I could make it up to you, but under the circumstances there is nothing I can do.'

'I can do better than post it for you,' she said.

Alf was surprised at her sudden change of attitude.

'What do you mean?' he said.

'I will deliver it by hand—that's if you behave yourself. '

Alf was over the moon and asked her name.

'It's Jennifer, and I might as well tell you I don't live far from you; in fact, I could walk there.'

'Then you must know my dad's garage and showroom? Just drop in, he would be pleased to meet you. Tell him I'm okay, and have a look at my old desk.'

'Don't worry, I will tell him you are just as clumsy as ever and that you have got your bucket and spade. I will tell him you are well and enjoying life, would that be okay?' She could see he was beginning to show his nerves and thought that it may help, especially as they were approaching the island.

The plane once again fashioned its wings for landing and then let its wheels down. At first glance the island landscape looked as if it was from another planet. It was peppered with lagoons. They could see a few buildings, but for the most it was a desolate place.

The door opened and this time it was a blast of warm air. Alf was up instantly, he wanted to see the stewardess once more. She was at the bottom of the steps talking with one of the other stewardesses, and quite frankly, he didn't expect much response from her. He approached her just in time before the Army took over his life again.

'What's this?' she asked.

'It's a map of exactly where my dad's business is located. The other note is for you, it's my last will and testament leaving my bucket and spade to you, I won't need it any more. Bye, Jenny Wren, sorry about your leg.'

She was unable to say one word and tried to touch him, but he was gone. All she heard was silence from these lads, then shouting from NCOs as they ordered them all into line before marching them away.

Good old Ginger, solid as ever, was keeping up the moral. Nobody said much, they just stood waiting to be reunited with their luggage, after which they were driven to the main camp.

Not all service personnel travelled by airline. Many travelled by troop ship, which took weeks, and a few travelled with the RAF transport command. There was a mixed reaction to their journey; nobody had expected to see so many places in the world. It was an experience of a life time, that is if you enjoyed travelling, on the other hand, if you suffered from travel sickness then obviously it was purgatory.

Stepping ashore at Port London after weeks at sea or arrival by air after a few days

9. WELCOME TO PARADISE GONE WRONG

To the untutored eye, the island presented itself as no sort of paradise, but then none of them had ever been to an island like this. They had, perhaps, read about a Pacific island paradise, with magnificent birds—both feathered and unfeathered.

The disappointment was to be seen on their faces, and being constantly tormented by the longer serving inmates did not help matters. The torment was fairly constant until one got a tanned skin, not by choice, but simply because of the mode of dress which was shorts, boots, bush hat and sunglasses. The sunglasses being essential due to the fierce glare from the sun. They were warned that a severe case of sunburn rendering one unable to work would lead to a case of self-inflicted injury being brought against you. Escape was futile, they were there, whether they liked it or not.

Looking around there was not much to get excited about, but their minds were quickly focused when they were brought together for a more formal introduction to their duties. It seemed that there would be no time to lose and they would be required to start work the very next day. It was recommended that a shirt be worn as they would be out in the sun most of the day. To Harry it was like having a ball and chain clamped to his ankle. They were again warned of sunburn, and stepping out of line would mean a charge, or a flogging as Alf put it. The warrant officer heard him and promptly reminded Alf that if he did not learn to keep his mouth shut he might well arrange a flogging.

After they had been dismissed they were allocated a tent. So their home turned out to be a tent with camp beds. Mosquito nets were essential; there were many flies and bed bugs. The loos left much to be desired, with little or no privacy at all. There were warnings of dysentery, and looking at the loos, etc., nobody was surprised. Their dismay at having to live so close to each other, with no fans to keep them cool in the relentless heat was a real shock to the system. Only a few weeks ago they were freezing in a hut, but at least they had fires to keep them warm. In this place there was very little in the way of comfort, which amounted to nothing short of privation according to Ted.

Pete suggested they try and find the cook house before getting their heads down. The entire camp seemed to be made up of tents, large and small, but the mess tent was an Army-style marque with the usual make shift tables and chairs. There was nothing palatial about the place, but everything would eventually be built to a higher standard, such as wooden huts for accommodation and a new cook house. There were also roads, other buildings, and even an airfield to help build and maintain.

The one consolation was the food. Issued with a tin tray, mug, and irons (knife, fork and spoon) they lined up for what was, by anybody's standards, some really good food. Under the circumstances the chefs had done a first class job, but then if the food had not been up to standard, they were trained not to argue. Leftover food had to be dispatched into dustbins, which were plagued with flies on a Biblical scale. The tray had to be washed in greasy water, not ideal, and certainly there was room for improvement. It soon became obvious that they were there to work, and according to their instructions, work started early.

Pete suggested that it was essential to keep clean. Wash your hands, and find a way to keep your tin tray, mug, and irons clean. Get plenty of rest, and remember the secret at a place like this is to drink plenty, otherwise you will suffer dehydration very quickly. It was excellent advice, but easier said than done. For starters the water was from a desalination plant and tasted foul. The alternative was to top up with a bottle of orange juice at the WRVS, or a few beers in the NAFFI, and get a reasonable night's sleep.

Feeling exhausted after their first day on the island the camp bed felt like a feather mattress, but to stop it sliding over into your neighbour's bed space it had to be fixed to an improvised wooden base.

Most of the lads were up early the next morning, except Harry who had to be reminded it was an early start. There was no way off this island, even if you decided to do a runner. In spite of his training Harry felt home sick, with the added feeling of being press-ganged into a life of unending purgatory.

After a quick breakfast they reported for their first assignment. They were divided up into sections, and given all manner of building projects. Harry, Ginger, Alf, Ted, Gary, Brian, and Pete all managed to stay together.

The sergeant ordered them into the back of a lorry which took them further down the island to where construction work was already taking place. The road, which had been carved out of the bush, made its way past the airfield where they had landed only the day before. On they went along a track, which in places was still under construction. Finally, they arrived at

Put to work the day after arrival

the site where a new runway was being built. This was going to be their work place for the next few months. Work had already started with a few buildings being constructed.

'Come on, let's be having you. Come on, shake a leg, I won't tell you again,' shouted the sergeant.

Ginger, Harry, and Gary were assigned building tasks which they carried out with no problems. Alf, Ted, Brian, and Pete would be drivers, transporting all manner of building materials and so forth between Port London and wherever they had to be delivered. Now they realised what all the training had been about.

Memories came back to Ted, he thought of the Saturday afternoon when one of the transporters had broken down. It seemed a long time ago, and a world away; he felt as though he would never see Penny again. Well, who cares if they run out of fuel this time? he thought. He could not believe how quickly they had been put to work, it was if they had been there for a week or more.

Nobody was left idle, but Ginger took some persuading to get on with it. He shouted out to the sergeant, 'I don't mind putting my back into it, so long as we all receive a mug of tea now and again, thanks Sergeant.'

The sergeant turned to Harry and said that he thought that Ginger's attitude was falling short and that he would have to watch his step.

'That may be true, Sergeant, but I can assure you he will do as he's told; please understand none of us are volunteers, we are reluctant national servicemen.'

The sergeant was sympathetic, but reminded them all of the work that had to be done and not to step out of line. Alf and Ted received orders to pick up a load of stores from the port. Brian and Pete were to remain on site Their first

day passed very quickly, but nobody was more relieved than
Ginger when they were able to get out of the fierce heat; no
wonder they were warned regularly to take extra care when
out in the sun.

They still felt tired after the long journey, and on their
return to the main camp, they had to eat whilst enduring
more banter from the longer serving sappers and airmen.
Ginger sat down at a table only to meet up with the airmen
on the plane. They had no idea of what was going on, but
their colleagues informed them that something really big was
being planned for the future.

None of them could care less though; they were hungry and
thirsty. The airman introduced himself and his colleagues.

'The name's Ken, I'm a technician. It looks as if I will be
working shifts. We are open all hours of the year.

'As far as I know there is some good fishing here. The
NAAFI has set up a place where you can buy a rod, and more
importantly, they sell beer.'

'That's an understatement about the fishing out here,' said
one of the longer serving airmen.

'We have caught fish that could win prizes back home.
But be very careful when swimming, this place is teaming
with sharks and other sea creatures capable of doing you great
harm. Look around you and you will find this place full of
wildlife, not just in the sea, but in the air. I have never seen
such a variety of sea birds. If you are interested, you can join
a group of us exploring the island on what time you have
off. Of course, you have to understand, it seems they have
ambitious plans for a demonstration of how to blow the world
to bits, so it's now or never. After their demo the whole area
may well be out of bounds to all except those except wearing
protective clothing.'

Ginger thanked them for the offer, he knew somebody who would be very keen to join them. As for himself, he had plans to meet the padre and offer his services. He was happy just to get on with what he was told to do, but at the back of his mind he couldn't help feeling he was working unwittingly towards something very sinister indeed.

Back in the tent Ginger began to realise that he was now involved and could do nothing about it. He decided to find the showers to freshen up after a long day and then read his Bible.

Harry was not in a good mood at all. It seemed that his work was not going well, and Gary was giving him a few tips over a beer. They had found the NAAFI tent and were joined by the others. Alf and Ted had already been nicknamed the Laurel and Hardy team. If it was not for these two clowns home sickness might have been a lot worse. Their very first journey to Port London saw them going the wrong way. The sergeant, tearing his hair out, tried in vain to stop them, only to see Ted turning this huge, lumbering lorry into the bush. Finally, they came back to the track and pointed the lorry in the right direction. Alf, always cheerful, jumped out and inspected this huge monster before giving Ted the okay to move on. The sergeant was beyond himself, but Ted pointed out that it was their duty to make sure the vehicle was safe to drive on the highway. The sergeant's reply was extremely colourful; there was no highway for about three thousand miles in any direction!

The first week passed quickly, mainly due to the fact that it was all work and very little time off. Pete pointed out they had earned their twenty odd shillings a week ten times over, but of course the Army had no intentions of paying an extra penny. Harry felt gross indignation, and in spite of his training,

Tent lines are shown on the left with the WRVS, NAAFI (Gladiator Arms), and church. The church was built by volunteers from the Army and Airforce. The new accommodation buildings including the cook house are on the right being sprayed with DDT.

became quite vocal in criticising the Army for failing to recognise their long hours. To Harry and several of the others it amounted to enforced labour on an island with an uncertain future. The acute home sickness and privation was enough for many of them to think that, if there was only a way off this place, they would indeed do a runner. For many the frustration was unbearable, with the added problem of stomach disorders resulting in frequent visits to the loo. Pete often reminded the lads to wash their hands, but that was not easy, working out in

The main camp, with new accommodation
in place most of the tents were abandoned

the bush. It seemed that sickness was catching up with many of the lads rendering them unable to work. Brian succumbed to an acute stomach disorder which left him shedding weight and almost attached to the loo. Everybody lost weight in spite of the very good food. It was the relentless heat and hard work that kept them below their normal weight.

Frequent drinking was an absolute necessity, and a reasonable cup of tea was made in the tent using a device called a grapple iron. This home made device, although lethal if handled incorrectly, would boil a mug of water almost instantly. The sappers and airmen made them from thick copper wire shaped into a loop and made enough of them to satisfy the demand. Other ways of satisfying your thirst, and a near perfect anodyne was, of course, a few beers. The temporary relief from the misery and ominous rumours about what was about to happen was more than welcome.

Letters from home would almost certainly improve their feelings. It would remind them that there was somebody back home that loved them, but on the other hand, for some a letter never arrived. The sight of the RAF Hastings returning from Hawaii with mail cheered them up to no end. Mail arrived two or three times a week, depending on the weather on route from the UK.

After a couple of weeks the lads started to expect letters, and most of them were not to be disappointed. Alf was surprised when he received one letter from home, and one from Jennifer the stewardess. Apparently she was warmly received by his parents, who were most grateful to her for her kindness. However, his father was not at all impressed with her wreck of a car, and would find something more reliable. She was shown around the business, and Alf's desk which looked sadly empty. It seemed his father was really proud of him, but wanted him off of this island and back home. Alf wrote back trying to allay any fears they might have.

Writing to Jennifer was completely unexpected and he started by saying how he felt responsible for hurting her. He wrote: 'I have not stopped thinking about you, I hope my father can find you a decent car. My bucket and spade will not be much use to me out here since I'm driving lorries all day, but perhaps one day you will grace this place once more by landing on the airfield?'

For once Alf was feeling that he would like to get to know this girl who took the trouble to write to him and make him feel so much better.

Ted was slightly disappointed at not receiving a letter from Penny, in spite of the fact that his sister had delivered his letter to the chemist shop. The only explanation he could think of was that she was back at university and it would take time for her to settle down. Nevertheless, he felt sure Penny should have responded by now.

Harry received news from his parents that his grandfather was very frail, but apart from this sad news his brother was about to leave school and looking for a career.

All the others received letters, but Brian was in such a bad way with this stomach bug he had no enthusiasm to do anything other than lie on his camp bed. Now and again he would dash out of the tent and head for the loo and would not be seen for some time. Pete was not happy and called for the medic to have a look at Brian, who was immediately admitted to the sick quarters where several lads had been admitted with the same problem.

With the sides of the tent rolled down it was time for the mosquitoes to start looking for blood.

'Fancy a beer?' asked Alf looking very pleased with himself.

Alf called the beer tent the Gladiator's Arms. There was a piano which led to some lively music and singing, it was also the place to air differences of opinion, which sometimes led to saloon-bar-style punch ups. Before these altercations got out of hand the military police would come and break them up, the culprits being led away to cool down and have charges levelled against them.

Weeks passed by and they were increasingly mindful of

what their runway would be used for. The work was going well, and all the other skills they had been taught, like fault finding on engines, had come in useful. With the runway completed, other skills were now required, such as electrical work on the runway lighting.

Although they still felt home sick and lacked the facilities they were used to, things were beginning to look up. The NAAFI tent was replaced with a large shed. There was no bar, just a hole in the wall to serve beer. It was suspected that this was so that the NAAFI staff had some form of protection when feelings ran high.

There was also a cinema being constructed. Spent oil drums were filled with sand, piled on top of one another to create an incline which was then covered with sand to produce a slope. The idea being, you could sit down on the sand and watch a film. Absolute luxury with a can of beer, what more could you wish for, other than let's get the hell off this place before all hell is let loose?

Harry was beginning to realise this place offered much more than cinemas and bars. Although he thought this place was a ghastly experience, and was not for the faint and weary, the island had a much more pleasant side to it if you looked for it. Harry was aware of the abundance of wildlife on this island, especially sea birds. He had never seen so many birds. From his working area he would watch these giant birds with their massive wing spans soar up into the sky and disappear into the clouds. Then there was the magnificent white birds that would fly alongside you as you walked, they had long tail feathers and made for a sight you were unlikely to forget. What are they? he thought. They seemed to be without fear of him, as inquisitive of him as he was of them. It was their home and no doubt these birds had adapted to this place over millions of years. He had no knowledge of them, but it was obvious that they found their food in the sea.

After yet another long, hard day Harry was glad to take a rest on his luxurious camp bed, but it was short-lived when Ted came in with a face as long as a clock. It was obvious there was still no mail for him.

'It's just as the lads said: don't bank on hearing from them again. At the back of my mind I was not entirely happy with her allegiance to me, but then I was daft enough to fall for it all.'

'Tell me something new, Ted. I went down that road and I can now say, with hindsight, that it may have been for the best. Come on, let's drink to absent friends.'

Outside the NAAFI tables and chairs had been placed with an outlook over the Pacific ocean. Harry could see his feathered friends diving into the sea looking for their meal of fish. What a spectacular sight it was. The Airforce lads who had travelled out on the same flight as them, joined them and mentioned that a whale or two had been seen swimming close to the reef with dolphins, porpoises, and a host of other species of fish. Of course, there was always the danger of sharks, and for that reason a watch tower had been erected. If the red flag was seen then there was a shark alert. Trouble was, the flag was always flown. One of the Airforce lads said he had bought a face mask so that he could peer into one of the thousands of pools left when the tide went out. According to him, these pools were teeming with tropical fish, and a host of other marine life. Anybody having a knowledge of these tropical fish would have a field day. It was truly spectacular. They were joined by two more lads, Andy and Dave. Their speciality was making wire tracers with meat hooks. This was attached to rope strong enough to haul in a shark. Business was brisk as they were in great demand.

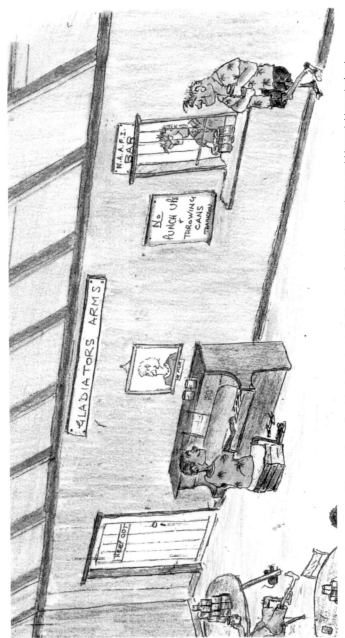

Happy days: one would remember going into, but not out of, this place. Serious altercations would be quickly sorted out by the duty NCO—who, shaking in his boots, would immediately call for back up from the military police.

The cook house was plagued by flies. In the background men work to repair the damage to the new huts after a storm. Many lost belongings in this storm.

Of course, not everybody had a passion for wild life and developed even less interest when they were bitten by mosquitoes and the dreaded bed bugs. The only way that you could temporarily rid your bed of these wretched bugs was to place the bed and clothing in the hot sun. The relief from flies and mosquitoes came from a light aircraft like a crop sprayer. The aircraft had been modified by Airforce ground crew and been flown very low over the camp spraying a noxious fly repellent. It was one thing being told not to get caught up in this dreadful cocktail, but it was another knowing when the plane was about to pass over you. Ginger got soaked walking back from the cook house, only to spend some time in the shower trying to rid himself of the smell.

Without doubt the island was a challenge to an outsider, but it was home to wonderful people who shared this island with a wealth of wildlife. As to whether they had had any say in their home being used as a nuclear test site, the lads had no idea. Harry pointed out that the wildlife would have been given no consideration, but then what could you do about it? Pete was more concerned about their own safety, which was only natural.

The new infrastructure was taking shape with wooden huts replacing canvas. The generator station, cook house and many other buildings were taking shape. Not only at the main camp, but also at Port London there were signs of improvement. To help with the construction the Fijian Troop were employed. They were giants capable of doing twice the work of the others and experts in mixing and laying concrete. The lads admired them, but they were used to the climate, and could work all day, unlike the lads who had to acclimatise to the relentless heat and very high humidity.

According to Pete and Brian there was much activity at

Royal Engineers at work with the Fijian troops.
With very high humidity and temperatures of about 85°Fahrenheit every day it took a couple of months to become acclimatised.

the southeast of the island where it was rumoured the nuclear tests were to take place. They had made deliveries to this place, where everybody was wearing white clothing. The airfield was ready with airmen moving in, and then all-white jet aircraft arrived. Harry was not that knowledgeable on aircraft types, so he asked one of the airmen. He explained the role of each aircraft and pointed out the aircraft, a Vickers Valiant, that would drop the bomb.

'Surely they are not going to drop the bomb on the island?' asked Harry.

'Good grief, I hope not. To be honest I have no idea what will happen, except that the bomb will be dropped by one of the Valiants.'

Harry was not at all happy and began to ask questions.

'What happens to us?' asked Harry.

'Don't ask me, I have no idea,' replied the airman.

Harry was none the wiser, and in a way was not the slightest bit interested. He rejoined his work mates, who had almost done their work, but then he spotted these magnificent white birds with the long flowing tail feathers. They flew alongside him, he could almost touch them. These little fellas had replaced the blackbirds back home in his affections, but these birds were like flying angels and might well be wondering what all these people were doing destroying their home.

Time had passed by more quickly with all the work they had to do, but there was much more work to be done elsewhere. Roads around the main airfield and the transmitting station had to be maintained. At times they might be asked to help out with other tasks such as minor electrical work. Under supervision, Harry learnt a great deal.

The mail plane brought with it a great shock for Ted. He received a letter from Penny after nearly five months.

Reading the letter he was barely able to contain himself, 'What am I supposed to do with a letter from somebody that might as well be on another planet? There's not even a hint of our passed relationship, and she signs off in a formal manner, as if I am just another client. Well that's that, I have no intention of responding to this kind of rubbish. Something must be wrong, but out here on the other side of the world, what can I do? I mean, in reply to my letters all she can say are words to the effect of: "To Mr Watson, I have received your letters and have wasted very little time reading them, and by the way, Daddy thinks you are a cad. Penny James."'

Ted went on a bit and then he realised the lads were listening, but with a smile on their faces.

'What's so funny?' he asked.

Pete answered saying, 'Well, Teddy boy, you hit the nail right on the head when you said something must be wrong.'

'You should say what you mean, Pete,' said Ted.

'Oh, I will, Ted. I mean what I say.'

Ted was getting a little annoyed with Pete. Why did he not say something sensible?

'Look, Ted, as you have since admitted, you were going out with a colonel's daughter, and, well, failing to take precautions was a hell of a risk. Has it occurred to you she might be in trouble? I mean, here you are having a ball on a tropical island, and the poor girl . . . well, I will say no more.'

'Pete's right, and if I were you I would write back for an explanation,' said Harry, trying hard not to laugh.

'Well, you are not me, and I think you are all wrong, I know this girl and—hang on, where are you all going?'

The lads had heard enough and decided to go for a beer, leaving Ted pondering over the colonel's daughter. Just as they were about to leave, their sergeant turned up giving them details of tomorrow's work plan. It seemed they all had to turn up at the main airfield for a roll call.

The next day was sunny, very warm, and humid as usual. They all lined up and were all accounted for. Further instructions were to follow. The Airforce was busy with several of the planes taking off, seeing them lined up, ready for take off, was quite a show for them.

Harry was told that the four-engine Shackleton could stay up for hours on end patrolling the sea.

Back to work, and Harry was instructed to clear a site for yet another building. Looking up, he could just make out a vapour trail, it was the Valiant on its dummy run. He started to think, what would it be like, the real thing that could reap havoc? Well, it would not be long before they would find out. It cannot be that bad, especially if it goes 'bang' a few hundred miles away; there is nothing to worry about, he told himself.

'Another day, another shilling,' was Alf's saying as he entered the tent.

'They say the fire works will go off tomorrow, lads.'

'So what? Quite honestly, I don't give a toss what they do, I just want out of this place,' said Ted.

'You're not still smarting over that letter? Surely you have got the message by now, Ted. Look, I have already told you twice, I will not tell you a second time. She either thinks you are a tosser, or you have put her in the club, and I think it's the latter,' said Alf.

'Yes, Alf's right, I think it's the latter,' said Pete. Think about it, if she has got tiny problems, then just think what big problems she might have with her parents.'

Harry agreed and then begged all of them to have a beer with him. He had received word from home that his grandfather had passed away. The lads could clearly see that it was a great loss to Harry, even Ted came out of his shell and apologised for being so miserable. There was nothing Harry could do, being so far away. It was a very difficult time for him, and his officer commanding could only offer his sincere condolences. He seemed to be very sympathetic, and even talked with Harry about his excellent work, and had high praise for all of them, singling out Ginger as being outstanding.

'You know you two should get together when you leave the Army. I can see a bright future for you. Go where your heart takes you. If I was your age, I would certainly take the opportunity of carrying on with what you are doing.'

Harry was grateful for the advice, it was almost like talking to his father, and made him feel much more relaxed. Perhaps he would talk to Ginger, but first things first, he had to write home and explain the situation. Above all, he wanted some flowers placed on his grandfather's grave and a message saying, 'Although I am a long way from home, I feel your presence here with me, and that you will protect me.' Harry cried his eyes out, and the other lads knew it and stayed out of the tent. Ginger was asked to go in first and give Harry some spiritual support, and true to Ginger's nature, he led Harry out, first to the temporary church, and then for a beer.

'I am sure your grandfather would have approved, Harry, so don't worry, everything will improve with time.'

Harry was steered back to the tent by his companions. The support, first from his commanding officer, and also from his closest colleagues pulled him through the week.

Everything on the airfield started to hot up. Most of the aircraft took off again, but it was just another dummy run. Ginger, Gary, and Harry had, between them, helped to build several miles of road, and had constructed many buildings.

During this building work Harry had often been visited by

the white birds who looked at him as if he was doing wrong. If they could have talked, Harry was sure they would be saying, 'What on earth are you doing to my home? Please go away and leave us alone.'

Once again, it was time for the mail, and sure enough the faithful Hastings came in on time. It took very little time for the mail to be sorted and the Army postman soon arrived at the collecting point. Sure enough, there was mail for most of them, but not for Ted, whose resentment was beginning to show through.

'I told you so, she's not interested, well I am not interested either.'

Harry had an unexpected letter from the nurse who had looked after his grandfather. She offered her sympathy and said she had spoken to his father. So it was good old dad who has given her this address, he thought. It made his day and without hesitation he wrote straight back to her.

Later on that evening, their sergeant turned up ordering them to be on parade early in the morning; they were to assemble for a roll call at the main airfield where they had been working for the last few days.

Harry failed to listen since he was thinking of what he was going to say to Helen. It had to be written in such a way as to make sure she would write back. He made no secret of the fact that he was very grateful and thrilled to bits. He mentioned the white birds that kept him company, there were two especially, although he did not think it would interest her a great deal. He certainly would not write about the purpose of being on the island. But Harry could at least mention Ginger reading stories from the Bible, and Ted's talks on court cases of long ago.

According to the longer-serving sappers, nuclear tests had already taken place near an island called Malden, and now preparations were being made for another test, but this time it would be near Christmas Island. Suddenly, the lads became very concerned, surely there must be a misunderstanding? None of the lads wanted to be involved with these nuclear tests, all they wanted was a return to civilian life, to earn decent money, or even start their own businesses. Harry thought they were losing precious time playing around in things they did not understand. Ginger became more vocal in his objections to being there at all. Realising he could do nothing about it, he would fight his corner by voicing his objections with regard to his beliefs.

One of the lagoons on Christmas Island

10. Too Close for Comfort

The next morning was as hot and humid as usual. The lads assembled near the main airfield and were informed that there would be a bomb run for real. This caused silent alarm, to put it mildly. Nobody in their right frame of mind would want to hang about. They honestly thought transport would at least take them to a safe distance, but no, they were told to sit down with their backs towards the drop zone.

Ginger was livid and shouted over to an officer nearby, 'I hope to God you know what you are doing, sir.'

'Your guess is as good as mine, sapper, now get down and keep quiet.'

Pete would have none of it and climbed into the back of a lorry undetected.

Tannoy messages were being broadcast telling them that the plane was on its final run. Harry looked up and he could see a vapour trail which must be the Valiant on its final run.

He dared not look back, and could only guess that the Valiant was close to the drop zone. What about the crew, he thought, would they get away in time? Surely the pilot would get as far away as possible as quickly as possible? He then overheard Ginger praying for all their safety, then the tannoy announced the bomb had been released. Harry was once again thinking, if I was the pilot, I would be out of there in no time—there would be very little time to gain a safe distance. Then without warning, Harry thought his life had vanished into a white abyss. With his hands over his face he could clearly see all the bones. The island was bathed in a white, searing light which made the lads gasp. All they heard was somebody shouting, 'Stay down, stay down! Totally confused and unable to think, they were suddenly hit by this searing heat, so hot that it burnt the backs of their necks. It felt as if all the oxygen had been sucked out of their lungs. Gasping, Harry became very frightened, and then the order came to stand up and turn around, but no sooner had they got to their feet than they were blown down again. At the same time, there was an almighty bang such as they had never heard before. The buildings took one hell of a knock, with debris flying through the air. Palm trees were bent over, some of which never returned upright.

Finally, they got to their feet and saw hell on earth. A massive fireball, just like another sun, was rising up and growing all the time. Lightning, thunder, and all sorts of colours could be seen. To their amazement the mushroom cloud grew larger and stretched way up into the sky. It must have been very close to the island, or maybe over the end of the south-easterly point. Who knew?

What Harry saw next was truly horrific. Birds of differing species came crashing down to earth. Many of them were still alive, blind and burning. Harry was devastated at seeing such senseless slaughter. He could only point and look on. These magnificent creatures, like the frigatebird, which had a nine-foot wingspan. Imagine soaring a few thousand feet up, then suddenly you are vaporised, or blown down with your feathers on fire. Blind and burning they fell to the ground, or into the sea. What happened to the marine life was quite another

Approximately thirty miles away the blast was still capable of causing damage: gamma radiation, heat and, about thirty seconds later, a blast from which we had no protection.

A bird's eye view of an RAF Shakleton monitoring Britain's first hydrogen bomb test

RAF Canberra flying into the cloud to collect samples.
This is a tribute to an old friend who sadly died many years ago.

God's animal kingdom: birds flying within twenty miles of the blast had no chance of survival. The author found the remains of birds many miles away from ground zero.

story. Before returning to the main camp, detailed parties of soldiers and airmen were ordered to pick up these birds. Those birds that were still alive had to be put out of their misery. On returning to the main base, damage to the tents was obvious. It was the worst day of their lives, but they had survived.

By the late afternoon one could still see the cloud drifting away. Normality was restored, but the shock of what they had seen remained. Ted spoke out by saying that the tempestuous last few hours had left an indelible mark on their minds for the rest of their lives.

'What on earth are you saying, Ted?' said Pete looking very serious indeed.

'Well, lads, you have just unwittingly witnessed one of the most hideous experiments known to man. The question is, why did we have to be there? I make no bones about it I——'

Pete interrupted, 'Yes, talking of bones, I saw all the bones in my hands.'

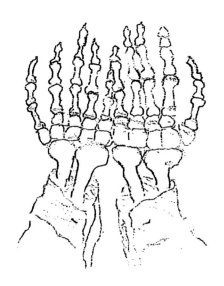

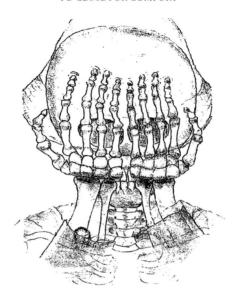

'I admit that's dreadful, but this country has to protect itself and others against terrible oppression. As far as I am concerned, these things have to be done in spite of the high cost and suffering. Somebody has to make sacrifices,' said Brian.

Alf was first in with both feet, he drew the line by saying, 'That's an argument that's likely to get you tossed overboard. I agree with you, up to a point, but tell me why we had to be lined up to witness this hideous moment of hell, with nowhere to shelter and no protective clothing. Don't forget that we have no idea if we have received a dose of radiation, our film badges were taken from us; some of the lads didn't even have a film badge.'

Things were getting a little out of hand, so Ted called it a day and thought a few beers would eradicate any ill feelings. When the Gladiator's Arms opened, Ted was the first in the queue. The conversation had become more subdued, although the consumption of beer soon loosened their tongues again. There was much speculation on this dreadful day, especially as to whether the radiation had affected them. Why had their film badges been taken away from them so quickly after the blast? And why had they not had protective clothing? Why were they not ordered to build a nuclear shelter for everybody? With the machinery they had it would have been easy to provide a nine-feet deep trench to protect them from the gamma radiation, heat, and flying debris. But no precautions had been taken; why? As it was tempers became short, not because of slight misunderstandings with each other; it was plain and simple to see—the looks on their faces said it all— some of the lads were acutely depressed. Having more than six months left to serve on the island surely did not help matters. Harry received a morale booster with another letter from Helen. Ted, on the other hand, received letters from his parents and one from his sister, but none from Penny.

'There you go, I told you that last letter was a "Dear John", so before you all start, I would rather you talk behind my back if you don't mind, I feel as if I have been done over again, good and proper this time.'

Nobody said a word, it would be pointless trying to console him. He was under extreme pressure, and as Pete put it, they should keep an eye on him.

Harry's letter from Helen got better with each line. It seemed that she was extremely interested in Harry's white birds and thought they were called tropicbirds. She had a keen interest in the birds back home, but wanted to know more about the birds on Harry's island. Harry wrote back that he had no idea, but he would try and draw pictures of them and give her a description. He was thinking that the only bird he was really interested in was her, but then look at what had

At RAF coastal command a Shakleton makes its final descent to the main airfield

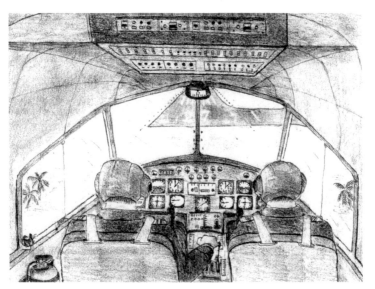

Among other cargo, the RAF Hastings brought the much
anticipated mail from home to the island

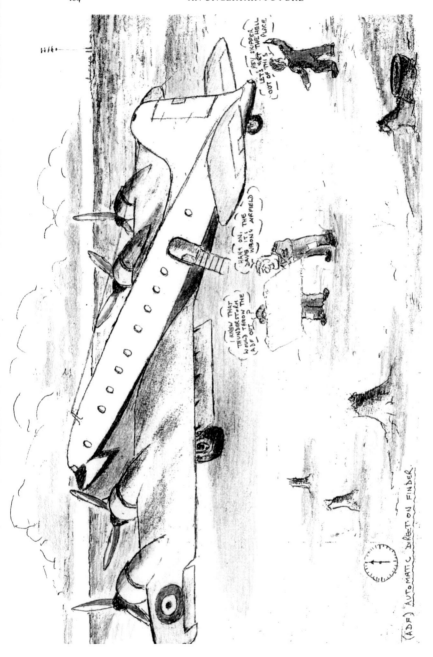

happened to Ted. The consequences of becoming too involved with someone when you were far away from home were not pleasant at all. Ted's situation was all too obvious. No, Harry would oblige Helen with all the information she wanted to know, but outside that he would exercise caution. Maybe he would meet her when he returned home for a well-earned leave, but he would not build up his hopes.

Christmas was almost upon them. It seemed strange to all of them spending the festive season on an island in the Pacific called Christmas Island, and in sweltering heat. Ginger was busy helping the padre, but for most it was business as usual. Ted was talking to some Airforce lads who had to work no matter what the time of year. Ted felt better when one of them mentioned his 'Dear John' which was quite common.

'Don't you feel down about it?' asked Ted.

'No, not really, some of us wrote to a department store, and quite unexpectedly the management circulated our letters to other branches. We ended up with a sack full of letters, some with photographs. I can fix you up with a bundle of letters if you like, all for a few quid.' He gave Ted his tent number and said there was a dating agency sign up.

Ted could not believe it, these lads must have given many of the other lads a great deal of happiness and fun. It would not only lift up your spirits, but may even create a union for life. Ted was tempted, but could not quite pluck up the courage. He decided to think about it.

Word had been passed around that, on no account, were fish to be eaten. This order was issued since it was all too easy to gather wood and cook fish. The enterprising Airforce lads had been making wire tracers with meat hooks ideal for catching sharks. Ted had joined a group one Saturday afternoon and had walked along the seashore to a place where sharks had been caught. One of the lads had a discarded piece of meat given to him by a chef, having fixed it on a hook, another one of the lads—who had drawn the short straw—would have to swim out towards the reef and drop the line into a deep gully. The other end of the cable was tied to the trunk of a large bush, with the line secure they would wait for the cable to shake the bush, signalling that a shark might be on the other end. However, it was rare to see a shark being caught, in fact, Ted could not see the point trying since, according to what he had heard, the bomb had destroyed countless fish of all sorts along with a countless number of birds.

Ted became very depressed, and became less interested in what he had left behind. He could see no future for himself, and being forced to carry out work which was beginning to make him lose faith in humanity, he felt totally alone in the world. The Christmas spirit was upon the island, but Ted had no interest. He was beginning to find more solace in the Gladiator's Arms, and drinking more than he should. It was pitiful to see him, he was almost out of control; finally he was arrested by the military police and later brought up before the company commander. He was not spared the rod, the officer reminded Ted that they were all in the same boat and whether he liked it or not he would have to complete his time on the island, or face a more serious disciplinary hearing which could lead to a military custodial sentence. Ginger, on the other hand, and knowing Ted's background, took him to one side and told Ted to talk to him. Ted gave all sorts of mixed reasons for his behaviour, and at one stage even tried to deny that there was a problem. Ginger told him to stop prevaricating and that the cause of his problems was not on the island but back home, and that the Gladiator's Arms was not be the answer.

'You are one of the brothers and I have to tell you the others are beyond themselves seeing you throw everything away. We need you, Ted, like both our arms, and, of course, we need your expertise with the law. It was good listening to you reading court cases of old.

'What do you mean?' asked Ted.

'I mean the lads found your talks very interesting, and it takes their mind off this place,' said Ginger.

Ted laughed and said, 'Would you care for a drink, Ginger?'

Ginger was perplexed, what is the use? he thought.

Then Ted explained, he did not need the drink, except perhaps the odd can or two with the lads. Ginger then invited him to the midnight mass service, which would be celebrated in the open air on the beach.

'You will never get another chance like this again,' he said.

Ginger was involved with the traditional Christmas midnight mass, and for all the services on the big day.

Most activities came to a halt and there was a brilliant Christmas lunch provided by the chefs. Christmas decorations adorned the mess tent, but although it was a great day for a celebration, it just did not feel quite the same as back home. How could it? thought Harry. He noticed one of the Airforce technicians; they had to work whatever day it was. Harry joined him for lunch with his tin tray piled high with all the traditional food you would have back home.

'What's this having to work today?' Harry asked.

'We have to maintain links with the outside world at all times, the transmitters have to be maintained, and now and again, we have to change the frequency due to the change in the ionosphere,' he said smiling.

Harry was none the wiser.

'If there is nothing to do, we will probably tune into radio

Australia, or anything else interesting. Maybe we might wash some of our clothes.

'What's wrong with the laundry service?' Harry enquired.

'What's right with it, you mean? Look at the state of my shorts,' and he stood up.

Harry burst out laughing. It seemed that he had received the wrong shorts back from the laundry—they were far too big for him.

The Airforce technician told Harry how they had made a fire place and placed an iron grill over the top. They then gathered up wood from the bush, and placed a large drum of water on top. With the water bubbling they washed their own clothes. Drying was no problem, but ironing was difficult. They had produced an improvised iron which just about did the job.

During this conversation another of the technicians mentioned the frigatebirds which gathered in the bushes near the aerial farm. Sometimes the cock birds would display their vivid red throat pouch to impress the hens; against their black feathers it was an impressive display.

Harry became interested and wondered if he could visit the place. He would then have plenty to tell Helen, and perhaps he would be allowed to take a photograph with his camera. The technicians undertook to take him, and said he could also join them on one of their walkabouts. There he would be able to see many sea birds. Harry was still very concerned for his white tropicbirds and mentioned them to the technicians. Yes, they had seen these birds and agreed they were magnificent.

Letters and cards arrived in time for Christmas and it was not uncommon to read letters more than once. It tended to calm things down and refresh the memory of life back home. It also gave one the feeling that time waits for no man; it would soon be home to freedom, just over five months and their plane would touch down at home.

Ted, on the other hand, was seriously suffering the loss of Penny. He had known that it might have been a serious mistake becoming too involved, and was now suffering the consequences. The feeling of utter despair had got the better of him and he now had the feeling that, even if there was a reconciliation, he would feel unable to respond to her. There was no way he would go through all those promises again.

His sister, however busy, still promised to investigate Penny's failure to write, even though it was not that important to Ted anymore. He was not happy with this idea, and made it perfectly clear that it was all over between them. Nevertheless, his sister managed to find out from one of the girls in the chemist shop that Penny had returned to university, but had since been seen locally with a woman who was, perhaps, her mother. The girl in the chemists could not be sure, but it looked as if Penny had put on a lot of weight. Ted's sister reminded Ted that there was a distinct possibility that he may have been responsible. Ted was nonplussed, but it might be his saving grace from a life of alcohol and further depression. Perhaps a letter would reveal all? But then Ted was thinking if she *is* pregnant, whose was it? And what could he do about it if she refused to write? What the hell, he thought, I must get back to my law books and take my mind off this ridiculous enigma.

The lads were cheered up no end by the fact that they only had about five months of service left. Two ladies from the Women's Royal Voluntary Service had started up a small recreation place for reading, or a game of cards, and so on. These were the only females on the camp and they had done a magnificent job of providing a place for relaxation. It made a welcome change from the Gladiator's Arms, where a few beers and a punch up were not everybody's idea of relaxation. Having said that, it may not sound idyllic, but the Gladiator's Arms made some of the lads—after a few beers, of course— feel that they were at home, which also took their minds off what might be in store for them in the next few weeks.

Harry's birds seemed to be missing, which was not a surprise considering the devastation that the last bomb had caused to all the other species of birds. The wildlife had, without doubt, suffered.

Work continued as usual. Harry was given an order to clear a patch of ground, and to his horror, he saw the remains of birds lying all around. He decided to dig a trench and bury them. The sooty terns were back, although they were obviously not the same ones as had been there before. Then to Harry's delight, he spotted two white birds away in the distance. So Britain had its hydrogen bomb, and Harry had his birds back.

Christmas was over and the new year was seen in way before the folks back home. The new year brought them a step closer to home. Shock and fear still lingered with the memory of that burning feeling on their backs to remind them that they had seen the devil in all his horror. Many of the lads would quite often drink in the Gladiator's Arms, perhaps to hide their feelings for one reason or another. The thought of more tests to come did not exactly fill them with joy. One or two drank more than they should, and Ted was no exception. Once again he was put on a charge for being drunk and disorderly. Ted's defence was that he was extremely worried about being exposed to radiation and that his health may have been compromised. Ted was reminded that there was no measurable radiation and there was no cause for concern.

'What the hell did you say, Ted?' asked Brian.

'Well I had to contain myself since I was already in trouble, so I put it very delicately by saying that I was not convinced since all the lectures we received on nuclear radiation had made it quite clear that it was very dangerous to be exposed to a nuclear bomb, so why would this bomb be any different? Not only that, it was very distressing, and quite frankly, I don't want to see anything like it again. I would rather be handcuffed to a bear with toothache.'

'Blimey, what did the captain say to that?'

'He replied with a smile, "I am not all that convinced you have a choice of alternatives, Watson, but under the circumstances you may be right. Having said that, your drinking habits are of more concern and maybe more dangerous to both you and your family. I am letting you off with a caution." I saluted and then he reminded me to not drink to excess; which is why I only have one can, or sometimes two, maybe three—I never could count.'

Harry and the lads kept an eye on Ted, and although very witty and clever at times, to a certain extent his entire future depended on getting off this island along with everybody else. The captain was right: Ted would have to be watched, or he would almost certainly go to pieces, and he might well be a dad.

The lads drank a little too much at times, and it would not be long before tongues were loosened to the point where arguments started leading to beer cans being thrown about. Often the target would be a pyramid of empty cans piled up just waiting to be demolished by some idiot trying to make the whole situation worse. The Army, Airforce and the Navy lads usually all sat apart. The Fijian troops also sat on their own, and it would take a very brave idiot to upset any of them. They were gentle giants, but it did not do to upset them. One punch and you would surely end up in the reef. The lads learned to respect the Fijian troops since they were experts in the arts of mixing concrete, building, and construction.

Everything would start off well enough, with a sing-song, some of the songs we did not sing in front of the padre. A piano completed the atmosphere of a western-style saloon bar. Now and again things got a little out of hand. The accusations of who was to blame for this catastrophic demonstration of how to end the world as we knew it came fast and furious. Of course, none of it had anything to do with anyone there. They were just venting their feelings, and perhaps the fact that they had no chance of getting off the island aggravated things. The lads were entitled to be frustrated and angry, and thought that they should be well away from the island, along with the local residents. Surely there was plenty of knowledge available at this stage of nuclear bomb testing? Why, Harry thought, should they have been made to face such a danger with no protective clothing and no concrete bunker to hide themselves in? Yet another cause for concern was the light aircraft which the Airforce used to spray a noxious insect repellent over the camp against flies and mosquitoes.

When tempers got out of hand, blood and teeth started to fly. This behaviour was promptly brought to an end by the orderly corporal who, shaking in his boots, would call in the military police. The ring leaders were arrested and frog marched away to cool off. The rest of them would stagger back to their tents with their memories temporarily numbed.

Getting off the island was impossible except for the lucky ones who managed to have a weekend in Hawaii. The journey was about four hours on the dear old RAF Hastings. It was a very welcome change, but was little recompense for what they had been through.

The author at the transmitting station and aerial farm

Approximately thirty miles away from ground zero was this small but essential convenience was unable to take the strain of Britain's first hydrogen bomb test explosion. It was demolished by the blast but fortunately there was no one in there at the time.

Harry was keen to see these magnificent frigatebirds, seeing one of the technicians from the signals station he asked him if he could still come and see them.

'By all means, I am on duty Sunday afternoon. It's a fair old walk, so if you can use your lorry come on in and you can have a cup of tea first. Drink plenty and wear your sunglasses as walking through the aerial farm can be like an oven.'

Harry was not disappointed, he turned up with Gary, who was also very keen to see these birds. The transmitting station was isolated from the main camp, so Harry and Gary kept their distance since he felt that they might be out of bounds. The transmitters were huge, giving off a lot of heat which, combined with the normal daytime heat, made the place almost unbearable.

Gary asked how they had fared when the bomb detonated. One of the technicians explained that there was some structural damage, and that their stand alone loo had been demolished. He hastened to add there was nobody in there at the time. They were told to go outside, sit down, and turn their backs to the bomb. They too had had a clear view of the bones in their hands and the blast sent all kinds of debris flying through the air.

Harry could not help noticing that one of the technicians, who was working on one of the transmitters, said very little. He sat down with a cup of tea and tried to speak but he seemed to be having trouble getting his words out. He was also suffering from stomach pains, which was of no surprise to Harry. He mentioned that he had been working elsewhere on the island, which had been most unpleasant, but declined to say what he had been up to. It seemed to Harry that a visit to the medical officer would be the only solution.

Walking through the aerial farm, Gary and Harry were amazed at the area it covered. Finally, they were brought to a halt, there in front of them you could see the frigatebirds roosting in these huge bushes. Harry took a photograph, thinking Helen would be thrilled to bits to see them. One of the birds took off, showing off its massive wingspan close-up: this was the icing on the cake.

Walking back they were offered another cup of tea, which was more than welcome after baking in the sun. Before they left they were invited to join the technicians next week on a walkabout and a swim in the lagoon, which Gary and Harry accepted.

'You won't regret it, we will be doing a spot of spear-fishing. We will make you a couple of spears; bring plenty to drink and a bite to eat, there's no telling when we might be back. Don't forget, next Saturday about twelve, pick-up outside the open air cinema you guys are building.'

Gary was over the moon. 'It's a substitute for climbing mountains, and time passes much more quickly being active,' he said.

Of course, he was absolutely right. As they were about to leave, Harry noticed water seeping up through the ground, creating large puddles everywhere. Small fish and crabs could be seen in them.

'What on earth is going on, where is all this water coming from? It surely is a strange place, almost as if we are on another planet.'

The mystery was explained by the airmen who were used to it, but still found it odd. 'It's all to do with the tide, these puddles will disappear when the tide goes out, taking the marine life out with it. Later on, when the tide comes back in the marine life will return. The marine life actually live down below the surface where there must be links with the lagoons. They couldn't remain on the surface in the baking hot sun— it would not be an option—beside that they would be rich pickings for the birds.'

Just before they left the technician pointed out the frigatebirds had taken off for a fly about.

'Look up there, they are just about to enter the clouds and will no doubt soar to several thousand feet. It's magical to watch, and quite honestly, they make my stay here tolerable. You will perhaps only see such wondrous things once in a lifetime. Hope to see you both on Saturday. Cheers for now.'

Back at the main camp, Harry got down to pen and paper. He wrote home and then a long letter to Helen giving her all the wondrous sights he had seen that day and telling her of his invitation to go walkabout with some pals. He mentioned nothing of work, or the events in the Gladiator's Arms. To Harry she represented a lifeline and he could well understand

Ted's feelings about losing Penny, even though he had nothing like as close a relationship with Helen as Ted had had with Penny. He would have felt shattered if he had had to face the same fate as Ted, and so he kept his distance and treated Helen as a pen friend.

Ted was beginning to recover from the loss of Penny and was caught reading a law book in the newly appointed WRVS recreational building. The lads were pleased with this turn around, but could not believe he would abandon the fun and games of the gladiatorial arena.

'I suppose you contestants for the next show of strength in the arena are wondering why I have abandoned you. Well, in case you haven't noticed, I am not about to run off down to the test site with a crate of lager. I have exams not far off and you would be doing me a favour if you would leave me alone with a non-alcoholic drink; no offense intended. While you are all here I would like to apologise for my behaviour towards you. I now realise that I am free from the clutches of this female's charms. Oh, and by the way, you never know, you may need my help one day, if so, it will be on me.

The lads could not believe how naive Ted was being, sure he had to concentrate on his future and look forward to being a lawyer one day—and good luck to him, he thoroughly deserved it—but he was completely failing to understand that he might soon be a dad.

Ted said that the WRVS would now act as his study. It provided the much needed peace and quiet away from the unruly behaviour of the Gladiator's Arms where justice was often meted out by the beer can and a free for all. The only common ground the various personnel had was that they all had an uncertain future.

Saturday proved to be a special day. Harry and Gary joined

A welcome drink of coconut milk

Fishing became a popular pastime, although any fish caught could not be eaten

the Airforce lads for a trip down the island. Both Harry and Gary had seen the end of the island before when working on sundry projects, but this trip would take them to a new area well away from where they had been working. On the way there they pulled over and went for a swim in one of the lagoons.

The water was shallow and crystal clear. Wading in it was not far before it was deep enough to swim, although Harry was not brave enough to as he knew that there could be sharks in the lagoon. He noticed some large fish in the clear water, he hesitated before wading out further as the fish came in closer. One was a green-blue metallic colour and about two feet long. Harry was stunned at their brilliant colour, he had never seen such a magnificent creature. Ivor, who was one of the airmen, said that it was almost certainly a parrot fish and that he was very lucky to see one. Ivor thought that it would be good to see a few sharks before returning.

Gary pointed out that they must be somewhere near the south coast, which was confirmed by the airmen who said the island was flat as a pancake, it took some careful navigation to find your way home. With that in mind, Harry wanted to know more about the place. One of the airmen had swum in the area before the bomb had been detonated and said that the place was full of deep gullies leading to other lagoons. 'Who knows how deep they are? It's the only way in and out for sharks looking for food. These lagoons seem to go up and down with the tide so there must be a link with the open sea. This island has evolved over millions of years and the wildlife has adapted to it.

'Now grab your spears and follow me,' he said.

Both Harry and Gary waded in up to about chest height. It was then one of the airmen named Jim spotted their first shark only a few feet away. They were fairly harmless.

'Sand sharks,' said Ivor. One was about four feet long and the other slightly smaller. Harry was not at all convinced the sharks were harmless, he had been told they might have been tiger sharks, which were known to be in the area, along with other very dangerous sharks. He turned back, he had had enough, it was time to eat rather than be eaten. One drop of blood and they would all be in trouble. On the way out of the lagoon he spotted a fish which seemed to change its shape. It was swimming in front of Harry and then it changed into a ball-like fish. Very strange he thought.

'Leave it, it might be poisonous,' yelled Jim. Harry had no intentions of picking it up, but was quite content climbing back into the lorry for a drink and a sandwich. They had all made bacon and egg sandwiches at breakfast time and one of the RAF cooks had made them a flask of tea, enough for all of them. Gary was not at all impressed with the sandwich he had made at breakfast, but he ate it all the same, he was really hungry for the first time in weeks as the stomach upsets had given him a great deal of trouble.

It was a day that Harry and Gary would remember for the rest of their lives. It was a fantastic experience for them, but one which carried a much more ominous threat than sharks, one which you could not see, hear, smell, touch, or taste.

They had seen the remains of dead birds on their way down the island, now new birds from elsewhere had taken over and laid their eggs, but had now deserted them.

Harry found the situation harrowing to say the least, he realised what these birds had suffered; this part of his adventure would not be included in his next letter to Helen.

'I wonder why those eggs have been abandoned?' said Jim. 'I think they belong to the sooty turn. The original birds must have been burnt to death when that bomb went off. It's a terrible shame when you consider this island is a paradise for sea birds and marine life. You pay a heavy price to the devil for power,' said Jim.

'Yes, but it's the animal kingdom that's paying the price, not us,' said Gary.

'I wouldn't be to sure about that, Gary, we may not come out of this too well ourselves. I mean, have you seen or heard of any evidence to suggest this island is squeaky clean?'

'Well, no, I guess not.'

'Exactly, I mean where is your film badge, how do you know that you have, or have not, received a dose of radiation?'

'I have no idea, our film badges were taken from us.'

'Precisely, and don't forget there will be another test in the near future. It's only a rumour, but you can bet your boots it's going to happen. We only have less than four months to do, so keep your fingers crossed it won't happen on our watch.'

Harry and Gary agreed with Jim, the sooner they were on that plane the better. They were still a long way from the end of the island and headed back to the camp with mixed feelings. Arriving back they thanked Ivor for an adventure of a lifetime.

Things got even better for Harry when he arrived back at the tent, there was a letter from his brothers and one from Helen, neither of which he had expected. His brothers mentioned that things had settled down after the loss of their granddad. His mum and dad were well, but were rather worried about what was going on out there in the middle of the Pacific. Apparently it was all in the news that Britain now had the hydrogen bomb, and Mum had jumped out of her chair. She was very worried and wanted Harry home. This was a few months ago, but his mother had never mentioned it. He must write to his parents and reassure them that all was well.

He would have to slightly mislead them, but what else could he do? Tell the truth and cause endless worry for them? No, he loved his parents dearly and would write immediately and put their minds at rest.

Helen had written a much more loving letter than her last one. It was full of apologies for not sending a Christmas present and that she was looking forward to him coming home. But then she had to mention that wretched bomb. 'What happened to all those magnificent birds, have they suffered, and what about you?' she wrote. 'I am very worried for you and how much longer before you come home?' Harry started to worry himself, he couldn't allow his family, or Helen to worry like this. Helen wrote as if there was a bond between them, although what kind of bond it was was not entirely clear. The couple of kisses at the end of her letter made him think, how do I respond? Do I respond with a kiss and then end up like Ted, bitterly disappointed? But then my situation is not like Ted's. Harry decided to respond with a kiss, thinking his natural instincts had got the better of him.

Harry posted his replies, hoping that he had dispelled any doubts about what was going on for Helen and his family. He was fit and having a great time, what more could he say? He never felt comfortable being careful with the truth, especially where his parents were concerned. As for Helen, he was happy to return a kiss; but what message the dear old RAF Hastings would bring back was anybody's guess.

Nobody was talking much and it seemed odd to Harry that many of the lads were spending an abnormal amount of time on frequent visits to the loo. Many of them were sick which made it impossible for them to work. Harry and Gary had been spared this debilitating illness, although they felt unwell with a stomach ache. Were the dreadful flies the cause, or something else? Who knew, the problem with the flies was partially contained by the frequent spraying of the noxious fly repellent by the RAF's light aircraft. This fine mist was sprayed all over the camp, and had a smell similar to diesel fuel, but they were told it was DDT. Whatever it was, it did have the effect of keeping the flies and mosquitoes at bay, but if you got caught up in the spray it was extremely unpleasant.

It was not long before manpower returned to near normal. Those who failed to recover fully were kept in the sick quarters for further treatment, those diagnosed as being fit for work were, in fact, fit for nothing. They were still weak and often had to run into the bush.

It was some time before Harry and the others regained their appetite. After a plague of illnesses and other ailments such as dry throats, and especially skins problems, many had lost weight. There was nothing wrong with the food, all provided by chefs from the Army, and later by the RAF chefs. The lads often remarked how good the meals were, taking into consideration the sort of environment the chefs were working in. After all, they still had to cook a meal, and provide sandwiches and tea, after the bomb blast had partially re-arranged their cook house. Never bite the hand that feeds you. Ginger often reminded them that it was the most important place on the camp, except for the new church that was being built by a team of Army and Airforce volunteers in their spare time. The building was built mainly with coral, wood, and other materials, truly a masterpiece of engineering and dedication. Surely it must be the only church in the world using coral as a building material for the main structure.

The sun came up as usual, a giant mass of hydrogen burning away into helium, a fiery ball giving us life and everything else we need on earth.

'So here we are producing a tiny replica of our sun, only this time to destroy life and everything we need. Can anybody get their head around that, because I can't?' said Harry. 'No, without doubt I would miss the fish and chip bar just down the road and a pint to follow. But seriously, I can't understand the rush to put us in harm's way, it beggars belief. I hope my wedding anatomy remains in order, that's what worries me.'

Everybody gave a nervous laugh and reminded each other that they had only a few weeks left to serve.

Harry reminisced about all the good times he had spent at his grandfather's home. His grandfather had had a nice house, with several acres of land, much of which was of no use except to graze sheep on, so he had made arrangements with a farmer who needed pasture land. There was a small vegetable garden and a fenced in area for chicken and bantams. The eggs were out of this world, and Harry wondered what his father would be doing about it.

It was quite early in the morning, the familiar sound of the waves rolling in could be heard. The workforce were almost back to full strength. The huts were all well on their way to being complete, and the new cook house was up and running, along with improvements elsewhere. The church was nearly complete, with Ginger inviting his long-standing mates to join him for at least one service before they left for home, which was less than three months away.

Letters from home brought very mixed reactions for most of them, not least for Gary. He yelled out and got up off his camp bed with the lads thinking it was some good news, but it was not to be. Apparently his girlfriend, Megan, was in hospital paralysed from the waist down after a fall up in the mountains. The mountain rescue team had saved her life. Gary started to shout and became so frustrated he stormed out of the tent. Ginger and Pete followed in hot pursuit, but kept their distance until Gary had settled down.

Gary was sitting on the sand looking out to sea and was extremely unhappy. 'It seems her climbing days are over, poor girl. What the hell can I do stuck on this damn island? I want to be with her *now* and look after her, she's everything I have.' He put his head in his hands. Pete tried talking to him and just touched his arm, but Gary pushed him away angrily. Ginger pointed out he had every reason to feel upset and frustrated, but perhaps things may not be as bad as they seemed. 'Have you any idea what it's like being stranded on the side of a mountain, freezing cold and with a broken back?'

'Well, of course not, but——'

'Ginger shut up and get out of my life, you're always poking your nose in where it's not wanted. I can't take much more of this, I'm telling you boy, I feel like a convict with everybody telling me what to do. Thank God the mountain rescue team found her, she wouldn't have lasted long up there.'

Pete was about to walk away feeling it would be better to let Gary cool down, but then the fateful letter was thrown at Pete with Gary shouting, 'If you don't believe me, read it for yourself, then you can both pass judgement.'

Pete picked the letter up and reluctantly read it. As often in the case when under extreme stress, one's judgement becomes somewhat clouded and Gary's was no exception. The letter was from Megan's parents and told him not to worry as their daughter would make a full recovery and that she loved him dearly.

'I think you owe Ginger an apology, don't you, Gary?' handing the letter back to him.

'What do you mean an apology, you've got to be joking?'

'I mean what I say,' said Pete and walked away. Ginger,

on the other hand, apologised to Gary and made it perfectly clear he would not interfere again. Gary read the letter again and walked away, not saying a word and feeling acutely embarrassed.

At last, the main camp was beginning to look more civilised with the new buildings well on their way to completion, but the lads were disappointed that none of the huts would be ready before they went home. They were fed up of sleeping on camp beds under canvas with bed bugs, giant land crabs, flies, and mosquitoes to keep them company. If that wasn't bad enough, it started to rain. It became heavier during the night and with the tide on its way in, water was beginning to enter the tent lines. The lads got short shrift from the sergeant who ordered them to dig trenches to drain away the flood water, which would have otherwise become a breeding ground for more mosquitoes. There was panic at one stage when Harry and Pete failed to find their letters from home, eventually Ted found soggy papers lodged under the duck boards.

Activity started up again with the Airforce much more active than usual. All the lads were interested in was the return of their UK uniforms, which had been held in storage all these months. Gary, feeling much more relaxed, apologised to Ginger and Pete and not before time. The shock had been too much for him, but as he put it, he took it out on the wrong people.

Ted, having recovered somewhat from his short-lived romance, vowed he would never get mixed up like that with a girl again. He was in touch with his sister and asked her if she could put his name forward to sit the law exams. He had coped much better with his studies without having to write endless drivel to Penny, or any other girl for that matter. He had become a different person, his personality had turned for the worst according to the lads. His ability to come to terms with his responsibilities seemed to have eluded him. In less than three months he would be home and the lads were confident that he would find himself again. Their main task was to keep him away from the drink.

The morning once again required them to wear sunglasses, Alf had had to repair his after the bomb blast which had blown them off his face causing the lenses to pop out.

The sergeant brought them into line and explained what had to be done. Ted, Alf, Brian, and Pete were to drive to Port London to collect several crates and so forth. The sergeant would be up front with the captain. They were not to stop, or talk to anyone. Ginger and Gary were also included as relief drivers. It would be a welcome break driving along with a sea breeze blowing through the cab.

Ted was paired with Alf, who let Ted drive there and Alf would drive back. The journey was uneventful and they arrived bang on time. For the first time since they had arrived on the island they saw many local people, and were absolutely amazed when they spotted a football match going on. Alf's eyes came out like organ stops when he noticed they had no boots on. Ted got out the cab to take a closer look, but was ordered back. Things were beginning to move as they were ordered closer to their cargo.

The Navy were now in full control and the lads were relieved to take a look around and have their lunch break. Out at sea they could see a large merchant ship anchored off the reef with large barges going to and fro bringing more building materials to the island. They were told that the Marines carried out these duties. The captain came over to the lads and mentioned that he wanted to be back on the road in an hour and then looked out to see cargo being brought ashore by the Navy and Marines.

'That must be the trickiest job on the island, rather them than me,' he said.

'Ah, yes, I totally agree with you, sir, but then they are not down at the sharp end, are they?' remarked Brian.

'That's correct, sapper, but for everybody's sake keep your voice down,' but it was too late.

What they hadn't noticed was a group of sailors nearby who had heard every word. One of them acquainted himself by reminding the lads that they often sailed around the island and close to the sharp end while they were still in bed. The captain made a quick exit.

'I should also remind you that all three services carried out the Malden Island tests about four hundred miles away. The Navy and Marines brought almost everything from the Merchant ships to this port, including service personnel. It was a logistical operation on a monumental scale right from day one.'

'Why are they testing these bombs here on Christamas Island? I mean it makes no sense to do anything other than get the hell out of it,' said Brian. The Navy lads agreed, but Ted was not interested and as usual went in with both feet. The look on the sailors' faces said it all: they burst out laughing and asked Ted what he could do about it.

'You are not the only one who has to get too close for comfort,' said one of the crew.

Ted was furious and rather foolishly started shouting, 'Who cares? All I want is to be off this island.'

'We can all agree with that, soldier,' one of the sailors replied.

Ginger saw everything and helped Pete try to calm Ted down. They apologised for Ted's behaviour and explained that he was not himself since he had been on the island

and had witnessed the first bomb. The sailors completely understood. The others grabbed Ted on both sides and were just about to put him back in the cab when their captain finally turned up. Ted was reminded that one of the Royal Navy's warships actually sailed under the nuclear cloud before returning home, leaving Ted with no argument and he apologised unreservedly.*

Much to the relief of all of them they set off back to the airfield, but the lead vehicle did not stop: they were meant to go to the main airfield where civilians took delivery. Men in white overalls were getting ready to offload the crates helped by the engineers.

Alf couldn't resist shouting out, 'Sign here, mate, it's your birthday, come on, open it up, don't keep us all waiting.'

'Very funny, you mind your own business and I will mind mine, now clear off.'

'Alright, keep your overalls on,' Alf replied laughing. He joined the others who had gathered around the captain, who seemed to be just as excited as all the lads at the thought of going home.

'Not long now, lads, and by the way, your uniforms should be available in a few weeks' time, having said that, we still have much to do. I must say it's been a pleasure working with

---

* The Royal Navy indeed played a major role in Britain's development of the hydrogen bomb, the initial test being carried out on Malden Island, four hundred miles away from Christmas Island. During these tests ships from the Royal Navy and the New Zealand navy were employed. The Royal Engineers carried out work on Malden Island before retreating back to an aircraft carrier along with all the scientific staff. Next came the Royal Airforce in a Valiant aircraft from Christmas Island to drop the bomb. Servicemen were lined up on the decks to witness the detonation. All three services, along with the New Zealanders, were involved. More nuclear tests followed using the southeastern point of Christmas Island as the test site.

you. Any problems, you know where I am.

'Just one more thing, would Sapper Watson report to me first thing in the morning. That is all for now, let's get back to the camp.'

Just as they were about to head back they spotted an RAF Shackleton coming in to land. The sea breeze was obviously quite strong, it was pushing the plane off the centre line, but the plane was slightly into the wind and it touched down with no trouble. Alf was impressed, he had been informed by one of the ground crew that these planes can fly the Pacific for hours on end, maybe eighteen hours or more.

Ted was not saying much on the way back to the main camp until Alf mentioned the fiasco down at Port London.

'I fully expect I will be on another charge, but quite frankly I'm not bothered, I mean it's this rotten place, I can't stand it. You wait, when I arrive home and I am out of the Army, I will be a changed person.'

'Well, I hope so, Ted, you have been through the mill, but I must hand it to you, having looked through one of your law books, I really don't know how you have managed to cope,' said Alf.

'I don't understand, what are you trying to say?'

Alf had to be careful what he said next, Ted seemed to be so unstable these days, in spite of the fact that he was going home soon.

'Well, I must say, it's all very complicated, justice and the law, I mean I've been done for speeding and illegal parking. I was in court just before I came into the Army. I reckon I was stitched up by the magistrate. She gave me a ten quid fine, and since I was about to enter the Army, she said she hoped it would teach me some manners.'

'Why was that Alf?'

'I called this bloke a prat for getting my name wrong, which raised a few eyebrows.'

Ted was in stitches, but felt that Alf was trying to say something else. 'Come on, Alf, what is it you were trying to say?'

Alf was going to dig a hole for himself if he was not careful, so he mentioned his friend Jennifer, the girl he had met on the plane during the flight out.

'She's been writing to me ever since and made her acquaintance with my family, and you know me, Ted, I operate carefully. So I am going home to an uncertain future.'

'We are all going home to an uncertain future; in more ways than one. Take my advice and don't become too involved, it may become problematic later on.'

'I'm not to sure you are right there, sometime or other you have to come to terms with your obligations.'

'Yes, that's fair enough, but don't make a relationship obligatory from the start, or you could end up being the court jester, like me.'

'I will remember that, Ted, and many thanks for the advice.'

Alf changed the subject, hoping that the talk had helped Ted more than it had himself. He felt he was sailing very close to the edge, hoping Penny would be kept out of the conversation. Quite unexpectedly, Ted said he was going home to unravel the mystery that had caused him so much grief.

'You are the only one who's not prepared to keep telling me what to do, saying you should have done this, why don't you do that, and get a grip of yourself. My head has been upside down for months, and so be careful. When, or if, I become a lawyer, come and see me when you get another motoring offence and we will both go down together.'

'You know, mate, I may hold you to that, well, here we are, back at Butlins holiday camp and I'm starving. By the way, don't mention——'

'Mum's the word, Alf, I know what it's like being ribbed all the time, especially the "Dear John" bit.'

Jumping out of the lorry, perhaps for the last time, they joined the others for a well-earned meal.

After a shower it was back to the tent and the art of trying to stay cheerful in a tent crowded with unwanted guests.

'No mail, I'm afraid, the mail has been held up by bad weather, so they say, lads,' said Ginger, who often collected the mail although there was usually little or no mail for himself.

Brian thought he was married, but there was hardly ever a letter for him. At one stage he received quite a lot of official mail and disappeared with Ted reading it. Nobody asked questions, and Ted was completely silent on the matter.

The captain turned up and reminded them that there was plenty of work to be carried out and that the time would go quickly before their return home in a few weeks' time. No details were available at this stage. Instead, their sergeant lined them all up for yet more orders. Tomorrow would be business as usual, but the day after there would be quite a lot of activity in the air. They were told not to worry as the Airforce were only practicing dummy runs. They would be told exactly what was going on, but they would have to be up very early in the morning and assemble for a roll call. They were to wear shorts, shirt, bush hat and sunglasses. There was nothing unusual about that; it was their usual working clothes. Harry wanted to know what was going on, and if there was to be another bomb drop would they be issued with protective clothing. The sergeant had no idea, and said he would look into it.

'I will inform the captain of your concerns, and by the way,

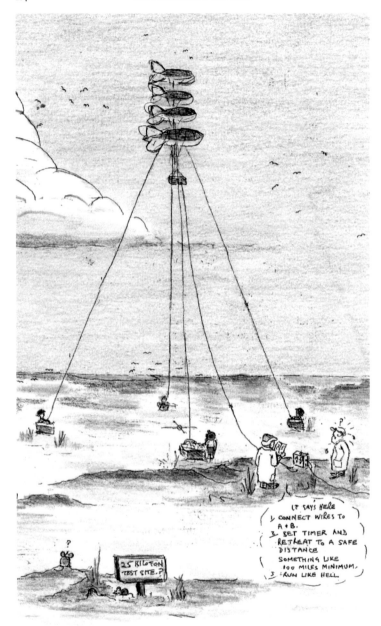

Atom bomb test

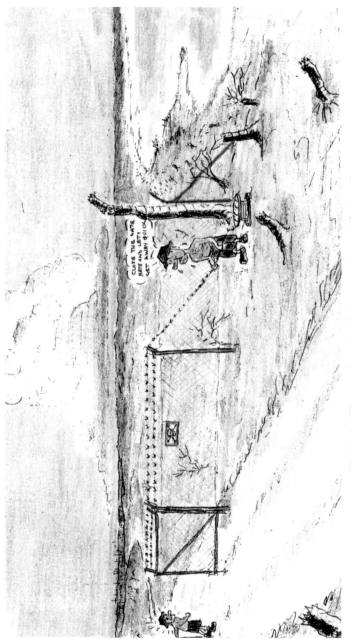

What looked like grass turned out to be green glass—vitrified sand?

I can inform you that mail will be in this evening,' said the sergeant.

It eased things a little to have letters arriving, and with great excitement and expectation they awaited news from home. However, that evening they heard the rumour that there would be a bomb drop tomorrow. For those who had witnessed the first bomb, fear struck them; the thought of having to go through all that again was too much for them to bear. Many of the lads resorted to the Gladiator's Arms to seek solace and to vent their feelings. The usual beer can throwing exercise took place with great effect, causing a retaliation of verbal abuse. Eventually, the arena was cleared, with the lads staggering back to the tents. Some slept where they fell, only to be reawakened by those who had remained sober.

Ginger looked after his mates, who had all climbed into a beer can, except Ted. He remained nonplussed about the whole business, but he had other ideas. In the morning, those who remained oblivious were placed under a shower so as to make them conscious of what could only be described as hell on earth.

After the parade, their names were been checked and orders were given that they were to be taken to a site near the main airfield. Harry and the lads drove the lorries and parked up near the airfield. Everybody jumped out but were told to wait for further orders. The Airforce had become busy with planes taking off and then the announcement that the Valiant with the bomb had taken off.

Everybody was ordered to a chosen area, and told to sit down with their back to the drop zone and there wait for further instructions. Harry became very frightened, but fear soon changed into anger. He had had no idea that his obligatory two years' service would include being subjected to such hideous experiments. Something was wrong, and this

Hydrogen bomb blast about to hit the airfield.

time he really would disobey. To Harry's knowledge there was
no choice; no option to wear white overalls and eye shields, or
go down into a concrete bunker with ten feet thick walls, or
better still go to the other end of the island, where you could
jump on a boat and steam away for a hundred miles or more.
No, it was simply 'Sit down,' and that was an order.

Ted was really upset, he stood next to an officer and started
talking to him. Harry could not quite hear what was being
said, but it was quite a lively conversation ending in, 'Sit down,
sapper, I have given you an order. I will take your name later,
but Ted refused to listen and shouted out.

'In view of what has already taken place here and elsewhere,
it would seem reasonable to ask the question that, since it
makes no sense to be ordered to line up to face these vagaries,
why should we then be the vanguard for these ridiculous
follies? It would seem appropriate, therefore, that we should
be allowed to dig trenches for everybody to shelter in. After
all, we have the machinery and the men to do the job. In any
case, I have no wish to shake hands with the devil and have
my neck burnt again.'

Under normal circumstances, Ted would have been
reported, but a colonel turned to Ted and said, 'I sincerely
hope you are wrong, sapper. I will talk to you later, now sit
down, all of you, and keep down as low as possible.'

Everybody heard the colonel who mentioned that he
thought he should know them all since they had all gone
through his training school. They had not let him down; their
work on the island had been outstanding. 'Well done, all of
you,' he said.

The lads would have appreciated what he had said, if
only they could have heard him. All kinds of emotions were
exhibited by these young men. They wondered why on earth

they had to line up once more. It beggared belief. Harry saw his chance when nobody was looking, he ran towards the lorries and climbed into the cab. He got down as far as he could. One or two others had done the same, but had hidden behind a building.

Young men could be heard praying for their loved ones, a few lads started to become very emotional, and one or two lost control of their bodily functions. They were obviously not that confident of their survival, which was why Harry became so angry. Nobody had given them any reassurances whatsoever, and with no protection it seemed completely wrong.

The man on the tannoy announced the arrival of the aircraft passing overhead. Ted looked up and could clearly see a vapour trail and then the final announcement that the bomb was falling. The tannoy ordered, 'Close your eyes. Close your eyes.' This was followed by the count down: 'Five, four, three, two, one.'

There was a pause before the penetrating, intense, bright light once again passed right through them. Once again they could see all their bones, which they had seen before, but then there was a horrendous heat, much more penetrating than before, it hit them but fortunately they had their shirt collars up, covering their neck. It made little difference, they gasped when this heat seemed to fill their lungs. This felt much more powerful than the last bomb, and when they were told to stand up they were proved to be right.

There was the most massive fire ball rising up into the sky. The shock wave had not arrived and most of the lads knew this and promptly got back down again. Those who did not were about to receive the shock of their lives. Not only could they see this massive fire ball, there came this terrifying shock wave. The buildings came under great strain which resulted in much damage. Coconut palms were bent double, with all kinds of debris flying through the air. Harry's lorry rocked and shook violently, but he felt safer being under cover, at least it protected him from the flying debris, it was a miracle that nobody got hurt.

Up and up went the fire ball, making an incredible noise like continuous thunder. How far away it was from them was anybody's guess, but it was something like thirty-odd miles according to one of the lads. He had been counting the seconds from the flash to the blast.

Still the fire ball rumbled on, but then this colossal cloud became frightening. It stretched high into the sky, but also got closer to them. Other clouds formed around them. What was going on? Forgetting to take Ted's name, the officer had left. He no doubt could see that things did not look well.

'Come on, let's get the hell out of it,' yelled the sergeant.

They climbed into the back of the lorries and drove back to the main camp. The damage to roofs and tents was obvious. Once again, it was back to work, quickly putting the tents up again, but still this massive cloud was going up thousands of feet into the sky. The problem became much worse when the clouds all around them got closer, eventually covering the camp. Then it started to rain, which did not help at all. Panic took over, with the lads staying firmly under cover. The rain stopped and the sun started to dry everything up again. They had remained in their tents until the rain had stopped, then they raced to the showers for a clean up.

They all knew that there would be no mail that day. 'No doubt he will turn up tomorrow. In the meantime, how about a beer, lads, after a meal?' suggested Harry.

To their surprise, even Ginger nervously agreed. It seemed that today had shaken Ginger to the core, he hoped that after a couple of beers with his mates he would hopefully regain his composure.

'Okay, anybody for the cook house?' asked Brian. When they went outside they saw there had been a fair amount of damage to the tents and some of the new buildings. The cook house had also received damage, but the RAF chefs had, as usual, done a fantastic job by still managing to prepare a meal. The lads lined up with their tin trays at the ready and rather sensibly they kept their mouths shut about any delay. Normally it would be, why are we waiting? But nobody would ever dream of thinking it was funny, not in front of the chef. You would no doubt receive an unwelcome invitation to the Gladiator's Arms where he would no doubt teach you why you should never poke fun at a chef.

It may well have been a sleepless night had it not been for a few beers. The next morning, the sun was on time. That baking hot feeling on the side of their tent forced them to get up, only to see the bomb cloud had gone away to reveal the damage that had been caused. Their captain was right, there was plenty of work to do. Debris had been blown all over the place, making for an untidy mess. Harry and Ginger never went back to their old job again, it would be general duties for them until they went home.

'Well, I guess that's it. I am not sorry to leave that job behind, but I could do with some of these machines back home,' remarked Ginger rather solemnly.

'You can always stay here, I am sure there would be no objections,' remarked Harry with a laugh.

'Perish the thought, me old mate, I will be first on that plane, don't you worry about that. I thank God for keeping us all safe, Amen.'

Ginger's prayer touched Harry and he then remembered

his two white tropicbirds, which prompted him to say a silent prayer for them, and all of God's creatures that had perished with them. He would go home with a very sad heart indeed, so much so that he just could not get the birds out of his head. He turned to Ginger and said, 'If we can't make these magnificent creatures ourselves, surely we have no right to destroy them, unless, of course, there is an absolute necessity such as food. I mean, we have helped to destroy not only their homes out here, but their lives as well. Then, on the other hand, we are told that it is all necessary for the sake of mankind.'

Ginger had no answer to Harry's question, except that he thought that, in God's eyes, we were probably no more than children trying to grow up, and that if there was to be another bomb test then he did not want to be there when it happened.

Harry was thinking that perhaps Ginger was right, maybe we are trying to grow up, so let us all hope that those who seek and hold power in all corners of the earth have the good sense and wisdom never to use these weapons.

Still no news came as to their departure date. Work continued with repairs to the buildings. Maybe the mail plane would bring them news from home and cheer them up, but rumour had it that the RAF Hastings had been held up due to engine problems.

Their captain had done everything to find out their return date and had been told it would almost certainly be in three weeks' time. He told them to be prepared for a quick departure. Packing their belongings presented no problem since they had very little. Money was still tight, so the thought of buying presents was almost out of the question, but they still had ideas in mind.

Harry gathered a few feathers and made an arrangement for Helen. Pete bought a gift for his girlfriend from the local people. These small gifts probably represented much more to them than to their loved ones. They had grown used to going without, and now they were only about two week from home. Without doubt, everyone of them had a changed personality, the Army and the bomb had seen to that.

The weekend was not much different to any other day with plenty of work still to do. Ginger met up with the Airforce lads. They too could not get away quick enough; they had seen enough for a life time.

'Don't get too excited, but air movements told me that new arrivals are due in two weeks' time,' said Jim.

Ginger could not thank them enough, and then Jim showed him his foot. It looked grim with an odd-looking skin disease right across the top of his foot. Jim reckoned that many of the lads had similar problems.

'Hope to see you on that plane, Ginger, all the best.'

As the bearer of the good tidings, Ginger went back to the tent to give them the news that they would be away very soon. It was jubilation all round, even Ted got away from his books for a moment of celebration. At the same time letters from home arrived, which kept them quiet for a while before a few beers to celebrate.

Ted announced that his name had been put forward for the law exams. His employer and sister had seen to everything. Alf was the first to congratulate him followed by all the others.

'Come on, let's celebrate everything, in one way or another this island has taught us much more than we think. It's held us all together, but under great stress. I have to admit I don't know what I would have done without you, believe me, many thanks to you all,' said Ted.

'In that case the drinks are on you, old pal,' replied Harry.

'Hang on a minute, not so fast, before we celebrate I need

to acknowledge that I might have other commitments back home.'

'You should say what you mean,' replied Harry.

'Oh I do, I mean what I say,' said Ted.

But that was it, Ted had no intention of saying what he meant, but the lads could guess that he had plans to find Penny again; it would be a very difficult time for him.

That evening at the Gladiator's Arms was, as usual, a lively one with much excitement about their return home with Britain's deterrent in the bag. One or two of the lads said that they had unwittingly been involved in producing a weapon capable of the mass extinction of life as we know it. And that sooner or later others would want this weapon—at the expense of feeding the hungry. Others disagreed and said that, without this deterrent, it would be like having one hand tied behind your back with the enemy just over the fence. The debate was going nowhere with tempers running high. The duty NCO, who was shaking in his boots, had orders to not intervene in these disputes on any account, but simply to call for the military police. Things calmed down somewhat at the sight of the military police. One would have been mistaken if they thought they had witnessed a vicar's garden party. Everybody behaved as if they were as innocent as the day they were born.

Staggering back to the tent lines after a few cans it was often the case where one would mistake somebody else's tent for your own. Eventually there was always somebody who would put you right.

In the morning the noise of the waves would remind you that you were still on the island. The smell of socks would be enough to get you off the camp bed. With a bit of luck it might be just a few more nights with their old bed companions the mosquitoes and bed bugs.

Many had the odd feeling that they would never leave; it felt as if they were on a prison island. One morning, when their sergeant was due to tell them if they had a seat home on a civilian plane, they were so keyed up that hardly anybody went to breakfast for fear of missing the chance of going home to freedom. But their hearts sank when the plane was seen taking off without them. Harry and the others were not just disappointed; they were gutted. When their sergeant finally turned up he almost had to read the riot act, but their training had taught them to keep quiet. Then the captain appeared and pointed out that he was just as disappointed as they were, but there was to be another plane next week, so to have their luggage ready.

'Ready, sir? I have been ready since this time last year, and I wager that all of us are ready right now, including yourself, sir,' said Alf.

'Spot on, sapper, I will see you on the plane,' replied the captain.

It was a fact that several of the lads had never actually unpacked since there was nowhere to put their belongings.

The captain, a decent man, came over to Alf and started talking. 'I don't suppose you have plans to stay on in the Army, have you Reynolds?'

'No chance, sir, come and see me and I might have just the car for you, as a matter of fact, there may even be a job for you if you decide to come out of the Army, my father is expanding all the time,' replied Alf.

'If you're not joking I may take you up on the offer, I am on a short-term commission and time is nearly up, so you never know, thanks.'

Alf had only meant it as a joke, this time it back fired on him, but then he had plenty of time to think about it. It would be an unlikely alliance, with the shoe being on the other foot, but Alf was more interested in his personality. Without doubt he was very smart, in both senses of the word, and spoke much better than he could. His knowledge of vehicles was second to none, and if his father had a vacancy . . . There would be no harm in swapping telephone numbers. Alf wrote his number down and handed it to the captain who looked at it with interest.

'I will keep this safe, I leave the Army in nine months' time and this will please my wife a great deal, especially where you live. I have your address on file, just in case, you understand.'

'Yes, I understand perfectly, and I have to say, sir, I feel I came within an inch of you having to open that file.'

'Well, thank God it didn't come to that, but I know what you mean.'

Alf stepped back and saluted, but the captain stepped forward and shook his hand and said it was a privilege to work with all of them.

* * *

It was now all over and back to reality. Would anybody miss the island? thought Harry. Not likely. It would be highly unlikely they would miss it, but they would never forget it.

At last they were back in their uniforms with what luggage they had and were ready to go. Walking out of the tent for the last time none of them looked back. They had put up with a camp bed for twelve months, along with bed bugs, mosquitoes, flies, crabs, smelly socks, privation, and who knew what else. They had seen a glimpse of hell, which would without doubt be an indelible mark on their minds for the rest of their lives.

Transport had arrived to take them to the airfield. New

arrivals to the island came in on their plane and were quickly taken away to twelve months of hell on earth. They would be shackled to a life of uncertainty. You could not see it, smell it, or taste it, but it was there. Although you were told there was no radiation to be concerned about, they all had their doubts, and who could blame them? It beggared belief that nuclear bombs of that magnitude would not result in levels of radiation to be worried about. In any case, they would never know if they had been contaminated, since their radiation film badges were taken from them immediately after the bomb had gone off. Nobody ever saw the monitoring team, and in any case, to monitor the entire island would be impossible, not forgetting the surrounding sea. Then Harry thought of Isaac Newton's theory of gravity, which he covered during his studies. What goes up, must come down, so if any matter had been taken up by the bombs it would have to gravitate back to earth. He decided not to think about it, he was going home and the transport was waiting for him.

The formalities of a normal airport were non-existent. It was off the lorry and wait your turn before boarding. Alf was, of course, remembering Jennifer when he last saw her twelve months ago, and now he was looking forward to seeing her again. However, she was not on board this flight, in her last letter she had promised to make every effort to find out his arrival time and meet him at the airport.

Harry was on board and got a window seat. He could see out across the airfield and into the bush. He could see the area had been working in from the window.

With everybody on board and doors shut tight the order was given to fasten seat belts, and with the engines running, the plane taxied along the runway. Harry was rather nervous at first, especially as the engines got to full power for take off.

Brakes were released and they were away, he could just about make out the last glimpse of the island before the plane lifted off and it was lost from sight for good.

The Bristol Britannia: the quickest way home via Canada

11. Take Me Away from This Place

The plane's engines settled down having climbed to its operational height of twenty one thousand feet and headed for Vancouver. Harry was looking out the window at nothing, his mind was still on the island. He was going home, having unwittingly destroyed the home of his little white birds. They had kept him company for months. He remembered them flying right alongside him with their long tail feathers streaming out behind them. How could you forget magnificent birds like that, but did they survive? He very much doubted it, the radiation would have seen to that, or that terrifying heat from the blast, nothing could have survived that. Helen would ask questions, of that there was no doubt, but she must never know. Other birds of the same species would re-colonise the island one day, but according to an airman sitting next to him more tests had been planned.

'Well, thank God we are out of it,' said the airman next to him. 'National service are you?' he asked.

'Yes, and only eight months to do, but we have just been granted four weeks leave. I must say I had no idea I would be involved with nuclear bombs.'

'No, neither did I, but it's now all over. I have less than a year to do, after serving five years, so when the drinks come

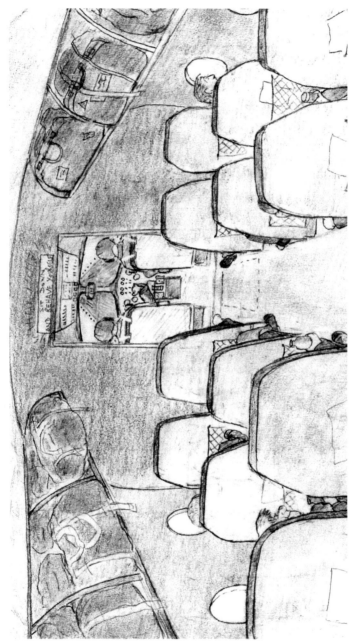

RAF Transport Command. Flying home the long way in a Handley Page Hastings took several days.

round please have a drink on me. I'm having a double; what's yours?'

'I will have the same, if you don't mind.'

Harry felt very much better after a couple of drinks. He was inquisitive enough to ask the airman, why his stripes were upside down, or was the drink playing tricks on him?

'For what it's worth I am a technician, which attracts more money than other ranks, especially national servicemen. Quite frankly, it's all wrong, I have seen you lads working long hours and for peanuts.'

'Twenty-nine shillings to be exact, and I agree it's derisory. Never mind, I have ideas for the future, but I haven't quite worked out the details yet. I have seven months to work it all out,' said Harry feeling tired.

There was no answer, the technician had fallen asleep. The plane was a Bristol Britannia with four gas turbine engines. It was carrying just less than one hundred people, although it could carry more. It called in at Vancouver, then climbed over the Rocky Mountains and headed for Gander in Newfoundland. Once again the plane only stopped to refuel. The final leg was to the UK.

The door opened and Harry breathed in UK air once more. There were a few farewells, but most were eager to go through customs and head for home. Harry thought customs would be no problem, but it was not to be. What belongings he had were searched thoroughly, which puzzled him somewhat.

'Is this all you have to declare, one bottle of spirits?' asked the customs officer.

Harry was not best pleased, and feeling tired after such a long journey and longing to get home, he reminded the customs officer of his meagre wage. He simply could not afford more than one bottle of spirits, he did not smoke and neither did his family.

All this was being watched by three Navy lads who were also returning from the nuclear test site. They seemed to be already celebrating with a bottle of whisky and shouted out, 'Get on with it, mate, we haven't got all day, we are due to drop anchor tonight.' The sailor took another swig from a bottle of whisky which he was sharing with the others. Harry felt better after seeing these sailors enjoying themselves, there was no doubt they richly deserved the bottle of whisky which would temporarily delete the memories of what they had witnessed during the last year. Harry shook their hands and wished them luck. 'Have a drink on us, mate,' they said.

One of them got up, swaying, and offered Harry and the customs officer a drink. Harry accepted gratefully, but the customs officer, who now had a smile on his face, had to decline but thanked them all the same. The customs officer quickly helped Harry pack his belongings—which amounted to very little.

He ticked Harry's case and wished him a pleasant holiday. Finally, he was free to catch up with the rest of the gang. Harry made tracks for the station where he rejoined Ginger.

It was a bit of an anti-climax arriving home only to be searched by customs. If it was not for the Navy, his home coming would have been dull to say the least. Most of the lads had gone half an hour ago, like Gary, Alf and Ted who were seen sprinting through the airport lounge to the railway station. Ginger was still waiting for his train when Harry joined him. Somehow, Ginger was not all that happy and Harry sensed his homecoming meant very little to him, although he dared not ask why. Harry reminded Ginger that he would be welcome to visit anytime; he would always be pleased to see him. Harry found it sad that it had to end like this, but perfectly understandable considering what they had been through. Having been on the island for twelve long months, all they were interested in was their homes and families.

Harry and Ginger jumped on the train and made plans to meet up while on leave.

'Don't forget, Harry, I will see you soon, but I will give you a call first.'

'I thought you were married, Ginger.'

'I have been asked for a divorce, Ted helped me with the papers and so on while on the island. There you go, you can't win them all, we all make mistakes. Take care, Harry, and mind you meet up with that nurse you have been writing to.'

Flying home on an RAF Hastings would
take several days calling in at many countries.

The author being taken home by his brother on his push bike to their parent's place in East Sussex.

12. Nothing Stays the Same

There was nobody there to meet Harry and he did not expect anyone. What with the loss of his grandfather still fresh in his family's mind, he realised everything had to get back to normal, and in any case, nobody knew exactly when he was going to arrive. He found the key and let himself in. The first thing to do was to make a pot of tea and sit down in his favourite chair; he had plenty to think about. He had this sudden sense of jubilation, I am home in one piece.

He was just about to pour a cup when the back door opened. Rushing out he spilt some tea, but who cares, it was his mum. With lots of hugs and kisses she was reduced to tears.

'We have been so worried about you out there, we know what's going on, it's been in the papers and on the radio. Nothing much was said, but your father has not been at all happy, and then of course losing granddad, it's been a very worrying time for him. Never mind, let's take a good look at you. My word, you do look tired, and you have certainly lost weight. I tell you what, pour me a cup of tea and I will make you a sandwich. After that perhaps you would accompany me to the shops, and later we will have dinner and celebrate. Did you ever hear from that young lady again?'

Three hours had passed when Harry's mother woke him.

'You fell asleep, my boy, and I'm not surprised, here's another cup of tea, the boys will be in soon, they have been looking so forward to this day.'

'I'm sorry Mum, I should have walked to the shops with you, I don't know what came over me.'

'You need all the rest you can get, your father is not at all happy with what you have been up to, and neither am I.

Harry was beginning to realise that from now on he would have to be very careful what he said so as not to unnerve his parents.

After a warm welcome from his father and brothers they settled down to an excellent dinner.

'What was the food like, Harry?' his mother inquired.

'Under the circumstances, it was first class.'

'What sort of circumstances do you mean?' asked his father.

'Well, Dad, the chefs produced cracking food under canvas, in terrible heat and high humidity, and with flies everywhere. From time to time, the camp had to be sprayed from the air with this noxious fly repellent—if you got caught up in it you had to shower to get rid of the smell.'

Harry's father wanted to know what work he had carried out and Harry was happy to explain.

'It was long hours and interesting. Quite honestly, I have learnt a great deal about plant machinery; site clearing; building roads and runways; and driving. Some of the lads even helped the electricians with electrical work such as the runway lighting. I have learnt a lot and it has given me ideas for the future; I would be grateful for your advice, Dad.'

Before Harry's father said a word, his brothers wanted to know more about this great big bomb that was exploded out there. How big was it?

'Oh, that was a long way off,' replied Harry.

'But you must have seen it, what was it like?'

His father was also interested, but his mother saved the day by asking more about this young lady that he was supposed to get in touch with.

'Yes, Mum, we exchanged letters, and what with your letters as well, they cheered me up no end, I will be for ever grateful to you.'

'Well, what about her, what's her name and when are you going to see her?' Her questions came in thick and fast, but it was a welcome relief from the questions about the dreaded bomb.

'Her name is Helen and she wrote often, and I must say she was very sympathetic when granddad passed away. She sent me a sympathy card and a kind letter. There was no way I could return home, and so she tried to represent me by putting some flowers on granddad's resting place.'

'So that's who it was, well I'm never,' said his father looking relieved that this mystery had been solved.

Time caught up with all of them, but his father thought it appropriate to have a wee dram before bed. The boys were not allowed to stay up late, but Harry promised to take them out during his leave. His mother had also had a long day and wished him a good night.

'You have no idea how thrilled she is having you back, Harry, and so am I,' said his father. 'But I make no secret of the fact that we are not happy with what has been going on out there. However, I will not press you on the subject, but maybe one day you will want to talk about it. Now then, what about this idea you have?'

Harry explained all the possibilities of starting up his own business, but was acutely aware of all the difficulties. He explained that if he could get his hands on some of the machinery he had operated on the island, he would not only be better off, but a lot happier than being a electrical engineer. He was sure he could earn more than my twenty-nine shillings a week.

'Well, I admire your confidence, young man, but have you thought about all the ifs, buts and maybes? I mean, it seems you have the skills to operate these monsters, but where are you going to keep them, and there's the little problem of money. No, Harry, think long and hard before you ever think of leaving your present position. However, you may have got over one hurdle, and before you go to bed I would just like to talk to you about your grandfather's old place.'

'What are you going to do with it, Dad?'

'Your mother and I are not getting any younger, and I must admit I can't take on such a task. I mean, as you know, there are quite a lot of repairs and, well, you know what I mean. So your mother and I want you to have the place as your inheritance. Your grandfather also left us some money, which we are more than happy with. We have this place, which quite frankly, I don't want to leave, and one day it will be shared between your two brothers, along with whatever else is left. I hope that sounds okay with you.'

Harry could not believe what he was hearing, and said he thought the place belonged to his parents.

'Oh, it does really, but what I am saying is that you can do something with it, and in any case you can't argue, the papers have been drawn up. Now, let's have one more dram before we go up the road, and by the way I will expect you to sign for it.'

In just one day Harry had drawn much closer to his dream of running his own business.

'Many thanks, Dad, from the bottom of my heart I thank both you and Mum.'

Harry slept soundly, he woke up still not believing what his parents had done for him. Downstairs his brothers were having breakfast, they called out to him to come down and tell them more about this girlfriend he was sweet on. His mother poured a cup of tea and asked what he wanted for breakfast.

'Just toast, thanks Mum, and can I use your phone, I have an important call to make.'

'If it's to that nice young girl then you should have phoned last night, my word, you are slow.'

'Thanks, Mum, and what about a walk this morning?'

Harry rang the hospital, it rang and rang until finally somebody answered. 'Sorry, Helen is not on duty, can I take a message?'

In many ways his mother was right, he should have phoned the moment he had arrived home, after all, that was the arrangement. She was on his mind all the time, why on earth had he not phoned her? On the other hand, he had been so tired that he had even fallen asleep when his mother was talking to him. He left his phone number with the girl who had answered the phone. Maybe Helen would phone him.

The boys left for school, leaving Harry to talk to his mother about her and his father's incredible generosity in leaving granddad's place to him.

'Your father and I don't want all the hard work that would need to be done, but at the same time we don't want to lose it, so we talked it over while you was sunning yourself on that island. We agreed that you were the best one to look after it, but, of course, we realise that it's in a bit of a state.'

'Mum, I tell you here and now, I will bring the old place back to its former glory, which is what granddad would have wanted.'

His mother brought him up to date with other news and

mentioned again that Sophie had left her old job and got involved with the boss of the new company she worked for. How on earth his mother found out all this was a mystery, but Harry had moved on a long way since then and nothing stayed the same.

Still feeling tired, he thought a walk would wake him up, but he met his two brothers coming home from school. It was Friday and the eldest one, Alex, was over the moon. He had found himself a part time job at a local airfield. There was no money, but he would have the odd flying lesson.

'I leave school soon, and with my inheritance from granddad I hope to become a pilot, but I have a long way to go.'

'Have you been up yet, Alex?'

'Four times and I really enjoyed it.'

'Get your licence and I would like to go up with you,' promised Harry.

The youngest though had other ideas. 'Harry, when is your girlfriend coming to see us?'

'Hang on, young fellah, she's not my girlfriend as such, more like a pen friend, after all I have only seen her once in my life.'

Next week he thought he might visit his old work place, just to see how things were. Perhaps he might find out more about his promised degree course.

His father came home from work looking tired and blamed the previous late night. 'Give me time to recharge my batteries and then we are going out to eat this evening,' he said.

Harry thought about his telephone call to Helen, he must call her again.

'Sorry, Dad, I was expecting a call and maybe—'

'Hello, what's going on? Got some girl already? You don't hang about, do you?'

Harry's mother was quick to point out that it was the nurse who had looked after granddad.

'She seems to know quite a lot about you, Harry, how long have you known her? asked his mother.

'Only since I was last on leave, I met her at the hospital when I went to visit granddad there.

'Well don't keep her to yourself; let us have a look at her. Why don't you phone her right now and invite her here, after all she looked after my father and I would like to thank her myself.'

Harry phoned from the hall hoping Helen would be in. The phone rang, for a long time there was no answer, but just as he was about to put the phone down somebody answered. It was Helen.

'Hi Helen, it's Harry, how are you?'

Before he could say anymore, she said, 'It's Harry? What a relief that you have returned safely, I was beginning to worry what had happened to you. Where are you, when can I see you?'

She never stopped talking and she seemed to be more excited than he was.

'I would like to see you this very minute, but I don't have a car so it would have to be the train,' replied Harry.

'Don't worry about that, I have a car. We could meet tomorrow, if you can make it?'

Harry made all the arrangements to meet outside his local railway station.

'I will bring my bird books with me, you can show me all the birds you saw out there. How do you feel after your long journey? I found your tiny island on the map.'

'By the way Helen, can you remember what I look like? I mean, it's been over a year since we met each other, and that was very brief. I won't be in uniform and my suit has taken a turn for the worse I'm afraid, so if you see a scruffy tramp looking for a couple of pennies it will most probably be me.'

'Oh, in that case I think I will give you a miss! Just be there, I really want to see you.'

'Yes, and my parents want to meet you and thank you for looking after granddad. They really appreciated what you did for him.'

Eventually, feeling on top of the world, Harry rejoined his family.

'It's all fixed, Dad, is that offer still on for eating out this evening, as I would like to go halves with you?'

'Not likely, lad, come on all of you, lets move, I'm starving.'

The meal was superb and Harry's father thought a wee dram would go down well at home.

'I have just the thing, Dad, a bottle of whisky, after all, it's about time I made my contribution. And I insist in helping you out, Mum, you can't keep feeding me for four weeks.'

'We will see about that, won't we? As far as I am concerned you are home and safe.'

His father never mentioned the island anymore for which Harry was grateful. His father later hinted to Harry that he might face redundancy.

'It's all to do with reorganisation and takeovers. If it comes to it, it will no doubt be within the next few months,' he said. Harry asked his father to reconsider handing over granddad's property, but he would not hear of it. 'Let me explain to you that this redundancy may work in my favour.'

'Yes, Dad, but what happens if it's not in your favour?'

'Then I will come and work for you, son,' he said with a laugh.

'No, you will not *work* for me; you come in as a partner or not at all.'

'What about yourself and your future? Surely you are not really considering packing in the engineering business after all the hard work you put in with your studies? You have a full city and guilds with a degree course to follow, I think you should consider very carefully before passing that up.'

'I appreciate that, and I realise starting a business is one thing, making a success of it is another, but you have given me another piece of the jigsaw by allowing me to live at granddad's place. Of course, as far as I am concerned, it will always be your place.

'The problem is that the Army has taught me a new trade, and during the last year I have enjoyed it. I fully admit the training was tough, but it was worth it. When I go back to the Army and they send me wherever, I intend to improve my skills in the use of heavy plant machinery.'

His father fell asleep for a while, or so Harry thought. But he was not really asleep, then he got up and said, 'You might have a good idea there lad, come on, it's getting late.'

Walking to the railway station the next day, Harry was a little nervous after waiting for so long to meet Helen. He was infatuated with her right from the first time he had met her, but would he still feel the same way now? On the other hand, he was not exactly cutting a dash with the sort of clothes he was wearing, but he had no choice. He had no money, no car, and had nothing else he could offer. He was beginning to feel it was a useless exercise to turn up looking like a tramp.

If that was not enough, it started to rain and he had arrived at the station far too early. Memories of the odd-looking rain that had followed the bomb test came back to him, giving him flashbacks of that terrible day: the frightening fire ball rising up into the sky. Feelings of panic surged within him. He sheltered inside the station, he felt safe there under cover from those clouds forming all around him. Looking at his watch he realised that he had time to spare, but panic took over again. The rain stopped and Harry made a dash for the door, just as he was about to walk away there was a car tooting its horn. There was so many cars, but then a car moved towards him, it was Helen.

'Jump in, soldier boy, welcome home.'

Harry stood there for a while trying to regain his composure.

'You *are* Harry the soldier boy?' she asked.

'Hi Helen, I'm sorry it's been a long time and——'

'Well come on, jump in or you will catch a chill.'

She looked tall, her long dark hair tied back in a pony tail. Fortunately for Harry, she was dressed casually, but very attractively, in a predominately all white arrangement. If that was not enough, she was wearing a perfume which somehow managed to calm his nerves. Without doubt she was way out of his class, and on twenty-nine shillings a week there was no way he could hold on to this beauty. How could he take her out to a first class restaurant and so on; the best he could do was sausage, egg, chips, and a slice of bread and marg. Oh, and of course a mug of tea.

Looking at her clothes, Harry had yet another flashback. He could see his little white friends, right in front of him, as clear as crystal. He could clearly see their magnificent tail feathers trailing behind them. It was a momentary glimpse of his past.

He was snapped out of it by Helen asking, 'Are you alright, Harry, you look very tired, perhaps it's best we have a coffee and have a talk for a while?'

'No, I'm fine, it's just the excitement of seeing you again, I have waited over twelve long months hoping this day would happen, and would you believe, I don't know what is happening to me, I feel so tired.'

'Remember me, the nurse called Helen? Okay, Harry my love, I will find a quiet place for us both and then we will see how you are. Time for a coffee and a chat.'

Harry was thinking he had blown it. What a first class idiot he was, but he just could not find the energy to come out of this unending tiredness. He could not keep on apologising, and he was beginning to feel that he had nothing to offer but a few feathers.

Helen parked her car and they made their way for a very welcome coffee.

Harry was forgetting she was a qualified nurse and would know exactly what she was talking about. Having said that, the last thing he wanted was to let her down.

'I don't suppose you brought your bird book? No? Not to worry, I have brought mine,' said Helen, eager to know what Harry had seen on the island.

The last thing Harry wanted was a long lecture on ornithology, and quite frankly, the only bird he was interested in was sitting across from him. If only he could muster up some energy and show a little more interest. He could clearly see that bird watching was her hobby, thumbing through her book she would ask Harry, 'Did you see this one, or was it that one?' Although he was bored to tears he tried very hard to show interest and then he remembered the feathers he had brought home with him. Taking her book he thumbed through the pages until he found the frigatebird.

'See that one? Well, I brought home one of its feathers in excellent condition. As a matter of fact, I have brought you home a selection of feathers from the island. I will bring them to you next time.'

'What about the little white birds, did you manage to find one of their feathers?' she asked excitedly.

'Oh yes, I managed to pick up one or two, but I must say it took me a very long time finding them.'

Nothing could have pleased Helen more, yet Harry had been thinking that it was hardly a worthwhile present.

The ribbons in her hair reminded him of his friends on the island. He just could not get it out of his head that many of them would have perished, along with all the other thousands of birds. He kept on saying to himself, look what is in front of you and not what has gone on in the past. He snapped out of one of his momentary glimpses of the past and found that Helen was looking straight at him.

'It's a pity you did not bring your bird book, Harry, but never mind, another day perhaps? What were you thinking about just then?'

'I don't need a bird book, I can see this beautiful bird right in front of me.'

She hesitated for a while and said, 'And what does this bird look like?'

He said nothing, then looking straight back at Helen, he told her what he could see. 'It is pure white with long tail feathers. It is flying right by my side, so friendly and pure, as pure as the day it was born. Sometimes I think it must be an angel from heaven trying to warn me.'

She touched his arm and said, 'Well this bird will warn you in a moment, but in the meantime try and cheer up, please. 'Now then, soldier boy, I think I should explain how I feel about today and——'

'I really am sorry,' said Harry interrupting her. 'I guess

I'm not what you expected, I can't help the way I feel at the moment, and in any case, you are well out of my league.'

'What on earth is that supposed to mean? Well I make no apologies for the way I look. Just take a good look at yourself, Harry. Perhaps you are right, you are not the person I expected, I thought I knew what you boys had gone through, but I'm wrong. Before I give you a lift home let me give you some advice. First thing Monday morning, go and see your GP. I think I know what is wrong with you, but your doctor will explain better than I can.'

'You say you know what us lads have been through, how can that be? I never mentioned a word about what we were made to go through and what we had to do. Well, I have had enough and I freely admit I don't feel well enough to meet you and I am truly sorry for that. I never said anything in my letters to you for good reason—it would have been wrong of me. Don't worry about taking me home.'

'Harry if you and I——'

Harry interrupted again. 'Helen, I think you are a little out of my league, by which I mean that there is no way I can take you out, I just don't have the means. The Army pay is derisory, I don't have a car, or anything come to think of it, but I can assure you that will all change very soon. I would be grateful for a lift to my grandfather's place, that is all I ask of you.'

She immediately agreed, and said, 'But first we must eat and it's on me, don't worry about a thing. Harry, can I be frank with you, I mean I would like to talk to you?'

By now Harry was finding it to hard to concentrate on anything, but here he was in the company of a very attractive girl who seemed to be doing everything she could to make this date a meaningful occasion.

'Please, go ahead, I don't mind at all, after all, people have been telling me what to do for the last eighteen months and I was never given a choice.'

Helen's eyes began to water up and she was beginning to think it had all been a waste of time. 'Okay, I will leave you in peace and I am sorry to have intruded into your life.'

'No, please, I didn't mean you, I need your advice, nobody else has offered me help, except my parents of course. They are eager to meet you, that's if you will forgive this miserable attitude of mine.'

'So long as you don't make any more remarks like the last one I will try to help you. You are really very tired and you may have a troubled mind. You don't seem to realise that you shouldn't have come here today, but purely from a selfish point of view, I am glad that you did. My guess is you are just twenty years old, give or take a year, but whatever, you should look a lot better than you do. As you know, I am a nurse and I cannot diagnose any further, so as I have already advised you, you should make an appointment with your GP as soon as possible. If you don't, then I will. I am very serious, do you understand? I know it sounds like I am telling you what to do, but I am just trying to help you become the better person that I am convinced you can be.'

Harry looked down at his coffee, thinking she was right, even his mother thought he looked terrible. With that Helen jumped up and said, 'Am I your little bird or not?'

It sounded like an ultimatum, come on, he thought to himself, wake up, she's right, you are tired, very tired. He took a chance and took her hand, reminding her of how much he had looked forward to this day and promised he would seek advice from his GP. The response from Helen was unexpected, she turned to him and kissed him, to which Harry responded warmly.

Helen spoke softly to him, 'I had mixed feelings about today, now I am glad that I came. Come on, I am on duty tonight, so if we want to see your granddad's place we must make a move.'

Helen was full of praise for his grandfather, she mentioned that he was never any bother, 'Unlike someone else I could mention,' she said looking at Harry.

'I really have no idea who that could be, patient confidentiality, nurse Riordan.'

'But of course, Mr Watkins, you can rest assured I will keep you to myself, so there.'

Harry was beginning to have real feelings for this lovely girl. Not many girls would put up with a grumpy so and so like him, but not to worry, there was suddenly a light at the end of the tunnel.

Granddad's place came into view. His house was down a country lane just off the main road. It was full of trees and without doubt needed some attention. Harry told Helen where to park. As they got out Helen said, 'Hey, just a minute, I didn't expect to be taken down a country lane and into the woods.'

'Ah, well, that's your own fault,' said Harry and started to chase her down the lane to his granddad's house. With a scream or two and many giggles, she stopped short of the house and waited for Harry, who was completely out of breath.

'Poor old thing, you couldn't catch me if you tried,' and then she started to taunt him. 'Come on, baggy pants, catch me if you can.'

She ran off round the back of the house, but Harry, who knew the place like the back of his hand, went around the other way and caught her peering around the corner.

Creeping up on her he shouted, 'Boo!' The response was a very loud scream, but it was too late and he held on to her.

'That's not fair, you don't play nicely,' she said. Wriggling free she ran away shouting, 'If you want a kiss you will have to catch me, baggy pants.' She stuck her tongue out at him and called him an ugly old man. She ran off and went to hide in one of many old sheds. Now and again she would taunt him until finally he could see her hiding in one of the sheds. She was looking through a hole, but had made a fatal mistake, there was only one doorway in. Harry shut her in and she screamed again. 'I'm going now,' he said, 'and I won't be back. Maybe I will bring an old crust around for you tomorrow. Bye, see you.'

Harry was walking away when he heard her shouting, 'I didn't mean it, I'm sorry, please let me out. I have to go to work.'

'Promise no more baggy pants?'

'Yes, I promise.'

Harry let her out, and with that she ran off again, shouting, 'Baggy pants, old baggy pants, catch me if you can.'

This time he was completely out of breath and sat down inside the house. Helen came in and sat down on his lap. 'I must tell you I really do have to go; time's up.'

Harry asked for her for just a few seconds longer, which turned into a few minutes. 'Come on, race you to the car, last one in is a ninny.'

'Well, I have to admit I am the ninny,' he said as he tried to run up the hill to the car.

Helen, realising what she had done, came back for him. Back on the road she was full of apologies, she should have known better, but she had enjoyed herself so much. Not for a long time, if ever, could she remember having fun like she had had today.

'It's a pity the place has to go, but at least I have seen where your granddad kept his chickens and his garden.'

'You wait, when I am back to normal, gosh you won't stand a chance, any more trouble from you, especially if you call me baggy pants again, I will catch you and lock you in the shed again. By the way, what makes you think the old place has to go?'

'Oh, I don't know, I'm sorry, it's none of my business. I just thought it was nice being there for the afternoon. Thanks for that.'

Helen insisted on driving Harry home despite his protests. A silence fell until they both spoke up at the same time with the same question: when could they see each other again? Harry was keen to see her as much as he could, but it had to revolve around Helen's shifts. She had two days off next Wednesday and Thursday, which was a bonus for both of them, and perhaps Helen just might squeeze a couple more days off.

'Don't forget the doctor first thing Monday morning,' she shouted as she drove away.

Harry could not believe his luck, Helen had turned out to be a very attractive girl, not only with a caring and loving way, but who was also young at heart. What more could any fellah want? But then he realised that he was missing her already.

When he got home, his family wanted to know how he had got on and when they would get to meet her.

'All being well, next week, but I have been ordered to see the doctor first thing on Monday. She agrees with you, Mum, I need to pick myself up, I feel a mess and no doubt look a mess.

'I'm inclined to agree with you there,' said his Father, 'I must say you don't really cut a dash in those baggy trousers.

I'm surprised she gave you a second glance,' he said laughing.

'Now, now, he doesn't need your jokes, he's just lost a little weight that's all,' said his mother, who could not help smiling.

But his Father had more to say with his dry sense of humour. 'I realise that your wardrobe may be a little outdated, and moths have rushed in and modified your entire collection of Stan Laurel outfits, but we have made arrangements for a fashion show to take place next Monday.'

'Well thank you very much, Dad, you have filled me with absolute confidence. Instead of wearing my Oxford bags perhaps I will show off a blazer and white flannels, sporting a carnation and a big cigar.'

'Of course, but a word of caution, my boy.'

'What now, Dad?'

'I somehow don't think your girlfriend will take too kindly to a cigar.'

'Well, what do you suggest?'

'Your dress sense leaves a lot to be desired, so perhaps a straw boater and a cravat will go well with your blazer and white flannels.'

'Excellent, I will see to it right away and——'

Their banter was interrupted by his mother bringing in a pot of tea before they had something stronger.

'Come on you two, stop all this nonsense, I want to know more about this young lady.'

His mother was asking questions which were impossible to answer. He had only met her for a few hours, all he could say was that she was a nurse and was very caring. She was very keen on watching wildlife and had written to him while he was on the island. And, contrary to what you may believe, Dad, she *is* keen on me, baggy trousers and all.'

'Well, I am surprised, my lad, I thought you were going to

say that she liked the trousers, but when are you going to take them back to the tailors?'

'Very funny, I must say, I know I don't come up to your expectations and I have let you down, but if on the other hand you could see your way to increasing my allowance, perhaps that would raise the bar on my social life.'

'Yes, I will think about your request in due course, but have you arranged for a formal introduction to your young lady?'

'I have already sent a letter of introduction for a meeting next Wednesday as social etiquette is of the utmost importance.'

'But of course, my boy, I haven't quite made up my mind, but I shall no doubt be wearing my clerical grey suit.

'Excellent, Father,'

Harry's mother interrupted all this banter and pointed out that the poor girl wouldn't come anywhere near the place if she knew what was going on.

'I am looking forward to meeting her and I am grateful to her for agreeing with me.'

'What's that, Mum?'

'That you should see the doctor, in fact you should *both* see the doctor and have your heads examined.'

His father laughed, his mother felt that the little bit of humour had done her son nothing but good. Then out came a tray of drinks served up by Harry's brothers. Wine for Mum, two large whiskies for Harry and his dad, and half a glass of beer for Harry's brothers. Everybody raised their glasses to granddad and said may he rest in peace.

Harry rested easy that night and slept solidly until late on Sunday morning. His immediate thoughts were for Helen having been on duty all night. She must feel tired out and no doubt would be fast asleep. It would not be fair to phone her, even though he was longing to hear her voice again.

Breakfast was long over and his mother was preparing Sunday lunch. That wonderful feeling of being home was appreciated much more than before he went away and the changes in just eighteen months had told him that very little stayed the same. One job he would never have contemplated before was to help his mother prepare the vegetables. Yes, the Army had changed him and his last six months of service would hopefully improve his knowledge of civil engineering. He briefly had a flashback to his life on the island, thinking about all the damage that had been done to his little white tropicbirds. It was a mistake thinking of them being engulfed in all that horror, it seemed to turned his head inside out. The only consolation he had was Helen, without her his tormented state would be unendurable. He wondered about Ted and what he had been through.

'I wonder if it was his?' he said thinking about whether Ted was a father, he had not realised that his mother was in the room.

'His what, who are you talking about my love?'

'Oh, nobody really, Mum. Shall I lay the table?'

'You can indeed, and after lunch perhaps you would like to go for a walk with me, your father will be back soon, but he often has a drink with his friends on a Sunday, so he won't come.'

At the table his father had some good news about the redundancy he was facing. There was a strong possibility that the new company would take on some of the old staff, however, it would not be in six months time but as early as next month.

The doctor examined Harry thoroughly and ordered tests immediately. Harry had already explained that he was in the Army and had been abroad building roads and general duties, but nothing about the nuclear tests. He was scared stiff that he may have been exposed to nuclear radiation and in any case there would be nothing the doctor could do, it was too late. His nerves had been shot to pieces on two occasions and now it had caught up with him.

'Are you sure there is nothing else you would like to tell me? I mean, what you are telling me doesn't seem to be that unusual, so perhaps you could tell me where you have been, it would help a great deal?

Harry prevaricated once more, which seemed to be trying the doctor's patience.

'Okay, it seems obvious that you have no intention of telling me what you have been up to in the last eighteen months, or where you have been, so take this prescription and I would like to see you in a week's time.'

Harry settled for that, but still felt dreadful knowing he had misled the doctor, which might have been a big mistake.

Meeting his mother for a coffee cheered him up, but he was reminded the next step was to replace those ridiculous baggy trousers. After picking up his medication they took a bus home. His mother was anxious to find out what sort of medication he was to take, but ended up none the wiser. Harry took his pills with an excellent cup of tea. It was not long before he looked for his bed feeling completely tired out.

That evening his mother answered the phone. It was Ginger Markham for Harry, but nothing could wake him. His mother shouted for him to come down, but it was no use, which left Ginger a little worried and saying he would phone again. No sooner had his mother put the phone down than it rang again. This time it was a lady's voice asking for Harry.

'Is that Helen?'

'Yes, hello Mrs Watkins, it's nice to speak to you.'

Harry's mother was delighted and relieved that Helen had called. She explained that Harry had been to the doctor and had been put on medication. Helen asked for details after explaining that she was a nurse. She was not surprised Harry was fast asleep and was careful not to upset his mother by saying he must rest and drink plenty.

'If it's okay with you, I would like to come over to see him and meet you all at the same time.'

'That's a splendid idea, Helen, you can stay as long as you like, I am sure the others will welcome you like the flowers in May.'

Helen was a little emotional when she saw Harry lying there. The medication had sent him into a deep sleep. Leaning over him she kissed him and touched his face. She had brought with her plenty of fruit and a bottle of orange squash.

'Come on down when you are ready, my dear, and I will make you a cup of tea.'

Helen once again reassured Harry's mother that it was perfectly normal for him to sleep and that after a few days he would be himself once more.

'To be honest, I think he has overdone things in the past, even though he has youth on his side, eventually the body has to rest. I also think he is not telling us everything that has been going on during the last year. Whatever it was, it has unsettled him to the point where now and again he just stares into space. What he can see there is anybody's guess, but whatever, the rest will do him the power of good and time is a great healer.'

Harry's mother pointed out that the island Harry had been working on was used to test nuclear bombs; Helen had been completely unaware of this.

'He has never said a word about it, but we know since it was all in the papers. It said Britain had tested a massive bomb. His father is very angry about it. It seems he knew somebody whose son was in Australia during the nuclear tests and his son became very ill. What happened there I don't know, and of course I am very worried about my son, but you have been a great help to me, you have no idea.'

'Can I see him before I go, Mrs Watkins, I am on duty this evening?'

'Call me Doris, please, and of course you can, perhaps you would take a glass of water up for him?'

Harry was still asleep as Helen placed the water ready for him. She sat down beside him and kissed him. For just a moment he seemed to come back into the land of the living. He looked at her and smiled and tried to lift his head, but the medication just would not let him reach her. She kissed him again, but this time her emotions were getting the better of her and so she left. Before leaving she made arrangements with Doris to come over on the Wednesday, but would phone first.

'I have two days off, so with your permission, I would like to be with him all day, please Doris.'

'I can do better than that my dear, you can stay here for as long as you want.'

Harry finally came back to life with a great deal of help from his very attractive nurse who at times even exceeded the wrath of the disciplinarians in the Army, but of course unlike the Army there were rewards for good behaviour. Feeling a hundred percent better he was signed off by the doctor who recommended he report to his Army doctor.

Harry thought that he might call in to his old work place and catch up on a few things, but he was to be disappointed. Nothing stays the same, even his boss had been replaced and nobody was that interested anymore. Well, that said it all to

Harry, he was even more determined to pursue his idea of starting his own business.

Back home and with time running out before returning to the Army he sat down and thought long and hard as to his future. Ginger would be a key part in his plans and he thought he would try and contact him until his mother told him that a Ginger Markham had already phoned.

'He left a phone number and said he would phone back. What did the doctor say?'

'Not much, Mum, he told me the results were okay and thought it would be a good idea to see a doctor when I went back to the Army.'

'Yes, and what else did he have to say? Did you tell him what has been going on out there on the island? You still look washed out and if things don't improve I will personally write to the Army and give them a piece of my mind.'

Harry had to smile and tried to change the subject.

'What did you think of Helen?' He had to shout as she was making a pot of tea.

Coming back into the room she placed the tray on the table and once again reminded Harry that she was serious about writing to his commanding officer and giving him a piece of her mind. His mother went on a bit and in a way she was right, but it would be like writing to a brick wall.

'And in any case, Mum, he almost certainly worked just as hard and may not have fared any better than me. You didn't answer my question, what did you think of Helen?'

'She's a lovely girl, Harry, and I must say she's very caring. I mean all those things on your table are from her. She was so nice to me, I have invited her to stay here for as long as she likes. I think she said she would be here Wednesday morning so she will be able to meet your father and the boys.'

'Here is a letter for you, come on now, it's getting late, Helen will be here any minute and don't wear those stupid trousers.'

Harry opened his letter hoping it would be news of his posting and that it was close to home. It was. He gave his mother a big hug and said, 'At last my luck is changing, I reckon I might be home weekends, and with a week's leave to come the next six months will go like smoke.'

The doorbell sounded and sure enough Helen was at the door looking as pretty as ever. She melted into Harry's arms and then wanted to look at him.

'How do you feel now and what did the doctor say? You shouldn't be outside, you haven't got enough on, you could catch a chill. Where is your mother?'

Harry felt like he was already back in the Army. One sergeant major was one thing, but two was ridiculous. With his mother nagging and now Helen, he was being attacked from both sides, he needed reinforcements but they would not be here for several hours.

Having taken the last of his medication he felt well enough to ask Helen if she would go out to granddad's place, but his mother intervened.

'Look here, my girl, you have just finished a night shift, now you just sit down with this cup of tea and talk to Harry while I make up a bed for you. Perhaps you could go to Harry's granddad's this evening, or better still go there tomorrow if it's a nice day.'

'She's a real dear, you are lucky to have such a nice mum,' said Helen in a whisper to Harry.

'That reminds me, you haven't mentioned your parents, do they live far?'

'I never knew my father, he didn't come back from the war.'

My mother has never explained things to me, even when I have asked her. All she said was that he never returned home and that there was never much between them.'

Harry found it difficult to understand. If he was killed during the war then her mother would have received an official notification of his death, or at least a missing presumed dead. On the other hand, her parents may not have married, in which case there would have been no official communication. Helen went on to say that her mother was married and had two sons, but she rarely visited them.

'I haven't seen any of them for the last three years I think, and to be honest, I never want to see my step-father again.'

Harry thought it best not to pursue the subject any further unless she wanted to. He did not want to make things more difficult for her, but he wondered why she was so quick to ingratiate herself with his own family. After all, they had not known each other that long, not that he was complaining, it was quite the opposite, he was lucky to have such a lovely girl. He thought he would ask just one question while trying not to hurt her feelings any more. Maybe she could use some help.

'Helen, has it ever occurred to you that your father may be still alive, I mean I don't want to interfere but——'

Helen swung round and gave Harry a look that frightened the life out of him. She just looked at him for a moment and then started to cry bitterly.

'I know he's alive, but my mother refuses to tell me his name. Well, I am not absolutely sure, but I have done everything to find out. Quite honestly, I have got nowhere and then you come along and say you will help me, I mean what can you do that I can't?'

Harry knew it was wrong of him to interfere in a very delicate matter, but his feelings had got the better of him and now he found himself in a hole. He was saved by the bell with his mother entering the room saying that Helen's room was ready.

'Come on, you must rest, you can't go on like this or I will have another one to worry about.'

'Thank you, Mrs Watkins, I am grateful to you.'

'Sleep well and rest assured there will be a cup of tea and a nice meal for you later. If you sleep on then don't worry, you will feel better tomorrow.'

Harry's mother knew she had been crying, but chose to say nothing, thinking that Harry may have had something to do with it. Come on, we are going for a walk. Harry felt like saluting; there was no point going back to the Army, he was already there.

The evening went brilliantly with Harry's father making a real fuss of Helen. His brothers could hardly get a word in, when they did, one wanted her to go and see him fly an aeroplane and the other wanted her to watch him play football.

The sofa became Harry's bed for the night with the radio for company. Suddenly, the door opened with Helen standing there in her dressing gown.

'Hello, baggy pants, I just thought I would say goodnight, your mum said we could have five minutes together.'

'Gosh, that's more than enough time, if you see what I mean,' said Harry.

'In your dreams, Baggy, and how dare you make a suggestion like that.'

'I have no idea what you mean, my little dove, and in any case, come and sit next to me, I have something to tell you.'

'I am not sure you can behave yourself, but just this once, okay.'

'Look, I have become extremely fond of you and with all

the good you have done for me, to be honest, it would be difficult to know how to thank you. Now I know where I am going to spend my last six months in the Army I have been wondering if you might pick me up at weekends, but only if it's convenient, it's not far and I can always use the train. Secondly, I wondered if you would like to visit granddad's tomorrow. Maybe we could take a picnic? And, finally, I am sorry that I upset you this morning. My intentions were entirely honourable, as they are now,' he said, taking hold of her hand.

This was the news Helen was waiting for, it all sounded too good to be true. As for upsetting her, she pointed out to him that her lack of sleep had got the better of her. She was mindful of his kind offer and then she got really close to him and whispered in his ear, kissed him goodnight, jumped up, and said softly, 'See you in the morning, my love.'

The next day was their last full day with each other and they planned to make the most of it. Time was running out for both of them. Helen had to return that evening and next Monday Harry was due back in the Army. Helen was looking forward to going bird watching but Harry had other plans, among them was to take a good look at the possibility of using granddad's place as a base for his business plans.

The weather was mixed, but was warm enough for Helen to go exploring on her own. Harry had brought with him drawing materials as he wanted to sketch out the land and the position of the main road, which was adjacent to one of the fields.

'Lunch in two hours, dear,' said Helen and off she went.

'Watch out for the big bad wolf, he sometimes jumps out and chases you around the field if your not careful,' shouted Harry.

'The only wolf around here wears funny trousers and I can handle him, he couldn't catch me if he tried.'

Harry had just about completed a plan of the area he was interested in. In the future he would complete the whole property. He went to find Helen who was preparing their picnic. She spotted a heron flying close to the stream, it landed giving Helen a first class view. Helen pointed it out to Harry.

'What else have you seen my love?'

Harry was surprised at the list she had made, including a bullfinch, maybe a kingfisher, and a bad, old, ugly wolf. Harry thought that was a tall story and said that he had seen a very beautiful bird flying through his granddad's garden.

'Oh, what do you think it was, Harry?' She was quite excited.

'Well, it was very pretty and I just couldn't take my eyes off her, you see it was a hen. Her feathers looked a little ruffled, but there you are you, can't expect her to look her best all the time can you? I have to tell you, I fell in love with her the first time I saw her.'

'And when was that?' she asked.

'Some time ago when my granddad was unwell, I saw her flying around the ward with her feathers a little ruffled. I thought she was going to peck me.'

'Your lucky she didn't do more than peck you, but the funny thing was this little bird felt the same way as you did. There was nothing that could be done at the time, but now we can make up for it.'

Helen just laid back on the ground there as happy as could be. Harry looked at her thinking he would never forget this day as long as he lived. In his mind he thought of Ted, who may well have been in a similar position before he left for the island, only then to be deserted with no explanation at all.

How would he have coped with that? Just looking at Helen said it all, he realised what Ted must have gone through knowing there was nothing he could do about it. Only now did he fully understood and found it as no surprise that Ted had nearly lost his mind by taking to drink.

Helen woke up and found Harry still looking at her.

'Good grief, what is the time? I have been asleep for two hours, why didn't you wake me? I have lots to tell you before you leave.'

'If it's not important then it can wait,' replied Harry.

'Yes, it's very important my love, I am not just here as a nurse for you, I have very deep feelings for you and I think you feel the same way about me, but I want you to know that you must be very careful with your health. Please don't under estimate what the doctor has advised you, and you can rest assured I will be watching you very carefully. I have no idea what you have told the doctor and quite frankly I wish you would explain to me what really happened. I mean you were near to a nervous breakdown and from now on I will be looking after you. Don't say anything you don't want to, but remember I love you dearly and, yes, I will make every effort to pick you up on the weekends.'

'You know you sound just like the sergeant major? However much you dislike being told what to do, the sergeant major and his disciplinarians will shout orders at you until it sinks in, but you begin to realise that they will always be there when you need them. Yes, I have learnt quite a lot in the Army. One day I might explain what happened, but in the meantime, while I am away, perhaps you would like to come out here and do some bird watching.'

'That would be fabulous, but what would your father say knowing I was walking all over his land?'

'He wouldn't say a word, believe me, and in any case the whole place belongs to me. I am not that happy about it, but dad feels he is happy where they live. He simply wouldn't be able to manage so it's down to me and my appointed estate manager.'

'And who might that be?' Helen asked, smiling all over her face.

'Oh, somebody pretty wild. Just one look at her and any intruder would run a mile.'

'That leaves me out then, but maybe I will apply for the position.'

Helen remained silent for a while, she just stared into space and then said, 'So it's Lord Watkins's estate, managed by Nurse Riordan, I just can't believe you have done this for me.'

She was so overjoyed she turned and held onto Harry, saying that however much she was enjoying herself, time was running out. They locked up the house leaving it ready for their first available weekend.

'We will hide the key under that stone at the back of the shed. Next time I will have another key cut just for you.'

'If you like, I will have a key cut this week and, in any case, who is the estate manager, my lord?'

Harry tried to chase her back to the car, but he realised Helen was right: his health was still not that good, all his energy had deserted him.

It was difficult to come to terms with seeing her leave, he had never had such fun, but he had much to think about. The plan he had drawn showed that there would be plenty of room for what he had in mind for his business.

Lying in bed that night, he suddenly thought of Ted and Ginger. He must call Ginger and find out where he had been posted. As for Ted, he had exams to sit, all arranged by his sister. Harry just hoped that Ted's health was a lot better than his own.

* * *

Ted's sister had wasted no time, she had already made arrangements for him to sit the most important exam of his life. Although under extreme pressure, Ted had hardly ever given up on his studies of the law. Even at home on leave his sister kept up the pressure. The exam was very difficult and he had to admit it was touch and go. His parents were proud of him nonetheless, but had serious doubts as to the state of his health considering the enormous pressures placed upon him during the last year. Youth being on his side, he coped well, but his sister was still puzzled as to why his girlfriend had abandoned him. Ted, on the other hand, failed to understand why, being divorced herself with a little daughter, she should want him to pursue what would be nothing more than a lost cause. She was a workaholic and bossy, which Ted had often thought was the reason why her husband had run off. Maybe that was just one reason among others which were of no concern of his, much the same as it was no concern of hers what he did. It seemed to make very little difference though; she would not let him alone and kept asking about Penny.

'Look, Christine, why are you being so inquisitive about my past, surely you have enough to think about? I would much prefer to forget the past and spend some time with my gorgeous little niece.'

'Well, that's really nice, Ted, and I appreciate that, but ever since you have been home you have looked miles away.'

Ted snapped back, 'Look, I am no longer interested, just leave it, and besides you have no idea what I have been through. Okay, I may have been miles away at times, and it is still in my head—I can't shake it off. But I just want to forget yet I can't, so please get off my back, Christine.'

Ted left slamming the door. He had simply had enough. Maybe he would go for a walk and think things through. He had very little time left before returning to his new posting. It would be great to meet up with his pals once more, at least they would understand, and then after the Army he would find another place to live, well away from interfering sisters who, in all fairness, did not understand what had happened to him.

Ted walked on until his conscience got the better of him, perhaps he should listen to his sister a bit more, she had given him a lot of support while he was on the island. Without her help he most certainly would not have been able to take his exams so soon after returning from the island.

Back at his parents house, his mother was as pleased as ever to see him. No sooner than they had sat down for dinner, Christine turned up. As usual, she was bossing everybody about.

'Oh, you're back are you, calmed down have we? You are just like a spoilt brat with little or no sense of responsibility. In future you can sort out your own arrangements. What's so frustrating with you is that it's your kind that leave all your responsibilities behind you, go abroad and enjoy yourself without little or no concern for what you may have done.'

'What the hell are you talking about? I haven't done anything. Who the hell do you think you are, flinging around wild accusations, you know what your trouble is, you're a frustrated old———'

That was it, their mother intervened, his father walked outside looking rather stern. Everybody had left the table, which displeased Ted's mother immensely.

'Christine, in the sitting room, now. Ted, you stay where you are.'

By now Ted was fed up with his sister and her bossy ways, but what on earth was she trying to say? He couldn't for the love of might understand any of her gibberish nonsense. He decided on another walk, this time a long one. As he walked past his sister's car he noticed she had left her daughter unattended. She was so full of herself telling everybody else their business that she had forgotten her own daughter was still in the car. Ted carried her in and said calmly, 'I think you should know that I found this gorgeous little girl in your car.'

'Good grief, Christine, what on earth do you think you are doing,' her mother shouted.

With that Ted found his dad in the garden.

'Come on, Dad, let's have a pint down the pub before the Army grabs hold of me again.'

'Good idea, son, let's get some peace.'

It was a fine morning that Ted made his way to work for the last time before returning to the Army. The rain came down heavily, but he arrived at his sister's estate office to see her on her knees cleaning the floor. He was ultra careful not to dirty the floor again and made his way to his desk. Why on earth she had to clean the floor like that was her affair. Money, on the other hand, was tight as the initial outlay to set up the business had cost her a small fortune.

'Look, Ted, I would like to talk to you please.'

'Fill in the appropriate application form please, madam, and I will give it my full attention this time next year. I can't do better than that, and by the way, I have tendered my resignation as of from today.'

'Please, Ted, I am truly sorry for what I said. Mum has read the riot act to me, I don't know what came over me, leaving Sophie like that. I was so scared at what I had done and I will be forever grateful to you. Dad has given me a very rare ticking off and you know how soft he is. Ted, I had no idea what went on out on that island, but Dad has told me. They are quite rightly very worried, as I am. What really happened, how did you all cope, it must have been hell for you? Please, I really am sorry.'

She was in a terrible state, crying and shaking like a leaf. Still on her knees, Ted reached for her and comforted her. She held on to him still crying and said, 'If any harm comes to you then whoever was responsible will have me to answer to.'

Yes, thought Ted, it would be interesting to see anyone incurring the wrath of his sister, but it seems she had not finished talking to him.

She sat down, looking a sorry state and hardly in a state to receive a potential customer.

'Come on, funny face, you can't meet customers looking like a dragon, go and put your face on and I will mind the customers. I will receive the first customer with a smart salute, 'Stand by your bed with your boots in your hands, sir, what can I do for you? And stand up straight when you're talking to me you insolent man.'

'Shouldn't you be holding *your* boots in——'

'Yes, yes, funny face, go on, push off before I really get into the Army mood. We can talk later, whatever it is you want to tell me, perhaps over a nice cup of tea?'

Christine came back into the room with a nice smile. Ted reminded her of an appointment in half an hour.

'Will have that tea with me later?' she said as she ran out the door.

In all fairness, Christine's hard work seemed to be paying off with several potential customers making enquiries and fixing appointments. Ted thought to himself, only a few weeks ago he and his mates were going through a living hell. It was very difficult not to think of what had happened since it was on his mind constantly. His nerves were still trying to recover, even when he tried to write down the details of customers his hand shook so badly that he had to make the excuse that he had sprained his wrist. I need a drink, he was thinking, but it was not the answer.

For once he was glad to see his sister return.

'I will put the kettle on, how did you get on?'

'Not bad at all, I think they will buy. They will confirm on Monday. How have you coped?'

'Quite frankly, you are going to be a very busy girl next week and at this rate there is no way you can cope without help. I tell you what, let's sort out the paperwork now, even if it means coming in tomorrow.'

'But I thought you had resigned?'

'Ah, yes, but due to unforeseen circumstances I have decided to withdraw my letter. I tell you what, sis, if we start the paperwork now you can take me, Mum and dad out for fish and chips tonight. You can take the money out of my wages, how about that?'

'You can't do that, I mean you don't have much money as it is. What have I done to deserve such a wonderful brother? No, Ted, you need all the money you can get.'

'Tell you what, we will go halves, that's fair, okay?'

Ted was adamant and Christine was also determined to explain what she knew about Penny, even though he may no longer be interested. The last thing she wanted to do was to upset him, but it was a chance she was prepared to take.

The look on his face told her that his mind was troubled in some way or another. Maybe it was the dreadful experience of having to witness the explosion of those terrifying nuclear bombs, but Christine suspected that he was still troubled by the sudden loss of Penny, even though he persisted in saying that he was over her.

Christine chose her time carefully; it was time to close the office, even though there was still work to be done.

'Ted, please tell me to mind my own business if you like, but can I talk to you about something which has given me a great deal of trouble, and I have often felt worried about it.'

'What are you trying to say, Christine? I mean you are babbling on about nothing at the moment, just get to the point and if I can help then you know I will.

'Well, Ted, I think I have already told you in one of my letters that I tried to find Penny.

'Oh come on, Chris, that was a long time ago, and to be honest, that's all behind me now. Why bring all this up again?'

'I have to tell you that I think I have found her, well, I have not seen her myself, but I have found somebody who has.'

'Has what? I mean this is ridiculous, it could be they were mistaken; it could be anybody. If I were you I would forget the whole idea, and in any case, I am back to my reluctant duties on Monday.

'I wonder what else they have up their sleeves to making my life a perfect misery. You have to understand, Penny, sorry I mean Christine, I feel like a fish out of water. Some of the others, on the other hand, have learnt new skills, but quite frankly I can't see myself ever taking up lorry driving, I simply don't have that sort of skill, or any interest in it.

Instead, I find myself driving to hell and back. We all got our fingers burnt, if you see what I mean. Perhaps you don't understand, and to be honest with you, it's just as well if you don't.'

'I really am sorry, but try and look on the bright side, I can't imagine what you have been put through, but I really am trying to help you. Please try and understand.'

'Understand what? You haven't said anything that has convinced me of anything yet.'

Christine knew the mystery of Penny was still on his mind, although he refused to admit it.

'I happen to know it *was* Penny, this person told me, she used to work with her. She was pregnant, and by now she would have had the baby.'

'So what's that to do with me? I mean if I am the father why on earth didn't she write to me? No, Chris, I'm not the father, otherwise she would have written and told me.' Christine, however, was not entirely convinced, the only plan of action now was to leave the whole messy affair to rest.

Ted suddenly had more to think about; maybe he was the father and maybe her parents had found out that he was the culprit. Maybe Christine was right, perhaps he should find out for himself, but in the meantime he was due back in the Army. There were too many unanswered questions, so why worry now? Perhaps one weekend he might go to see the old place, and who knows, he might meet Penny again. He decided to keep this idea to himself.

That evening it was pleasant having the company of his family. Christine had simmered down somewhat and was pleasant company for a change.

'Christine, you will have to recruit some help in the office, there's no way you can cope, for a start why don't you try an agency?'

Her parents agreed and her father tried to go one further by mentioning that maybe all this hard work had caused her to be so difficult.

'You have been nothing but a pain in the backside, young lady, Ted's right, you need help.'

'Now, now come on all of you, we have enjoyed this evening, so don't lets have another row. Shall we go and have a pleasant drink at the King's Head?'

'Excellent idea, Mum,' said Ted having a flashback of the Gladiator's Arms.

It was not only his sister who had problems, he had his own. Was it the excessive drinking that was causing his hands to shake so badly, or what he had witnessed? The loss of Penny certainly didn't help, and without doubt had led him to drink in the first place. Then he came face to face with nuclear weapons, which left him with a memory that would take time to heal. First bitter disappointment, then the dreadful memory of the bomb. Ted had to make up his troubled mind and maybe finding Penny would be the answer.

13. MATES FOR LIFE

Ted felt sure he might catch a glimpse of some of the other lads on the way to the camp, but it was not until he got off the train that he saw Brian and Pete walking in front of him.

'Hey you couple of scruffy, good-for-nothing, big, useless twits, get your shoulders back,' Ted shouted.

They halted fearing the worst, but then they saw Ted. There faces said it all: blimey, it's our Ted the lawyer.

Pete was now married and the baby was his world. Brian, on the other hand, had fallen out with his girlfriend, but he was delighted at being godfather to Pete's daughter.

'How about you, Ted, did you find Snow White?'

'As a matter of fact, I did, but I'm afraid——'

'Don't tell us you let her get away?' said Brian.

'It's a long story boys, will explain later.'

Transport was laid on to take them to their new camp where it seemed that most of the lads knew each other. Many of them were ex-members of Operation Grapple, but it was soon discovered that one or two were missing. For starters, where were Ginger and the others?

The camp was huge, with tanks and all sorts of heavy transport. There was no shouting, or maybe not as aggressive as before. They were allocated hut numbers, bedding and instructions for their daily routine. Work started early, but all Ted was interested in was whether he could go home for weekends. Well his luck was in, it seemed that for most weekends it would be in order for them to go home so long as they were ready for duty first thing on Monday morning. What time you would be released on Friday afternoon was very much up to the company commander, who turned out to be the same officer as they had had on the island. Ted, of course, had already met his acquaintance when he was put on a charge, so it would be prudent for him to lay low for a while.

'I would love to have a go on one of those tanks,' said Brian.

'No chance,' said a voice from behind.

It was Gary and Harry looking a lot better than the last time Brian had seen them.

They greeted each other as if they had not seen each other for years.

'Anybody seen Ginger or Alf ?' asked Ted. Nobody had.

'Perhaps they have been deployed elsewhere on this massive camp, or maybe another camp, who knows?' said Pete.

Harry felt more relaxed, especially meeting up with his pals again, but he was disappointed on not seeing Ginger. He needed Ginger as a partner in this business venture and he realised it was all his own fault for not returning Ginger's call back home.

With very little to do until the next day, Harry laid on his bed thinking of all the support he had had from his family and the gift of meeting Helen. Without Helen's loving care, he felt sure his health would have taken a turn for the worse. As it was, Helen's professional nursing skills had without doubt helped him through a very difficult time. He had fallen in love with her and for the first time in his life he felt sure he was heading in the right direction. He was determined to start his own business and he wanted Helen to be part of it. He had also found his little white bird again and given her the freedom of his granddad's garden. Her life had been a difficult one, based on what she had told him. Starting life on her own and learning the many skills required for nursing was indeed a wonderful achievement, but coupled with the fact that she had little or no family, it must have been a lonely experience. She had managed life on her own, but now she had chosen him for perhaps her life-long friend. He had not realised until now how lucky he was and how much he already missed her.

Feeling homesick, he wondered if any of the lads fancied a pint—maybe Ginger and Alf would be there.

Not surprisingly, Pete declined: bringing up a family had cleaned out his pockets; but Brian insisted, along with the rest of the lads. The idea being to wet the baby's head.

When they got to the bar the conversation started up again.

'By the way, Gary, how's Megan?' asked Harry.

'She's making good progress thanks, in fact I think I must have pushed her the length of north Wales. She can just about stand and walk a few steps. We hope by the time I get out of the Army she will have made a full recovery, well almost, fingers crossed, which reminds me I owe an awful lot to you Brian, or was it Pete, for sorting me out on the island. I was finding it a tough place and then that letter arrived. I couldn't take too much more, especially with what they had asked us to do.'

Brian interrupted Gary by saying that it was Ginger who had helped him, in fact Ginger had held them all together.

'Yes, I agree,' said Ted.

'I have to admit I would have fallen to pieces had it not been for Ginger. Perhaps none of you know of his own problems. At the time, of course, it was strictly confidential, but now I can tell you, he was going through divorce proceedings. He asked for my help dealing with the papers and so on. I have to say it hurt him a great deal. Having said that, he found time to help me with my ridiculous folly. My foolishness—recklessness, call it what you like—lead me into hell in more ways than one. You know nobody gave a damn when we came home? It was just get on with your life of uncertainty.'

Everybody agreed with that statement, nobody had been interested.

'Just a moment, Ted,' asked Pete. 'What do you mean by saying a ridiculous folly? You certainly bottled everything up while on the island, you had us all worried, was it all to do with that girl and the thrashing you got back in training?'

'You could say that, in fact, according to my lunatic sister, she's pregnant, or let's say she was.'

Everybody laughed and congratulated him.

'Hey, just a minute, you're just as batty as my sister. For starters, it could well be my sister has got it wrong, and for another thing why didn't she write to me? No, it's nothing to do with me.'

'Men in your position always say that, Ted. Well, if it's not you, then whose is it?' said Pete.

'How should I know? You're all jumping to conclusions, and in any case, none of you know what happened before we left for twelve months hard labour.'

'You should say what you mean, after all, you spent many hours in the Gladiator's Arms trying to forget. So, come on, there's no smoke without fire as they say.'

'Oh, I mean what I say, it's nothing to do with me. The girl I knew was obviously just after my money,' he said with grin.

'But, of course, we all know that, but what else was she after?' said Brian.

By now everybody was in stitches of laughter, even though the feeling of being let down was mutual. Nevertheless, he saw the funny side of it all.

'By the way lads, there is something I haven't told you and then perhaps you will understand my odd behaviour. This girl I was going out with was the colonel's daughter. While they were away the cat will play as they say.' Everybody was absolutely taken aback by Ted's bravery, or lunacy, and nobody said a word until Pete spoke up.

'Ted, are you seriously telling us that you were seeing a colonel's daughter?'

'Absolutely, old chap, and what's more, you ate a slice of her cake she made for me, remember?'

'Well, I must say you have guts, and good luck to you.'

'Hey, just a minute, you said that as if I was still involved.'

'You are, Ted, right up to your neck, come on, we think you should do the honourable thing by marrying the girl without delay.'

Ted nearly choked on his beer.

'Oh I see, perhaps I should ingratiate myself at the colonel's house by introducing myself as Sapper Watson. "How nice to see you Colonel, I hope you don't mind, but I was wondering if your daughter would like to come out to play?"

'Can you imagine the response, asking him if his daughter would like to come out to play? "But of course, Ted, come on in, can I offer you a drink?" Shouting up the stairs, "Oh darling, Teddy has come to play with you." Come off it, Pete, I may look daft, but I'm not—or that brave.'

'Well you seem to live dangerously, what with the colonel's daughter and then nuclear bombs, I am quite sure I would not like to be in your shoes. I mean, it must be like being between the devil and the deep blue sea, or like jumping out of the pan and into the fire. It's a pity you chose the wrong island.'

'You could say that again,' Ted said with a groan.

'Anyhow, as I said, you have guts, so let's see if you can do the honourable thing by going to the colonel's house and asking for his daughter's hand. What do you say, lads? We shall read the papers with interest: solicitor in shotgun wedding with colonel's daughter, read all about it.'

The decision was unanimous, he was to go public and marry the girl as soon as possible with invitations all round. The drinks are on Ted they shouted, laughing until the manager came over to quiet things down a bit. It was just like being in the Gladiator's Arms again. However, Ted was far from amused.

'Very funny, I would rather be handcuffed to a bear,' he said, having to laugh in spite of himself.

It was all Ted's own fault really, he should have known the lads would rib him, and in any case, he would do the same to them if he had had the chance.

Harry leaned across to Ted and said, 'I am sure you already know that all this taking the mickey is just a bit of fun, but seriously, they all wish you well with your exams. The pressure must be enormous on top of the loss of Penny. Go and find her, Ted, release yourself from this mystery. After all, Penny is still one of the team and we want her back, if only to thank her for the cake. We have both lost girlfriends on the way, in my case it was hopeless, but you still have a chance, so go and do your investigations. Or we will do them for you: I think a little visit to the colonel's house would be in order, what do you say lads?'

'So long as you go first, Harry, we will be right behind you,' said Brian.

'No, that's enough, I give in,' replied Ted nervously.

That was the sort of thing they would do, although they obviously would not really knock on the colonel's door, but they would find Penny somehow or other, so he capitulated to their blackmail and agreed to find Penny.

'Look, Ted, I have got myself into a somewhat similar situation,' said Harry. 'You remember the nurse I was writing to? Well it turns out that she is absolutely wonderful and after only a few days I am a little in love with her.

'She made me see a doctor and I guess she was right. I still don't feel that well, and what's more my hair is nowhere near as thick as it used to be. At the rate I am loosing it, I will be bald as a badger before leaving the Army.'

'I can see that, Harry, but you never know, it might grow back again, so in the meantime why don't you have a short haircut. You ask some of the others, they all seem to have problems like skin complaints, for example. Look at the state of my skin? It's early days, but I have to say I am worried for all of us.'

The banter soon ran out of steam, it was now the turn of Harry, who was still concerned as to the whereabouts of Ginger and Alf. They all agreed that somehow it did not feel the same without them. Harry explained that it was all his fault for not returning Ginger's phone call. Nevertheless, he would find him, come what may, since there was no way he could ever think of starting his business venture without Ginger.

'The sad reality of all this is that in just a few weeks' time it will all be over. In spite of what we have all been through, I suspect the moment the gates are opened many of us will never see each other again. It will be just another chapter in our life here on earth as Ginger would say.'

'Well, I hope you are wrong there, Harry, but I have to say I think you are right,' said Brian.

Later on, Harry checked his own skin and found no signs as far as he could tell, but the idea of having his hair cut very short seemed to be worth a try.

It seemed to be a little more relaxed than their training days. Reporting for duty they were told that their duties would mainly be driving tank transporters, but first they would be on building projects, which suited Harry. This was his real chance of finding out if he could master the skills required for his ideas.

Weekend passes would be granted from sometime on Friday afternoon, reporting for duty first thing Monday morning. There would also be a further two weeks leave during August. That cheerful note was all they needed to arrange their return to civilian life once more. Gary, though, was having trouble trying to sort out a route home until Brian showed him his map.

'It's not that bad, Gary, I reckon you could reach home way before midnight. It all depends on when we are released on Friday afternoon. You will be home with Megan late Friday, all day Saturday, and if you can meet me at Church Stretton station sometime Sunday afternoon, say about five o'clock, then I will give you a lift back to camp on my motorbike, how about that?'

The others had already worked out their train times, including Harry who decided that maybe it would be unfair to ask Helen to drive after a night shift, a quick phone call would suffice to tell her he would be home Friday evening.

They were soon put to work, but there seemed to be no great urgency, all they were given was labouring jobs for the first week. The days dragged on and Harry was not best pleased and tried to make a complaint, but it fell on deaf ears. He was really keen to start work using the plant machinery which came to the ear of one of the NCOs.

'You haven't got the experience we need on this job, sapper, but your enthusiasm has been noted,' said the sergeant.

Harry would not give up since his experience was more than enough. He could complete this job with his eyes shut.

'Sergeant, can I just say I have just spent the last twelve months building roads, foundations, and even a runway for the Airforce.'

'Have you now, well in that case, we shall see what you can do starting Monday. Report to me first, okay? And by the way, you can all go home for the weekend as of from now.'

You couldn't see them for dust, with Gary and Brian out of the starting blocks first. They thumbed a lift with no trouble at all straight to Ross-on-Wye. All they needed now was a lift heading north to Shrewsbury and the A5.

It was just gone six when a smart looking car pulled up.

'I'm going to Church Stretton, any good?'

'I say it is, many thanks,' said Brian and was in like a greyhound.

Brian introduced Gary, who for some unknown reason was a little shy.

'My friend here is heading for the A5. The driver smiled and introduced himself as Max. 'Been in long, lads?'

'Too long,' said Brian who went on to say that they were reluctant national servicemen with five months left to do.

Max laughed and said he had finished his time about three years ago.

'I took a short term commission in the Army and I must say I had mixed feelings about it before going in, but I have to say I got off lightly with decent postings, so I know how you feel. Have you been anywhere decent?'

Brian explained the dreadful experience they had been

through and that it was still indelible on their minds, maybe
for a lifetime.

'I still can't get it out of my head, I just see this massive fire
ball and I can hear the noise ringing in my head. The heat put
a rash on the back of my neck.'

'I'm sorry, Brian, I must correct what I said: no, I don't
know what you have been through, and I hope to God I never
do. Brian, what do you know about cars, I mean have you got
a car?'

'If I had a car, Max, I wouldn't be in this magnificent car.
No, I am the proud owner of a motorbike and I am just about
ready to fix the engine and hopefully then I will be able to take
Gary back to camp on Sunday. Thanks to you and your lift I
can start working on the engine this evening. The girlfriend
nearly gave me the push after the bike broke down miles from
nowhere.'

Max laughed and said he had been down that road himself.

The car drove effortlessly to Church Stretton and soon they
were pulling into a drive with a large house. Brian and Gary
got out, but Max told Gary to get back in the front seat.

'I just want to explain to my wife that I am taking Gary to
the A5 and before you go, Brian, here's my card. As you can
see, I am a senior sales manager. If you are interested, give
me a ring anytime, that's if you are not already fixed up. I sell
these cars for a very big company and perhaps you might be
interested in joining us as a sales rep, it's up to you, just give
me a ring.'

'Yes I will think about it,' said Brian. It sounded too good
to be true. Brian shouted out to Gary, 'Try and fix yourself up
with a helmet and have a great time, see you Sunday.'

Sunday soon came around. Ted was the first one in, but then

his weekend had not been that pleasant, what with all day Saturday spent working for his sister. His mother was not enjoying the best of health, leaving his father looking after her. His sister was busy all day Sunday, so he returned to camp for a quiet pint in the NAAFI. Brian and Gary were back in time to join him and for Gary to buy both of them a pint.

'I really enjoyed the ride back on your bike said Gary to Brian. 'Hopefully you could give me a lift again next time? I will pay for the petrol.'

'We will see about that and next time I will drop you off on the A5.'

'By the way, Brian, what did you make of that bloke in the posh car. Quite frankly, I wouldn't trust him further than you could throw him.'

'Fancied you did he?' said Brian laughing with Ted.

'He's married and in any case you saw his wife,' said Gary who was having none of it.

'What difference does that make? And in any case that may have been his sister,' replied Brian.

'Well, it certainly wasn't his mother,' said Gary, who was still laughing.

'Don't worry, mate, I have no intention of becoming one of his reps, I have my own plans, thank you very much.'

'And what's that?' asked Ted.

'Selling motorbikes,' replied Brian.

On Monday morning the lads started work early, taking the sergeant by surprise.

'Okay, Sapper Watkins, lets see what you can do.'

They studied the plans carefully enough to figure out what needed to be done. Harry was away and hardly stopped for a break.

'Blimey, he's keen, where has he learnt that? He's almost done a day's work already,' remarked the sergeant.

'Most of us are ex-Christmas Island, sergeant, and to be honest we are still there, it's still in our heads. I can't forget what I was ordered to do, none of us can,' said Pete.

Pete was still talking to the sergeant when the captain turned up with a set of plans. He was looking straight at Harry and remarked that at this rate the job would be done in half the time.

'I know these lads, sergeant, well almost everyone of them. He turned to Pete and shook his hand, how are you sapper, how's the baby? I must say you are looking a little tired and I must say I feel the same. They keep you up all night; sometimes I feel I would rather be back on the island, but then, with hindsight, I think not.'

Pete agreed and pointed out that several of the lads had felt unwell while on leave and remarked that they were still not themselves.

'Yes, I know what you mean, but in the meantime, carry on with the good work and I will have a word with the major to see if he could arrange a long weekend. At the rate you are all going, we will be way ahead of schedule.'

Pete thanked the captain, stood back and saluted, but he was still staring at Harry beavering away and then asked, 'Is that Sapper Watkins down there? If it is, please tell him I would like a word sometime.'

The captain walked away as the sergeant looked at the details of the new plans. He eventually brought them all together and explained what had to be done and the good news that if progress carried on at the present rate then they would try to arrange a long weekend.

Two weeks passed and most of the hard work had been

completed. Harry was interested in what happened to the plant machinery when it became redundant, if only he could find out, he would be interested in raising the capital against his granddad's property to buy some of them. It would be worth the gamble, but he realised it was not just raising capital, he would have to be granted planing permission as well, but above all he needed Ginger as his business partner. He must find Ginger before making a decision. His father was also a key part of his plan.

The long weekend was granted, allowing them to go home on the Thursday. Ted, feeling more relaxed within himself, took full advantage of his extra day off. His priorities were his mother's health and perhaps trying to find Penny. The latter point would satisfy his mates, since he felt sure they would do something daft like try and find her themselves—however unlikely that might be—if he did not. Then, of course, there were his exam results to come, which for some odd reason had escaped his mind, mainly due to his mother's failing health.

Ted's sister was surprised to see him. She soon put him in the picture regarding their mother: she was to rest and take life easy. Their father had negotiated to work part time at his job, which suited everybody, but Christine was not happy; she wanted them to sell up and move to her place, what did Ted think? Ted thought it was a good idea and at least the pressure would be off their father, and in any case there would be no overheads for them.

There was, of course, a sting in the tail where his sister was concerned. However thoughtful and kind his sister was to her family, she was still nosey.

'Ted, I would be grateful for your help tomorrow, but I would like you to go and find Penny on Saturday. Now I know it's none of my business, but I think you still have feelings for her, however slight they may be. If you don't want to do it for yourself, then would you do this for me?'

She was as crafty as an old fox. She came up to Ted and put her arms around him and told him how much she loved him.

'Okay, you win, sis, I will go sometime soon, I promise you, but I am a bit short these days as you know.'

'You will go on Saturday and take this,' she said.

'What's this? I can't take all this money, old love.'

'Less of the old, it's only twenty pounds, and let's face it, you have never taken a penny before.'

'Is that supposed to be a pun, you know, take a *penny*?'

At last they found time to laugh, which seemed to lift Christine's spirits to a point where she was a totally different person.

'By the way, sis, if a letter arrives at home with my results, would you open it and let me know immediately.'

Christine needed no persuading, but pointed out it may not be the result he wanted, in which case she would use her discretion. He would have to come and work with her. In that case, he thought he had better get the right result.

Chasing after a lost cause was not Ted's ideal way of spending his day. The train pulled up at the station and old memories came flooding back. He walked through the town thinking that this is where it all happened: getting a good hiding; meeting Penny, all the good times they had had together, and now this. It felt ridiculous, but at the same time he had to be honest with himself, he felt slightly better for coming to this place again. It was all so long ago, Penny may be miles away by now.

He arrived at the coffee shop where he had fallen over and Penny had looked after him. Moving on, he came to the place where they first met; it was at this point he had to admit to himself that he had missed her more than he had thought. Looking across the road, there was the chemist's shop, busy as ever. He decided to have a cup of coffee before going in to make enquiries, but then just as he was about to leave, there was Penny. She came out of the door and started running down the street. He tried shouting, but with all the traffic and people it was a waste of time. He tried running after her, but she was gone without trace. Thinking it might be a good idea to go into the chemist's and get some information, he set off back to the shop. Just as he was about to go in three girls came out one of whom he recognised; she had come out the shop with Penny when they had first met.

'Excuse me, my name's Ted Watson, I was a friend of Penny, remember me, the bloke with a face like he had been in the ring for ten rounds? She was very good to me and——'

'Yes, she certainly was, and it's about time you showed your face, lover boy. I mean, you blokes think you can have your way and then swan off somewhere abroad and enjoy yourself; look at your tan.'

'I can assure you I have not been "swanning around" as you put it and, in any case, what do you mean?'

She burst out laughing and was joined by her two friends who found the story equally funny.

'Fancy that, it's lover boy come to claim his princess, well push off, we are respectable people in this town.'

It would not have been so bad if she had not blabbed it all down the street, but one of the others was a little more co-operative and told him where Penny lived.

'But I thought she lived with her parents on the Army camp?'

'Yes, she did, but things move on, you will find out, lover

boy,' and they went off giggling like a load of old hens.

Time was moving on and he wanted to go home and spend time with his mother. Now that he knew where Penny lived he was satisfied with his day's work; but what had happened? Why had she moved? Maybe she had moved in with an eight-foot bull of a man; he sincerely hoped not, he did not fancy getting another good hiding. His mind was wondering all over the place, but at least he had found out where she lived and he had actually seen her. It was a result; but would it satisfy his sister?

Back home his mother was resting. His father had been asleep and looked tired out, so Ted asked if he could prepare a meal for them, which was gratefully accepted. Everything was quiet and peaceful until the dragon turned up.

'Come on, where is he?' she asked Ted's mother. Then, seeing Ted, she said, 'How did you get on, what did you say to her?'

'Hang on, I'll get you a lamp since this is going to be an interrogation exercise, with maybe a bit of torture thrown in for good measure. I don't fancy the rack so I guess the thumb screw will have to do, what do you say, Dad?'

'I don't know what you are talking about son, but it don't sound good.'

'Well I do, so how did you get on?'

Christine was really fired up and ready to turn the screws.

'To be honest I didn't actually meet her——'

'You big, useless, twit, how come I have been landed with an idiot for a brother?'

The verbal abuse levelled at Ted was too much for his father. He ordered his daughter outside for a very rare reprimand. All Ted could hear was that she should learn to respect her mother's illness and her brother's business.

'Come on, let's go down the pub,' said his father to Ted when he came back inside, 'I think your sister wants to talk to your mother,' said his father looking rather annoyed.

'Well then, young man, what's this that I hear that you have got a young girl into trouble?'

'Might have, Dad, in any case, I'm sorting it.'

'Good lad, and by the way, when will you be called to the bar?'

'I have no idea, and I don't think you have quite got the way it all works, Dad.'

'Oh, I think I have, I'm talking about that bar over there; it's your turn for a round. Just one more thing, lad, about this young girl, do you think I could meet her sometime?'

Ted admired his father, he would never interfere, but would always be there when he was needed.

Everything was going well for Harry, the kind of work they were doing was perfect experience for his business venture. He needed all the experience he could get, and one way was to talk to the sergeant. The sergeant was more than helpful and mentioned that the captain wanted to speak to him. While they were looking at the plans for a bridge, a corporal turned up asking for Ted. He was to report to the company commander without delay.

'Clean yourself up, Watson, and good luck,' said the sergeant to Ted.

Ted had no idea what it could be; what had he done? Maybe he had been rumbled and the colonel had found out that it was him who had been seeing his daughter. Maybe he would be thrown to the dogs and given a dishonourable discharge for disgracing the colonel's daughter and family. What me, sir? I have my reputation to think of, and I assure you that these wild charges are as inaccurate as they are preposterous. Case dismissed. Ted's nerves were on edge as he was marched into the major's office.

'Ah, now then, stand easy, Watson, I have some very good news, and some very bad news for you I'm afraid. Now then, first of all the colonel and myself——'

That was it, the colonel had found out. Ted's mind went wild. 'Sir, if only I could explain, you see I was rushed abroad and——'

'What on earth are you talking about, Watson? Allow me to be the first to congratulate you on a job well done. You are now a lawyer. Your sister asked the colonel to pass the message on to you.'

The major went on a bit, saying the Army could use people like him, but of course he was mindful of the past twelve months Ted had spent on the island, and he expected Ted would want to think about it.

Ted had already thought about it; the Army had already used him enough for a lifetime. Ted reminded the major that he and the others had not only sweated blood working out there, but had shed many tears and were fearful of what they had seen. Ted was dismissed without comment, but not before being told that work had to continue throughout the weekend: there would be a long weekend to follow.

Some of the lads were not at all happy with the news and Harry was no exception. His plans to contact Ginger would have to wait awhile, but in the meantime he would explain to Helen what he had in mind. He called Helen who agreed to meet him and go straight to granddad's place.

The time passed quickly and soon Harry was being driven by Helen to his granddad's place. It felt great to be back at his granddad's once more with Helen, who surprised him with lots of food already in the house. She had cleaned the place up and since the electricity had not been cut off she cooked them a meal.

'I must say, nurse, that was delicious, and I was thinking perhaps you would consider a more permanent position here? I know it's a little sudden springing this on you, but I for one am not keen on the title of estate manager for you. I am asking you to marry me.'

Helen's reply was swift with a big hug and a kiss, but she had an ultimatum: they must wait until Christmas and Harry had to help with the washing up or she might change her mind.

'It's a deal, but I was wondering what we could do after the washing up, if you know what I mean.'

'Yes, baggy pants, I know what you mean, we are going to find Ginger,' she said laughing.

Ginger was not hard to find and he was soon introduced to Helen. He was happy enough and had found a girlfriend, but he had no plans for the future and found Harry's idea brilliant. 'Yes, I will come and work with you Harry,' he said.

'No, Ginger, you come in as a full partner or nothing, so what do you say?'

Ginger pointed out that he had no money and neither was he likely to have any, so Harry put him in the picture. He would put up the cash in the form of a loan from the bank so long as Ginger managed the hardware. Ginger seemed to be happy enough, but insisted on a meeting the moment they were released from the Army and went back to their old jobs. He made no bones about it, the bills had to be paid. Harry agreed and showed him his plans.

Ted had no plans to tell his sister that he was about to attempt another fiasco with Penny. Naturally Christine was over the moon with his exam results and his parents were relieved and very happy for him. He chose not to say anything of his plans, except that he would not be available on Saturday.

On the train once more he decided this time he would make a real effort, it could not go on. He was due to leave the Army and needed to sort out his career very soon.

14. The Reunion

He found the place where he had been told Penny was living. Fortunately, all the flats in the block had name plates. The lift was out of order and so was Ted by the time he had walked up three flights of stairs: he had been celebrating his exam results the night before and it had really caught up with him.

Looking a little untidy, he pressed the bell and waited. Finally, the door opened, it was Penny.

'Oh, hello, somebody told me they had seen you a few days ago. Well, I suppose you had better come in.'

'Thank you, and it's lovely to see you again. I must say you look well.'

There was no reaction at all, she would not even look at him. Closing the door, Penny asked Ted into the kitchen.

'Well, I suppose you want an explanation as to why I finished with you: I will come straight to the point. When you left over a year ago I went back to university, only to find out I had to leave. My father became very ill and my having to leave university did not help matters. I felt so ashamed of myself, and what with you not writing to me, I swore I would never see you again. Okay, I received two letters from you, but unfortunately my mother found one of them. She decided not to tell my father, but told me not to write to you again or my father would be informed of our relationship. If that was not bad enough, you never even tried to get in touch with me when you came home. Why has it taken you so long to find me?'

Penny was beginning to raise her voice slightly, which prompted a voice from another room to say, 'Are you alright, darling, if it's another salesman tell him I'm not interested.'

'It's okay, Mum, it's only somebody I used to know, I won't be long. I will bring you in a coffee in just a moment.' That told Ted everything, he had very little time to explain his side of the story.

'First of all, Penny, I am very sorry to hear about your father. I have similar worries with my mother, she's not at all well.'

'With all due respect, I am not interested in your problems, I have plenty of my own, thank you, so if you don't mind, just say what you want and go.'

The ship was sinking fast, there was only one last stand to make. Tell her the truth, as Ginger had taught them.

'Penny, I will not make any excuses because there are none, not for either of us. It seems to me we have been the victims of circumstances beyond our control. Remember what I said to you before I left, when things became hard to take I would always be there for you? The pen would keep us together. Never mind it didn't quite work out, but nobody can say I stopped thinking of you. I got myself into a lot of trouble Penny, and I have to say it was my mates that held me together. It has been a very tough year for me as well, believe me.

'Yes, I know, I think my father went out there twice, but not for long. I have no idea what he was doing, he wouldn't talk to Mum about it. He was not well enough.'

'May I ask how he is, Penny?'

'He died about two months ago, so you see we are not quite ourselves at the moment,' she said quietly crying to herself.

Ted, for the first time in his life, was absolutely devastated, he did not know what to do. He wanted to comfort her, but he controlled his feelings by just touching her hand. She made no attempt to withdraw, but simply looked up at Ted and said, 'I have to make a coffee for Mum would you like one?'

'Thanks, Penny, I have a great deal to tell you, especially about my feelings for you.'

'Well, you had better sit down, you're making the place look untidy. Later on I want to show you something.'

She came back in after seeing her mother.

'It's okay, my mum is fast asleep so we can talk; but first, follow me.'

She took Ted into her bedroom and went over to a cot and carefully picked up her baby. She presented her baby to Ted and said, 'The last time I made you a cake, this time I made you a baby, and of course you had an awful lot to do with it.' Ted was absolutely bowled over. He took the baby in his arms and walked over to the window, he had to since his emotions were beginning to take over. He walked back to Penny and said it was the greatest gift he had ever had. This time he threw caution to the wind and kissed her gently.

'I love you, Penny, and you can rest assured I will be back for you and our baby.'

'Ted, don't be too hasty, I have to tell you, there is somebody else in my life, but nothing serious, I can assure you.'

'I don't understand, you said to me it was my baby, so what's going on?'

'So it is, Ted. Look, I have always loved you, in spite of my reluctance to see you again. When things went so badly wrong, desperate measures had to taken, none of which were my decisions. My parents gave me no little option other than to have the baby away from home, but then my father was sent away to where you were. He came home and made arrangements for me to stay in this flat. Our baby was born in the hospital and then my father went away again. When he came home again he was not well according to Mum. I never saw him again. He died after a short illness about two months ago. Mum, for reasons only known to her, became very angry, which is most uncharacteristic of her, she moved here with me about two weeks ago and has been here ever since.'

'Penny, I am desperately sorry for you and your mother, please accept my sincere condolences to you both. Penny, you say your father came out to the island on two occasions, when was that exactly, can you remember?'

'I have no idea, I was never told anything; except what to do all the time. Why does it matter what time he was there?'

'It doesn't really, my love, and I shouldn't intrude into your family affairs. Look, I would love to see my—just a minute, I was so carried away I forgot to ask the baby's name.'

'You have a son and I decided to call him Harry.'

'You chose well, but just before I go I would like to say that no matter how much we have been through we have made it back together today. I don't care if you have a boyfriend, I will be back one day and take you and Harry away from this place.'

'There is no boyfriend, well I should say he is just a friend of the family and has been very helpful during these last two months. He is a lieutenant and is very ambitious. He visits Mum now and again, helping her with my father's affairs. I have nothing to do with it.'

Ted was beginning to feel slightly unwell after the night before. The celebration on his recent success had been a low key affair, but he had had one or two drinks too many, which had now caught up with him all of a sudden. He had felt so tensed up before meeting Penny, now he felt more relaxed and asked if he could sit down, if only for a couple of minutes. Penny was slightly concerned, and asked what was wrong. Ted explained he had been celebrating, but fell short of saying what it was all about. Penny would have none of it and demanded to know if there was somebody else in his life.

'Look, Ted, I want you to tell me the truth, or otherwise you can go, I have told you everything, well almost, what else can I say?'

Ted felt dreadful for a moment, sweating slightly and feeling completely tired out. He never heard what Penny said but he felt he had better take his leave before he felt worse.

'I am sorry, Penny, what were you saying? Oh, yes, of course I forgot to mention . . . Do you remember me telling you I worked for a solicitor as a clerk? Well, I studied law while I was away. My sister helped me by sending all the books I needed. My sister is a solicitor come estate agent and put me up for the law exams. Well, I managed to pass, so I must be the only sapper who is now a lawyer, but for the moment I have to serve a few more weeks shovelling stone and driving lorries. Hopefully my old firm will take me on again and I will be able to earn a little more than twenty-nine shillings a week. Nevertheless, I know my responsibilities and will support you both the best way I can. In the meantime, if you have any problems send me a signal, and hopefully we won't get it wrong this time.'

'What do you mean, Ted?'

'Well, my love, I guess we have lost a great deal of time, but I am back to claim what is rightfully mine. I know I have been a bit of a clown, but I can assure you that from now on I won't let you down. You know what I mean, don't you?'

'I think so, but then you were always saying daft things, weren't you? Okay, you had better go, and I hope your mother gets better.'

There was no attempt to renew their relationship. Ted felt that Penny had not once made any attempt to come close to him, or even ask if he would come again. He had to make all the moves by saying he would call again. The response was half-hearted, you can visit if you want to. He could only put it all down to the fact of losing her father, and all the bitter disappointment her parents had had with her pregnancy and her losing her place at university. She had lost her father but gained a son.

Going home on the train he felt a sense of guilt at all the stupid things he had said about the colonel. It all seemed so ridiculous; he needed to grow up. From what Penny had said, Ted believed that he may well have spoken to her father before the bomb went off back in April. In fact, he was certain the man had been Penny's father, he could see the likeness now he thought about it.

He had no idea where things would go with Penny, what with her unpredictable behaviour it would be touch and go. But his happy memories of the times when they were together, and the fact that he was now a father to her son, were compelling reasons to go back and regain her trust.

15. An Unexpected Christmas Present

Ted called his sister to give her the news of his reunion with Penny, after which Ted felt a little more relaxed. He also planned to explain the good news to his mates, who no doubt would have plenty to say about their own ventures. Although what had really happened was none of their business, he could at least say he had finally met Penny, and therefore lay the whole affair to rest. He would mention nothing about his son or the colonel's death until their release from the Army when everybody would go their own way again, and no doubt would have too many things on their own minds to think much of his affairs.

Following the next day's hard work, Ted decided to give the lads some of his good news in the mess hall.

'By the way, lads, I wonder if I could have your attention for just a few seconds? If any one of you require the services of a qualified solicitor then my bed/office—or better still the NAFFI bar—will be open for free advice.'

The reaction was immediate with cheers, whistles and a good deal of congratulations all round. The rattle of mugs and spoons on the tables caught the attention of the chefs who, after being told what was going on, came over to Ted and shook his hand. Ted had never expected a reception like this.

His news about Penny he decided to keep until he was with his closest mates. Harry stood up and gave a short speech, he said that although life in the Army had been unexpectedly tough, without Ted it would have been even more tough. Even in the midst of testing two very powerful nuclear bombs he had studied the law, but Harry was confident that Ted would see justice was meted out according to the law.

Back in the hut the lads decided that a celebration in the NAAFI would have to wait, and with pay day a few days off a cup of tea was about all they could afford. Not only could they not afford a pint, but with demob coming up fast many of the lads had other commitments to consider, such as Pete who had a young family. Or Harry and Brian who needed every penny to start their business venture. Brian suggested, which came as a great deal of relief to the others, that a joint celebration would be in order just before they went home for Christmas.

Ted was more than relieved since he had to find more money than his pay provided to support his new family, however tenuous the situation might be. Hopefully, Penny would have recovered a little from her ordeal when they next met.

Gary came back from a weekend with Megan looking a lot more cheerful. Megan had made excellent progress, so much so that they were engaged to be married sometime in the future. Finding a place to live was not easy, especially somewhere close to his work, so it may be some time before they set a date, but all his mates were invited.

'One more reason to celebrate near Christmas,' said Brian, whose relationship with his girlfriend had improved.

All seemed to be going well, Ted had managed to save money for Christmas presents, but he was woefully short of the money he needed to support Penny and his son. Perhaps his sister would be a little more generous with his pay provided he worked all day Saturday; he could visit Penny and his son on the Sunday and return to camp in the evening. That was his plan, but then he remembered the savings account he was encouraged to take out well over a year ago. Why on earth had he not thought of it before, after all, the interest was derisory?

It's a poor return for very hard work, he thought in describing the investment. Suddenly he felt like he had a little more money, making him feel like a new person, but he was still concerned for his relationship with Penny. Why was it that she seemed to be quite happy for him to be with her, but showed little or no interest in him whatsoever, there was no comparison with their previous relationship. He became rather depressed one weekend and decided to look in on his former employer.

He approached the house and found his boss, Mr Williamson, in the garden. He was delighted to see Ted and even more with his exam results.

'It's best we go up to the house, Ted, where we can talk. I take it that you want your job back, so if you are happy, then I will make all the necessary arrangements. Of course, you will want a little more remuneration than the Army pays you, say another five shillings? Yes? Well that's settled.'

He had always liked to joke and would string you along until you broke and Ted was no exception.

'Anything is better than the Army, Mr Williamson, and I ungratefully accept, but I must warn you I am hopeless at dotting the i's and crossing the t's.'

'That's very kind of you to say so, young Ted, but I am sure we can make allowances, your spelling always was atrocious. Well, now that's all done and dusted would you like some suitable refreshment just to celebrate?'

'Just a small one for me, thanks, I am due at my girlfriend's place now,' replied Ted.

'Oh, in that case we must not hang about, just a small one for the road.'

As he was pouring the drinks he said, 'You know what they say, you should never look a gift horse in the mouth, but thirty-four shillings a week, that's a real bargain. At this rate I shall be able to retire.'

He turned to Ted smiling and said 'Come on then, what's her name?'

'Penny, sir, and if I don't get a move on there won't be a penny left.'

'Here, you haven't got into trouble? I can't afford to have my firm's reputation brought into disrepute, now we don't want that do we?'

Ted downed his drink and replied, 'On thirty-four bob a week, I couldn't afford to now could I? Who do I say I work for, Ebeneezer Scrooge?'

'You can do, if you don't want to keep your job,' he said laughing.

'Have a nice time, Ted, and thanks for coming to see me, and by the way, we are having a Christmas party. One of the girls will send you an invitation. Take care now.'

What more could he wish for, having a boss like that? He now knew how Bob Cratchit felt. If only he could have a nice time with Penny it would make his day. He was already three hours late, but then did it really matter? He doubted Penny would be that bothered.

After ringing the door bell a few times he was just about to give up when the door opened.

'Penny's out, so you might as well go away, or come back another time.'

It was Penny's mother, looking extremely tired. Ted had bought some flowers for Penny, but instead he gave them to her mother saying, 'On behalf of myself and my colleagues, we would very much appreciate it if you would place them on the colonel's resting place.'

'But you didn't even know him, young man.'

'Yes, we did, we trained in the Royal Engineers and the colonel felt he should know us all, if you see what I mean. What's more, we met him while we were on the other side of the world. He spoke to us when we all needed him, after it was all over I looked for him, but he was gone.'

Looking a little puzzled, she thanked him and promised she would place the flowers on her husband's grave the next day. She said it was the nice to know he was appreciated. She invited Ted in, but he was so disappointed at not seeing Penny that he declined the kind offer and left a message for her instead, saying that he had been delayed due to his new appointment as a solicitor at his old firm.

'She may not be long, she has gone out with some friends, and to be honest I don't know what she's doing. Take care, Ted, and thank you for the flowers, and please thank all the others for me. Goodbye.'

'So sorry, Mrs James, I forgot to write on the card.'

'It's not necessary, Ted, but I would be grateful for your telephone number if you please.'

Ted felt a bit of a fraud, he had intended the flowers for Penny, but under the circumstances he thought it was better if they were placed on the colonel's grave.

He was half way down the steps when he realised that he had forgotten to hand in his son's present, so he went back and left it by the door. He looked all over for Penny, thinking he might see her, but his time had run out and he was due back.

It was nearing Christmas and had turned bitterly cold, which reminded him of the day he was conscripted into the Army and how things had changed since he had joined.

Back at camp the mood of the lads was surprisingly sombre. There were no more questions and all the banter had disappeared. Maybe things at home were beginning to catch up with them.

Ted jumped into bed and pretended he was asleep. His mind was troubled once again, he just could not get to sleep, but then he decided that all his efforts had been in vain, it was a waste of time trying to regain that loving care that Penny was so good at. What could he do, she was slowly drifting away from him, perhaps it was best to leave her alone and let her come to him. He was far from comfortable with that idea, but it was the only thing left for him. Having no money did not help matters, but that was life, he did not miss what he had never had. Having thought that, he realised money would have helped. He would have been able to drive up in a nice car and take her out to a posh restaurant. Instead, he couldn't even afford sausage, egg, and chips.

The morning was bitterly cold and it was raining, but work carried on until Harry decided he was only making more of a mess rather than a decent tidy job. He retreated to the shelter where a fire had been lit by one of the lads who was trying to make toast.

Harry was eager to get back out there when the sergeant turned up.

'There is no point carrying on, lads, but before you go I have some good news for you. Although it has yet to be made official, you are to be released from the Army before Christmas. That means that you will not have to return after your leave. Okay, carry on.'

Back in the hut it was a strange feeling for all of them. Naturally they were elated with the news, but it came as a complete surprise. The sudden feeling that they would be on their own in just a few days' time changed everything. It was beginning to sink in that they would be on their own. They had worked and lived together during difficult times, so much so that they would live through what they had seen for the rest of their lives. They realised that nothing stayed the same, but they would be mates for life and hold reunions every year.

This unexpected Christmas present changed everyone's immediate plans, especially for Brian and Harry. Brian went out to make urgent phone calls, it seems he had been offered a job over the Christmas holiday and could earn some real money for a change. Not only that, he still had serious plans to sell motorbikes. Harry joined Brian at the phone box, wanting to give Helen the good news. He would have to go back to his old job before he could move forward with his own business ideas.

Without doubt there was a certain amount of panic among the lads, some more than others. No longer would there be a guaranteed place to live, a meal on the table and a job to do—however ridiculous the pay. There was security here of a sort, but outside it was a very different story; there is no such thing as a free lunch, once you are outside those gates it was a very different story. The Army had taught them many things, they had visited other countries and an island far from civilisation where they worked hard in blistering heat. Home was a tent with a camp bed, which after a long day's work felt like a feather bed, if only you could master preventing it from tipping over and causing an embarrassing situation. There had been little or no luxuries and nowhere you could put all your belongings. Harry and most of the others had lived entirely out of their suitcases.

With little or no recreation the main entertainment came from the animal kingdom, which provided perhaps some of the finest fishing in the world, and many different bird species had made the island their home for many thousands of years. They provided a spectacular display diving for fish and then soaring high into the clouds. Harry remembered them and Ginger, who described them as all part of God's creation to be enjoyed by all until man came along with his quest for perfecting the most dangerous bomb known to man, the hydrogen bomb. The memory of all these magnificent creatures was joined by the memory of the most hideous weapon on the planet. Bombs of unimaginable power were detonated one after the other near or on the island. Those young boys who were ordered to witness these nuclear explosions, and those who were ordered to work there after all of the tests, had a very uncertain future. Without doubt they had served their country well and had helped give it a deterrent against any aggressor, and all for twenty-nine shillings a week. On anybody's reckoning that represented pretty good value for money, but for those who took part, it represented a nightmare for the rest of their life.

Their last few days went by completely unnoticed; apart from reading the official release notice, a final pay parade, and a medical, they were ready to leave—but not before a final celebration. Many promises were made, none of which they would keep. They would be scattered all over the country so the chances of meeting again would be slim. Gary would send a wedding invitation to all of them and reminded them that only one was missing. Harry had found Ginger, but nobody had a clue where Alf had disappeared to.

Without going into details Ted mentioned that on behalf of all of them he had placed flowers on the colonel's resting place. It was a sombre note for all of them since they had regarded the colonel as one of the team.

'I don't understand, Ted, are you seriously saying he was on the island with us?' said Harry.

'Yes, but only for the nuclear test, you know the really big one that frightened the life out of us? I think he also witnessed the first test in the November, went home and came back again. If you remember he was the officer telling us to keep down and stay down. He was going to take my name after I started shouting it was all madness to make us all line up. He must have known it was all madness himself after standing up only to be knocked down again. As you know, it was panic stations after that and when I finally regained control of myself he was gone. In short he went home, became ill and died of some form of cancer. I have never asked details as it's none of my business, but I do know it has made his family deeply unhappy and in a way I am partly responsible.'

'That's ridiculous you can't blame yourself, Ted, after all you couldn't possibly have known who he was,' said Harry.

'Are you seriously telling me he was the father of the girl you were seeing before we left for the island,' said Brian.

'Yes I am, Brian.'

'Well, that really is tragic and frightening for us all, not forgetting you were jolly lucky he didn't know who you were when he was talking to you. Ironically the bomb saved your skin,' said Brain.

'Well, apart from being burnt on my neck, I suppose you are right Brian. I still say he was a decent sort of a man, even though I didn't know him.

'May God bless and keep him forever,' said Brian.

Their last day came and Gary was first out of the blocks, back to Megan and his beloved mountains. Brian and Pete followed, leaving Ted and Harry shaking hands and looking back into an empty room.

'All for twenty-odd shillings a week, come on, mate, let's go home,' said Harry.

With their uniforms no more they walked outside the gates for the last time.

Waiting for the train, Ted explained the true story of how he had found Penny and that he had a son.

'*Now* you tell me, you know perfectly well we would have celebrated the good news. Why on earth didn't you tell us Ted?' said Harry, who was very disappointed.

'No, Harry, it's complicated. Penny has changed, and to be honest, I have all but given up on her. I might as well not be there and all that holds us together is my son. Nothing stays the same does it? You know, Harry, it would be fitting if we carried a parcel under our arms. How long were you banged up for, mate? Two years, but with six weeks remission for good behaviour, spare us a couple of bob will ya?'

'Parcel or case, Ted, what's the difference?'

'I guess you're right.' Harry laughed, he desperately wanted to talk to Ted but his train had come in.

'Keep in touch, I mean you are only a few miles away, something will work out for you.'

'Will do, mate. My love to Helen.'

The train pulled away leaving Ted standing there. Pulling the window down, Harry shouted back to Ted, 'Don't give up and don't let me down, Ted.'

Harry felt so sorry for him, especially after what he had gone through. Of course, he began to realise that Penny would be finding it difficult to come to terms with the loss of her father, and then there she was holding Ted's baby. Yes, indeed our Ted always seemed to be sailing very close to the edge.

Walking back towards his parent's home it had suddenly turned very cold, reminding him of the day he was ordered to join the Army. With hindsight he had mixed feelings about the experience, but above all he was grateful for all the training and experience he had been given. The memories of having to face those terrifying nuclear bombs still lingered in his mind, but above all it was the loss of all of those thousands of magnificent creatures, dying in the most horrific manner that disturbed him the most. Any closer and it could have been him, but instead it was his little white friends, the Pacific tropicbirds that had perished—along with their home.

16. Wedding Bells

Harry was almost home and was feeling slightly emotional, thinking it was all over, he had returned from a truly dramatic adventure and met some of the best mates he could possibly wish for.

Without doubt his whole demeanour, personality and confidence had changed from that of two years' ago. He realised the experience was questionable and then, of course, his hair had completely changed from a fashionable hairstyle to a crew cut—which he maintained mainly in an attempt to stop his hair falling out.

Done time have you mate, how long was you banged up for? Harry couldn't help laughing, Penny doesn't know what she is missing he was thinking to himself.

Passing a phone box he just could not wait to phone Helen. He tried a few times, but no answer, so he phoned the hospital who told him she no longer worked there. He failed to realise that she had told him that she was trying to find a job at a hospital much closer to his granddad's place. Of course, how stupid of him.

He was just about to ring the doorbell of his parent's house when the door opened and there she was. Throwing her arms around him Helen kissed him again and again. She held on to him and took him in to see his mother and brothers. They had laid on a party for him with bunting hanging ready for Christmas.

'Welcome home, my love,' his mother kissed him and held onto him for a while.

'How are you now? I have worried about you ever since you came home from that place, they should never have sent you out there.'

'It's all over now, Mum, and I must say all your letters helped me a great deal. Thanks to you and Helen, neither of you have any idea how much it helped me, especially last Christmas. Never in a million years would I have thought I would one day spend Christmas on Christmas Island.'

'Why did they give the place that name?' asked his mother.

'It was Captain Cook, Mum, he discovered the island on Christmas Eve, the largest coral atoll in the world, with an abundance of wild life.

'I must say we have enjoyed having Helen here, she works so hard, your father treats her as his own daughter. By the way, he will be home any minute, he's so looking forward to seeing you and I believe he has some news for you.'

Helen brought him in a very welcome cup of tea and said she would be busy in the kitchen helping his mother.

'The boys are in the other room, they are so looking forward to talking to you,' she said.

Harry's father came in his usual manner.

'Where's that boy of mine? You know, that big useless twit?'

'He's in there', said his youngest son.

'Oh, so you know who I am talking about? That's good. How are you my boy, it's good to have you home and to have somebody who I can talk a bit of sense with. Can't get a sensible word out of either of them,' looking straight at his two younger sons with a broad grin.

The boys retaliated by saying, 'You know the other day he said he couldn't understand why a beautiful girl like Helen would go out with an ugly thing like Harry. "She must be off her trolley," that's what he said.' The place erupted with Harry's father chasing them out the room. He shouted out to the kitchen, 'These two clowns are not to eat with us this evening.'

The reply was swift with Harry's mother saying, 'And if you don't behave yourself, Jack Watkins, you won't be dining with us either, now go and get everybody a glass of wine. I really don't know what you think of us, Helen, you must think this is the mad hatters tea party.'

The truth was that Helen, for the first time in her life, felt as if she was in her own home. She was happy with these people who had taken her in as one of their own.

'Did you say we are all going to Harry's place tomorrow, sweetheart, my dearest and most precious love of my life?' said Harry's father, handing a glass of wine to his wife.

'Yes, so long as you can behave yourself, now come along everybody, up to the table.'

Harry could never have wished for a better homecoming and he started to wonder how the others were getting on.

Would he ever see them again? He very much hoped so, but then he thought of his own situation: he would never have the time if his plan to start his own business came to fruition. But before he could do anything he had to find Ginger.

It was soon time for Helen to start her night shift. Harry thanked her for a wonderful surprise and said he did not expect to see her until she had slept, but she mentioned that his mother had said that she could sleep in Harry's bed.

'Wow, I will certainly settle for that, Jenny Wren,' he said holding on to her.

'I'm sorry to disappoint you, my love, but you have your orders to take your family to your granddad's first thing in the morning.'

'But surely just five minutes, just to say hello, I promise.'

'No, remember our last five minutes turned into an hour?' she said with a smile.

All he got was a long, wonderful kiss and a hug.

'It's wonderful to have you home, please never go away again.'

She was gone, with Harry thinking how lucky he was compared to Ted. Yes, his mother was right, they don't come better than that, he had made up his mind. His family were obviously taken with Helen, but what had been going on in his absence. Which hospital did she work at and where was she staying? His mother must know, since she had already pointed out that Helen worked long hours.

'What hospital does Helen work at, Mum, and where does she stay?' Harry asked. He was completely in the dark.

'As I said, she works all hours and quite honestly she is hardly ever here, but fancy moving to our local hospital.'

'I didn't know this, Mum, how long has this been going on?'

'Don't tell her I told you, I expect she wants to keep it a secret.'

'Fat chance with you being around, Mum.'

'Really, my boy, I don't know what you're talking about. Has she got any family, she never talks about anybody? What about those pills, do you still have to take them?'

'Where is she staying, has she found a room?'

'No, Harry, she has found that very difficult, so your father and I said she could stay here until she could find her own place. She has only been here a week, so I hope you don't mind using the sofa.'

'Quite frankly Mum I have slept on a camp bed for a year so the sofa will be no trouble, and I must say I really do appreciate what you have done for her.'

The following day was bitterly cold with a keen easterly wind. Even with the cold they all left early, leaving Helen to rest.

'That's odd, who's been tidying the place up?' said Harry.

'It's nothing to do with us, son, so that only leaves one other,' said his father.

Even the outside of the house looked tidy, but inside it was a picture, with Christmas bunting all around the living room. The fireplace had been cleaned and was ready to be laid. The boys soon saw to it and got the fire going with plenty of wood out in the shed. Just about everything had been taken care of.

'Tell you what, shall we spend Christmas day here?' asked his father. 'I mean just for lunch, and then go home or maybe go for a walk around the fields, and then perhaps you would tell me more about your plans, you see I may be able to help you; I will explain later.'

Harry's father was delighted to see his old home looking like it used to in his childhood days. The boys had got the fire going giving the room a warmer feeling.

'Here's a nice cup of tea for you all and that lovely girl has left us biscuits and a cake,' said Harry's mother.

His mother was certain Helen had not only been working at the hospital, but had also been working hard at granddads. It was a splendid day, and was all due to Helen, but now it was time to return home. Harry hoped that Helen had rested. Sure enough, she was up and made them all a welcome cup of tea.

Christmas Day was splendid and everything was prepared. The boys were in charge of the firewood, closely watched by their father. After lunch Harry and his father did the dishes while the girls took a seat by the fire.

Later Helen and Harry decided that they would brave the cold and went for a walk around the fields, it was a little too cold for Harry's parents who preferred the log fire. Before they left, Helen reminded Harry to wear something warm as he had been out in the tropics for so long.

Helen said she had changed hospitals. Harry was over the moon, 'But where are you going to stay?' he asked.

'I mean I can always put you up in the shed, it wouldn't cost you much, or on the other hand you could always stay in the house for as long as you like.'

'That's very kind of you, Mr Watkins, but I think I must decline your very kind offer and sleep in your bed, and for your cheek you can remain on the sofa, so there.'

'You drive a hard bargain, young Jenny Wren, so I must offer you an alternative plan. How about you and me living here in this house as soon as possible? I mean, of course, it would need improvements, but to be honest I don't want anybody else in my life except for you. When I find the money I promise you I will turn this place into whatever you want. I am serious, but take as long as you like, I have no plans to go anywhere.'

Helen was looking straight ahead and began to turn away from him; she was crying. Harry quickly held on to her, wondering what on earth he had said to offend her. She eventually looked at him and said, 'Are you really asking me to marry you?'

'Yes, I am, but please take your time.'

'When shall we get married, my love?'

'So I take that as a yes?'

'Yes, I will marry you Harry,' and having said that she held on to him.

Walking back to the house she pulled him into the old shed where she kissed and held on to him. She made it clear she loved him and asked him to never leave her.

'I am sorry for those few tears, but you see I have never been loved like this before and your family means everything to me. You will promise me, won't you?'

'I have dreamed that one day I would meet somebody I would truly love; and here you are. There was one time when I actually prayed for my family and you. One of the lads heard me calling out your name. I was so scared at the time, we all were. I'm sorry, I shouldn't have said anything.'

'Harry, I have no idea what you have been through, but I will look after you, believe me, my love.'

'Yes, I am a very lucky fellah, that's for sure.' Holding each other Harry mentioned that he had had a good idea.

'Tell you what, why don't you stay in the shed until you find a place of your own, you know, just until we get married. It won't cost you a penny. I can make all the necessary arrangements to have the place cleaned up.'

'In that case, baggy pants, if you think that you can get off the sofa tonight you can think again. I have got your bed, so what do you say to that?'

'Double drat, I knew it wouldn't work,' said Harry and chased her around outside the house.

She was happy at last. For the first time in her life she had a real family that would look after and love her.

'Shall we tell them?' she said all excited.

'It's up to you, Jenny Wren, I will buy a ring from the

market just as soon as I find the time.'

'Oh, so that's all I am worth is it, baggy pants? Well, we will see about that.'

'If you don't behave yourself, young lady, I will sell *you* down the market, but I wouldn't think you would fetch much, maybe sixpence.'

She chased him back to the shed. Inside Harry remembered his granddad's tins and boxes full of old bits and pieces.

'What are you looking for?' asked Helen.

'There you are, lets see if it fits.'

It was an old ring in need of a clean, but polished up it would do until Harry could afford a proper engagement ring. Helen needed no persuading to go into the house and announce their engagement. At last she had found her own family and her own home. Harry had found a gem of a girl, he only hoped that Ginger and Ted would manage to settle down.

17. TED ACTS ALONE

With the new year celebrations over, Ted had settled into his new office with enough work to keep him working late most days. There had been an offer of a property put to him by his employer, but he had given it very little thought until Mr Williamson came to see him.

'Look, Ted, would you like to make me a reasonable offer before I go to an agent? I have the responsibility of selling this place on behalf of a deceased client, so have a look at it and get back to me within a couple of weeks. There are no relatives to deal with, and nobody has come forward to make a claim. I must have an answer soon, you understand? When are we going to meet your girlfriend by the way?'

Ted said very little in that direction, he simply said he would promise to give a decision on the property just as soon as he had looked at it and the deeds.

Even though he took Christmas presents to Penny and his son he found nobody answering the door. He simply left the presents at the door. After walking around the town thinking by chance he might see Penny he returned home feeling like a lost soul.

He did not even get a phone call from Penny, which depressed him a great deal, and living at his sisters house was not exactly exciting either. Christine had shown empathy, but was in no hurry to make matters worse after her last ill-fated intrusion into his private life, she had been through all that herself. Nevertheless, she realised her brother needed something to take his mind off the past few months which had been like hell to him.

'Ted, that property you wanted me to look at, I have looked into a few details, and to be honest it's worth looking at, so how about this evening?'

'I suppose so, just let me change and we can go. What about Sophie? You can't leave her here.'

'Of course not, you big useless twit.'

'Everybody calls me that, I wonder why?'

They arrived at the entrance where, according to Christine, the property started but the house was not to be seen. They drove on down the track, carefully hoping Sophie would not wake up. There was a bank on the right side of the drive with woodland behind it, slightly elevated and surrounded by trees they saw one large house. They eventually arrived at what was supposed to be an old timber frame cottage. It was nothing short of a mess, completely overgrown with what looked like an old barn ready to fall down. To the left hand side of the drive was a couple of fields, one of which had been neglected, and more woodland over on the far side.

'According to this deed, the woodland on the right would be yours and the fields, but not the wood over the far side. Hang on, there is a river separating the fields and the wood.'

'There is no way I can afford all this, I mean look at the state of the house, I couldn't live in that.'

'No, Ted, of course you can't, but think of the potential. I am sure you could get permission to knock down the house and replace it with a magnificent new timber frame house. If you can get it at the right price, I am sure you could make a handsome profit.'

That word 'profit' meant nothing to Ted, he wasn't interested in making big, fat profits, all he wanted was a home to bring up a family and settle down to a peaceful life. Why can people not be satisfied with what they have, he wondered. There was no harm in making a profit, but it was the manner in which profits were made that was the problem, like taking advantage of others who had very little.

He was thinking what would Ginger advise? Since his offer would go to a charity only known to his employer he would make an offer that would be fair and honourable. Whatever happened, his conscience would be at peace.

'Hello, hello is anybody there?' Christine said waving her hand in front of him.

'Sorry, Chris, I was miles away, but I know what I have to do, I must go and find Penny and my son before it's too late.'

'Well, that is maybe, but what are you going to do about this place?'

'I will let my conscience decide what is fair and proper, don't worry. And thanks for helping me Chris.'

Ted just walked away, not giving any indication of what he intended to do, leaving his sister very worried about her brother's state of mind.

The following week Christine had just about finished for the day when Ted turned up.

'What's this?' she said.

'What does it look like? It's called a car you know.'

'When did you buy it? You never said anything about buying a car.'

'Well, I have and you might as well know my offer on that ridiculous property has been accepted, thanks to Mum and

Dad, and yourself of course. I don't know what I have done without your support. To be honest though, Chris, I have slept on a camp bed for twelve months, so I don't think living at that place would be much different. The mortgage is a little steep, along with paying back Mum, Dad, and yourself in kind, but at least I had enough left over to buy this old banger. By the way, I have permission to put a caravan on the site which will be a lot better than a tent.'

'That is maybe, but you can't live on your own, so I insist you continue to live with me, that's if you can put up with Sophie and me and continue to work for me on the weekends.'

'That's more than kind of you, Chris, all I need now is a bucket full of luck.'

Looking at Ted's latest acquisition, Christine was thinking that must be the understatement of the year.

'Don't worry, Chris, I know what you are thinking, the Army has taught me many things and one of them was engines.'

'Yes, well I am sure you know what you are doing, but are you aware of the state of your rear tyres?'

'As soon as I get paid I will fix all that, along with one or two other minor problems; I mean it won't start that well at the moment.'

'No, I'm not surprised,' said Christine smiling. 'Well, I have to say, it's only fair that you should be helped by Mum, Dad and myself, after all, Mum and Dad supported me financially through university and now it's your turn to have some support.

Time passed quickly and Ted had made good progress with his plans, but the requirement for a splayed entrance would be more expense. The drive was in one hell of a mess. Who could sort out such a mess, then it struck him: Ginger and Harry. I wonder if they have started their business yet? It would be great to speak to them if nothing else.

Ted's boss, Mr Williamson, popped his head around the door, 'Got a minute Ted? I won't keep you long. As you know we are ahead of ourselves at last and it has not gone unnoticed that you have been working long hours, so I would like you to take a couple of hours off; naturally you won't be paid!'

'Naturally, Mr Williamson, I wouldn't expect to be paid, I am indeed most grateful to you for being so generous. I must say your new car looks splendid, it's a pity you have to park it next to mine. I make no apologies, of course, since I don't get paid a great deal for my services.'

'Oh, I don't know about a raise in your salary; but take three days off and then just maybe we can talk about it. But first I have an important client I would like you to take care of on Friday evening, I hope you don't mind. Next week they are buying a farm not far from your place, so who better than yourself to act for them? Just before I go would you mind telling me how you feel these days, you see I popped my head around the door yesterday and you were fast asleep. I left you alone thinking there was no way I could increase your salary. No, seriously Ted, I am asking you as a friend, are you feeling unwell?'

'First of all, I really am sorry for that, but yes, I have been feeling below par just lately. Maybe it's because I don't eat enough, I simply can't afford these highly inflated prices these days.'

'I hope you are not making unfounded insinuations, young man, that you are seriously out of pocket here, because if you are then I will have no alternative but to withdraw your three days off. If I catch you asleep once more I will have one of the girls in the office make you an appointment at the surgery, and by the way, what happened to that young lady, it must be getting on for six months or more since you told me about her.'

Yes, indeed it seemed some time ago and Ted was no further forward, but he had made up his mind he would drive to see her soon. He did not feel that optimistic about this visit, but he was at least entitled to see his son. He had been sending money to Penny, but there was never an answer to his letters. Nevertheless, he was determined to see his son.

The car ran surprisingly well—he had now sorted the ignition. He parked up and made his way into the unknown, wondering what kind of reception he would get. Would it be, 'Hello, Ted, how nice to see you. Come on in,' or would it be, 'Oh, it's you, what do you want?' He rang the bell to find out, thinking what he had to say.

Eventually the door opened, it was her mother.

'You had better come in, please excuse the mess, Penny is in the bedroom, you can go in if you want.'

'No, thank you, Mrs James, I would rather wait if you don't mind. How are you?'

'I feel fine thank you, but I get very tired, perhaps it's your son keeping us awake all night.'

'Well, I don't know what to say, except I am sorry,' said Ted.

'No, you are not, you men are all the same. Would you like a cup of tea?' said Penny, still in her dressing gown and looking rather tired.

'He's been fed, Mum, and he's ready to go, if you would like to take your grandson out for a few minutes I would like to talk to Ted.'

Ted said goodbye to his son as he did not expect to be there when he came back. He walked to the door and made a fuss of him and said, 'It's nice to see you, little fellah.'

'He has not been christened yet but as you know we have called him Harry, what do you think Ted?' said Penny's mother.

'I couldn't have chosen better, but what about the boss inside? Don't forget I am on borrowed time. The time has come my, little man, to talk of many things.'

'Please call me Molly and before I go please just let me tell you, Penny often cries herself to sleep. I have never been able to find out why, my true feelings are that she has never forgotten you. Maybe I am wrong, but I think she found out about what happened to her father and . . . well you know what I am trying to say.'

'What you are trying to say is that maybe she thinks the same will happen to me and . . .'

Ted stopped to think before he said another word, but Molly carried on, saying Penny might be very frightened and couldn't face loosing him the same way as she had lost her father.

'Well that's a sobering thought for anyone, I must say, and something I shall have to live with for the rest of my life,' replied Ted.'

'I am sorry, Ted, I could at least be more tactful, please forgive me.'

'Don't worry, Mrs James, I'm not planning to go anywhere just yet.'

'Oh, go on you daft thing,' she said laughing, but then she became serious again.

'Please, Ted, go back in there and bring my daughter back to me, because at the moment I just don't know which way to turn.'

Molly had to go, but not before saying she wanted to see Ted again soon. It would be a private matter and nothing to do with Penny.

Ted went back in to face the music. Penny seemed to be just a little like herself, she never asked once why he had not been to see her or anything like that. Molly was right, the moment he sat down, Penny wanted to know how he felt in himself.

'You don't look at all well, Ted, have you seen a doctor?'

'Look, Penny, I feel fine, but like everybody else I sometimes feel a little under the weather, and in any case you don't look too good yourself.'

'I am sorry, I will get dressed and maybe you would like to tell me what you have been doing these last few months, why don't you come into the bedroom and you can talk to me there.'

'Just a minute, I don't think that would be a good idea, I mean the last time you took me into your bedroom you cast a spell on me and I have to tell you the spell has never left me. You took full advantage of me and then I was sent away, well this time I intend to stay.'

At last she laughed and told him to sit down and behave himself or she might cast another spell on him.

'Fat chance of that with you beside me,' Ted replied.

'Tell me, Ted, what have you been up to? Have you been well? I have always wanted to know.'

Well she's got a funny way of showing it, he thought to himself, but he told her anyway.

'If you are sitting comfortably I will begin.

'That last day we spent together was truly magical for me. I took memories that I believed would help me through the next few months, however, I was wrong. If you remember, I also took with me most of your perfume all over my uniform. You have no idea the looks I got and I almost made a date with the sergeant—in a negative sense I hasten to add.'

Penny started to laugh and said she always wondered how he had managed.

'It's a joke now, but at the time it certainly was not. When I left your house I'm afraid the children next door were looking out of a window and saw me. I then heard the church clock strike seven. To put it mildly I was in deep trouble, fortunately a motorcyclist gave me a lift but we were stopped at the main gate for security checks. Once again, I was seen. To be honest I was terrified and then there was a misunderstanding with an officer who ordered me to the guard room for a reprimand. It was a mystery at the time why I was not put on a charge, and a huge relief to realise nobody had reported seeing me leave your house. Flying over the Atlantic we were told that we were going to a nuclear test site, but I could not care less, so long as you were safe from military investigations and real problems with your parents.'

By now the tears were running down her face; she had had no idea how difficult it had been for him and wanted to come closer to him, but then the door bell rang.

'Who on earth could this be, it won't be Mum that's for sure,' said Penny feeling very annoyed.

She opened the door and sounded a little surprised.

'Oh, it's you, Anthony, my mother is out at the moment, perhaps you would like to call back later?'

'What has your mother got to do with it? I have come to see you and take you out, how are you today?'

That was enough for Ted, he came out of the bedroom and made for the door.

'Who's this?' said a rather tall and well-built man looking seriously at Ted.

Penny looking acutely embarrassed introduced Ted as an old friend, but Anthony was having none of it. He immediately realised that Ted was the father and started to lecture him on normal human behaviour. Whatever that means, thought Ted.

'I don't suppose you have a job, yes, it's people like you who bring a wonderful family like this down to your level and then think you can just walk away.'

Well he has got that last bit right, Ted thought; he had every intention of walking out regardless of all the verbal abuse. He was not going to listen to any more derisory and unfounded remarks made against him, and as for Penny she was partly responsible for him having been beaten up before; and now all this. He would always honour his son, but for now he was getting the hell out of this mad house.

Ted picked up his brief case and closed the door behind him. All he could hear was this man shouting obscenities, but Penny was crying and shouted back saying, 'He is a lawyer and he is my lawyer, and you should have been more careful what you were saying you stupid fool. He is perfectly entitled to see his son. All you have done is barge in here and upset his few precious moments with me and his son.'

Ted was so confused he made for his car, but on the way he stopped by a cafe for a cup of tea. He had been in there before with Penny, he remembered the day he fell over and cut his leg.

'Can I help you?' the young waitress said behind the counter.

'Can I have sausage, egg, and chips with two slices of bread and butter and a pot of tea please?'

'Anything else while you are lashing out, I thoroughly recommend the baked beans?'

'Alright can I have two spoonfuls please.'

'You can have the whole tin if you like, but I don't recommend it if you value your friends.'

'Yes, of course, I see what you mean.'

Ted selected a table by the window still smiling and thinking what a funny girl, she would hardly make top class restaurants, but she had a great personality and Ted enjoyed chatting to her. It was like a breath of fresh air and he was already feeling better. Thinking he should have gone back to support Penny, he decided that it would have been a waste of time, especially after trying so hard to get back with her. She would have to make up her own mind from now on. Disappointment had turned into he disinterest. Wasting no more time, he read through some important legal papers which prompted him to write up some notes.

'Would you care for our apple pie or rhubarb crumble with ice cream or custard?

'Apple pie with custard, thank you.'

It was just like being back in the Army, although he had no wish to return, all he wanted was a return to normality. Taking care not to soil the important papers he was going through, he noticed a slight mistake which he corrected and then he looked up; he had not noticed the person who sat opposite him. He couldn't believe his eyes.

'Hello, Penny, where did you spring from? Gosh this is a surprise, how on earth did you find me, would you care to join me for a cup of tea?'

Without waiting for an answer Ted signalled to the waitress who was already one ahead.

'Coming up, would you like one of these delicious cakes?' she asked.

'Thank you very much,' Ted said without consulting Penny.

There was no 'Hello, Ted,' she just sat there looking as pale as a ghost. Finally she said sorry for the terrible confusion he must be feeling. Ted was not that interested, he had a letter to write, which under the circumstances was very important.

'Just allow me to complete my work and then you can say what you want to before I go, I have an important client to see,' said Ted looking at his watch.

Please, Ted, that man means nothing to me, please understand.'

'No, I don't understand, Penny, after all the accusations and slanderous remarks made against me I deserve better than that, don't you think? And I also noticed that you were not exactly overly enthusiastic in coming to my defence. Why on earth you haven't told me all this before heaven knows, for crying out loud, what am I supposed to think? Now unless you have something sensible to say to me I think I will be on my way, but don't think I won't be back to see my son.'

'Ted, I have never had a life of my own, this man was forced upon me by my parents, although my mother doesn't like him any more than I do. Please, if you are thinking that I have let him——'

'Penny, I don't think anything, that's your business and your life to lead as you wish.'

Penny was looking increasingly desperate. Her face changed to a very pale colour and her eyes were no longer looking at him. In fact she looked as if she was about to be ill or faint. Whatever, he had to act fast. Once again the waitress was there just when you needed her.

'What's the matter with her? Just a minute, I will fetch a glass of water.'

Ted was at a loss to know what to do, but the waitress was there to make up for his incompetence. Giving Penny a sip of water she turned to Ted and said, 'She has a temperature and her little heart is going flat out, I mean just look at her, she is two penny worth of nothing. When was the last time she had a decent meal, or a drink? I mean she hasn't taken anything here. The best thing you can do is keep her warm, take her home and call a doctor.'

She then looked after Penny while Ted went to fetch his car, hoping it would start. Eventually he turned up at and the waitress helped Penny outside to the car.

'You don't honestly expect to get her home in this do you? There are names for cars in this state, go on off you go and put her to bed.'

Ted was relieved that Molly had returned and she immediately took Penny to her bedroom. Ted explained the situation to Molly who understood and thought it was high time she explained to Ted what was going on.

Ted had no time left, but said he would return at the weekend.

With more letters to deal with on his return to work he was relieved by the fact that Penny was feeling better. Molly phoned his office and said she was looking forward to seeing him, but he had to be honest with himself, he was not looking forward to going—except to see his son.

He took his mind off things by phoning Harry, who was over the moon hearing from one of the gang. They agreed to meet at the property with Ginger, who would not miss seeing Ted for the world. They would require a site plan of his house and a rough outline of the drive, after that it would be a drink to old times in the nearest Gladiator's Arms which made Ted smile. That was one meeting he really was looking forward to.

Molly was pleased to see Ted, which made a pleasant change from his last few receptions. Penny had been diagnosed with flu, but further tests were still being done which might reveal something a little more sinister. Molly was very worried that Penny may have glandular fever and that the doctor said for the moment it would be a good idea to keep the baby out of Penny's bedroom.

'He is in my bedroom at the moment, go and fetch him if you like, and by the way, Ted, please don't get too close to Penny until we know exactly what's wrong with her.'

Ted looked in on Penny, she was fast asleep in this rather dull room. He had not noticed before, but it was obvious she had very little of her own. He went back to Molly and asked her if she would take him and her grandson into town where he would treat them to lunch.

'I know you want to talk to me, so what do you say? I mean we can't be too long because of Penny, so what's it to be?'

Molly needed no persuading, she was ready with her grandson hoping he wouldn't have another little mishap on the way, having just cleaned him up.

Molly admitted that things had gone badly wrong with Penny's upbringing. 'It was our own fault really, her father was very strict with her and I never interfered when I should have. The trouble was he never knew any other way, it was his whole life and then it had to end so tragically, which is something else I would like to discuss with you.

When they returned, Ted placed flowers with a letter in Penny's room. She was still fast asleep, so without disturbing her he spoke to Molly, promising to return the following weekend.

On the way home he felt that Molly was doing all she could for her daughter and young Harry. It must be very difficult for her, but somehow Ted thought that the only way out for all of them was to move to an entirely new area. Just get away and start a new life.

The meeting with Ginger and Harry was just like old times. The site was no problem and they promised a good price for the entrance, drive and to knock down the old house.

'Don't worry about a thing,' Ginger said who had not changed a bit.

He had re-married a girl called Caroline who was a Jehovah's Witness and they had a son who they had called Gary.

'Incidentally, we have never heard from Gary in North Wales,' said Harry, 'we sent an invitation to him for my wedding, but never received a reply. This is your invitation, Ted, but we didn't quite know what names to invite.'

'That's fine, Harry, and thanks; as you know my life never seems to settle down and the present moment is no exception. My girlfriend, if you remember, you know the one that never wrote to me, has suspected glandular fever, so who knows, I may be the only one at your wedding. At least I was able to keep my promise and find her.'

'Are we talking about the same girl, Ted, you know the one that was a complete mystery to you? I remember you having a tough time on the island,' said Ginger.

'Yes, the very one.'

'So you are a father, well I'm damned,' said Ginger looking as if he was about to give him a lecture on moral standards. 'Congratulations to you both, what's the baby's name?'

'It's Harry,' Ted replied laughing.

'Well, I am not going to argue with that,' said Harry.

'We always said you sailed close to the wind, but this is not only fantastic news, but is worthy of a celebratory pint in the Gladiator's Arms,' said Ginger.

Ted was in full agreement, but his thoughts were for Penny; he hoped she would be well enough to attend Harry's wedding.

'As for Gary, we are at a bit of a loss, he was so keen to keep in touch and Ginger reckons Alf was also keen to meet up again.'

There was no mention of Pete or Brian, they never left their addresses and simply disappeared.

'Look, lads, how about you trying to find Alf and I will find Gary?' said Ted.

It was agreed, but Harry had one other piece of news. 'Do you remember Rex?' he asked.

'No idea,' replied Ted.

'Well that's for you to find out at the wedding.'

18. Penny's New Home

Ted contacted Molly each day, but there was no change in Penny's condition. If there was no improvement soon she would have to be admitted to hospital. Ted was beyond himself, but Molly seemed to coping well under the circumstances; she did mention one thing, Penny wanted to know where Ted was.

'The sooner you get up here the better, Ted, perhaps you would like to stay, but you have to sleep on the sofa.'

By now he realised Molly was shedding a few tears and tried to reassure her. He would be there first thing Friday evening.

Bad luck seemed to follow Ted, but he was about to have one stroke of good luck. Mr Williamson popped his head around the door, 'Ted, I have Mr Townsend here who would like to speak to you about your house and the new entrance.'

'I think it might be worth your while, but before that Susan told me that your girlfriend's mother has been on the phone to say her daughter has been admitted to hospital. She left a message hoping to see you on Friday evening. Now look, tomorrow I would like you to sort out the contract for the farm Mr Townsend intends to purchase. It will require a site visit, but after that you must go and visit your girlfriend. I will see you on Monday morning. Good luck, and please give her our best wishes.'

Mr Townsend was indeed a business man and came straight to the point, 'There is no time to beat around the bush, young man, I know you have more urgent problems, may I ask your young lady's illness?'

Ted explained the situation with Mr Townsend reassuring Ted that it may take a long time, but she would pull through.

'I know, my daughter suffered with the same illness,' he said.

'Incidentally, my daughter will be running the farm. We breed horses and the farm land is ideal, but for a public footpath. In the interest of public safety I would like you to negotiate an alteration to the existing route to a more favourable and interesting route. Naturally, I will pay for any expenses. Secondly, I don't know if you realise it, but I will be your new neighbour down the lane. At the moment I have a very unsatisfactory entrance, so I was wondering if you could see your way to allowing me free access to my house via your lane. I don't expect an answer here and now, but I would be grateful even if you looked at my proposal. What do you say, mate?'

Ted explained it would be some time before he could finance his plans. He showed him the plans and pencilled in a possible route to Mr Townsend's house. He also mentioned that he was expecting a price to have all the work done by a couple of old friends.

'Their qualifications are second to none. You name it they can do, from building roads to buildings, even surviving nuclear bombs.'

'Blimey, don't tell me they were at Maralinga? Rotten business all that nuclear stuff in the Woomera area. I come from Ballarat and then moved to Adelaide, nobody goes out that way if they can help it.'

'No, sir, we served on Christmas Island more or less in the middle of the Pacific Ocean. Anyhow, I don't really see a problem to be honest, naturally I would have to draw up an agreement, but as I say, if you can wait a few months I don't see a problem.'

'How about if I financed the entrance, including the drive down the lane as far as my place? These friends of yours could carry on with my drive to the house. Would that help?'

Ted nearly fell off his chair.

'Sir, I have to tell you that's the best offer I have had in a long time if ever, but fifty–fifty would be fair.'

'Look, young man, you know what they say; never look a gift horse in the mouth, I insist, so that's one fence jumped.'

He was a highly intelligent man with a great sense of humour. Ted was interested and would look at all the legal details that would suit them both. Ted needed the money, but he was a little concerned about the whole project being paid for by Mr Townsend, he decided to get advice from his boss. Maybe if the money was paid direct to him and then he settled the final bill with Ginger and Harry? He need not have worried, Mr Williamson said he would draw up the contract so that both parties would be happy.

Ted was amused by his neighbour's humour and looked forward to living next door to him, even though Ted's house was way down the lane.

The worry about Penny had been temporarily taken away by this unexpected change in his fortunes. Walking around the farm looking for this public footpath he realised the problem his client faced; but the proposed route would indeed be an improvement, and he could not see a problem in making a formal application to have it re-routed. The rest of the day was his to walk around the fields and think about

Penny and their future—if there was a future. His priority
was his son, and the last time he was getting on well with
Penny all hell let loose when the boyfriend walked in. It was
just like a relapse, but this time he intended to redeem the
situation just as soon as she was well enough. To see if there
was to be any meaningful relationship he would invite her
to see his home.

He arrived to find that Penny was at home. She had been
in hospital for two days. With youth on her side she had
responded well to treatment, but was left very weak simply
because she had not eaten properly, and in Ted's opinion her
life had been controlled with such strict discipline that she
had no mind of her own.

Molly allowed him to see Penny, but not to get too close
to her.

'Doctor's orders apparently,' she said.

However frustrating, Ted held Penny's hand and talked
about his change of fortune. 'I can see a light at the end of
the tunnel,' he said.

'When you are well enough would you like to see my
latest acquisition and I am not talking about my car?'

'No, Ted, we don't talk about your car,' she said laughing.

'Well, of all the sauce, I can assure you my car is well
sought after.'

'Yes, in scrap yards maybe,' said Penny, teasing him all
the more.

'Yes, I would love to see your home, and to be honest I
would go this very moment if I was well enough.' By now she
was speaking very softly, it was obvious just those few words
had exhausted her. She just about had enough energy to say
she had missed him.

'How right you were about the angel in that dark tunnel

helping us through difficult times, but now even I can see a light at the end of the tunnel.'

That was it, she had said all she could before falling asleep. Feeling much more confident that she would overcome this dreadful illness, he kissed her gently and felt that at last they might well have a future together.

Weeks passed by and with the arrival of spring Penny made good progress and was soon fit enough to travel. Ted had worked on his car putting in better brakes and a heater that worked.

The boot was packed with Harry's things and enough food to last them all for a week. Molly insisted they took plenty just in case. Penny had made lots of her famous cakes and had piled in just about everything one needed for an Arctic expedition.

'The car is groaning at the thought of moving it all, let alone getting to end of the road,' Ted said looking rather worried.

'Are you sure this thing will start?' said Penny, not helping matters at all.

'No, I'm not sure, it has serious doubts about its power-to-weight ratio and may launch an official complaint half way down the road, by which time it will be too late. However, if you are all sitting comfortable we will ask it to start.'

Molly found the departure highly amusing, but was more thrilled to see the three of them together on their own at last.

The entrance and driveway had been completed, except for the top surface, all the way down to the old house.

He explained everything, but Penny said nothing. Her face said it all, she looked so sad.

'What's the matter, my love, have I said something wrong, do you want to go home?'

She was looking at the house and then turned to him, and

for the first time in what seemed like aeons, she held onto him.

'You can't stay in that old house, you will catch a death. No, please Ted, I would worry myself silly for you.'

'I have no intention of staying there, my love, take a look around the other side of the old barn and you will see a mobile home. It's a temporary arrangement until this place has been rebuilt. Take a look at the plans for the new house.'

He explained just about everything, with young Harry doing his best to tear the plans apart and laughing at the same time.

'Hey, little fellah, if that's what you think of it then I don't know what to do,' Ted said pretending to chase him.

Penny, on the other hand, was less vocal, she walked back to the old house and turned to Ted asking, 'Is this where the new house will be?'

'Yes, the old house can be knocked down and the new house will take its place, but on the condition that it will be of a traditional timber frame construction. I can start just as soon as I arrange the mortgage, but it seems I am one penny short.'

'What do you mean, my love? It's a magnificent place to live and you thoroughly deserve it,' said Penny looking rather puzzled.

'Yes, but it doesn't answer my question, I am still one penny short.'

'What do you mean silly boy,' she said looking straight at him.

'I mean what I say: would you like to live here, Penny?'

'Yes, I would, I could only dream of a place like this. Yes, Ted, I can stay with you, but then I . . .'

There was a pause for a moment; it was Ted's moment to ask the big question.

'You won't live here with me unless we are married, is that it?'

'Yes,' replied Penny clinging on to him even more.

'Well, will you marry me, Penny James and become Mrs Penny Watson?'

'Of course, of course I will, I would have married you the first day we met.'

She was so excited she kissed him like the first days they were together. Penny picked up their son and walked back to the old house saying, 'Look, Harry, this is our new home and Daddy is going to look after us. Joy quickly turned to tears, Penny found it all too much to take in. Ted comforted her and took them both into the mobile home, where Penny calmed down. Her tears quickly changed to a very happy smiling face. It was little Harry's turn to shed tears, and by the look on Penny's face she was not surprised.

'I will change him, my love, if you would be so kind and fetch his things in here and when I have done you can bring the picnic in here, it's too cold outside.'

During the picnic Penny had a lot to say.

'I can't leave Mum on her own, I mean I want to come here right now, but I couldn't leave Mum on her own.'

'You're quite right, sweetheart, I have been thinking of that myself, so that's something else we have to think about.'

Ted knew it would be at least twelve months before they could even think about moving in, so they both had plenty of time to think. To there amazement there was a knock on the door.

'Who on earth could this be?' Ted said getting up from the table.

It was Mr Townsend, he had been taking a walk, and seeing the car he thought he would say hello.

'Please come on in and meet the gang,' Ted said with a broad smile.

He introduced his family, and Mr Townsend introduced himself as Bill and their neighbour. Penny seemed to be quite happy with this unexpected visit and quickly made a place for Bill.

'I will make you a cup of tea and please help yourself to my cake, or whatever you like,' she said.

'Well, I must say you two—or I should say three, sorry young man.'

With that young Harry thrust out his little hands which were covered with food.

'If you don't mind, I would rather not shake hands just at the moment, thank you, but I am sure we will meet again.'

Everybody was amused and Bill forgot what he was going to say which was even more amusing.

'Bill comes from Australia, Penny.'

'Yes, I actually came from a farm not far from here, but my parents took off for Victoria. They settled in Ballarat with a farm, but I took off into the Australian Army, became a major, and spent a great deal of time up north in the Northern Territory and Queensland. I went back to live in Adelaide with my wife and daughter, but my wife died and my daughter decided she wanted to come here and so here I am.

'That's fascinating—and sad,' said Penny, 'But you are always welcome here, so long as you can put up with Harry's grubby little hands.'

It was a pleasant end to their first visit. Ted walked back with Bill and explained that the final layer on the lane would be completed just as soon as the bulk of the house was finished.

'Just one more favour, Ted, I have a couple of horses that are very dear to me. For their retirement I was wondering if they could run around in your field now and again, my daughter thinks I am a sentimental old fool, but they have given an awful lot to me over the years. I would have to have it all fenced off so let me know what you think. I know what you are going to say, I haven't got the money to fence it all off, so I would take care of that, plus a shelter for them. By the way, their names are Poppy and Hector.

Penny couldn't wait to get home and break the good news of their engagement, but she suddenly realised there was plenty to think about. What with a wedding and a house to furnish there was no time left to think about the past. Yes, Poppy and Hector would be as welcome as the flowers in May.

'What amazing names, are you going to let them run around the field?' asked Penny.

'I don't see a problem, but it's entirely up to you, it's your field as well sweetheart.'

19. Ted Remembers Ginger's Advice

Having seen a doctor about a lump on his neck, Ted went to hospital to have it removed. He was told it may only be a benign cyst and quite common, on the other hand it might be malignant: a biopsy would reveal the truth.

Ted became extremely anxious, especially when the doctor wanted to see him again. The doctor recommended a course of treatment and after that he would review the situation. Ted obviously wanted to know more and asked why he needed treatment and for how long. The doctor seemed to evade the question, simply saying the treatment would last for six weeks after which he may well need a further three weeks to rest, transport would be available if required.

In view of the difficulties with the loss of her father he was acutely aware of the possible reaction from Penny, but he was wrong. Penny was relieved to know that he had at last done something about it, but Molly was a little more sceptical and concerned, having seen her husband go through similar treatment. She felt sure it had something to do with exposure to radiation.

Ted explained what he had been told, and that he felt fine, which was a slight departure from the truth. He had always remembered what Ginger used to say, always tell the truth otherwise you just end up making a rod for your back. He decided to explain to Molly exactly what was going on.

'I have six weeks of radiotherapy treatment for cancer. The doctor won't tell me exactly how serious the situation is so I can only hope the treatment works and I make a full recovery.'

'I sincerely hope you are right, I think the world of you and what you have done for us, and goodness knows what my daughter thinks of you, she never stops talking about you.'

It was then Ted noticed a familiar face, 'May I, please,' he asked, picking up a picture of an Army officer.

'It's my late husband, Ted, you thought you all knew him.'

'It's difficult to believe I stood right next to him.' Ted stopped short since he thought it would be very unwise to upset her by explaining what had really happened. Instead he told Molly he had seen him only once, in fact the colonel spoke to him, but that was it, he disappeared and no doubt he must have been very busy. Putting the picture back he could only say the lads thought he really looked after them. Molly smiled and saved him from further embarrassment.

'It's just as well he didn't know who you were at the time, Ted, but to be honest I know he would have got on well with you, now be off with you, Penny has been eager to show you something.'

Penny couldn't wait to take him outside to see her car, which Molly had bought for her. It was a Morris Traveller, absolutely perfect for Penny and all of Harry's things.

'What do you think, darling, would you teach me to drive? I have taken several lessons already, I just need to get a little more experience, perhaps I could drive down to the house one weekend and I can drive you to the hospital for your treatment.'

The house was taking shape with Penny wondering how she wanted her kitchen and what she would wear at Harry and Helen's wedding, but the most important priority was Ted's treatment. Penny wasted no time in terminating her part-time job and made arrangements to move in with Ted, but most important of all were her own wedding plans and young Harry's christening.

20. TWO WEDDINGS

Ted's treatment went without a problem, but a complete rest was welcome towards the end. He became extremely tired, so Penny suggested a holiday in North Wales. Her driving test went without a hitch and Ted thought she drove far better than himself.

With young Harry firmly placed on the back seat, they set off for North Wales. They had a holiday cottage with a view looking up to the mountains.

'We have to go up there,' Ted said.

'No way could I climb up that, you will be on your own, won't he, my little man?' Penny replied picking up their son so that he could see this huge mountain.

'According to this map that mountain is called Carnedd Llewelyn and we could take the car up so far and get a fine view.

The week passed too quickly and it was time to go home. Ted wanted to go back to work, but on their way home Ted enquired if anybody knew of a Gary Owen.

'There are plenty of Owens around here, which family do you want?'

It was hopeless until two young girls knew of a Gary Owen who was in the building trade.

'That's the one,' said Ted getting rather excited at the prospect of seeing his old mate again.

There was a lot of talk between the girls in Welsh.

'Yes, now let me see, I think he was the one that had an illness. His parents buried him at the chapel. We don't know were they live now, did you know him?'

'We were in the Army together,' replied Ted.

'Yes, that's it, he was in the Army, national service I think they called it. There was quite a row about it, his father was extremely angry about his son's work abroad, but that's all we know about it, sorry.'

Ted thanked them both and said it was a very sad ending to a fine holiday, but they would be back one day.

The first port of call was to visit Molly, who had prepared a fine meal for them. After a lot of persuading, Molly finally consented to stay with them for a while. Molly would have the second bedroom and young Harry would go in with them. To Molly it was quite an adventure to sleep in a mobile home down a lane full of creepy crawlies, but in a way she was looking forward to it.

Ted went back to work and said he was feeling a little better. Waiting for him was a pile of work, among which were the amended deeds for the right of way down the lane. He quickly confirmed this to Bill in writing and promised to call in just as soon as possible.

Not feeling one hundred per cent he realised that pacing himself would be the only option. The memory of Gary didn't help, but he had seen his homeland, especially his beloved mountains. He would most certainly go back there, and he had found out that Penny had a passion for gardens.

Arriving home one evening Penny was full of it, 'We had a visit from your sister, only for a cup of tea, but it was a lovely surprise. She had Sophie with her and promised to put Mum up while we go to the wedding. She has invited us for Sunday lunch before we take Mum back, and by the way your parents will be there.'

It was typical of his sister, full of heart, and Ted realised that although they had had differences in the past, she was always there when you needed her.

After their evening meal, Molly was keen to speak to Ted on his own.

'Can we walk up the lane please, Ted, I know you must feel tired, but I would like to speak to you.'

Ted obliged and said anytime she wanted to talk he would always be there for her. Molly had several things to ask him; the first was would he mind if she moved closer to them permanently? She felt a little isolated and above all she wanted to get away and take the good memories with her.

Ted was delighted and said it was the finest thing to do and he would help in any way he could. 'For starters you already have a lawyer, and it won't cost you a *penny*,' he said laughing.

'Well, you see, Ted, your sister knows of some bungalows that are yet to be built, but she wants to show me the area. Can I stay on for a few more days?'

'You, above all people, need not ask, as Penny sometimes says, you are as welcome as the flowers in May.'

'Ted, I really appreciate this, but can I ask you just one more question? I know it may hurt you, but I would just like to know what happened on that island, that is the time you saw my husband, it would help to settle my mind. You see, nobody at the time of his illness would tell me a thing.'

Ted had no wish to rekindle what had happened on the island, it felt like having a relapse, especially when things were going so much better for him, but if it would make her feel a little better he would explain what had really happened for her sake.

'We expected a medical when we came home, but we didn't get one. I will tell you straight, Mum, I feel pretty rotten letting the colonel down, and yourself of course. I had a hard time during those two years, I loved Penny so much, the boys will tell you, they used to say I sailed very close to the edge when Penny stopped writing to me.'

'What do you mean, Ted?'

'Oh, I took to drink, and quite frankly before the bomb was dropped near the island I couldn't care less. When they made us all line up I was standing right next to Penny's father; naturally I had no idea who he was, but I can tell you this, he made absolutely sure that we stayed down with our backs to the bomb.'

'But surely you were given protection, I don't believe none of you were given shelter, or at least taken well out of harm's way.'

'I have no idea, but it became obvious we were far too close for comfort. Airmen were also lined up on the airfield for an unexpected glimpse of one of the greatest firework displays on earth. There was no place to hide, not with a bomb that size.'

'You did speak to my husband?'

'Oh yes, I think I was letting off steam and objected to being lined up for another roasting, the colonel told me to keep quiet. He wanted to know my name.'

'And did you tell him?'

'No, but he said he would speak to me later.'

'He made absolutely sure we stayed down, but I have to tell you he knew we were frightened out of minds. Some lads prayed for their families. Believe it or not, I prayed for Penny. One or two became emotional and the rest, well, you don't want to know. The first bomb was bad enough, which frightened us to a point where some of the boys became very confused and terrified.

'Please, Ted, if it hurts you to tell me then don't say anything.'

'No, it's okay, it's just the thought of these weapons ever being used that bothers me. There is always somebody who wants to rattle the sabre. "Look, if you don't get out of my way and do as you are told then I will drop a bomb on you." It's really frightening, especially when you know what these things can do. God forbid these weapons are ever used, it scares me, Molly. Diplomacy and trust is the only answer. The daft thing is we are all made from the same blueprint, but have grown up with all sorts of different beliefs, most of which all point in the same direction. One of the worst elements of man is greed, our motto being, "What's mine is mine and what's yours is mine. So get out of my way." The little guys have no say whatsoever. Sorry Molly, I got carried away, so where was I? Oh yes, somebody was talking over a tannoy, bombs away, close eyes, close eyes. The colonel was still shouting to us, keep down and then silence. All I remember was seeing all the bones in my hands quite clearly. With my collar turned up on my shirt I managed to avoid being burnt on my neck by the heat, but the heat still sapped the air from my lungs. I gasped for air, but the heat was so intense I honestly thought I was going nowhere fast. From then on I felt as if I was on my own, I just sat there not wanting to get up. The heat was unrelenting and I knew from the last time it would be very unwise to stand up, the full impact was yet to come—with devastating power.

Still, your husband shouted at us to keep down, but for reasons only known to themselves one or two lads foolishly got to their feet, only to be blown over by a very powerful afterblast.

Later we were told the bomb was something like thirty-odd miles away. The noise was out of this world, I finally stood up only to see this huge fireball rising up. To be honest, it looked incredible, roaring away at us with different colours shining out of it. You could still feel the heat and then this huge cloud formed, getting larger all the time. We stood there until we realised that more clouds were appearing. We ran for cover by getting into the back of a lorry. Debris had been thrown all over the place and some of the palm trees took quite a beating, some of them were snapped in two.

We saw a glimpse of hell; hundreds of birds were seen falling, some were still alive but blind and burning. Seeing all this I felt sick. We had seen enough and we decided to get the hell out of it. The driver drove away as fast as he could with clouds forming all around us. One of the lads thought it was the end for us all, especially when it started to rain. We stayed inside the lorry for a while since it occurred to us it might be fallout, but later on we were told differently. There was so much confusion and panic we lost sight of the colonel. He must have done the same as we did and run for cover. I feel upset, Molly, especially when I think he was young Harry's grandfather, but also he was our commanding officer looking after us right to the end.'

'So he was. Well, thank you, Ted, you have eased my mind knowing the truth at last. I am sorry to have burdened you and I am sorry to have to put you through reliving such a dreadful experience. It seems to me you have every reason to be upset, why on earth you were all lined up like that without any protection beggars belief. Well, I don't know what to do, so I would appreciate your advice.'

Under the circumstances it was perfectly understandable that Molly should seek some justice, Ted reminded her she may be entitled to make a claim for a war pension, but it would be advisable to let him look into her case before taking any form of action.

'There are more than one way to skin a grape. Just sit back and let me handle everything, and in any case, hopefully you will be moving close to us before long and that in itself can be stressful.'

Molly agreed and said it was time to get back and enjoy a nice cup of tea before it rained.

'How do you like it here, Molly, I mean you won't be too frightened living like we are at the moment will you? We have lots of wildlife here, including owls at night and also you may hear a fox screaming, don't worry it will only be the vixen.'

'What does Penny think of it here, bless her? I have often worried about her in the past, but now she seems to be so happy.'

'She is happy here, I very much doubt she will ever go back, so the sooner you come down here the better. Penny wants to take you home, but just to pick up a few more things and then bring you back. After all, it's Harry's wedding next Saturday.'

The big day arrived. Christine played host to Ted, Penny and Molly. As usual she had worked her heart out for her family. There was an early breakfast, leaving plenty of time for Penny to get herself organised with young Harry, who by now was beginning to walk. Christine would be taking Molly to see her new bungalow taking shape, and then it was out to lunch before taking her to see Ted's parents while Ted and Penny attended the wedding.

Waving them off, Christine could not help feeling that at

last that lovely brother of hers had got his act together, bless him.

Having plenty of time, Ted pulled into a cafe. He asked Penny to hold out her hand and then placed her engagement ring on her finger, which was long overdue. Ted admitted he could have chosen a better place and time, but he felt she should have her engagement ring for the wedding.

Penny did not mind, at last she could show off her engagement ring to the world.

After lots of kisses and hugs, Penny carried Harry inside for a coffee with Harry telling everybody he was there. Ted followed after locking the car, but in his eagerness to join his family he fell over making one hell of a mess of his suit.

'What on earth have you done, my love.'

Penny reminded Ted of when he had fallen over and cut his leg, but fortunately this time he had only made a mess of his suit.

'Stand up and lets have a look at you.'

She couldn't help laughing, cleaning him up, she described his suit as looking as though it had been dragged behind the car.

'You will do, I don't know what we are going to do with him, Harry, perhaps he can hide at the back of the church, what say you?'

Harry slept all the way to the church with Penny saying to Ted she could easily join him. Ted agreed and held on to them both. Ted could see nobody he knew at the church.

Once they were seated Penny nudged Ted and said, 'Are those your friends up the front?'

But it was difficult to see. Just in front of them was a large family, all girls, who were later joined by what had to be their father. Ted was certain he had seen him before, but could not quite place him.

Suddenly, the organ stopped playing, but soon struck up again as the bride walked in. Harry was awake and in fidgety mood until he spotted the bride. That was it, for some reason he wanted to touch her with his arms outstretched. Helen gave a nervous smile at him, leaving young Harry burbling away, he then lost interest and turned to his mum.

At last Ted could see Harry and Ginger, having lost their youthful looks as he first remembered seeing them, but who was the man in front of him? Ted felt sure he had seen him before.

When the wedding ceremony was over Penny handed young Harry over to Ted. Helen and Harry walked past them with a big smile from Helen for baby Harry, who pointed a tiny finger at her. Not surprisingly, Harry failed to spot Ted. Then it was all over, the ceremony had gone well and now it was the turn of the photographer.

The sun felt just a little too strong and Penny was anxious not to let Harry get caught by the glorious sunshine, so leaving them sheltering under a tree, Ted dashed off to find his son's hat. Suddenly, Penny was approached by the best man.

'Excuse me, the young man with you a few minutes ago, I wonder if you could tell me where he is please?'

'You are Ginger, I am sure you are? You can speak to him yourself, he's just gone to fetch his son's hat.'

Ginger looked at little Harry and said, 'Well, well, this is his son and you must be Penny, the girl who made us a cake. I am so pleased to meet you, my dear, you have made a dream come true. That boy talked about you so often, Penny, and my God he certainly loved you.'

Penny just had to show him her engagement ring and then thanked him for all the work he had done for them.

'Just a minute, you are the colonel's daughter, well I must

admit I didn't see much of him, but I did hear him talking to Ted.'

Realising that he might have put his foot in it he said he had to dash back to the reception.

Ted returned with Harry's hat and they made their way into the reception. Taking their seats, Ted saw the man he had recognised before, but this time the man was looking at him.

'Hello again, you obviously don't remember me, the name's Rex, Rex Harper, and these are all mine; five of them at the last count.'

His wife, Sarah, was introduced to Penny and then Rex turned to Ted and said, 'Remember Port London? We picked up a few crates and you had a narrow escape from those Navy lads. We had a talk the next day if you remember, Ted?

'Blow me down, it's Captain Harper, how are you, still in the Army?

'Good heavens, no. I left about a year after you and found life a little tough for a while, I remembered Harry giving me his home number and here we are. I work for them now and I must say it has been the best part of my life, apart from this horrible bunch of rascals,' he said, waving his fist at his children. They giggled and obviously thought the world of their dad.

'What about yourself, old chap? Fancy a beer later and then we can catch up on a few things.'

Ted agreed, but above all he wanted to see Harry and Ginger. He did not have to wait long; the four of them soon went for a couple of beers. Harry had very little time to talk, but arrangements were made to meet up as a reunion every year. Ginger and Harry left Ted and Rex, who also was about to leave.

'The little one is not that well, has to take regular

medication. She was born with very poor vision, which I am pleased to say has improved somewhat. Costs a fortune, but she's a little darling to us. I got out of the Army realising I just had to earn more, and thank the Lord, here we are. The boys tell me you are going to marry the colonel's daughter; how did you manage that? Sorry, none of my business. They say you are a lawyer, defended any rogue traders lately, have we?' he said laughing.

Soon the evening had to come to an early end. Rex rounded up the scallywags, as he called them, and shook hands. Penny got on well with Sarah and invited them all over just as soon as they had moved into the new house.

It was getting late and Ted drove them home. It was not long before Penny and little Harry were fast asleep in the back of the car.

Christine was waiting for them with Molly ready to go home. Molly had thoroughly enjoyed her day and had committed herself to buying a bungalow.

'I will tell you all about it tomorrow, I think we are all a little too tired at the moment.'

Without doubt the position of the bungalow was ideal for Molly with a park and shops nearby, and a bus service and railway station. Molly had enjoyed her weekend, especially visiting Ted's parents. Feeling rather pleased with herself, she had thought through what Ted had said about the island and her husband. She decided that it might not be very wise to enter into complicated matters now that she had committed herself to buying a bungalow. Molly felt that it would be an investment for all of them and all she really wanted was to start a fresh life. Both Penny and Ted were really pleased for her and promised to help her in any way they could, but Ted reminded Molly to not rule out the possibility of filing a claim for a hearing at a war pensions tribunal. He would look into her claim and produce a statement for her and then submit a claim. He would represent her at the hearing, and would be in a position to answer any questions on her behalf. Molly had to go home, so Penny thought it would be a good idea to go back with her and stay the week and then return the following Friday. Ted was happy with that and said he had much to do, perhaps during the week she could start looking for her wedding dress?

'The time has come, my love, to talk of many things, of wedding dresses, wedding bells and, finally, wedding rings,' mumbled Ted in his usual jovial fashion.

The wedding was to be in three month's time. Time enough to send out invitations, and for Molly to move into her new bungalow. Their own house was taking shape with the possibility of them moving in before the winter. Penny had one rather difficult problem though. Who would give her away in the church? It then suddenly occurred to them both that perhaps Bill would do the honours.

The next day Bill called round looking for his usual cup of tea. He always liked to see young Harry, especially now he was walking quite well.

'By the way, Penny, many thanks for the invitation. I look forward to it. What do you want for a present?' asked Bill.

That was it, Penny saw her chance.

'Bill, I don't have anybody to give me away, you see, my father died about three years ago, he was with Ted during one of those awful nuclear tests. He came home and fell ill.

'Obviously he was much older than these young lads, was he in charge of them?' asked Bill.

'I am not sure what he did in the Army, all I know is he would go away now and again, but as I said, he became very ill, so I have to find somebody to give me away and I was wondering——'

'Wondering what, my dear? Look, don't beat around the bush—don't cry whatever you do.'

Penny's eyes were beginning to go red and she was about to shed tears.

'I know, you want old Major Townsend down the lane to do the honours! Bless you, my dear. Don't worry, I will do my best for you.'

Penny knew her mother would approve and she was right; the wedding plans were complete, all was ready except for the house which would take at least two more months according to the builder.

Molly was delighted with her bungalow and had no regrets on the day she moved in. The difficult times of the past were over, she had found new friends in Ted's sister and mother, but she still found it difficult to overcome the loss of her husband. Ted paid a visit, wanting to explain the latest details of her claim for a hearing at a tribunal. He made it clear to her that dropping the whole idea of going to a court was the right choice. He explained why it would be very complex and would require the services of a very good lawyer experienced in such matters.

'If you approve the content of the case I have made on your behalf then all I need is the go ahead from you. Take your time and let me know just as soon as you are ready. I will represent you at the hearing, all you have to do is sit with me.'

Molly didn't hesitate, she read carefully the case notes while Ted admired the view from her window.

'I can't fault these notes at all, I can understand most of it, I think, but I suppose you lawyers understand it all.'

'Don't give up, Molly, never give up,' said Ted, thinking he very nearly gave up on more than one occasion.

'It may help others: let us see if it works,' said Ted feeling a little optimistic.

'What happens if I lose, will there be any bills?' Molly asked looking a little concerned.

'Oh dear, I was expecting you to ask that. Well, they may throw you in jail for six months and, of course, there will be my fee—unless you make me a nice cup of tea. No, Mum, there will be no fees whatsoever, so don't worry, we will look after you, I think you will find the members of the panel will also be very nice to you. It will be me answering all the questions, unless you wish to add something you think important.'

It was not exactly the right time for a wedding, but under the circumstances, and with another baby on the way, it was just as well. Penny had had it confirmed that she was pregnant, so with the wedding plans now set, they sat back and relaxed.

Penny said that the first time she had found out that she was pregnant she was beyond herself and unable to think straight, with her parents up in arms.

'Well, let's see if we can make up for those dark days, my love, we have shed light on many things since then, so come here and let's have a good look at my pretty bride to be.'

The house would soon be ready with the added luxury of heating, and by the look of the weather they would need it. Ted had spent a fortune based on his sister's forecast that inflation would take off. That was fine, but would his salary match inflation? He doubted it very much.

The big day arrived with Bill looking very smart and proud to give Penny away.

'Major Townsend and foster dad at your service, my dear, and I must say you look fabulous, let's take a look at you.'

Having his own camera he got the driver to take pictures

outside their new house. On the way to the church Bill said how pleased he was to have Poppy and Hector in the field and that he hoped she liked the shelter he had built for them.

'Okay, sweetheart, here we are, just hold on to me and look straight ahead.'

Bill noticed that she was shaking a little.

'Okay, soldier, this one is for your dad, hang on girl, and let me cover for you. Right, charge.'

By the time she reached the altar she felt much better.

Bill had been wonderful to her. He was a gentleman of the old school from Australia and Penny had found a foster dad.

The weather was not good, with heavy rain and strong gale force winds. The photographer found it impossible, so he recommended a few more pictures inside the church and the rest back at the reception.

Harry, being the best man, made a cracking speech and avoided talking about the past, which was a relief to Ted. However, Harry did mention how Ted took enormous risks just to see Penny, and how he turned out to be the worst barrack room lawyer, only getting them into more trouble. Bill found that very funny since he must have had many Australian lads' misdemeanors to sort out while in the Australian army.

Ted's speech was rather short as he knew that many of the guests were rather concerned about the weather outside and were anxious to take the road for home. Before Harry left he made arrangements for all the lads and their families to meet at his place before Christmas.

Christine, who was always one ahead, asked Molly if she could take all the buffet and drink back to her place. Molly jumped to the idea and everybody was invited. As it turned out there was only Bill and his daughter, Molly, Christine, and Sophie and her parents.

Penny and Ted went home with little Harry, who had fallen asleep. She put him to bed and then Ted just wanted to see Penny in her wedding dress once more before changing.

There was no honeymoon, simply because there was no money left, but Ted had plans for next spring and asked Penny to choose. Penny had her heart set on Cyprus, but it was not possible because of the problems out there. In the end she chose Cornwall, which suited Ted.

Ted thought Ginger had looked unwell at the reception. He obviously could not say anything; but he had seen Ginger looking better. One other worry was that Ted had received a letter from the bank detailing his recent expenditure. He was on the edge of being called into account. This called for drastic action, he had to call in the troops.

Two months passed, and there was yet another letter from the bank.

'Everybody on parade,' he shouted.

'What's the matter, darling, is there anything wrong?'

'Yes, indeed there is, Sapper Watson. Today I received a final warning from the bank that unless steps are taken to reduce the overdraft then drastic measures will be taken; maybe a complete foreclosure, which could mean the bailiffs banging on our door. Well, we will see about that, won't we, Sapper Harry? What's going on, he's fallen asleep—this is an outrage.'

'Permission to speak, sir.'

'Yes, of course, but I don't want excuses, carry on, Sapper Watson.'

'I represent Master Watson's interests in this matter and we think it's all your fault. If you can't come up with the goodies then you are fired.'

'Oh, so that's it? Well, my financial affairs have always been beyond reproach. This is an outrage, I shall speak to my bank manager immediately. Do I see one soldier still asleep?'

'Yes, he thinks you are a Wally dodger, fancy getting us into debt.'

With that the door bell rang, it was the major come for his cup of tea, no doubt.

'Hello all, fallen out already have we? That's the spirit,' he said laughing.

'We have all been on parade, Bill; he's only got twenty-nine shillings left so my little man and me are leaving.'

21. MIXED JUSTICE

Many years passed by with Penny and Ted solving their financial problems. The boys were growing up fast with Harry at university and James about to leave school. James was not interested in furthering his education, it seemed his interests were in cars and he found a part-time job at a garage in the sales department.

'It's not easy, Dad, there is a lot of hard work preparing a car for the road these days, and it's going to get tougher, believe me.'

Ted was impressed with his son's progress and gave him an old car to work on in the barn.

Driving home one evening Ted met Penny down the lane tending to her shrubs. She had made a splendid job of making the lane look a riot of colour during the spring and summer.

Winding the window down he said, 'Would you care for a lift, young lady?'

'My mum said I was not to talk to strange men, but in your case I will make an exception,' replied Penny with a broad smile, but she could see that Ted looked a little tired and was certainly not himself. Calling for her little cat, Mitzie, who followed her everywhere she jumped into the car.

'Is anything the matter, darling, you look a little depressed?'

'First of all, I have the rest of the week off, so how about you and me taking off for the weekend, anywhere you like, just pack and we can go?'

'In that case, soldier boy, if you want your way with me you had better put your foot down, I might change my mind.'

It was the honeymoon they had never had, Ted had already pre-booked a hotel in North Wales as he had felt certain that Penny would jump at the idea. James was left plenty in the fridge and they were away with not a moment lost.

'You seem a little down today, my love, do you want to tell me what's wrong?' said Penny.

'I suppose it's good to talk sometimes, especially when you have lost so many good friends,' said Ted.

'When I lost my mother it was a great loss to me. I mean she suffered a great deal, and in a way her loss was a blessing. We then lost our dear old friend the Major, but your mother was one hell of a shock to us both. We were lucky to have had such wonderful and supportive mothers; and to win your mother's case at the tribunal was a great moment for me. She thoroughly deserved to win.

'Today I received a phone call from Harry saying that Ginger was very ill with cancer and not expected to live beyond a couple of months. I can't begin to tell you how depressing that is to me, and I could only think there was only one solution and that was to go away for a few days with the girl I love dearly, she always cheers me up.'

Visiting some of the places they had seen before nothing much had changed, even the cafe was still there where they had found out about Gary.

'It's all very sad when you think about it, he was so young, which makes me think something is wrong. Think about it: of all the lads I knew out on that island many of them have had one problem or another, some of them losing their lives prematurely, including your father.'

They drove up towards Carndell Llewelyn, parked the car and walked through some of the most magnificent surroundings one could wish for.

'I agree with what you are saying, Ted, but in my parents' case, things were not that happy. There was increasing acrimony between them and my father was spending more and more time away from home. I remember when I was pregnant my mother supported me, but my father became really angry and threatened to leave. He, of course, ended up with you and I have always felt guilty, feeling that it was me that sent him out there.'

'For the love of might, I don't think you should be blaming yourself, sweetheart. If you have to blame yourself then I have to take the blame as well. No, my love, there is something wrong, too many of the lads have developed health problems over the years. I mean there is your father, young Gary, and perhaps I didn't tell you, Harry found out that Alf had died in a car crash, but he knew he was dying of cancer. Harry had no other details except that he was married with no children, which I suppose was a blessing. So you see there are few green bottles hanging on the wall.'

'It's true what you say, it is suspicious, Ted, do you think it's worth representing Ginger at another tribunal?'

'If he agrees, then yes, and while I am at it I will ask Harry if he is interested.'

'What for, there's nothing wrong with him? I know he has a heart condition, but outside of that I don't think he has a case,' argued Penny.

'That is as maybe, but perhaps you don't know he had real problems when he came home, which may have affected him badly, and he had no children. It's a very delicate matter, of course, and something which must remain confidential.'

'You are absolutely right, my lord, even if you did tell me, and I know you won't, I wouldn't understand all that legal jargon, I might as well listen to my cat Mitzie, so come on, let's walk over to that old house there, maybe nobody lives there.'

'That's outrageous, if you think I am going in there with you think again, young lady, the last time you cast a spell on me——'

'You're right, and knowing you it should still be working. Come on in, I won't bite.'

Arriving home they found their son Harry had come home with good news, he had been offered a job in a bank, but it was in London and so he would have to find digs. Ted was very pleased for him, and all his offers of help were gratefully received, but it appeared that his new employer had been very generous in offering a mortgage, so long as he could raise a deposit.

It seemed only fair that he should be helped to buy his own house since they had already helped James, but James was entirely different, he wanted to be his own boss, which was fully supported by both Penny and Ted. Penny still had her mother's bungalow which Christine had advised her not to sell but to let.

Ted strongly suspected that Penny was financing the purchase of cars, so Ted thought it only fair that he should help with Harry's house.

Ted reflected on his own youth: he had been called up to the Army for two years' compulsory service and put through rigorous training. He had met a girl, fallen in love with her, got her pregnant, and became involved with nuclear bombs; and all on twenty-nine shillings a week.

All his mates had a mixed story to tell and it was at the next reunion that Ted mentioned the possibility of representing them at a tribunal. He presented good sound reasons, but of course it was their final decision. Harry was sceptical, he did not think they would stand a chance as they had all been of low rank in the Army. He thought that the War Pensions Tribunal would have looked more favourably on the colonel's claim due to his rank. Rex disagreed, after all, he was a captain and he saw no valid reason for discrimination.

'Why on earth should there be? And, in any case, I think it's very kind of Ted to think of us,' said Rex.

'What is all this going to cost? And may I remind you, Rex, Ted's track record in getting us off a charge in the old days was not exactly good.'

Ted realised Harry had not changed a great deal, he always remembered him as being a bit of a moaner who spoke without thinking. Not to worry, he would make one last offer.

'Okay, lads, what's it to be? Do you want me to represent you at a tribunal or not? And by the way, I have no intention of charging you a penny.'

Rex was extremely grateful, but thought he had been lucky; his little daughter had not had perfect health, but she had a normal life and had grown up to have a boyfriend who thought the world of her. Nonetheless, he was very grateful to Ted.

Harry never mentioned he was grateful at all, he said he was interested, but what about Ginger, he was too ill to be here, so he would give Ted the details. Ted made it perfectly clear he could not deal with Ginger's case through a third party, he would have to speak directly to Ginger, or Caroline his wife.

Things had not gone according to plan, but then they never do, Ted was thinking. He would make an urgent call to see Caroline and Ginger, but first he would make one more call on Harry to gauge his opinion once more.

He found Harry at home, looking out over a magnificent landscape with two large ponds and an island in the middle of one.

'Helen spends hours spotting different birds down there; it was all Ginger's idea. Quite frankly, I would never have made it without him, Ted. Come and sit down and enjoy his creation, I will make some tea. I am sorry to have to break the news to you, but Ginger has only days to live. Helen is with Caroline at the moment, but should be back any minute with Megan.'

Harry finally admitted that he had a problem and that was why they had no children. He was really bitter about it and mentioned that after trying for a family they tried to adopt a baby, but their age was against them.

'Helen accepted the situation and is now helping Caroline come to terms with Ginger's illness, at the same time taking care of Megan who is finding it very hard to see her father suffer, so you see, we love Megan as our own. By the way, how are your two boys getting on?'

Ted felt really sorry for him and remembered the time when Harry became very frightened after that last bomb. His nerves had been shot to pieces and now his heart was not good. On top of that, he had struggled to explain that he was to blame for them having no children. Ted was not surprised, and felt more determined to pursue a claim for a war pension.

Harry brought in a mug of welcome tea.

'There we are, old friend, get that down you, Army style. By the way, Ted, I have been thinking, Ginger will be in no fit state to talk to you. You know what he is like, he won't blame anybody for what happened. Leave it with me and I will get back to you, in the mean time, please go ahead with my claim, and many thanks, Ted, for all the efforts you are making. I know your record on previous occasions is . . . well, shall we just say it is unfortunate,' he said laughing.

'The point is, Ted, I think you are right to pursue these matters, it all seems very odd to me; we were taught all the dangers of nuclear weapons and then lined up in front of them, not forgetting all those youngsters who had to stay behind and work in a very dangerous environment. I shall never forget you, Ted, just before the bomb detonated——'

'Sorry, Harry, if you don't mind, I would rather forget that part of my life. If I am to make up for all the bad advice I gave you all back in training, then I have much to do.'

'Good on you, Ted, win or loose, we should get together, all of us. Please don't take it personally, we all know you mean well. Rex has been telling me that there has been quite a lot of news lately dealing in health problems with nuclear test veterans. Rex intends to find out more and will let us know at the next meeting.'

With that the door opened, it was Helen and Megan.

'Hello, Uncle Harry, how are you?' said Megan giving Harry a kiss, but it looked as if she had been crying.

'Ted, this is a lovely surprise,' said Helen.

'Megan, do you remember Mr Watson who used to be in the Army with your dad and Uncle Harry?'

Megan was not sure, but she remembered her father talking about him and was very pleased to see him. Helen wanted to know how everybody was keeping and would Ted stop for lunch? But Ted had things to do that afternoon. Harry saw Ted to the door and said he would keep him informed.

It was a sad week for all of them when they received the inevitable news of Ginger's death. The funeral took place with a huge turnout, many of Ginger's workforce being ex-Army. Harry and Caroline closed the business down for the day in memory of Ginger and all his colleagues who had left this world. Helen invited them back to her place where Caroline looked surprisingly happy, saying that she was privileged to have known such a good man and thanked everybody for coming. As Caroline passed on Ginger's message she pointed out that he never blamed anybody for anything and always had a kind word for everybody. He was always trying to find his inner self. His efforts here on earth to improve his allegiance to God were often compromised by earthly demands and laws, leaving him with a far from perfect account, full of sin even though he tried hard. Ted smiled and turned to Penny, pointing out that in his opinion he did not think Ginger had too much to worry about, apart from letting the fires go out one night back in training when it was bitterly cold, even though it was unintended.

'We nearly froze to death,' said Ted.

'Good heavens, what do you mean?'

'I mean what I say. We were freezing, but Harry helped Ginger raid the coke yard in a howling blizzard. If they were caught it would have been hell for both of them, but we can only assume there must have been divine intervention. With Harry's courage, Ginger had redeemed himself. Both Harry and Ginger risked the wrath of earthly law just so that the rest of us had a fire for the night. Ginger admitted it was all his fault and instilled in us to always confess your mistakes by telling the truth. "It's all recorded in you," he said. "Read Psalm 139."

I must confess, I didn't understand it at all. He used to say, "Don't let others suffer, redeem yourself by admitting your mistakes, everything is recorded in you." It's an enigma to me, I mean I seem to open one door only to find two more and so on. My confusion goes up by the square law. Back on the island, Ginger would often read to us verses from Psalms. In return I would read more down-to-earth court cases of old, which caused quite a lively debate at times.

* * *

Ted was in no mood for optimism, his faith in justice had gone clean out of the window. Clearing his desk, he was thankful it was Friday.

'See you Monday, Bob.'

'No, Ted, you are due a week off, so take it, you deserve a break,' said Bob.

Arriving home Penny was still out, so he phoned James.

'Where's that dodgy sales lady, can I speak to her, James? It's urgent.'

'You won't believe this, Dad, she sold a car today.'

'Well done, but would you tell her if she gets back here right now, I will take her to Eastbourne for the week.'

'She heard that, Dad, and has already left. Have a great time.'

Ted had just one more call to make. He needed to speak to Harry and explain his disappointment at losing all three cases. Yes, Harry was right, his success rate was not good, but Harry would have none of it, as far as he was concerned they had only lost a battle, not the war. Yes, Harry was disappointed, but at least Ted had made a start and as he had often said, there are more ways to skin a grape. Harry would speak to Caroline and Gary and explain.

'I seem to remember Caroline mentioning that Ginger was very unhappy at having got involved with these evil weapon; he should have refused to cooperate,' said Harry.

'He did refuse, if you remember, during training and on the island he made his views quite clear. Not that anybody listened, of course, everybody couldn't wait to get off the place and weren't interested. One other point, you never saw Ginger line up with the rest of us, did you? I don't know what happened to him, he never said, but to my way of thinking he did the right thing.'

'Well, I must admit, Ted, I never knew that, but when you come to think of it, it never did him any good, in fact, it never did any of us any good, there was so much panic, with nowhere to hide. Safe or unsafe, it's still difficult to comprehend why we were all lined up. Well, that's what I think, and I can't seem to get the whole business out of my head, to be honest I would rather forget the whole affair, but it wouldn't be right.

'Rex has found out that there are others questioning what happened, not just on Christmas Island, but the Australian and Malden Island nuclear tests. According to Rex, others have collected and collated information regarding the health of many ex-veterans from these nuclear test sites. He thinks there is an association being formed and would like to call a meeting in the pub. Maybe we can at least get the satisfaction for Ginger which he richly deserves.

'Have a great holiday, Ted.'

'Thanks, Harry, I agree whole-heartedly, but to my way of thinking, Ginger has won his war. He was such a great man to know, but I agree he should be recognised here on earth.

'I look forward to hearing from you, take care, Harry.'

Harry put the phone down and remembered the day he

had set off on the train with his girlfriend Sophie waving him off. How things had changed since then. He had learnt a great deal, and looking back on his two years in the Army it had, without doubt, changed his life. Both himself and his colleagues had seen a glimpse of hell on earth, which was now indelibly imprinted on their minds for the rest of their lives, and in many cases had left them with very poor health.

One thing was certain, he would never have started his business with Ginger had he not gone into the Army, but unknown to them at the time the price was far too high, leaving them with a very uncertain future.

EPILOGUE

With the scars of nuclear bombs left behind in Australia, the Pacific, and the minds of those who took part in these tests, it is fair to say that the contribution these servicemen made towards giving the UK a deterrent has, to a large extent, gone unnoticed and ignored in spite of many of them becoming ill.

I received a medical before, but not after, my tour of duty on Christmas Island. The medical included a chest X-ray and a full blood test. With a clean bill of health I was on my way to a nuclear test site where, if I had been issued with a radiation film badge, I would have been in a much better position to know if I had been exposed to radiation. However, I never had that privilege. Those who were given a radiation film badge before a bomb was detonated had the badge taken away from them, so they had no idea if they had been exposed.

Finally, I left the Airforce and studied at Bletchley Park before moving to Shropshire working with communication, radar, and computer engineering. I retired to Herefordshire where I spend much of my time hill walking in the Brecon Beacons. I continue to enjoy spectacular flying displays by ravens, who have replaced the giant frigatebirds of Christmas Island.

In all the time since I left Christmas Island, I have not

enjoyed the best of health, which I feel is indicative of nuclear radiation. Climbing hills and mountains in Wales has, without doubt, helped me to overcome these health issues, along with much appreciated care from my GP and the staff at Hereford hospital.

After all these years I still find it difficult to forget how badly God's animal kingdom suffered. Apart from thousands of birds and marine life which perished, I found the skeletal remains of birds well away from ground zero. We need to understand more than ever that we are the custodians of God's animal kingdom. Without them we will surely suffer.

Whatever happens in the future, we must try harder to eliminate these dreadful weapons before the situation in this world becomes unstable enough to use them, but I am afraid power struggles, greed, the lack of food for everyone, the threat of serious disease, and a lack of faith makes for a very uncertain future.

Before finishing this story I have to say that in reality these veterans of nuclear testing may well have been forgotten had it not been for the untiring efforts by early pioneers who campaigned for recognition of the service these lads carried out by helping to give this country the ultimate deterrent to any aggressor.

Atom bomb test in the Woomera area of South Australia, home to Aborigines

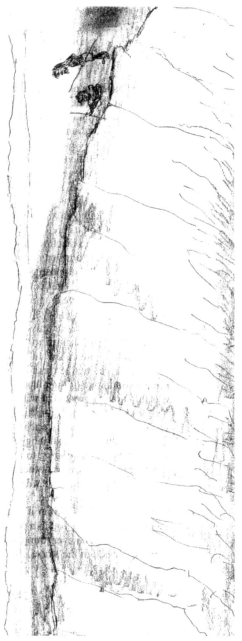

'I suppose that's one way of looking for a meal.'

ACKNOWLEDGEMENTS

I will always be grateful to my late parents who wrote to me frequently while I was away in the RAF from their home in East Sussex. My younger brother wrote to me with all the news of the countryside, while my elder brother, John, who was serving as a chief petty officer in the Royal Navy, wrote to me from Malta.

Both of my brothers encouraged me to write down my memories of the island. It has not been easy, but with help from ex-members of Operation Grapple, I have managed to put together a story so that nobody who took part will be forgotten.

Finally, I would like to acknowledge Daniel Smith of Aspect Design who helped me to put this book together.

British Nuclear Test Veterans' Association

The early pioneers who collected and collated a great deal of the information about the ill-health suffered by these men and their families has lead to the formation of an association with branches all over the British Isles.

Sadly, many of the founder members have left this world with a younger generation taking over. The association is now under the chairmanship of Nigel Heaps, it has to be said that without their dedication and commitment the veterans of nuclear testing would have been forgotten.

LITIGATION

Many servicemen claim that their exposure to radiation has caused their failing health, and compensation is being sought through the courts. Towards this aim, Neil Sampson and his legal team have worked hard to secure a settlement for these men and their families. Work continues in this area and I would like to thank everyone for their untiring efforts.